GOODBYE EARL

A
REVENGE
NOVEL

GOODBYE EARL

LEESA CROSS-SMITH

**GRAND
CENTRAL**
New York Boston

Copyright © 2023 by Temple Hill Publishing, LLC
Cover design by Laywan Kwan
Cover photograph of pie by The Picture Pantry/Alamy Stock photo
Cover photographs by Shutterstock, Getty Images, and Stocksy
Cover copyright © 2023 by Hachette Book Group, Inc.

Bible verses on pages vii and 234 are from the King James Version.

Grand Central Publishing
Hachette Book Group
1290 Avenue of the Americas, New York, NY 10104
grandcentralpublishing.com
twitter.com/grandcentralpub

First Edition: July 2023

Grand Central Publishing is a division of Hachette Book Group, Inc. The Grand Central Publishing name and logo is a trademark of Hachette Book Group, Inc.

The publisher is not responsible for websites (or their content) that are not owned by the publisher.

The Hachette Speakers Bureau provides a wide range of authors for speaking events. To find out more, go to www.hachettespeakersbureau.com or call (866) 376-6591.

Library of Congress Cataloging-in-Publication Data

Names: Cross-Smith, Leesa, 1978- author.
Title: Goodbye earl : a revenge story / Leesa Cross-Smith.
Description: First edition. | New York : Grand Central Publishing, 2023. |
Identifiers: LCCN 2022053135 | ISBN 9781538707654 (hardcover) |
    ISBN 9781538707678 (ebook)
Classification: LCC PS3603.R67945 G66 2023 | DDC 813/.6--dc23
LC record available at https://lccn.loc.gov/2022053135

ISBNs: 978-1-5387-0765-4 (hardcover); 978-1-5387-0767-8 (ebook)

Printed in the United States of America

LSC-C

Printing 1, 2023

For everyone, seriously.
(Everyone but Earl.)

Greater love hath no woman than this, that a woman lay down her life for her friends.

—John 15:13 (KJV, paraphrased)

Act I

My friends are my estate. Forgive me then the avarice to hoard them.

—Emily Dickinson

2019

1

KASEY FRITZ

Yep. That electric slut-red cherry on top of the Goldie Dairy Dee sign was zapping like always, even though Kasey Fritz hadn't been back home to see it in fifteen years. She rolled the rental car window down and stuck her hand out—like maybe she could touch the ghosts she knew were there, like lightning bugs wisping through the summer dark.

The old used car lot was now a family-style Mexican restaurant. The gas station where she and her girlfriends stopped to get slushies after school got turned into a fancy new gas station with more pumps and glowing bulbs hanging overhead than the one before. It was lit up like a fish tank as Kasey drove past. She went through the green light, knowing the next turn would put her right in front of where the laundromat, the KFC, and the liquor store once were. They'd been replaced by a brand-new boutique hotel, which she'd read about online right after Taylor sent her to the wedding website.

Enjoy Goldie! You can visit a farm, stroll around the old-fashioned town square, get a mixed cocktail with your fried chicken at the swanky hotel restaurant...

The town decided to knock down a KFC to build a hotel that sold a plate of fried chicken for thirty dollars. Kasey wowed as she remembered checking the price twice, so sure she must've read it wrong. She stopped the car in front of the hotel and pulled the brake. She'd refused the luxury rental they attempted to upsell her at the airport thirty minutes away and gotten a little hatchback stick shift instead. The hotel's valet parking wasn't optional and Kasey tipped well, but she wheeled her luggage to the front desk on her own as a tiny act of defiance.

The receptionist was young, *so* young. Was that how young they were making hotel receptionists now? Kasey was only thirty-three, but this girl behind the counter didn't look like she should be allowed out past ten. Kasey gave her the wedding hashtag—#*PlumBMarried*—as Taylor had instructed her, guaranteeing the discounted hotel room. The Plums had more than enough room to house her, and it was true that Kasey had grown up counting every penny; it also felt ridiculous to be paying so much to stay in some fancy hotel in *Goldie*, of all places. Still, money wasn't an issue anymore, and Kasey liked having her own space. She insisted on staying at the hotel for the entire wedding week and not imposing on anyone—yes, wedding *week* because nothing, not one thing, was too much for little miss Taylor Plum.

The receptionist gave Kasey a small, stiff card for free drinks with her first and last name and #*PlumBMarried* written on the back in frilly cursive. Kasey pocketed it and glanced around quickly, betting she'd see someone she knew.

Thankfully, she didn't.

Whew and praise Jesus. She wasn't ready for that just yet.

The hotel lobby was piping out a comforting lavender-vanilla scent to go along with the coffeehouse acoustic playlist—brushy voice and guitar, soft and low. Both the smell and the music hemmed Kasey in as she made her way to the elevator. There was a big digital screen inside flashing a slideshow of Main Street and the town square. The green hills and blue sky. Smiling, sunglassed families. Rich-looking tourists. *Enjoy quaint Americana!* slid across in a fat yellow font so bright Kasey squinted at it and scrunched up her nose. The screen jumped to black and she almost laughed at the ridiculous reflection staring back at her.

———

Once Kasey got to her room, she plopped on the bed and promptly tapped the Devon messages to text her fiancé and let him know she was safe.

He responded, So glad to hear it. Do you feel like talking? It's ok if you don't.

> Not really, but thanks. So freakiiiing weeeeird being back...but...I don't know. Maybe seeing everything in the sun tomorrow will make a difference.? I hope so.

It will. Have you bumped into anyone you know yet?

> Weirdly and thankfully, no.

Did you go to the farmhouse?

> Nope.

Gotcha. Call me in the morning? I love you.

> I will. I love you too.

As Kasey texted Devon, she undressed and took a speedy shower. Brushed her teeth. By the time they were finished, she was in bed with the lamp off, the blue light of the television glowing the room. It'd comforted her ever since she was a little girl, sleeping with the TV on. She turned on a home-renovation show and drifted away easily as a couple timidly argued about whether to go with Italian or French marble for their kitchen countertops.

———

The blackout curtains did their job a little *too* well. Kasey was knocked out for a full eight hours, something that rarely happened back home in New York. Between her job as finance manager of LunaCrush—the third-largest beauty company in the world—and traveling for work and meetings at work and drinks after work and emails and phone calls and Devon and her girlfriends and and and, the thought of getting a full eight hours of peaceful, dreamy sleep at night in New York City was ridiculous. Being in Goldie gifted Kasey the luxury of being dead to the world.

She sat at the table by the window in her matching underwear, the sunshine warming her face. She drank the surprisingly good hotel room coffee, sipping carefully and scrolling through the wedding group chat Taylor had added her to, although Kasey had never written in it. The last one from Taylor read,

> Good morning, bitches! I love you all so much and I'm so glad you're here to celebrate our special weeeeek! Get your asses to the Plum house as SOON as you can for mimosas and cupcakes. Srsly, there's so much food! GET. HERE. NOW.

The other girls began chiming in quickly, at least a million of them.

> *OMW!*
> *I LOVE YOU SM BITCH!*
> *Can I bring anything?*

Are we doing dressy-dressy?
Of course it's dressy-dressy, this is the south! :P Dress up like you're
going to a football game!
Can someone come pick me up? I am NOT walking in these big-ass
heels.

Kasey set the group chat to Do Not Disturb before calling Devon and telling him her plans for the day. Devon was a Listener and stayed quiet as she complained about the embarrassing fawning, the possible tension, and all the questions she knew were waiting for her.

"Well, Kase . . . I offered to come with you, but you said you wanted to do this alone. Do you still want to do this alone?" Devon asked when she was finished. "You have a hard time admitting you need help. I wish you didn't. It would make things a lot easier sometimes," he added. Kasey heard New York City clichés over the line—quick honks, rumbly construction, overlapping chatter.

"Yeah, yeah, I know," she said. Devon meant well. She was sure he could hear her loud facial expressions over the phone; he'd told her plenty of times that her face could use a volume button. "Thank you. I'm okay, I am. Just venting. I can take care of it, and trust me, there's no point in you coming here. At *all*. Pfft, let's talk about something else. Tell me something good, please."

Although it frustrated him, Devon was used to Kasey deflecting whenever he wanted to dig deeper about Goldie and what life was like for her growing up. She gave him—along with everyone else—the bare minimum: she was from a small town, didn't have much family, had an asshole stepdad, both of her parents died when she was young. Orphaned, she left right after high school and never came back, never *looked* back either. She'd ditched that town in the dust because Kasey Fritz was so much bigger and better than Goldie, that was for damn sure.

Devon launched into the things he saw on his early morning run in the park. Described the dogs in full detail for Kasey's pleasure. Two scrappy Yorkies in matching yellow bows. A hyper golden retriever living its best life. A tiny brown-and-white mutt with a tennis ball in its mouth.

"You're very good at loving me," she said, sighing.

"You're easy to love" was his reply.

"Yeah . . . uh-huh. *Super* easy and agreeable and never annoying. Sure."

"It's true. Even when you're fussy," he said.

"Righto, D. Okay. I'll talk to you later."

"Please do. Here for whatever you need. Just say the word, bird. Just tell me the plan, Jan. Let me know the deal, Neil . . ."

After laughs and *I love you*s, Kasey finished her coffee and got dressed.

Two *hope you have a good time, safe travels, love you* texts from her girl-friends in the city. She sent them both kissy-face emojis in return.

One missed call from Rosemarie.

Two missed calls from Ada, and one text.

One text from Caroline.

Kasey left them unanswered.

RACK: Rosemarie, Ada, Caro, and Kasey. They'd been best friends since they were babies. Taylor was Ada's younger sister. Kasey would see them all soon enough and they'd fall into place like they had ever since they were little. They were her sisters; they'd made their own family and gotten through their darkest moments together. They could get through anything—they could.

This is it. It's happening. I'm back and I'm going to see my best friends again.

———

Kasey's heart cartwheeled as she walked toward Plum Bakery—still smack-dab in the middle of the town square. The building was lavender and pale pink with green polka-dotted letters, the windows filled with pastel-colored sweet treats, cupcakes, cakes, and pies. Right next to the bakery was the restaurant, Plum Eats. Down on the corner, Plum Florals connected to Plum Designs. The Plum family had run a small bakery in town for over a hundred years before Ada and her mother turned Plum Inc. into the monster of a local empire it was today. There'd been a headline on the front of the *Goldie Gazette* last year: ADA PLUM-CASTELOW, GOLDIE'S STAR AND SOURCE OF STYLE. Caroline had emailed it to Rosemarie and Kasey when it happened, along with *RACK NEWS! Look at our girl!* Rosemarie replied from Barcelona, *No surprise, this beauty. I love her so much.* Kasey had written back, *Oh wow look at our girl indeed!*

Rosemarie, Ada, Caro, and Kasey tried their best to keep in touch with one another as much as they had in the past, but at times it was impossible with their busy schedules. Rosemarie was leading hunger-relief initiatives both domestically and all over the globe. Ada had the Plum Inc. empire on top of her husband and four(!) boys. Caro had recently gotten married and was forever busy with baking.

Ada and Caro stayed in Goldie, and since Caro ran Plum Bakery now, they were the two who saw each other most often and remained as close as they were in high school. The foursome had gotten together every now and again when their schedules aligned in the fifteen years since they'd graduated from high school, but never in Goldie. Always in NYC or Seattle. Seattle: Rosemarie's new home base whenever she was stateside. Who could resist a girls' week/weekend in either of those cities? Well, in truth, Kasey *had* tried resisting it the first time, but Rosemarie showed up on her doorstep hollering KASEY FRITZ, IT'S ROSES! I LOVE YOU AND I FOUND YOU! Ada and Caro flew up the next day. Kasey knew Rosemarie would be the first to come see her; Rosemarie also had been the first to email her after she left. She kept emailing even when Kasey took too long to write back or didn't reply at all.

When they all got together that first time in New York, the girls sat

Kasey down and again demanded answers. Kasey listened, they cried. She told them what she'd always told them: that she'd felt like if she didn't leave that night, she'd be trapped forever. When Rosemarie was the last to go, she told Kasey she'd get the girls to lay off from asking her to explain herself, as long as she promised to never go completely radio silent on them. Kasey made that easy promise.

The old-timey movie theater was still there and so was the whipping American flag on the pole shooting up from the courthouse lawn. A small group of laughing teenagers got into a car in front of it. The video store was gone but Myrtle's Diner hadn't budged. So much looked exactly the same. Kasey walked slowly, taking it all in.

"Hot damn! Kasey Fritz, as I live and breathe, I'd know you anywhere, lookin' *just* like your mama," a voice next to her said from underneath a navy-blue ballcap. Duke Nichols took off his hat. Duke was a former marine, a Vietnam vet, who had worked at the grocery store with her mom back in the day. Last time she'd seen him he'd been skinnier with a full head of hair, a smooth face. He was a big, bald, bearded sweetheart now. He'd been so kind to Kasey when she was growing up, sneaking her candy and pops on her way out of the store when she stopped in to visit her mom. Now, Duke owned one of the busiest bars in town. Seeing him bloomed her heart into a swirly mess of happy and sad. Duke Nichols had been such a good friend to her mom it was perfect that he was the first to welcome her home. She felt safer in his shadow; she wished she could tell her mama that.

"Hi, Duke," Kasey said, smiling, pushing her sunglasses atop her head.

Duke swallowed her up in one of his bear hugs and she melted in his arms.

"You ain't been back here in what...?" he asked.

"It's been fifteen years, just about. Since I graduated from high school," Kasey answered as they pulled away to look at each other. Duke still had his hands on her shoulders, and Kasey's eyes got watery.

"You're back because the Plum girl's getting married," he said, squeezing her again and returning his arms to his sides.

"Yep. Little Taylor. I'm headed there now," she said.

After she caught up with Duke—and promised to stop by his place for a piece of his wife's cherry pie before returning to the Big Apple—she kept walking. An older gentleman walking a chocolate Lab with a red kerchief around its neck excused himself past her after saying hello. Kasey made a mental note to tell Devon about the dog when she texted him later to say that the sunshine *had* made a difference. Goldie really did sparkle in the morning awash in the golden light it was named for, the lemony sun cutting across the rolling hills.

June in Good Ol' Goldie's town square still smells the same—hot ice cream and garbage, she thought. It *was* comforting, she admitted to herself. It made her feel two-faced, telling the good-parts truth about Goldie. How could the place she'd grown to hate so much look so pretty? How could even the rotten parts make her wistful? She thought she'd feel downright miserable when she saw the WELCOME TO GOLDIE sign as she drove into town...but she hadn't.

All Kasey felt in those last moments making her way to the Plum house was hot; her face was starting to sweat. *Good Ol' Goldie, humidity's best friend.* She'd gone half dressy-dressy and put on a brand-new white V-neck eyelet dress, her small strand of real pearls, and her tobacco-brown cowboy boots. So unlike the minimalist, clean lines she wore in New York. Stepping into that white dress and those boots felt like stepping into a time machine—the *ghost of Goldie Kasey's past.*

———

The Plum house sat like a big pink trilevel cake on a tray of green grass. That morning it was festooned—from the mansard roof down to the historical plaque announcing it as the oldest house in Goldie—with Instagram-worthy balloon arches and fresh flower decorations. Peony bouquets the size of small children lined the steps. A big banner that read CONGRATULATIONS, TAYLOR AND BEN hung across the porch columns, the letters glimmering and catching the light. Pink, pink, pink! Everylittlebit of it. It'd been both Taylor's and Ada's favorite color their entire lives.

The inside of the house adhered strictly to the theme—pink twinkle lights and tulle, pink streamers and ribbons, T-A-Y-L-O-R in huge, individual rose-gold balloons. Kasey put the bag holding Taylor's bridal shower gift on a table covered with a pink tablecloth, and it was no surprise when Ada herself appeared in pink chiffon bell sleeves squealing Kasey's name.

"Oh oh oh, you're here! I'm *so* glad you're here. *Finally!* Tay, Kase is here! In Goldie!" Ada said the last part up at the ceiling, her bouncy brown-blonde hair falling down her back, although Taylor was nowhere to be seen.

"I'm so glad to see you. Everything looks *annoyingly* perfect. I mean, of course...you did all this. It looks...amazing. You look amazing," Kasey said, staring into Ada's hooded smoky-blue eyes. Kasey had to bend down a bit to hug her properly.

"Oh please, thank you. But you! It's been too long since you've been in front of me, and I hate that. I need to see you more. In real life! Why weren't you texting on the way here? Why didn't you call last night?" Ada asked, letting Kasey go.

"I'm sorry—I am. It's bizarre being back, but all that matters is...I'm here now! *Aaand* I need a drink," Kasey said as a woman she didn't know stopped next to them and kissed the air. Ada leaned her cheek over to the woman's mouth.

"Kasey? Kasey Fritz!" a high school acquaintance of the foursome said from the staircase. She was with some other girls Kasey only vaguely recognized; they'd gone to the other high school.

"Hi!" Kasey waved up at them.

"Of course. Go! Get a drink and go out back. I'll be right there," Ada said to her.

Ada's husband, Grayson Castelow—tall in a lilac seersucker suit—

smiled and boomed, "What up, Fritz?!" and hugged Kasey like the old friends they were. Grayson, a year ahead of them in school, had always been a gem. Kasey got on her tiptoes to hug his neck and asked him about their boys.

"Mama has the little ones upstairs," Grayson said, gesturing vaguely, "and the twins are playing outside with their friends. Oh, wow, it's *really* good to see you. Welcome! Can I get you anything?"

"No, but thank you, Grayson."

"All right, just let me know if I can do anything. This should feel like your home," he said as he was nudged and pulled into a conversation with a rowdy gumball group of men dressed in bright suits.

"*KaseyEffinFritz?*" a girl from junior year seventh period leaned over to squeal at her.

"Hey! It's me," Kasey said, smiling.

"The *hell?*! I swear we thought you'd died or something!" The girl threw her head back and laughed like it was the funniest thing she'd ever heard.

"Ta-da," Kasey said weakly, still smiling.

Bless Rosemarie Kingston's heart with her God-given timing. She stepped into the foyer in an earth-colored linen short suit, Birkenstocks, and giant hoop earrings, strikingly out of place amidst the candy-colored sundresses.

"I assure you Kasey Fritz is alive and well and I do need to borrow her for just a bit; please excuse us," Rosemarie said to the girl from high school. Saved! She took Kasey by the arm and led her to the back deck, where Rosemarie promptly plucked two bubbling flutes of champagne and handed one to her.

"I love you," Rosemarie said as they hugged, careful not to spill.

"I love you too," Kasey said. "So much. Look at how *beautiful* you are."

"*You're* the one. You have the best ass out of all of us. I'm *way* too skinny. I've already had a cupcake and a slice of cake," Rosemarie said, all brown skin and coconuts—her forever shampoo. Kasey noticed her long lashes swiped with mascara and barely tinted lip gloss, which was about as fancy as Rosemarie got makeup-wise. She had her hair pulled up with a white scarf tied in it, the loose knot and leftover fabric like petals at the base of her neck. "Take a cupcake," Rosemarie commanded. Kasey obeyed, grabbing one with a cloud of lime-colored frosting and pink sprinkles. "There's Caro. Have you seen her yet?" she asked and pointed, taking Kasey's cupcake hand by the wrist.

They snaked across the deck, through the buzzy crowd. There were a couple gasps from people Kasey knew, more smiles and squeals. Kasey's face was already tired from smiling, but that didn't matter when she saw Caroline leaning against the railing on the other side. Goddess-like, her thick red hair flamed over the shoulder of her white long-sleeved turtleneck minidress. She was sipping something honey colored from her champagne flute, the stem tied with a white ribbon. Without a word, the three girls got close, pressed their foreheads together. The tension Kasey had worried about was there, but it wasn't as thick as she'd anticipated. And it disappeared in a blink as soon as Taylor appeared.

"Oh me, me! Lemme in!" Taylor said, squeezing in next to Kasey and kissing her cheek. "Kase, you're here and I can't believe I'm looking at you! I love your boots!" she said, putting her arms around the girls.

"Hi, Taylor! Yes, yes, I'm here," Kasey said.

"Tay! I haven't even seen your *ring*. Where's Ben? I haven't seen him either! Where's the groom?" a woman said a bit too loudly from behind them, and that quickly, the embrace was broken. Taylor was gone, replaced by Ada, who reached out for Kasey's hand but laughed as Kasey used it to take the first bite of her cupcake.

"This is so good, Ada. Caro, this is so good," Kasey said to them. She took another bite. She hadn't eaten all morning and that cupcake tasted as if it'd been baked by God Himself.

Rosemarie's finger got the rebel frosting from the tip of Kasey's nose, and she licked it off. Caro smiled at them and retrieved the small, round flask she had hidden behind the flowerpot on the railing. Refilled her flute.

"Day-drinking Foxberry Bourbon? *Tsk-tsk*, Caroppenheimer, you naughty *minx*," Rosemarie said, calling Caro by the nickname they'd given her in kindergarten. Caroline Oppenheimer turned into Caro Oppenheimer turned into Caroppenheimer. Even though she was Caroline Foxberry now, the nickname was forever stuck like glue.

Caro winked at them. "Cheers!" she said.

Her new husband's family came from a long line of slaveowners and tobacco farmers, and they owned the brewery, the winery, and the two large distilleries near town, as well as several others spread across the South. The list went on and on: Foxberry Beer, Foxberry Gin, Foxberry Vodka, Foxberry Bourbon, Foxberry Wine, Foxberry Moonshine. At Halloween? Foxberry Pumpkin Ale. Christmas, Foxberry Winter Spice. *Why not Foxberry Resurrection Communion Juice for Easter? Or start calling it Foxberry Rain when the heavens open? Aren't they all soaking up the Foxberry Sun?* Kasey thought as she watched Caro drink.

Caro offered her flask to them, and Rosemarie and Kasey took small sips.

"Honestly, Ada. Taylor's so lucky. You've outdone yourself," Kasey remarked. She finished her cupcake and put her arm around Ada's waist, nuzzling in. Ada nodded because she knew it was true. She was a woman who always went above and beyond what was expected.

The foursome looked out at the crowd spilling from the house into the backyard— colorful knots of people milling in and out of the white tents, feasting on pink-confetti cupcakes, sipping cold champagne and prosecco in the high noon sun. A plucky bluegrass band was playing in one of the tents; the happy, quick music hung on the wind. The whole deal was not unlike the high school graduation party they'd had in that same spot fifteen years ago. That party was the last shot of sunshine before the storm, and for so long afterward, there hadn't been a rainbow in sight, not even a slip of light.

Everything was different now, but somehow—like strange, humming magic pulled through time—to Kasey, it all felt the same.

2004

2

Kasey and the girls were on the front porch of the Plum house after school, each one of them with a piece of banana pudding icebox cake and a clinky glass of tea. The March air still carried a chill, but the afternoon sunlight was slanting in a dreamy way—hope for warmth and good things to come. They were supposed to be going over graduation party plans, but Caro and Kasey had fallen into a fit of giggles talking about one of their teachers.

"No, seriously, though! The last day of school is, like, *two* months away and he's already given up. He's not doing *anything*. All he talks about is his divorce. Oh, Shelly has a new boyfriend...Shelly took the dog..." Caro said, mimicking their teacher's deep voice.

"He's such a loser! He told us the same thing yesterday!" Ada chimed in.

"Hold on, Juno is a *really* adorable dog, though. I'd be pissed if someone took my dog," Rosemarie said with her bare feet in Ada's lap. Being a dog person was a strong part of Rosemarie's personality and so was doing spot-on impersonations. "Give me Juno back, you bitch!" she said, sounding exactly like their teacher.

"Wait, waitwait! Forreal. Don't y'all think he's *kind of* cute, though?" Kasey said.

"Who?! Mr. Chandler?! Absolutely not," Rosemarie said with a full mouth.

"Don't judge! I said *kind of*!" Kasey said.

"Y'know...I can see it..." Ada said. She and Rosemarie had Mr. Chandler for English first period, Caro and Kasey had him for fourth.

"Ada, you're basically already Mrs. Grayson Castelow, so your vote doesn't count. It's distorted," Rosemarie said.

"You have so many girl crushes; your vote is distorted too," Ada said, sticking her tongue out. She took her last bite of cake.

"Hey! I have boy crushes too, just not freaking sad bastard Mr. Chandler!" Rosemarie said. She sat up and pushed her ears out like Mr. Chandler's, and the girls started giggling so much Taylor smacked open the screen door and asked what was so funny. "I was being ridiculous, Tay, that's all," Rosemarie said.

"What are y'all gonna do now?" Taylor asked, hungry for attention. Ada's little sister was the RACK mascot with her whole eleven-year-old heart. She was forever attempting to tag along and tried her best to stay up late when the girls slept over. She'd even decided TRACK was just as good of a combo name as RACK, and she always reminded them how easy it'd be to slide her *T* in front.

"*You're* going to do your homework, and *I'm* going to start dinner before Mama and Daddy get home. Everyone else is heading out," Ada said, collecting the girls' empty cake plates.

"I'm off to work. Diner's a-callin'," Caro said. She stood and brushed her hands off on the teeny strawberry jean short shorts she loved to wear so much. "Bye, y'all." She touched each one of them on the top of the head like they were in a quick game of duck, duck, goose before walking away.

"Fritz, are you tutoring today?" Rosemarie asked.

"Nope. But I gotta go because *Dumbass* needs the truck, and if it gets him out of the house, I don't care what it's for," Kasey said, standing too.

"You can spend the night here whenever you want, Kase. You know Mama and Daddy never mind," Ada said.

Kasey stared down the street until Caro's long red ponytail and strawberry shorts got lost in the hazy buzz.

"My parentals have the gig at the bar. They won't be home until, like, two in the morning. Regardless, you're more than welcome to crash with me anytime too, Fritz," Rosemarie said.

"Thanks, y'all. It's...fine. I'll see you in the morning. Love you," Kasey said after hesitating, taking in their offers. She walked down the porch steps, got into her truck, and waved as she pulled off.

———

The farmhouse Kasey lived in was a six-minute drive from Ada's pink mansion, a three-minute drive from Caro's cute trailer park, and a five-minute drive from Rosemarie's wind chimey house. The girls had grown up knowing every inch of Goldie—the shortest shortcuts to the lake, the ditches with the best crawdads and turtles, the bushes and flowers, every patch of wild onions, dirt, and grass. They'd grown up at one another's houses, could find their way through them with their eyes closed—every notch in the wood, every doorknob, every screen door and window they had to jiggle just right to open up. They knew Caro's driveway had the sharpest rocks to hurt their bare feet, that Rosemarie's driveway was smooth. That they could see both Goldie High's *and* South Goldie High's Friday night lights from Ada's balcony, that Kasey's backyard was the froggiest on summer nights, and that the water at her farmhouse was choppier than the water on the other side of the lake.

The girls never hung out at Kasey's anymore, though.

Not since her dumbass stepdad, Roy.

The farmhouse that her real daddy and his friends built with their bare hands was on the edge of Goldie, almost like if Kasey stayed there too long, she could slip right off the map.

She promised herself that one day, she'd actually do it.

Roy truly was a dumbass and an angry ass and a violent ass too. Kasey hated him more than she ever thought she could hate someone. He hit Kasey's mom when he got drunk and nasty, and when Kasey's mom wasn't there, he'd smack Kasey around too. The last time he'd done it, Kasey took a steak knife and told him if he ever touched her again, she'd stab him without thinking twice.

It'd been a month since.

The girls knew some of what Kasey's home life was like even though she didn't tell them *everything*. She didn't tell them Roy pulled her hair and smacked her across the face once when she was doing the dishes "too loud." She didn't tell them about the time he'd pushed her into the wall for talking back when all she'd done was ask him to repeat what he had said. Kasey couldn't bring herself to tell the girls those things. It was all too dark, too embarrassing.

Kasey's dad, Isaiah, was killed by a drunk driver when she was only six months old, and by the time Kasey was in elementary school, her mom had gone through a lot of different dickhead boyfriends, although most of them didn't hang around too long. Losing her dad flicked a switch in her mom. Kasey's dad was a good man, and since something so terrible happened to him, it was like it scared her mom into dating *only* assholes from there on out. Like some sort of desperate defense mechanism. Even though her mom's boyfriends sucked, none of them were as bad as Roy. None of them ever laid a finger on either of them until him.

Her mom and Roy got married when Kasey was in middle school, and her mom was so tough, so staunch about everything, Kasey couldn't get through to her when she tried to talk her into leaving him. On one hand, she resented her mom for it, for tying herself to a no-good man like Roy, but on the other, it terrified Kasey—thinking of secret reasons why her mom would stick with him. Like there must've been something Kasey didn't know, something she couldn't ever understand. Maybe when you got to a certain age and had a kid to take care of and you let yourself be sad enough, let grief slice you deep enough, you forgot who you were. Maybe the *who you once were* escaped through those slits the grief-knife made. So you let people treat you all kinds of ways you never would've before, because you *just got so tired.*

Maybe her mom *just got so tired*.

Kasey's mom saved her dad's truck for her and signed it over on her sixteenth birthday. She didn't like to let anyone else drive it, because it was all she had left of her dad outside of the farmhouse besides a pair of his old jeans and some of his T-shirts. But when Roy needed the truck, he didn't ask, and Kasey was scared to say no. Plus, Roy needing the truck meant he would probably be gone with it for two or three days and things would feel normal for a little while.

Until he'd pop up again and ruin everything.

Dumbass put a cloud over that farmhouse, but Kasey felt her daddy there, even now. In those hardwood floors he'd measured, cut, and sanded himself. In that kitchen table he made with his bare hands. She fantasized about her daddy returning from the grave and saving them, taking his house and his family back. She kept a picture of him tucked in front of the permanently lit-up check engine light in her truck. In it, her daddy was young and shirtless. Smiling, shielding his eyes. Sun-kissed—his deep-brown skin even browner from working outside so much that spring she was born.

She never left the picture in the truck when Roy borrowed it; Kasey shut the engine off, put the picture in her backpack, and went inside.

In the kitchen, Kasey tied her hair up, turned her iPod on and tucked it in her pocket, put her earbuds in. Filled a pot with water for the pasta. Rosemarie, Ada, and Caro had pooled their money together and gotten her that iPod for her birthday. Kasey had cried; it was her second-favorite material possession after her truck.

She listened to the Chicks album as the pasta boiled, and she sang along, chopping mushrooms and onions for the sauce. She made meatballs from scratch, rolling them across her palms and carefully setting them to sizzle in the hot pan. Her mama taught her to make meatballs when she was a little girl, told her it was her daddy's favorite recipe—from *The Godfather*, his favorite movie. Kasey felt a lift in her heart, thinking about her and her mama having the house to themselves for a couple days, maybe. She was stoked to surprise her with spaghetti and meatballs and the fancy garlic bread she'd just taken out of the freezer.

One of her earbuds was snatched out.

Kasey gasped. Roy, behind her. She hadn't heard him come in.

"Your mama's working late tonight," he said.

"Oh. She didn't call me—" Kasey began, rabbit-hearted.

"I was just at the store. I just talked to her."

"Okay . . . well, I was making us spaghetti dinner, so I guess we can eat it later."

He moved next to her and started filling up his big plastic cup with water. She was never scared of Roy when she was in the kitchen near the knives; the one she'd been chopping with was right by her pinky on the cutting board. She eyed it and looked out the open window at the sleeping vegetable garden waiting for her to put seedlings in, come May. She'd already started some basil, tomatoes, and sweet peppers under grow lights in the garage next to Roy's weed plants. Like every spring, she was looking forward to planting berries. Even when the world was a sinkhole, little green sprouts made Kasey feel all right.

She could almost taste the metal of Roy's sweat now. She wanted to die thinking about him getting on top of her mama smelling like that. Kasey heard them sometimes—the rhythmic thunking of the bed frame against their shared wall.

"I'm taking the truck until tomorrow night, so you'll have to get another way to school," he said after he was done filling up his cup and taking some gulps.

"Yeah . . . okay."

"Did you put gas in it?"

"Nope."

"So, you expect me to fill it up?"

Kasey turned the stove burner off and looked Roy right in the eyes for the first time since he walked in. She glanced at his red neck. *He's literally a redneck*, she'd say to the girls.

"If you want to use it? Yep," Kasey said, popping the *p* out in an annoying way. She was sweating now, and the cool air coming in through the window made the hair stand up on her arms.

Or was it the nasty look on Roy's face?

"Well, if you can't fill the truck up with gas, then you ain't eating no dinner tonight," he said. He snatched the spaghetti noodles off the stove and poured them down the sink, flicked the garbage disposal switch. It rumbled so hard the glass in the cabinets rattled and shook. He threw the sauce and meatballs down there too, cussing and growling about how hot everything was.

Kasey's adrenaline tingled and spiked, then her blood went cool. She refused to cry in front of him, so she went to her bedroom to let the tears out. She allowed herself one big scream into her pillow, then she threw a change of clothes in her backpack with her books, left, and slammed the screen door behind her. She walked through the grass until she reached the edge of their property. She heard Roy start the truck engine in the driveway and peel out as she made her way along the path beside the lake, back toward town.

She didn't have to say a word when she showed up on Ada's porch crying.

"I'm making lasagna" was all Ada said, holding the screen door open for her. "It's even better than last time. Now I do a mix of Italian sausage and ground beef. Also, fennel. Did I tell you I started adding fennel?" Ada now stood with her hands on her hips in her kitchen, wearing a ruffly yellow apron. There was a fingerprint of tomato sauce on her cheek; Kasey took her thumb and gently wiped it off. "Oh, and you're staying here tonight," Ada commanded. Kasey nodded her okay.

"What can I do? How can I help?" Kasey asked.

"You're just in time for the layers, girlfriend. Start grating that mozzarella," Ada said, pointing. "Taylor, set the table for one more.

Kase is spending the night." Kasey took her backpack off, set it by the kitchen door, and washed her hands.

———

The Plum table had a vase of red tulips in the middle of it. Kasey helped Ada make a simple garden salad, and she entertained Ada while she made lemon bars for dessert too. Ada said she wanted to make lemon bars because lemon bars made everyone happy and Ada was one of those girls who really did want everyone to be happy. Ada was easily the sunshine of RACK, and Kasey tried her best not to be the gloom. Even in the dark times, Kasey fought to keep a light inside herself, and it was that light and hope that would give her the wings to leave the darkness behind someday—she knew it. She could feel a faint, pulsing power deep in her heart, burning, revving up.

Holly Plum sat at the table pouring wine into her glass, praising her girls for the beautiful spread.

"Above and beyond, as always. I sure did raise y'all right," she said as her husband took his seat at the head of the table.

"Does this mean we can get a puppy?" Taylor asked as Kasey dug into her food. She'd been hungry when she started dinner at the farmhouse, before Roy showed up and ruined everything again. She was so hungry now her head was throbbing. She took two big bites of Ada's lasagna.

"Are you going to ask for a puppy every day until we say yes?" Mr. Plum smiled at his daughter as he picked up his fork.

"Yes" was Taylor's reply.

"Then my answer is...maybe," he said, winking.

Ada's parents started jokingly arguing about whether or not there'd be a new puppy in their house anytime soon, and Kasey loved being witness to normal domesticity. The Plums had two older twin boys who'd be home from their second year of college soon. She couldn't help but be a bit jealous that Ada had such a big family and could make dinner in peace. That the Plums had homemade lemon bars and a long table in a fancy dining room. A chandelier that spilled little rainbows down the walls. Crystal doorknobs and tulips in a vase. Kasey daydreamed it was *her* daddy sitting where Mr. Plum was sitting. That it was *her* mama drinking wine from a fancy glass, laughing about getting a puppy.

And Roy? Oh, Roy was dead dead dead and Kasey could go spit on his grave.

"It's so good, right? Best lasagna you've ever had?" Ada asked Kasey, snapping her out of the daydream. "Tell the truth. Don't you *dare* lie, 'cause I'll know if you're lying."

"Yes. It's the best lasagna I've ever had in my entire life, Ada Plum."

"Told you," Ada said, scrunching up her nose.

——

After dinner, Kasey texted her mom to let her know she was staying at the Plums'. She didn't bother telling her what Roy had done with the food. She'd see it for herself once she got home; Kasey left the kitchen a mess.

Sorry about our dinner date. I can't turn down extra shifts. We can use the money.

i know mama. it's fine. c u after school tmrw.

Love you, Kasey Jo.

luv u 2.

Ada and Kasey were up in Ada's big bedroom doing their home-work. Taylor had hung around in there until Mrs. Plum told her for the third time to go to her own room and get to bed. Mrs. Plum's voice was so starry and wine-drunk Kasey couldn't help but shake her head and laugh as she refocused on the AP calculus on the page in front of her.

"Ladies and gentlemen, my drunk-ass mama," Ada said.

"She cracks me up, though," Kasey said. Mrs. Plum had plenty of ridiculous moments, but Kasey preferred wine-drunk Mrs. Plum to *everything has to be perfectly perfect* Mrs. Plum.

When the girls heard the plinks of gravel against the glass, they both hopped up to look down. Ada pushed open the window.

"Come out," Grayson whispered. He knew very well Ada's mama took her wine to bed and that her daddy slept like the dead.

"You can't call me like a normal person?" Ada whispered back at him.

"This is more romantic."

"Well, I can't come down every time you ask. You'll get tired of me. I read about something like this in a magazine last week."

"Never. I'll never get tired of you, Ada Plum. You're my favorite," he said, putting his hand on his heart.

"Kasey's spending the night," Ada said, nodding toward her.

"Fritz is up there?" Grayson's brother, Silas, whispered, stepping out of the shadows.

"Hey," Kasey said down at him. She twinkled hearing her last name in his mouth.

She shouldn't have been surprised Silas showed up too. Silas Castelow was everywhere all the time and everyone loved him, even the teachers. Kasey knew of at least two who'd tried to set him up with their daughters. He was as much a part of the town as the water tower and the lake. When she got special attention from him, Kasey felt lucky to be in his light. The Castelow boys were kind and fun and wild, in the best way. Almost too good to be true if Kasey hadn't

25

known them herself. They had trees for middle names—Grayson Sycamore and Silas Hickory—like their mama just *knew* they'd grow up to be that tall and strong.

"You brought your *little brother* with you to whisk me away on some romantic rendezvous?" Ada's fake fussing made Kasey laugh.

"Damn, girl. Just get down here," Grayson said.

Ada grabbed her pink cardigan off the chair and stepped out onto the balcony. Kasey got her Goldie High hoodie off the bed and pulled it over her head, her stomach swirling like cotton candy.

The boys had parked their truck around the corner, and the four of them were quiet getting in. Grayson was behind the wheel with Ada scooted next to him; Kasey and Silas were smooshed together in the backseat. Grayson started the engine and drove toward the lake in the dark.

"This is my favorite kind of surprise," Silas said, leaning close to Kasey's ear.

"What is?" Kasey asked.

Silas Castelow's long, lean body was next to her, smelling like woodsmoke and apples in brown jeans and a red-and-black buffalo plaid flannel. He loved that outfit, wore it all the time. She'd committed a *lot* of Silas info to memory. Like the time RACK bumped into him at the bakery last summer. How it'd just finished raining and he stopped whatever he was doing and somehow grabbed all four of them at the same time, gently pushed them out the front door without explaining why, and pointed up because he wanted to make sure they saw the big rainbow pouring over the hills.

"Finding you...on a night like this," he said.

They'd grown up hanging out occasionally and a lot more ever since Ada and Grayson got together sophomore year, but for the past few months, Kasey and Silas had been circling each other like sharks. He'd had a girlfriend and the day before they broke up, Kasey started half dating a boy from school who worked at the bakery. She and Silas kept missing each other, but she liked him so much. *Too* much. She hadn't even brought it up often to the other girls, for fear of jinxing the whole thing, even though for the past few weeks she'd been whispering *Silas Castelow* quietly to herself as she was falling asleep because his name sounded like the wind.

Kiss me. Kiss me, Silas Hickory. I want to climb you like a tree. I've had the shittiest day and that would make it better, forreal, she thought as he put his arm around her. It was dark-dark in the truck when the streetlamps weren't flashing through. It smelled like boy plus girl in there—gas and gum, gray and pink. His brother gunned it.

When they got to the lake, the sky was clear, the stars were out, the curved slip of moon was shining its milky light on the black water. The radio was on in the truck. Ada and Grayson were already kissing on a blanket in the back and Silas and Kasey looked for a spot.

"Here's good, Dandelion," he said to her as he put the blanket down on the grass.

Kasey giggled. "What's that? *Dandelion?*"

"You. Because you popped up outta nowhere and you're stubborn and tough...pretty too."

"Oh! Thank you. Thanks for saying that," she said. It felt like she'd been strapped to a rocket, firing up. "That's a really sweet thing to say to someone. I don't know how else to respond."

"Don't need to. It fits, because I think you're really sweet," he said, sitting and leaning back, looking up at the sky as "Cowboy Take Me Away" by The Chicks came on the radio.

"I think you're really sweet too," Kasey said, sitting next to him with a mouth full of words she kept in.

The romance of the water. The swelling symphony of chorus frogs. It wasn't long until Silas asked if he could kiss her. He asked if she would go to prom with him and finally be his girl. He told her he'd been wanting to ask for so long but was working up the nerve. Kasey hadn't ever thought of herself as someone a person would have to work up the nerve to ask out, and she never thought of Silas as the type of person who had to work up the nerve to do anything either. Him saying that made her feel upside down—heavy and light at the same time, like a wet petal. Wonderful. Enchanted.

Kasey smiled and said yes as he leaned in to kiss her, her ears roaring so loud she thought they'd up and burst.

Three! Two! One! Blast off!

2019

3

CAROLINE FOXBERRY

Caro, half-dizzy and buzzed on Foxberry Bourbon, stared at her swimmy reflection in the mirror. She and Kasey were alone in an upstairs bathroom of the Plum house; Kasey was peeing. Caro had missed Kasey so much she even missed going to the bathroom with her.

"Should I get bangs?" Caro asked. She hadn't had bangs since freshman year of high school. She pulled some of her hair over her forehead to make fake ones—*A longish fringe would look good*, she thought.

"Okay, what's wrong? Spill it. Whenever you talk about getting bangs, it's because you're going through some sort of crisis," Kasey said, reaching for the toilet paper.

"Zooey Deschanel had those bangs in *New Girl* and everyone loved her," Caro said.

Kasey wiped and got up from the toilet, stood at the sink to wash her hands. Caro scooched over a bit.

"Seriously, what's up?" Kasey asked.

"Why'd you come back for Taylor's wedding but not mine?" Caro asked her for the first time. She'd *wanted* to ask before but couldn't find the right moment. Although Kasey had said she was coming for

Taylor's wedding, she was a bit vague about it and Caro had half hoped it wasn't true. "When Trey and I got married, you said you couldn't do it. Only six months ago, you said you couldn't set foot in Goldie, that you had too many bad memories and that's why you never came home. I *know* we promised we wouldn't bring it up anymore if you didn't want to talk about it. We were too scared of pushing you away—but lo and behold, here you are, Kasey. Your ass is here in Goldie, just like that! And for Taylor? I mean, we all love Taylor, of course we do, but she's not one of *us*. You never came back for *us*, and that hurts, Kasey. It really *fucking* hurts!"

They were both crying now. Caro had held it in for so long that when she finally let loose, it was like a natural disaster she had to let happen. Simply brace herself for the aftermath. Her breath got short. Kasey stood close.

"Caro, I'm sorry. I'm sorry I missed your wedding. It wasn't easy for me to come back now. Trust me, it took a while to talk myself into it. I'm sorry I can't come here more, I . . ." Kasey said.

Caro knew how hard things were for Kasey growing up, knew how hard she took her mama's death. She never knew her maternal grandparents, and her dad had been adopted by a single woman who didn't have much family, who'd died of a broken heart not long after Kasey's dad did. She had a few distant cousins of her mom's scattered farther south but had never met them. Kasey's mama was all she had, and everything in Goldie reminded her of it.

Caro was sensitive to what returning to Goldie could dredge up for Kasey, but she needed to be honest with her too. She'd accepted the fact that Kasey left and they had to go to New York or Seattle to see her, so Kasey was going to have to accept the fact that after fifteen years, Caro could get buzzed and stand in the bathroom and ask some tough questions. Finally. She and Kasey had *always* been able to be real with each other before Kasey left Goldie. Theirs was a special bond because of the shared disfunction when it came to their families and since they were the only ones in RACK without siblings. She wanted them to get back to the way they'd been before. Somehow.

"But *why*? Why did you finally come home? Why now?" Caro asked, after taking some deep breaths.

Kasey had sent four hundred dollars' worth of lingerie to Caro for her bridal shower, in absentia. Kasey had sent wineglasses and dish towels and eight-hundred-count bedsheets to her and Trey for their wedding, in absentia. Caro had asked Kasey to be her bridesmaid and Kasey had declined. The wedding photos weren't the same without her. RACK was RAC.

"I..." Kasey started. "It was just time to come back."

"Was it Silas? Did you come back for him? He's out there, y'know," Caro said, flicking her hand toward the open window facing the backyard—the smell of fresh-cut grass, and chatter, laughter, birdsong. The air-conditioning was on full blast, but Caro had opened the window as soon as she walked in, convinced it would sober her up a bit. "Did you see him? He looks the same. He hasn't changed. He's everywhere all the time. I see him practically every day. He looks good. I mean, it's *Silas Cas-te-low*, y'know?"

"No!" Kasey's mouth twisted into a snarl. Caro couldn't help but think she was ridiculously cute. Caro was pissed, but it was so good to be this close to Kasey again, to see her grouchy face right in front of her. "I didn't come here for Si! I'm engaged. You *know* I'm engaged to Devon. What are you talking about?"

"I haven't even seen your engagement ring in real life," Caro said, taking Kasey's left hand, separating her ring finger from the others. She touched the square diamond, gently pulling it closer to her eyes. "It's gorgeous and it's *huge*. Devon must be loaded?"

"Yours is bigger than mine. Please! *The diamond as big as the Ritz.*" Kasey smacked her lips and snatched Caro's left hand up to her face. They both eyed the ice flashing in the sunlight. "Um, you're married to Maxwell Mason Foxberry the *Third*." Kasey held up three fingers with her free hand. "That long-ass name alone screams money. It's,

31

like, probably illegal for a poor person to have a name like that. Get real. His family owns more than half of Goldie...so yeah, now *you* own more than half of Goldie. Puh*lease*!"

No, Caroline didn't exactly hate becoming town royalty by default when she'd married Trey. The girls had teased her about it for a bit, calling her *Princess Caroline* and *Princess Caroppenheimer Foxberry the Third* in their emails and texts. Ada was one to talk, with how much money she'd always had, and Rosemarie was content with non-profits and working for Christian charities. Apparently, Kasey was now rolling in it too, which made Caro so happy. Kasey grew up with practically nothing and went off to an Ivy League and now had this amazing job and apparently an amazing, loaded fiancé, and all of that would have been lovely if Kasey had bothered to return to Goldie even once during the last fifteen years. Caro's fresh round of tears was angry and it wasn't stopping. She wanted to know why Kasey was back, but of course Kasey wouldn't budge. She had been as stubborn as a Mississippi mule since the day she was born.

"I'm not here for Silas, trust me," Kasey said softly.

There was a knock on the bathroom door.

"Yeah?" Caro said.

"It's Roses," Rosemarie said. Kasey opened the door and wiped her eyes.

"Tell her. Tell her Silas is out there somewhere," Caro said, stepping back to whip some toilet paper off the roll. They were so used to seeing one another cry Rosemarie didn't even mention it. She just smiled at them.

"Oh, he's out there, all right. Forever hot as shit. You haven't seen him?" Rosemarie said, finishing the champagne in her flute. Caro honked her nose and wiped her face some more. Rosemarie touched the top of her head, then Kasey's.

"Y'all, please! I haven't seen Silas in fifteen years! And lemme check! Oh yeah, I'm *still* engaged," Kasey said, holding up her hand.

"You wouldn't be this mad if you didn't care. Look at you—you're sweating!" Caro said, moving Kasey to the mirror.

"What do you expect? It's hot in here! Damn!" Kasey said, fanning herself.

"Look, girl, we're only telling you the facts. The facts are: he's out there," Rosemarie said. She thumbed toward the window.

Trey was handling business at the distillery and said maybe if he had time, he'd swing by the Plums' later. Caro didn't care either way. Not anymore. The bourbon slipped itself around her like a jacket with a hood, and she could feel it working, blocking out some of the bad. She put the empty flask back in her bag, which she'd left in Ada's old bedroom, and met Kasey—leaning against the wall, texting—in the hallway again.

"Show me another picture of Devon," Caro said to her. "Are you texting him about Silas?"

"Caro, you're—"

"I'm what? Go ahead—tell me." She smirked and put her hand on Kasey's cheek. "You're so beautiful. I can't believe I'm looking at your face."

"*You're* so beautiful. Honestly, I don't want to fight. I really mean it when I say I'm sorry. I—"

"Show me another picture of Devon, please," Caro said again.

In high school, Silas used to call Kasey "Dandelion," but to Caro right then, Kasey looked like a brown-haired daisy in her white dress. Her mom was white and her dad was black, and both those things came together perfectly in Kasey's features. She had a heart-shaped face, the cutest nose, pink lips. A delicate dimple in her chin like a fingerprint press in soft dough. Kasey was the oldest of them but looked the youngest; she was mistaken for a freshman all throughout high school.

Kasey pulled up a picture of Devon that Caro hadn't seen and handed her the phone. Devon Allbright, sitting up on his elbows in the grass in Bryant Park, wearing a pair of Wayfarer sunglasses. He was ultra-preppy in a white T-shirt and navy shorts rolled once, summer-brown skin, hair combed back. Caro told Kasey that the photo was literally "Boys of Summer" by Don Henley come to life. RACK knew every word of that song by heart. They used to scream-sing it in high school, driving the country roads in Ada's convertible. Now Caro—buzzed as a fat, pollen-drunk bee—sang part of the chorus to Kasey with their faces so close.

"I know, right? I've probably told him that before. He thinks I'm crazy for it, I'm sure," Kasey said.

"Why didn't he come? Why don't we get to meet him?"

"You will—I promise. He's busy. He's a workaholic."

"Environmental law for the PineLight Project," Caro said, proud of herself for remembering exactly whom Devon worked for, even in her tipsy state.

"Right. And I don't know if I'm ready for Devon in Goldie, honestly. Being here alone is overwhelming enough." Kasey took her phone back and they both waved at a short line of girls in swishy pink dresses slinking past.

"You're *not* alone! You have us, whether you want us or not," Caro said.

"I *want* y'all. Of course I want y'all," Kasey said, sounding like she might cry again. Caro held her hand.

One of Ada's twin brothers walked by with Ada's youngest thrown over his shoulder.

"Hi, Auntie Caro!" her little boy said.

"Hi, boys," Caro said. Kasey smiled at them. It'd only been about an hour since Kasey had met Ada's babies in person. The girls regularly shared pictures of their lives with one another, but this morning was the first time Kasey had ever seen Ada's boys in the flesh. Caro felt those all-mixed-up flickers of frustration and abandonment, anger and sadness. Those leftover feelings that crept up whenever she thought about Kasey leaving without a real goodbye, days after their high school graduation.

"I'm still mad at you, though," Caro said once they'd passed.

"I know, I know. I'm sorry."

"Stop keeping secrets and stop keeping everything bottled up. You know we're here for you and we'll do anything for each other! Talk to us!" Caro said, dodging the hypocrisy of her own words. She'd been feeling like a shook-up bottle of pop lately—violently bubbling with the cap on, waiting to explode. She thought for sure Kasey would have been able to sniff it out, but if she had, she didn't let it show. They put their arms around each other and hugged tight.

---

still @ work

Trey never texted with sweetness anymore. He rarely used any punctuation. When they were dating, he'd tried harder and given Caro no reason to think he'd *stop* trying, but the sweetness had faded away like the end of a song.

He sent two more not long after the first one.

Busy

not gonna make it

Caro felt relief, cool on the back of her neck, when she read those texts. She didn't respond. She left her phone in her bag upstairs and was glad to be outside now with her girlfriends and more cupcakes. She grabbed a full flute, deciding to quit the bourbon and switch to something non-Foxberry: champagne.

"Come here. Quick!" Rosemarie said to her. Caro had always been wild with love for Roses, RACK's heartbeat. Rosemarie also left Goldie after high school and traveled the world like Carmen Sandiego, but she returned as often as she could. Most of the time her visits were a surprise, and Caro loved to find herself at the end of a long shift at the bakery—flour snowing her hair as she boxed up the hundredth birthday cake, the millionth cupcake—and suddenly see Rosemarie's pretty brown eyes in front of her.

When Caroline walked to her, Rosemarie subtly signaled to the right, then did it again.

"What?" Caro asked, confused.

"Well, *lookee* there who Miss Kasey found," Rosemarie said, nudging her.

Caro leaned over to see Kasey talking to Silas Castelow. He was behind the portable bar shaking a drink and smiling so much Caro thought maybe his face would split open like hot fruit. Silas loved women and women loved Silas, but Silas had *really* loved him some Kasey Fritz since they were teenagers, and everyone in Goldie knew it. The girls watched Kasey giggle with her whole body at something he was saying.

"I knew he wouldn't be mad at her. He *never* could stay mad at her. He's probably as crazy about her now as he was back then. Do you think this will be a problem?" Caro asked, taking a sip of champagne, which felt like water after all that bourbon. She put her flute down and got a pink cupcake off the table, removed the paper. She and Ada had spent two full days with their team at the bakery making those cupcakes.

"I think our Kasey might be full of surprises. Who knows? There's a whole chunk of her life we know nothing about, and right now, all I see is two lovebirds yukking it up in the grass," Rosemarie said. Caro offered her the cupcake and she took a bite. "Trey's not coming? Figured this would be his kind of thing. Isn't he usually Mister Popular, Never Misses a Party?"

"Pretty much, but he's at work. Where's Esme?" Caro asked about Rosemarie's girlfriend of three years. "I'm sorry I forgot to ask earlier."

Rosemarie waved her apology away with a quick flick. "She's stuck in Seattle. Plus, this is the *exact opposite* of her kind of thing."

"Well, Trey and I got in a big ol' fight last night, so..." Caro trailed off for a moment. "Let's just say I'm thankful for the space," she finished. Her stomach dropped again as she thought of how angry he'd been over nothing. How hard she'd cried, still standing her ground. Part of her wanted to go upstairs and get her phone, text him back to test the waters, but she killed that impulse real quick by finishing the cupcake and letting the champagne glitter her mouth before downing the rest of it.

"A fight about what?" Rosemarie asked, going straight to the heart of the matter. The girls knew never to bring anything up to Rosemarie unless they wanted her to get right down to it. Caro loved how honest Rosemarie was and had told her that plenty of times. Rosemarie would shrug it off and say it was easy because she didn't know any other way to be, but it inspired Caro to want to be more honest too.

"Nothing. He was just in a bad mood."

Somewhat honest. Definitely not a lie.

"Is that why he's not coming? Because you had a fight? Is Trey *super* petty? Because wow," Rosemarie said. Caro opened her mouth to weakly defend him, but nothing came out. "Look, look!" Rosemarie said quietly, nodding toward Kasey and Silas. Silas had stepped around the bar, and Rosemarie and Caro stood there watching them hug. Silas lifted Kasey off the ground a bit, holding her way past the length of a regular hug. So romantic—Caro felt jealous of both of them. The champagne slurred through her bloodstream. When they pulled apart, Silas put his hand out and Kasey lifted hers to show him her engagement ring. Caro was grateful she and Rosemarie had something else to focus on besides Trey, and she was even more grateful for the distraction of Ada showing up next to them, asking what they were looking at.

"Your brother-in-law and our darling Kasey Jo back at it, apparently," Rosemarie said.

"Really? Oh wow. I don't know how to feel! Tell me how to feel!" Ada said, looking back and forth between Rosemarie and Caro for answers.

"She reminded us she was engaged," Rosemarie said.

"Isn't Silas seeing someone?" Caro whispered. Her champagne-tongue tripped over the *s*'s, which made them all laugh. Then she snorted, which made them laugh harder.

"Not anymore. Not since Christmas. I told you this," Ada said. Caro had a vague memory of it, but it was gone as quick as it'd appeared. Every now and then Silas would bring a woman to the bakery for treats or occasionally show up with someone new when they were all hanging out together, but he seemed committed to being a chill bachelor, which made him *that* much more desirable to the women of Goldie keeping tabs on him.

"I love it, truth be told," Rosemarie said. "I mean, Devon seems like a great guy, but nostalgia is a *hell* of a drug."

Kasey and Silas shifted their position, and the girls were peeking through the bushes now—a good and proper covert operation.

"I just want her to be happy," Ada said.

"So do I," Rosemarie added.

"Me too. Devon *does* seem like a great guy. If Taylor Swift saw him in the park back in the day, she would've gone straight home to her cats and written a song about him. Seriously. Have you seen that picture? I was like, *damn*, girl," Caro said.

"What picture? She didn't show me!" Ada said.

"Ask her about it. Tell her exactly what I said," Caro said with a bubbly *ha*. "And I *love* that Silas is wearing a pink suit. I *love* it when men wear pink. Trey's too macho to go near it."

"Yes, I do love that suit. He and Grayson went shopping for theirs together. They were real proud of themselves. Uh, where'd they go?" Ada asked, getting on her tiptoes. Rosemarie and Caro leaned over to help look. It was Caro who turned first and noticed Kasey standing right behind them.

"Okay, wow—y'all are sad. Sad!" Kasey said, smiling and shaking her head.

Caro—close to *really* drunk at this point—went upstairs alone to check her phone for texts from Trey. Again, there were three.

> so youre still mad about last night
> even tho i apologized even tho you
> working there embarrasses me
> sometimes and ive told you that
>
> its not like im not busy too
>
> response ?

A question mark, his lone use of punctuation. Caro sat on Ada's old bed and wrote him back.

> I know you apologized and I do
> believe you're sorry. I don't know
> how I feel right now. Mostly,
> I'm sad.

The gray bubbles appeared almost immediately and Caro tried her best to focus on the glowing screen.

> well im sorry youre not perfect and
> neither am i

> I never said I was perfect, Trey. I
> said I was sad!

Caro was crying again, shuddered a deep breath in.

then ok im sorry youre sad

Even that tiny bit of sweetness was a comfort to her. They'd talk more when she got home. Caro was sure he'd be fine. She'd gotten in late the night before because of a huge festival pie order that she'd forgotten about, having been so lost in making cupcakes. Trey had to heat up dinner for himself, something he hated to do, and it took too long because Caro forgot to thaw out the leftovers. As soon as she closed the front door behind her, he made his anger known. Again, he brought up wanting her to quit working at the bakery, and again, she flat-out refused.

But. He only called her a *bitch* once.

And. He (half) apologized when they'd gotten in bed together.

She'd roasted a chicken early that morning before she left; she made his favorite fried potatoes and peas with Irish butter too. Thinking of the woman who could wake up that early and cook a full dinner for a man who scared her so much the night before made Caro feel detached from herself—like she'd been unsnapped from gravity and could float away.

Thank you for being sweet to me, Trey. I NEED you to be sweet to me sometimes. Do you understand that?

ok caroline

2004

4

Caro's grandma Mimi was thirty-seven when Caro was born; Caro's mom was only eighteen. People who didn't know better thought Mimi was Caro's mother. Caro's mom was twenty when she realized being a mom wasn't what she wanted to do with her life. She tried (barely) but repeatedly fell back in with the men and friends who brought out her addictive, self-destructive behavior—meth, pills, alcohol. Caro's daddy wasn't much better, but at least he sent checks. Sometimes.

When Caro was a baby, her grandma started a knitting group at the church and that was where RACK was born. The girls had been best friends since crawling around together on that church floor.

They were about two months out from high school graduation, and Caro knew for sure she didn't want to go to a four-year college. What she wanted was pastry school; it was like she'd known it her whole life. She could tell her feelings were right and true because she didn't detect even the slightest twitch of jealousy about her best friends' plans after high school. Kasey had already been accepted to her dream school on the East Coast. Rosemarie was taking a gap year before going to school in Seattle, and Ada was interested in culinary school or interior design, but her family had so much money it didn't even matter what she did after high school, because she'd be fine no matter what.

There were times when Caro felt guilty about *not* wanting to leave Goldie; it seemed like everyone else couldn't wait to leave the small town they'd grown up in. There were countless country songs and movies about this, and it was all Kasey talked about sometimes. That was what hurt Caro's feelings the most—the fact that Kasey acted like she couldn't escape Goldie fast enough. But Caro knew how desperate Kasey was to get away from that monster Roy, even if she was scared to leave him with her mother. When she saw Kasey close her eyes in a silent wish listening to "Wide Open Spaces" while they were driving with the windows down, faces turned to the sun like flowers, hair blowing in the wind, Caro's heart hurt.

Caroline *liked* the comfort that came with thinking about staying in Goldie and perfecting her pie recipes at the diner for the day in the far-off future when she and Ada would open their own restaurant—*Oh Plum*, after both of their last names—together.

Caro liked that Goldie was a small, touristy town that had such cute, trendy boutiques and shops that it *felt* like a big one. She liked living so close to the lake and the little fuzzy ducks that her grandma stopped for on their drives home so they could cross the street. Caro wasn't ashamed of living in a trailer park either. Their trailer was nice and cozy. The outside of it was a skyish pale blue draped in twinkle lights. There were kitschy gnomes next to the steps and, for as long as she could remember, a ladybug welcome mat in front of the door. Whenever it got too faded, her grandma bought another exactly like it.

That was what her grandma had always called her too, her whole life: *Ladybug*. There were lots of places she wanted to go and things she wanted to see, but Caro loved living in Goldie, and she didn't have plans to leave her grandma alone. Simple as that.

———

At Myrtle's Diner, Caroline built on the recipes her grandma passed down from her mother and her mother's mother. "All the way back to Eve," Mimi would say. Caro loved baking anything—cookies, cakes, tarts, doughnuts, cupcakes, cobblers, pies. Being in a kitchen with sugar in the air made her feel better about the world.

Caro was thinking about turning her grandma's gooseberry pie into a special at the diner. She'd made the crusts a day early and par baked the bottom one so it wouldn't get soggy. Now she was in the diner kitchen boiling down a mess of gooseberries she and Kasey had picked at Kasey's farm over the summer. Her grandma taught them both how to can them; Mimi knew how to do everything.

Myrtle walked around the corner.

"Your grandmama ever tell you about how when we were little, we used to try and sell those mud pies we made down by the church?" Her laughter twinkled like small, sunny bells. Miss Myrtle was one of Caroline's many surrogate mothers. Her real mom might've been a bust, but Mimi made sure Caro grew up surrounded by women who could run the world.

"Oh yes, I do remember her telling me about those mud pies, Miss Myrtle," Caro said, smiling. Myrtle had some hilarious stories about her grandma, and Caro never got tired of them. She listened to Myrtle talk while she waited for the gooseberries to pop; then it'd be time to add the sugar, flour, and nutmeg. And! Her new additions: orange and ginger.

"Okay then. Well, let me know how your pie turns out, but since *you're* making it, I already know it'll be good. I'm heading home. See you tomorrow," Myrtle said, getting her white fringe purse off the hook.

"Bye!" Caro said, stirring. She was going to make the pie real pretty with pastry circles and a couple of gooseberries on top. She loved decorating with lattice crust and cutout designs as much as she loved making them. A week ago she'd decorated one of her new favorites— honey pear pie—with little hearts on top.

When the pie was cooling, Caro put it in front of a couple of her favorite customers—two older gentlemen named Louie and Pete who came in almost every night for black coffee and warm treats after dinner. They looked like Statler and Waldorf—the grumpy old men from *The Muppet Show* who heckled from the balcony—but they were never mean. She cut two slices.

"So, whatcha got for us tonight, Reds?" Pete asked.

Reds. It was what a lot of the customers called her. Between her girlfriends and her grandma, she had a million nicknames already, and her red hair added even more opportunities. She'd heard every possible nickname for a redheaded girl. *Big Red* because she was five foot ten. *Red Delicious* by some of the guys who liked to holler out their truck windows as they whizzed by.

Ginger. Ginge. Fire Crotch. Do the carpets match the drapes?

She didn't mind when the old men called her Reds. They were harmless and they loved her pies.

"Brand-new recipe, testing it out. I could wait for it to cool down some more but since you're here now, give it a try. It's my grandma's gooseberry pie. Canned the gooseberries myself! And then I added some secrets," Caro said, winking at them.

They both took big bites and dramatically *mmm*-ed at how good it was. Caro refilled their coffees as they talked to her about the Goldie High baseball team. They tipped more when she pretended to care about sports, and Caro didn't mind listening.

When they left, there was a crisp twenty-dollar bill slipped underneath the pie plate.

More people had been coming from all over the country to eat at Myrtle's ever since it'd been featured on one of those American road trip shows on the Food Network some months ago. Caro's red hair made it onto the broadcast, whipping around the kitchen corner. Rosemarie, Ada, and Kasey liked to tease her about having a famous ponytail.

Myrtle's was well-known for its double bacon burger platter, its grilled cheese too. Almost every day after school, Caroline was waitressing, sliding plates of fish and fries, meatloaf and potatoes, barbecue sandwiches, and cinnamon apples across the tables. The diner sat down the street from Plum Bakery, next to the antique shop, right where it'd been for almost fifty years after Myrtle's father had opened it, naming it in honor of his only baby girl.

———

Mimi was waiting out front in her yellow Wagoneer right at ten, and like always, she asked Caro if she'd had time to do her homework.

"A little," Caro said, lying.

Sure, she'd had the time to do it, but no, she hadn't done it. Instead, on her breaks, she had sat out back and smoked with Beau, her favorite cook. She'd asked him to teach her how to French inhale, and he was trying his best. Caro didn't normally smoke, but she smoked with Beau.

Beau had served in the military and now he was home. Beau had a fuzzy shaved head, a pretty mouth, and a way of looking at Caro that made her feel like she was a hologram floating in space. He smoked Camel Lights and loved Cash and Coltrane, drove a white truck with a tackle box in the back. Sometimes when he didn't know she was looking, he'd put his unlit cigarette between his teeth and flick it back and forth with his tongue the same way Leonardo DiCaprio did in *Titanic*. And sometimes Beau called her *Muffin Mix*. He looked at her one day and said it out of nowhere. For all the nicknames she had, *Muffin Mix* was definitely her favorite.

Beau was twenty-two and she was seventeen, and she knew that could get him into some trouble, but she liked flirting with him anyway. Flirting with him passed the time when she was in between boyfriends, and she and her ex, Mateo, had broken up a month ago.

"Ain't that the Foxberry boy?" Mimi asked as Caro put her seat belt on. She looked over to see two shadows shoving each other by the garbage cans in the alley. She quickly recognized Trey by his height and the way he was moving his arms. He was a big boy.

"Yep," Caro said as Mimi drove away.

"Boys sure can act like dumbasses sometimes, can't they, Ladybug?" her grandma said, coasting through the yellow light.

Caro mm-hmmed and turned around, waiting to see if the boys would spill out of the alley, but from where she was sitting, everything looked pristine and peaceful. Like a backlot from a comforting movie with a happy ending. Even though she knew it was the furthest thing from the truth, as she looked down that small-town street, it seemed Goldie was a place where nothing bad could ever happen.

———

The next morning at school, first thing, Kasey took Caro by the elbow and led her to the corner by their lockers.

"Girl! Silas kissed me last night and asked me to prom. Asked me to be his girl. It was wild...I wasn't expecting it, but of course I said yes. It was...it was wild—" Kasey said.

"Excuse me?! What? Tell me *everything* right now!" Caro said.

As Kasey filled her in, Caro couldn't help but feel like she'd missed out on something super *you had to be there* important. It hurt her feelings that Ada knew all this before her. Also, Caro was jealous because she still didn't have a date to prom, but she was happy for Kasey too. They talked until the bell was about to ring, then went their separate ways.

Caro saw Trey Foxberry on her way to class. Most of the time he ignored her, but they'd gone to the same schools since elementary. He was looking real dumb but kind of cute in his Goldie High hoodie and jersey shorts, slowpoking down the steps with a copy of *Wuthering Heights* and a busted lip.

After school, the girls went to Rosemarie's, where there was a tray of fudgy brownies waiting for them. Rosemarie's parents had lived on more than one commune as they made their way from California down south, and in true hippie fashion, their house was forever stocked with far-out after-school treats. Spinach salads with apples, pepitas, and homemade dressing. Cookies made with carob chips and tofu. Sun tea with fat lemon wedges, fresh mango, and banana smoothies with almond milk. Vegan cheese grilled between the bread Rosemarie's mom, Leilani, made. When Leilani baked "special" brownies, she pretended like they'd disappeared, never asking if the girls had eaten them.

"Those are the pot ones; these are the boring ones," Rosemarie said, pointing. The pot brownies were in purple glass, the regular ones in a metal tin. Caro had to be at the diner in a few hours, so she put a boring one on her plate; Ada did too. Rosemarie and Kasey dug in with their fingers, chomping fat chunks of chocolate they took from the purple glass.

Rosemarie picked up her guitar and played for a little bit as the girls hung out in the kitchen, talking and laughing and touching things. Rosemarie could sing anything; she had a soft, angelic voice like her mom. One of those light, wistful voices that could make you cry before your heart caught up to it, like Dolly Parton or Billie Holiday.

Rosemarie turned on Grateful Dead's "Sugar Magnolia" as the girls walked through the beaded curtain separating the kitchen from the living room. The Kingston house was an explosion of color—the kitchen walls were psychedelic purple, the fridge was orange, the back door was Grecian blue. And so much green: hanging pothos in macrame holders that Rosemarie's mom had made, aggressive unidentified vines wrapped around a trellis. The girls climbed into the conversation pit, where everything was tie-dyed pillows and marigold velvet. The Kingstons' beloved mutt, Jerry Garcia, followed them and flopped down onto a triangle of sun on the floor.

"Y'all should paint stars on the ceiling," Kasey said, and Caro knew she was feeling the brownie already because of how she said it, all dreamy-like.

"Yes! Like fractals repeating and repeating from this end all the way over there. Or like *The Starry Night*," Rosemarie said, letting her arms go wide and keeping them that way.

"Wait. Is this Roy's weed? Please don't tell me your parents get their weed from Dumbass," Kasey asked.

"Pshh, y'know Daddy grows his own. Organic. My daddy wouldn't *touch* Roymont's weed," Rosemarie corrected her and rolled her eyes, giggled, and kept giggling. "By the way! *Why* is he named that?"

"His mother thought it was a great name. She made it up," Kasey said.

"I hate this conversation," Rosemarie said.

"I do too. Fuck you, Roymont! Why won't you die?!" Kasey said as loud as she could. Rosemarie repeated it and belted the last part like it was the big finale of a musical. They kept saying it and singing it until they were both laughing so hard they had to stop. The two of them were off in their private purple haze.

Ada and Caro didn't even mind being left out, because they were happily talking about boys—which ones were ramping up their cuteness as the school year drew to a close, which ones were slacking off.

"All the cute boys smell like wood, don't they, Kasey? We've agreed on this point," Caroline said.

"Yes! It's true! It's totally true! It's a fact from God. Cute boys smell like wood, *aaand* boys love wearing socks, like, constantly. What's up with that?" Kasey asked.

"Dude! Dudes *love* socks. I don't know why, but they do. That's a God-fact too, it is, so write it down somewhere," Rosemarie said.

"Seriously, though, are you and Grayson getting married? Is that what you want? He's never going away to college?" Caro asked Ada, as Rosemarie and Kasey slunk away to their weed-world again. Grayson had graduated last year and now he worked for his family's construction company, and Mrs. Castelow owned and ran the adorable B and B off the town square. The power-merging of the Plum and Castelow families would be such a big deal their families probably would've wanted to arrange it if it hadn't happened on its own.

Ada leaned her head on her hand. Rosemarie and Kasey were cracking up about something new that Caroline had missed. Rosemarie was literally rolling from one end of the couch to the other while Kasey did a poor job of catching her breath. The girls were making so much noise Ada and Caro could barely get through their conversation.

They always had the most fun at Rosemarie's. Her place was cozy and enchanted, with the ever-constant music from the bamboo wind chimes mingling with the birdsong. There were hand-painted feeders on both the porch and the back deck, several birdbaths, and birdhouses in the yard.

"I think so. I think we really will get married. Someday," Ada said. "Okay, my turn. Do you continue to have a lethal crush on Beau?"

"Wow, interesting, but the thing is, I *don't* have a crush on Beau," Caro said, squinting her eyes at Ada and playfully slapping her bare leg. The girls liked to tease her about Beau, and although it didn't bother her, there was a part of her that was protective of him. She didn't want anyone getting the wrong idea about their friendship. She didn't want him getting into any trouble for it. He'd never been inappropriate with her, although yes, she thought about . . . stuff. He was cute and young and strong, and she liked how, even when the diner scent hung heavy on him, he still smelled a lot like the fresh wood shavings she used to put in her guinea pig's cage. One of her favorite smells.

"Who do you want to go to prom with?" Ada asked.

"I don't know," Caro said.

"Hmm, let's see! Who would it be? Who do you have a megacrush on? Hmm, maybe *Beau*?" Ada said.

"Shut up!" Caro laughed.

Rosemarie gasped and stood; Jerry Garcia's ears perked up. The girls turned sharply to look at her. "Should we invite *everyone* to our graduation party? Like, the *entire* town?"

"That's basically what my mama is already doing, Roses," Ada reassured her.

"Sweet. Graduation isn't that long after my birthday, so I'm gonna milk it. Free second party!" Rosemarie said, sitting down again and closing her eyes.

"Hey, Roses, how does Caro feel about Beau?" Ada asked.

"Caroppenheimer is *obsessed* with Beau and his witchy hazel eyes. What are we even talking about?" Rosemarie said, opening her eyes, looking hilariously confused.

"*Witchy* hazel eyes? What in the world does that mean?" Caro asked.

"Sounded good to my ears and my mouth…*witchy* hazel…hazel… same thing. You love everything he's got," Rosemarie said.

"You heard it. Perma-Truth Serum over here cannot tell a lie. So, it's a fact, Jack," Ada said, satisfied.

Caroline smiled wide and gave them the middle finger. Kasey gave it back and kept laughing with her eyes half-closed as she slow-motion-totally-stoned pushed her brown curls out of her face.

Later, Rosemarie and Kasey braided each other's hair into fishtails and decided they wanted to jump on the trampoline in the backyard. Ada needed to get home to start dinner, said there was a warm steak salad with blue cheese dressing she was trying to get right.

She and Caro left and walked as far as they could together before they hugged in front of the diner. Caro went inside, started her shift.

———

Caro took the ginger out of the recipe and made another gooseberry pie. Beau and the old men at the counter agreed—they liked it better without. They left her twenty dollars again because she let them tell her about how when they went to South Goldie High, they played football and almost took state. They liked to tell that story about once a month.

She didn't finish her homework. She smoked with Beau out back and tried her best not to laugh out loud thinking about *witchy hazel* eyes. She hung out with Rosemarie, Ada, and Kasey some more—they brought the Castelow boys with them too—because the girls always came up late on Thursday nights for ice cream. This time Caroline gave them pieces of gooseberry pie to go with it, demanding they tell her the truth about whether they liked it or not. Ada was the only one who offered up a fix. "More nutmeg," she said, tapping her short pink fingernail on the plate.

As they left, Rosemarie handed Caro a little purple glass container of pot brownies *for later* with a wink.

"Psst. Beau, do you want a *pot* brownie?" Caro whispered once her friends were gone. She stood behind him in the kitchen.

"Sure. You gonna give me one?" he asked, turning to look at her with his bright-as-a-firefly face. Too cute. He had both hands in the soapy water of the deep sink. It wasn't even his job to do the dishes, but he did them sometimes anyway. Said it was therapeutic.

Caro unsnapped the top of the glass container and broke off an ice-cube-sized chocolate square, held it out for him. When Beau opened his mouth, she put the whole thing in.

"Thank you," he said, chewing.

"Bye! See you tomorrow!"

"All right now, Muffin Mix," he mumbled out.

Her heart pressed Record everysingletime he called her that, and she listened to it over and over again on the ride home.

———

In her bedroom, after finishing her homework and after her grandma had gone to sleep, Caro ate a brownie as slowly as she could, savoring every gooey bite. She wrote in her baking journal.

Next pie stuff to try messing around with:
    blueberry lime (with a cream wash)
    blueberry lavender peach
    lemon chess
    raspberry honey/cinnamon meringue?

Next cookies to try:
    red velvet
    hot chocolate

Also:
    pick up demerara sugar from the grocery store.

When she turned off the lamp and lay down, she was thinking about her girlfriends, her sisters. She got floaty, wondering if they were in bed already too. Rosemarie and Kasey were night owls, but she and Ada were usually early birds. She imagined the four of them as real birds, kaleidoscopic and fat and soaring. She wondered if Kasey was at home or staying with Ada again. Tomorrow she'd tell her she could sleep over if she wanted.

Like a lone puff of cloud smoothing the blue, her thoughts drifted to Beau—Beau being in that bed with her, Beau in his military uniform, Beau's hair, Beau's beard, Beau's chocolatey mouth, Beau falling in love with her after eating her pies, Beau getting in a time machine so he would be young enough to take her to prom, Beau's cedar smell. She didn't try to stop them. She opened the window, took off her clothes, got under her cool sheets. Let those thoughts warm her up.

2019

5

ROSEMARIE KINGSTON

Rosemarie was already partied out. She didn't know how she was
going to get through an entire *week* of wedding festivities. She took a
breather alone in the bathroom, texting Esme.

> How goes it? Y're coming down
> soon?

Soon as I can! How is everything?

> It's fine. Kase actually showed up!

Are you serious?

> Totally serious. It's kind of surreal.

Well good. I'm glad you get to
spend time together. How are you
feeling? Are you sleeping enough?
Drinking lots of water?

Wow. I'm fine. Yes, mom.

Stop that.

Sorry (not sorry). ☺

Have fun! Call me later. Ilu.

Ilu too.

She texted Leo.

Wyd?

Depends. Wyd?

Missing you, honestly.

Gross. I miss you too. Where's
Esme this week?

Seattle. Last week was Vancouver.

For how much longer?

Few days? IDK. Can I come over
tonight?

Sure you feel up for it?

Absolutely.

Well, then you better.

GOODBYE EARL

Wanna sing together? Practice for
the wedding . . . IF we get around
to it?

Dumb questions, Ro.

:p XO

Love.

Rosemarie put her phone in her pocket, and after she used the bathroom and washed her hands, she patted the cold water on her cheeks. She stared at her reflection so long she started to dissociate.

———

She went into the backyard and got a peek at the lunch spread. Fishy finger sandwiches and blue cheese romaine salads with rings of red onions. Big glass bowls of grapes and every kind of berry, plums, and peaches. More fruit floated in the pitchers of water in the middle of the tables. Too much. Her brain might've been hungry but her stomach wasn't on board. She'd go home and nap instead. She told Ada and Kasey that and went upstairs to find Caro and tell her too. She moved toward Ada's old bedroom and heard Caro behind the door, talking and crying. Rosemarie stood quietly listening. She wouldn't usually eavesdrop, but Caro's mood had been bordering on gloomy lately, and there was something odd about the way she'd said she'd had a fight with Trey. Something dark. Rosemarie didn't want to think the worst, but her intuition was rarely wrong. She closed her eyes; she *had* to close her eyes whenever she thought about Caro hurting. Rosemarie couldn't make out everything Caro was saying, but she heard the fear in her wavy voice, the pauses and trembling. When Rosemarie couldn't stand it any longer, she pushed the door open.

"I've gotta go," Caro said quickly, ending the call.

"*Girl*, what's up? Was that Trey? Seriously, if this is still about last night, he needs to get over it."

"No. It's fine. I'm drunk and he's an asshole sometimes no matter what I do," Caro said, hugging her phone to her chest. When she looked up at the ceiling, she began sobbing.

Rosemarie put her arms around Caroline, closed her eyes. She didn't ask any more questions, didn't say anything at all. Just held her and let her cry.

Rosemarie convinced Caro to sleep it off. She'd seen Caro drunk plenty of times, but this time she was *sad* drunk. So early in the day too. While Rosemarie sat next to the pillow, petting Caro's hair, she was in and out of sleep, apologizing. For being too drunk, for not asking about Esme enough. Caro even apologized for a stupid fight she and Rosemarie got into back in middle school over which famous artist to pick for their group project. Rosemarie wanted to do Van Gogh and Caro chose Georgia O'Keeffe. They had to do O'Keeffe since Rosemarie was outnumbered.

"I picked her because everything she painted was a vagina and I love vaginas. You love vaginas too, but I'm sorry, Roses," Caro said.

Rosemarie cackled and touched Caro's cheek.

"You're right. You're exactly right, sweet Caroline. I do love vaginas." Rosemarie shushed her. "Go to sleep."

"I'm *very* drunk."

"I know. It's all right. Drink some more water and take these. You'll feel better, and I'll see you later tonight," Rosemarie said quietly. Caro sat up enough to swallow the ibuprofen. Rosemarie made her drink one more big gulp of water before she lay down again and closed her eyes.

* * *

Caro's phone lit up with messages from Trey.

> i get so mad at you
> but you married me so it cant be
> all bad bc
> you love me
> why else would we be together
> i wasnt hurting for a fucking
> woman when i asked you
> i may swing by dukes
> text me later
> and yes the chicken was good

Rosemarie knew Caro's passcode; RACK had always known one another's favorite numbers and passwords. She put it in, and feeling guilty—but not guilty enough to *not* do it—she read the texts from Trey. Caro snuggled up in the blankets and rolled away from her. Rosemarie could smell the alcohol sweetening her sleeping breath, warming up the room. The song the bluegrass band was playing ended with a quick flair of fiddle, and another took its place. "Blue Moon of Kentucky."

Rosemarie's stomach hurt as she read through Trey's nasty responses to Caroline. Rosemarie had never really known or liked Trey; none of them had except Caro, and obviously she saw something good in him, peeking out from behind the dark clouds of that much money and his family name. And although Trey's looks were tolerable, Mr. Darcy's words ran through Rosemarie's head oftentimes when she saw him: *Not handsome enough to tempt me.*

She considered responding to Trey from Caro's phone. Properly telling him to fuck all the way off forever. Instead, Rosemarie looked down at her best friend's thick river of red hair washing across the sunlit pillow and put the phone back on the bed.

———

Rosemarie was at her parents' place now. Home. Her parents were out of town for a couple more days, playing a folk music festival in Tennessee. So, for now, the whole colorful, cozy house was left to her and her Australian shepherd, Basie. The dog demanded Rosemarie's total, undivided attention when she met her at the door, so Rosemarie gave her some love and let her out to do her business in the backyard grass.

Basie was sleeping warm across Rosemarie's feet on the couch when her phone woke her up. She'd opened the windows and climbed into the conversation pit, even though it was a tad too hot to have turned off the AC. She felt better than she had earlier in the day, and it seemed like a bit of magic, how good her body could feel in the sun when she ate the right things, drank enough water, got enough rest. Sometimes all she needed was her dog and some softness, some color to make her feel like everything in this world was going to be okay. The humidity had plunged her into an even deeper sleep, and now she found herself pleasantly dreamy and drowsy, stretching as much as she could without disturbing the dog, when she answered the phone and heard her mom's voice.

"Hey, baby, I was gonna leave a voicemail. I didn't think I could catch you, considering little Miss Taylor is basically holding you hostage the whole week," Leilani Kingston said to her.

"I'm napping in the sunny conversation pit. Basie and I are worthless right now, two lazy summer pups." Rosemarie rubbed the dog's head, and the dog returned the love with a deep groan of pleasure.

"Sounds lovely. Your dad and I have, like, a two-hour break until we need to be on stage again. It's been fun! Almost everyone else is younger than us, but we're trying not to let it make us feel *too* bad about ourselves." Rosemarie could hear the high lonesome sound of a fiddle somewhere behind her mom's voice, some scattered applause and birdsong too. She put the phone on mute so she could yawn properly.

"You will always be young and beautiful to me," Rosemarie said when she was finished.

"Thank you. Esme's not there yet?"

"No. Everyone keeps asking me about her, though. This is why I don't like telling people things. Too much fuss."

"I'm sorry. Do you not want her to come?" Leilani asked. Rosemarie heard her dad's gruff voice in the background. "Your daddy says hi."

"Hi, Daddy. And sure, I want Esme to come. Sure, I do. I'm just tired of talking everything to death. Who has the time?"

"I know that's right."

Rosemarie had stripped out of her linen suit before her nap. She slid her bare legs from underneath the dog and rolled over to stand. She turned her phone on speaker so she could read her text messages while her mom chatted away.

From Kasey.

Should we let Caro sleep?
I'm not drinking much tonight. Are
you?
I feel too old for this already.

From Ada.

Are you still at home?
What time are you going to Duke's?

From Esme.

I hope you have/had a nice nap!
Proud of you for resting, honestly.
Resting is healing and don't forget
how much you need it. You never
turn your little engine off!
Love you.

After seeing Kasey's texts, Rosemarie got pissed all over again about Trey's messages to Caro. She bent to snatch her suit off the floor.

"Well, that's about it. Call us tomorrow. Try to enjoy yourself. We love you so much it hurts," Leilani said. "Oh! If you talk to your brother, tell him to call or text his damn mama. It's been, like, two weeks now."

Her brother was a DJ based mostly in London, and he was terrible at communication. Eventually, when he did finally pop up in the group chat, he'd announce he was somewhere else, like Seoul or Athens. Or Barcelona. A year ago, she and Esme had met him there and gone to one of his shows.

"I will. I talked to him Wednesday. He's fine. He's been in Spain since Monday. Love *y'all* so much it hurts," Rosemarie said.

She texted everyone back. Asked Kasey to try getting Caro up in about two hours and told her she wasn't planning on drinking much tonight either. Told Ada she'd meet everyone at Duke's at seven. Told Esme she loved her too and sent her the train emoji because of its little engine. Then, Rosemarie headed out the door for a short walk with Basie excitedly prancing on her leash.

———

Goldie Golden Hour came early. It was steamy, but the sky was a dream—wildly blue with fat puffy clouds slowly shadowing the hills. Rosemarie strolled through the town square in the comfy clothes she'd put on after her nap—a pair of cutoffs and the black, threadbare Amnesty International T-shirt she'd had since college with her Birkenstocks—knowing full well Taylor and her girls would be dolled up like bachelorette piñatas. She'd smudged some red lipstick across her mouth and given Basie an extra treat as an apology for leaving again.

Caro and Kasey were standing outside of Duke's waiting for her.

"Well, how're you feeling?" Rosemarie asked Caroline. She hugged both of them.

A small pink group of Taylor's girlfriends whooped and hollered as they made their way inside. One of them was carrying a giant purple inflatable dick and had to try three different times to tuck it down enough so she could get it through the door of the bar.

The girls laughed about it, all of them. There was a riot of intense female energy on the sidewalk in front of Duke's, and Rosemarie let the power wash over her—heavy, hot, and buzzing.

"I slept for, like, five hours, puked twice, and drank so much water my stomach is sloshy. So, yeah. Better," Caro said.

"Good," Rosemarie said.

"Uh-huh. Y'all had some *lol*s teasing me about Silas, but look who's strutting out of the Burrito Barn," Kasey said, tilting her head to motion across the street. Rosemarie spied Leo with his hands full, using his foot to hold the door open for someone walking in.

"Ha-*ha*," Rosemarie said wryly, lifting her sunglasses and waving at him.

He looked both ways and waited until a car passed, then half jogged to their section of the sidewalk.

"It's early, ain't it? Figured y'all weren't coming out until later. Didn't know I'd be lucky enough to see *you* right now," he said, stepping close to Rosemarie. He said hi to Caro and Kasey and readjusted his bags of food.

"No rules, only lawlessness. It's the Wild West this week," Rosemarie said.

"Seems like it," Leo said, squinting to peek inside of Duke's. Rosemarie turned to see what she could. One of Taylor's friends was still wrestling with the inflatable dick, and another was standing on a chair, attempting to keep the balloon from getting whacked by the ceiling fan.

Smiles, some small group talk. Leo told Rosemarie she could let herself in later tonight if she wanted.

"You look good," he said to her.

"Thank you, Leo. Now, get," she said.

He leaned down to rub his nose against hers and turned away.

"All right," Rosemarie said, irrationally shy that Caro and Kasey were witness to what just happened. They knew Leo. They knew their relationship. So what? But still. *Irrational.*

"Enjoy your evening, ladies! Don't do anything I wouldn't do," he said and turned back around. "Then again, I'll do anything. You can ask Ro about *that* if you want to." He winked at them and almost stepped backward into traffic. He turned at the last second and disappeared around the corner. As quick as he was gone, Ada and Taylor walked around the same corner toward them.

"Well, it looks like you and Leo continue to be completely obsessed with each other, but just in case I'm missing something, I need an update. I'm gonna need to know *everything*," Kasey said to her.

"*Everything*," Caro chimed in, taking Rosemarie's hand.

Ada and Taylor were followed by another small group of girls in short dresses and sandals. Two of them were carrying pink balloons. One of the girls was visibly drunk, a light rain of mascara across her cheeks. Taylor doled out quick kisses to RACK and disappeared with her friends inside; Ada stayed out on the sidewalk.

"Did you literally run into Leo Bell?" Kasey asked her, pointing.

"Yeah, almost. Why?" Ada said. She was in her pink dress from earlier. One thing about Ada Plum was that she loved being in a pink dress, period. Rosemarie let it in—how good it was being back together like this, the four of them in Goldie again. She glanced at Kasey one more time to make sure she was real.

"Why? Because Roses and Leo are out here rubbing noses in public, but she's being shy about it, and maybe she has a *lot* to tell us—that's why. So, let's go sit down so she can do that," Kasey said.

Rosemarie shook her head at them. Snatched her sunglasses off and hooked them into the collar of her shirt. Caro gently nudged her toward the front door of Duke's, and time slowed as the music box of the glossy white ice-cream truck lazily made its way up Main like a languid raft on water.

She felt a lift in her heavy, latent sadness. Thought of Leo on his walk home and his ex-wife, what she was doing now. Rosemarie had been *so* jealous when he told her that he was getting married, but she'd stood next to him in her slim tuxedo anyway and smiled and cried. She thought of Leo walking into his empty rental house alone. She thought of him waiting for her to come over later. How he'd say *Ro* again like his mouth tasted good when he made the sound. No one else called her *Ro*.

She thought about Esme too. How humid her Seattle heart would find Goldie, how she'd want to get barbecue because she'd never had Southern barbecue. She imagined Leo and Esme meeting for the first time. How Leo would say something smart and funny to make Esme laugh, how effortlessly Esme would match his energy. Leo and Esme knew about each other, knew Rosemarie considered herself to be in a relationship with both of them, and they accepted that and agreed that it was certainly possible to be in love with more than one person at a time, because they'd experienced it too. Rosemarie had always been open with them about everything, but it was impossible to explain exactly *how* she could love them both so equally and differently. How life was way too short to worry about the *specifics* of love since it all felt so warm to her. So warm and so *home*, no matter what anyone thought or said.

The girls moved through the dark of the bar and out the back door. Onto the patio, into the sun again. Rosemarie sat at the table and put her sunglasses back on, thinking too much. Filled with love and wonder and a whirlpool crush of emotions. Happy and sad at the same time. Hot and dizzy as a june bug.

2004

6

Rosemarie's mom had made taco filling with fake meat and homemade salsa with cilantro and hothouse tomatoes from their greenhouse. She roasted corn in the green Spring Blossom Pyrex and grated cheddar cheese into a matching bowl before she and Rosemarie's dad left for a gig in Adora Springs, thirty minutes away and two towns over. Caroline had come home with Rosemarie to snack after school but didn't stay long, because she had a diner shift. Ada was at a prom committee meeting. That left Rosemarie and Kasey, too full to move, in a patch of sunlight on the trampoline.

"We *have* to go hunting for a prom dress for you. Tomorrow! Everything good is probably gone already! Why are *you* the one slowpoking when you actually have a date?" Rosemarie asked.

Ada and Kasey were going with the Castelows, Caro didn't have a date yet, and what Rosemarie *really* wanted was to ask Sparrow Kim to prom because Sparrow Kim was her crush. Sparrow had been her crush for months. Sparrow was half-Korean and half-black with skin that held the sun. Her parents owned the one Korean restaurant in town: KG. *Korean Gold.*

Rosemarie and Sparrow were friends and maybe the *tiniest* bit more if Rosemarie counted the one time their humanities class went to the movies and she and Sparrow sat next to each other and Sparrow held her hand during the scariest part and then they kept holding hands even when the scary part was over. They held hands walking out of the theater together and only let go when they went into separate stalls in the bathroom. They locked fingers again on their way to the rumbling buses in the parking lot. Sparrow's hair was thick, crow black, braided down her back when she played field hockey. She was captain. She clipped her pens to her shirt collar and, for reasons unknown, was usually almost late for their English class, barely sneaking in before Mrs. Perkins closed the door. Sparrow sat right in front of Rosemarie— *Kim, Kingston*—and smelled like Bath & Body Works Cucumber Melon mist. Rosemarie hated the smell of cucumbers and melons coming from anywhere else, but when they came from Sparrow, they were her favorite.

Rosemarie hadn't crushed this hard on a girl in real life before. Celebrities, yes. Especially Old Hollywood. There was a photo of Dorothy Dandridge above the light switch in her bedroom, a postcard of Elizabeth Taylor—in her slip from *Butterfield 8*—in her bathroom. Thinking about them was fantasyland and so was imagining being able to ask a *girl* to prom in Goldie. Sure, she was raised by hippie parents who loved every bit of her unconditionally, but Goldie was in the South, and she, along with most people in town, had been raised in the church.

Her romantic feelings for girls crept to the first boiling point the summer between middle and high school when she decided to let Ada, Caro, and Kasey know she thought Lisa Bonet was hotter than any boys in town. Ada had laughed and brushed her off, but Caro and Kasey knew what she meant. When Ada realized it too, she'd said, *Just so you know, I will never care who you want to touch your itsy-bitsy, Roses. As long as it's what you want. It's your business, not mine.* Then Ada went on a rant about how maybe she was kind of lesbian too because she totally would've kissed Marilyn Monroe if they'd been alive at the same time.

Later that afternoon, when it was just Rosemarie, Caro, and Kasey, they'd asked her if she ever had a crush on either of them, since she wasn't shy when it came to talking about liking girls anymore, and Rosemarie *did* lie a little when she told them she never thought about it, because they were like sisters.

She'd *thought* about it, but it hadn't gotten very far. She'd only been testing out the feelings, like a new pair of shoes. They were her *sisters*, so she didn't want to hurt their feelings by telling them if she *had* to date one of them, it'd be Kasey because with her dark hair and eyes, Kasey looked the closest to the girls Rosemarie crushed on.

Rosemarie didn't have a role model for how she was feeling, and she didn't know how long her feelings would last. Maybe they were temporary? Maybe they'd be forever? She hadn't suddenly stopped liking boys or anything. It was both. Why couldn't she like them both? It made way more sense than it didn't.

One neighborhood over, there was an older lesbian woman who was friends with her mom. She and her daughter visited about once a month to buy eggs from their chickens, and occasionally, the woman's girlfriend would tag along. They were both kind and affectionate and called her Little Rosemarie no matter how big she got. Sometimes the woman's girlfriend wore a rainbow pin on her jean jacket.

And everyone knew Gary Green was gay. He was friends with her parents and taught ceramics at South Goldie High. The kids called him Gay Gary Green so much he wore it like a badge of honor. He disappeared to Mexico for winter breaks and summers and sent the Kingstons pears and chocolates for Christmas. Rosemarie knew of quite a few gay people in Goldie, but it wasn't like there were any *aggressively* openly gay couples in town she could look to.

"Ugh, I don't know. The dresses are *so* expensive. I do have money saved up, but I don't want to spend it on something I'll only wear once," Kasey said.

"I saw a powder-blue dress on the rack at Lily's that would look so good on you it makes me want to die. We're getting it tomorrow. It's not that much! I'll buy it with my own money—I don't even care! I was going to let you do this yourself, but you've left me no choice, Fritz," Rosemarie said. She sat up so Kasey could see her roll her eyes properly. Rosemarie was going to wear the dress her mom got married in, which was the only thing that made it a wedding dress— it was a pretty, petallike purple dress with ruffly straps and a dip in the back.

"How much was it?" Kasey asked.

"Like, ninety-nine dollars."

"I have ninety-nine dollars, but it feels like a waste when I could save it."

"You won't be saying that when it's on Silas Castelow's bedroom floor at the lake house. You'll be looking at it there on the floor next to his nightstand where he keeps his..."

Kasey nodded a *go ahead*.

"His...I don't know! What's he keep on his nightstand?"

"Last time I was there, it was a *Garfield* book; like, a half-empty can of pop; and his wallet. He also has this plastic Yoda next to his alarm clock," Kasey said, showing Rosemarie how big it was with her fingers.

"Wow. Okay. So, you'll look at that blue dress on the floor next to Silas's *Garfield*s and think to yourself, *I'm glad I let him take it off me. Rosemarie was right.*"

"I don't know if we're gonna have sex on prom night or not, though. I haven't decided yet." Kasey put her hands behind her head, keeping her eyes on the sky.

"Right, I know. Okay, so, think of this as one of *many* possibilities. You need the dress anyway. Listen! We're getting the dress, damn it!"

"Yes, ma'am. Now that that's out of the way, are you gonna ask Leo to go with you or not? Who's Sparrow going with?"

Ada, Caro, and Kasey knew about Rosemarie's crush on Sparrow, and they teased her about it the same way they would've if Sparrow were a guy. No one else knew, not even Rosemarie's mom. Even though her mom was one of those women who was excellent at intuiting things, she and Rosemarie hadn't spoken about it outright—at least, not yet.

"I don't know. I heard maybe Frankie was gonna ask her," Rosemarie said, shrugging and lying down. The spring sun was warm, not hot; the wind, refreshing and cool. Rosemarie could've stayed like that all day with the big oak tree half shading them and the birds happily clicking at the seed in the feeders, even though they reminded her of Sparrow.

"Are you too jealous to talk about it?"

"Eh, I don't know," Rosemarie said, imagining Frankie Mattingly with his hands all over Sparrow, the two of them dancing together, what color her dress was and how she'd do her hair. "Yeah. I guess I am," she said, unable to keep it in.

"For what it's worth, I think she likes you back. Maybe she's shy about it too. She's always talking about how cool and funny you are. I've heard her!"

"Leo ain't too bad of a second choice," Rosemarie said after some quiet. He was cute and breezy. Charming. They'd been friends their whole lives. Leo was a brilliant musician and could play every instrument. He was going off to Boston to study music theory in the fall. He was cool in an important, nerdy way and reminded her of Dave Brubeck, whose bespectacled face she found adorably smiling back at her from her dad's jazz albums. Leo had dark, floppy hair and glasses, plus a pair of dimples that she and a lot of the girls she knew went crazy for.

Rosemarie really did *like* Leo in a huge way; she'd never liked a boy this much. She liked him in a way she *had* to like somebody she spent so much time with. Meaning his mouth didn't make too much noise when he ate and she liked his natural smell and he was extraordinarily easy to be around. He wasn't a know-it-all like so many other guys, and he had a Mister Rogers gentleness about him.

Also, he was a good kisser. They'd made out a few times, the last time being less than a month ago at one of the Castelow parties by the water. They sat outside roasting marshmallows and warming up, and when Rosemarie went inside to use the bathroom, Leo pulled her into one of the empty bedrooms and asked if he could kiss her again and she said yes. They turned the lights out and stayed in there for so long by the time they emerged, some people had already left, and Kasey and Silas were asleep on the couch.

Rosemarie and Leo hadn't had sex; she hadn't had sex with anyone. She'd made out with Leo enough that she thought she could imagine what sex with him would be like, and it was pleasing to think about from time to time and keep it separate from the times she thought about kissing Sparrow or being in a dark bedroom with Sparrow for so long they had to squint when they walked out.

Rosemarie knew a lot of girls at school were jealous of her because she was the one whom Leo was so into, and he had been for so long. Maybe she and Kasey should walk to his house right now so Rosemarie could ask him to prom. Kasey's mom was working late, and Kasey was spending the night at the Kingstons' to get away from Roy again, and neither of them had any homework.

"He's *obsessed* with you. That's a plus," Kasey tacked on. She nudged herself closer to Rosemarie and put her head on her shoulder.

"I wish Caro could go with Beau somehow. He's the only boy she likes."

"I know. Sucks. But! Ada is on the case to find her a date. One of Grayson's friends, apparently."

"Aha. Of course she is. Okay. Get up. Let's go. Let's go find Leo. Time to lock it down," Rosemarie said.

"Can we stop by Myrtle's so Caro can hook us up with some pie and ice cream first?"

"How can you be hungry?! We just ate, like, *four* tacos!"

"But doesn't raspberry honey pie with vanilla bean ice cream sound *so* good?" Kasey asked, making far too much sense for Rosemarie to object.

On the walk to the diner, Rosemarie listened as Kasey told her about the latest evil, dumbass thing Roy had done. He'd backed into a pole in Kasey's truck and dented it good, but he wouldn't pay to get it fixed. Kasey didn't have the money and said she wouldn't even care if it weren't her daddy's truck in the first place, but it was, and she loved that truck. Silas had offered to get it fixed for her, and she was thinking about it.

"Tell me the truth: Has Roy ever done *one* nice or good thing for you?" Rosemarie asked. They sauntered through the neighborhood, making their way past the last cul-de-sac before they got to the main road. Kasey was wearing her knockoff flowered Dr. Martens and a short, breezy white skirt with scientific drawings of plants on it—her favorite, Rosemarie knew. RACK had one another's clothes memorized. Kasey's lime-green T-shirt had a tiny, useless pocket over her left boob. *Put an acorn in it*, Rosemarie had said one time when they were blissed out on pot brownies. They'd gone outside to find an acorn and put it in there. Came inside and laughed for five minutes straight about it, putting it in and taking it out over and over again.

"He won a lion plushie for me at the Goldie Fair back in seventh grade. One of those ring-toss games. He got pissed at me the next day when my dog chewed it up. Does that count?" Kasey said, kicking at a rock. They were at the intersection now, so they stopped and waited until it was clear to go. Three boys from school drove by in a black Jeep, honked and hollered at them, then disappeared down the road into the sun.

"Fuck him," Rosemarie said, taking Kasey's hand so they could cross together. "No, seriously. I know how bad it is to hate somebody, but I *hate* him. There's nothing good in him." Rosemarie continued her short rant about Roy's shittiness, leaving Kasey's mom out of it completely, although Kasey's mom, Angie, was way too smart and sweet to be with a guy like that, so none of it made sense. Rosemarie only saw Roy when she caught a glimpse of him driving through town in Kasey's truck or the handful of times Rosemarie would come to pick Kasey up at the farmhouse and see him out in the yard or on the porch. Not a week went by without Rosemarie asking Kasey if she was scared to stay in the house with him. Rosemarie's parents offered up their home to Kasey, day or night, for whatever she needed.

Rosemarie's dad was laid-back about everything and could get along with anyone, but he didn't like Roy one bit. *Bad news. Real bad fucking news*, he'd said to Rosemarie once, and Rosemarie would always remember the look on her daddy's face when he said it, because it was a new expression she'd never seen him make. There was none of his usual chill there, only fire.

"Like...I...fantasize about someone killing him. Genuinely *good* people get murdered all the time. How is Roy still out here walking around? No matter what he does, no one cares, no one helps, no one will do anything about it. Not even my mom! It's infuriating. I just—" Kasey stopped and found a fluffy cloud above them, watched it like it held an answer.

"*I* care. You know how much I care," Rosemarie said, stopping and looking up with her. She reached over to brush the hair from Kasey's forehead.

"I know you do," Kasey said, and they walked again, quiet for a little bit.

———

Caroline fed them pie and ice cream and took her break with them afterward. Beau was out back too with a lit cigarette dangling from his lip, rooting around in the back of his truck. The girls sat at the umbrellaed picnic table, trying not to be too obvious about watching him.

"Okay, y'all. I'm gonna ask Leo Bell to prom with this delicious piece of pie," Rosemarie said, lifting the box into the air. Caro had cut her an extra piece for the occasion.

"You two are BFFs! Don't try to act like you're worried he won't say yes," Caro said.

Beau pulled out a toolbox, set it on the ground, and let the tailgate down. He had an *extremely* cute ass. So perky! The girls watched him bend to get whatever out of the toolbox and lift himself up into the truck bed. They didn't know what he was doing and they didn't care. Free BeauTV.

"Nah, I'm not worried. It just makes me feel caged in when I should be free," Rosemarie said, spreading her arms out so wide Kasey scooted so she wouldn't get smacked in the face. Rosemarie made herself feel better by imagining everything that would come after graduation—traveling the world, living on the other side of the country. Doing whatever she wanted. All of it far from the prying eyes of Good Ol' Goldie.

"Free as a *sparrow*," Caro said, poking her shoulder.

"Exactly," Rosemarie said.

"I feel like a loser for getting Ada to hook me up with one of Grayson's friends," Caro admitted.

"Grayson does have some hot friends, though," Kasey said. "The one who's on the soccer team. Will. He drives the loud red car. He's cute! He's an airhead, but he's cute!"

"Yeah. He *is* cute, actually," Caro said with a newfound spark of interest.

Beau put his stuff in the truck and walked toward them. He didn't say anything, just handed Caroline his half-smoked cigarette, and she took it. She smoked and blew it out of her mouth, sucked it in through her nose.

"Hot damn, Muffin Mix! Told ya you'd get it down. A-plus," Beau said. Caro's cheeks got red from the extra attention; she was beaming. He took a seat next to her, but not too close. "Am I interrupting girl talk?"

"We forgive you," Kasey said.

"Trying to find Caroppenheimer a date to prom who is worthy of her," Rosemarie chimed in, knowing not to look directly at Caro, who was surely giving her the stink eye. Rosemarie kept looking at Beau. The sun was warm on the top of her head and it made her feel like a thirsty little flower, drinking up the light.

"Any guy who hasn't asked you yet ain't worth a shit," Beau said seriously.

Beau sat with them for a little longer, making corny jokes and listening to the girls talk until his break was over.

"Okay, he's gotten cuter, right?" Kasey said when the coast was clear.

"He's a lot to deal with. *Damn*," Rosemarie said.

"Yep. We are indeed agreed on this, ladies. Solidarity. Thanks for coming to see me," Caro said, standing.

"Love you," the girls said to her as they left for Leo's.

———

Leo opened the door with a pencil between his teeth and another behind his ear, the eraser nub poking out from his black hair like an itty-bitty pink nose. He was holding a spiral notebook.

"You know what? I'm gonna go sit by your pool and give my mom a call. Is that okay, Leo?" Kasey asked, pulling her flip phone from her pocket. She'd told Rosemarie she would make herself scarce while Rosemarie asked Leo to prom, and Rosemarie had told her she didn't need to. It wasn't a big deal! Rosemarie only gave her one instruction: don't be weird. So naturally, Kasey was being hilariously weird and stepped off the porch backward with her phone to her ear, giving them both a thumbs-up.

"Oh yeah. Go ahead," Leo said with the pencil still in his mouth. He took it out and gave her a thumbs-up back. "Come in. My mom made cookies if you want some," he said to Rosemarie, holding the door open for her. Leo was always doing things like that—opening doors for her and being the best. If she could like Leo and *only* Leo, she could free up the part of her brain focused on Sparrow.

"Please, no! I'm so full I could puke. All we've done today is eat! I brought this pie for you, though. A Caro special: raspberry and honey with cinnamon meringue. She said she dreamt the recipe," Rosemarie said, stepping into the Bells' cozy home, all soft furniture and plush rugs and photos of Leo and his two sisters. There was a glossy black piano in their dining room, an acoustic guitar in the living room corner. One of Leo's little sisters played the harp, and Rosemarie spent so much time at the Bell house she even knew it had its own special closet downstairs next to the bookshelf.

"Well, I can't turn down a *dream* pie," Leo said, taking the box. He put everything else he was holding on the coffee table and opened the pie box to take a peek, telling her how delicious it looked. One of their three cats meowed into the living room, wanting attention; Rosemarie bent to pet it. Leo told her that his parents were at the church and his two sisters were downstairs watching *The Fellowship of the Ring* for the billionth time. "Like true nerds," he added.

Leo was chatty by nature. In fifth grade, their teacher made him sit at a separate table by himself in an attempt to keep him quiet, but it didn't matter. He'd *psst* Rosemarie to let her know he saw a squirrel on the window ledge or that a hot-air balloon was flying by or that a cloud looked like a doghouse with a dog in it or an ice cube on a pizza.

"Leopold," Rosemarie said. Leo was Leonardo, not Leopold, but Rosemarie liked to call him that sometimes anyway. "I have no clue why I'm so nervous about this, so I'm just gonna come out and ask you. Will you go to prom with me? It's why I brought you the dream pie." Rosemarie curtseyed in front of him, pulling her baggy tie-dyed T-shirt out at the bottom.

"I figured you wanted to go by yourself. Figured you didn't want me to ask you. I would've asked you first," Leo grumbled.

"So, yes?" Rosemarie asked, half-annoyed.

"I mean, *obviously* it's a yes, Ro," Leo said, also half-annoyed.

"My dress is purple."

"Noted. I'll rent a tux and we'll get the *stuff*," he said, using his hands to shape what Rosemarie guessed were flowers or a boutonnière box. She laughed at him.

"What?"

"Nothing. Not a thing."

"Come here." He reached for her, pulling her close. "We'll have a good time." He rubbed his nose against hers.

"I mean, duh. We're *us*," she said, leaning in to kiss his mouth.

———

When Rosemarie and Kasey crawled into her bed that night, she forced herself to think about Leo and only Leo, and upon seeing a *sparrow* at the birdfeeder first thing the next morning, she sighed dramatically and asked Kasey if she wanted coffee or tea.

2019

7

ADA PLUM-CASTELOW

Ada didn't have time to be hungover, but hungover she was. Grayson was standing next to her, holding a glass and two ibuprofens. Their four-year-old, the youngest, sat at the edge of their bed, earthquake-shaking it by kicking his feet.

"Thank you," she said to her husband, chasing the pills down with the cold water. "Pacey, *please* stop kicking. Go see what your brothers are doing." She sugared her voice because she felt guilty enough for waking up hungover, and Pacey was their most sensitive child. Their eight-year-old twins, Noah and Nash, were confident and stubborn, ace leaders for the brood. And the six-year-old middle child, Gabriel, was usually as angelic as his namesake, unless the twins got him riled up.

Ada—the planner—had gotten pregnant on purpose at twenty-four. God—the even better planner—surprised them with two boys at once. With Gabriel, they had been trying for a girl so Grayson could go ahead and get his vasectomy. Gabriel wasn't a girl, but they couldn't imagine their life any differently and didn't want to. And although they couldn't have loved him more, Pacey had been their *oops* baby after they'd put the vasectomy off. Grayson got snipped the same week Ada peed positive.

All four boys had their daddy's dark hair and eyes and a decidedly adorable Castelow nose, but they had Ada's mouth too. The four of them looked so much alike; if they were the same age, they could've been quadruplets.

Ada needed to get showered and dressed. She had errands to run before the RACK brunch at Caro's. She hadn't drunk *that* much at Duke's, but even two glasses of rosé gave her a slight hangover now. Last night she had three and it'd been so much fun! Her baby sister was getting married and Kasey was back in Goldie! Ada had gotten borderline trashed and kept telling everyone Madonna called rosé *summer water*, and that was why she called it that too! She had a blast with her girls!

When she and Grayson finally decided to leave, Kasey and Silas were on the karaoke stage singing "Summer Nights" from *Grease*, drowning in neon light. At home, Ada and Grayson paid their baby-sitter and had quick sex, half-hanging off the bed. Grayson had only been a *little* drunk and kept pulling Ada closer to him and laughing at how much everything was making her laugh. Afterward, like always, Grayson went to the kitchen for a pop.

Pacey hummed out of the room and down the hallway to his brothers' bedrooms.

"Love you, baby," Ada said as she watched him disappear.

"Boys, we'll head to Gram and Pop-Pop's in twenty minutes," Grayson said with a raised voice, leaning out of the doorframe. A scatter of small *okay*s lifted through the air. Grayson came back into the room and sat next to Ada on the bed.

"I'm so sorry I'm hungover. I have a lot of stuff to get done today," Ada said to her husband. A bad mood would creep up like an itch if she strayed from her schedule.

"You're fine, just a lightweight. Ease up on yourself." Grayson was naturally like this—laid-back, flexible—the exact opposite of who Ada was. It was why they worked; when she spun, he was still.

He was wearing a short-sleeved button-down with anchors on it, a pair of peanut-butter khaki shorts, and black flip-flops. He had plans to take the boys to his parents' to grill out and swim for the day. A few of his friends were bringing their kids too. Ada appreciated how much Grayson took the boys and let her have time to herself. She had girlfriends whose husbands had never changed a diaper or given their children a bath. Grayson had been hands-on with their boys since day one, and while Ada didn't set the bar so low for men that she thought the smallest things deserved praise, she was exceedingly thankful for how good of a husband and father he was so she could keep her worries to everything else in life.

"Will you be gone most of the day? I will," Ada said. She was up now, walking to the bathroom. She heard Grayson get up from the bed and follow her. She sat on the toilet and looked at him leaning against the counter.

"Probably. We'll connect later. It's fine."

"Did you *see* how Kasey and Silas were last night? Roses and Caro were excited about it. I don't know how to feel."

Ada stood and washed her hands, continuing the conversation with Grayson in the mirror as she brushed her teeth. Four little feet pattered in the hallway—two of the boys were running and laughing. Usually, she'd remind them to be careful if they were getting too rowdy, but today she pretended like it wasn't happening.

"It's been a long time for them. Maybe *too* long. I don't know what I think, since I haven't thought about it much, honestly," Grayson said.

"What happened with him and that woman who worked at the bowling alley or the bookstore? Was it the bookstore? Did she work at both?"

Grayson shrugged.

"Y'all don't talk about this stuff?" Ada said with a mouth full of toothpaste.

"I mean, sometimes we do. Not all of it, though. You know I love to mind my business," he said.

"But...he's your *brother*," Ada said. She spit and returned the toothbrush to its cup next to his.

It drove her crazy thinking there could be something potentially important about Silas's life going on and Grayson wouldn't know because he minded his business. It was his brother! Whether they wanted it or not, they had some *shared* business!

"Kasey's engaged, though. I mean, right?" Grayson asked. He scratched at his beard, crossed his arms. He was watching Ada suds up her face with her expensive LunaCrush cleanser. She splashed it off and her sinuses ached. Grayson handed her a soft bamboo washcloth.

"Well, yeah, right. But! She and Silas have *fifteen* years of unfinished business, and it's so weird she's finally back here after all this time anyway. I don't feel like I know anything about what's going on." Ada dried her face and leaned against the counter too, patting rose toner on her forehead and cheeks. Swiping it across her neck, tapping it down her nose. She'd exfoliate her face in the shower, finish her routine. She was in her lacy pink bra and panties, and although the AC was on full blast, she could tell how hot it was outside already. The morning sun slanted through the window and onto the tiled floor, warming her bare feet.

"Are you going to ask her about it?"

"I don't know. Maybe I should mind my business," she said to him quickly. She kissed him and left the bathroom.

"May*be*," he said, turning off the light and following her.

She slipped her arms into the coolness of her robe and tied it closed, stepped into the hallway on the hunt for their boys so she could properly tell them good morning and goodbye before getting in the shower.

———

In her orange-slice sundress, Ada stopped by a crowded Plum Bakery for a tray of strawberry-lemonade thumbprint cookies, and by a packed

Plum Eats for eggs, plain pancakes, and toppings to put together the pancake board. Then she drove to Caroline's mansion off Main. It was down a small side street not far from the pink house Ada's parents still lived in.

Mansion is what she, Rosemarie, and Kasey called it sometimes, but not to Caro's face. Ada had grown up in a huge house, and the house she and Grayson lived in now was about the same size as Caro and Trey's, but somehow it was *different*. Ada felt bitchy and judgmental for thinking it, but it was true. The Foxberry family had old money like the Plums, but the Plums weren't flashy or gaudy. The Foxberrys behaved like new money, and of course, since Caro *was* new money, it made sense that some of what she did was over-the-top. It wasn't the fountain out front or the fairy garden statues by the pool or Caro's brand-new white SUV with tan interior. It wasn't when Caro drove Trey's sports car around town either. It was just a *feeling*.

That *feeling* returned in full force when Caro opened the front door for her.

Now Ada was inside the mansion scooping the scrambled eggs into a crystal bowl. Caro stepped next to her holding a black velvet box and opened it, revealing the glossy luster and glow of a pearl necklace. Ada took it.

"I was talking about how Tom gave Daisy a three-hundred-and-fifty-thousand-dollar pearl necklace in *The Great Gatsby*, and I guess Trey got jealous," Caroline said, smiling. Ada watched her and waited for the smile to reach her eyes. When it did, Ada smiled back at her. "I mean, obviously he didn't spend *that* much, but I've never had real pearls. I was telling Kasey that yesterday because she had her pearls on."

"It's beautiful, Caro. *So* beautiful. What are you going to wear it with first?" Ada asked with wide eyes. She tilted her head and looked at the necklace one more time before handing it back to her. Caro put the box on the kitchen table and pulled the cookies from the bag.

"Probably jeans. Girl, you know me," Caro said. She giggled and shook her head. "It embarrasses me when he does stuff like this, but obviously I love it. He says I'm two-faced about it, but that's a little harsh. I mean, I love nice things and like being pampered, but I grew up in a *trailer* with my grandmother and, like, look at this." She motioned at the sea-monster-sized chandelier hanging above them, the humid bottle of Veuve Clicquot on the counter.

"Right. I mean, I get it. Being spoiled suits you—it does. You deserve it," Ada said truthfully. Caroline was a natural sweetheart, and there wasn't a thing she could do to change that. Her mom was trash, her daddy was trash, but her grandma was an angel, and Caro got an angel heart from her.

"I'm sure he felt like an asshole for being so mean to me yesterday . . . and the day *before* yesterday." Caro said the last part under her breath, taking her time transferring the cookies to the tray. "So pretty. Who made these?" she asked, perking up again.

"Pammy," Ada said, referring to the new girl they'd just hired. Even when Caro wasn't working, she was working; the bakery was her baby. It had the Plum name on the front, but it may as well have been called *Caroline's*.

After Ada's parents basically gave the restaurant to her five years ago to rebrand and run while her mom took over their interior design and floral businesses, having Caro stay in charge of Plum Bakery made the most sense. The bakery belonged to Caroline in every way except paperwork and name, and sometimes Ada convinced herself that was good enough.

"Are y'all still fighting?" Ada asked.

Yesterday she'd overheard Caro talking to Rosemarie about a big fight with Trey, but she'd been too busy with everything else to get the full story. Plus, Caro and Trey were *always* fighting and making up. Ada went back to the bag to get the box of pancakes, started putting them on the big wooden board next to the fruit and eggs.

The huge house was empty except for them. Ada asked Caro once if she wanted to adopt a cat or a dog to keep her company, and Caro scoffed. Told her no since neither she nor Trey were home enough to take care of anything. Even though the house wasn't exactly Ada's taste, it did earn its beauty by simply existing, and Caro looked stunning in it. She was barefoot, wearing a white button-down and cutoff jean shorts. Her long, milky red hair was pulled back off her face in a high ponytail, her gold hoop earrings swinging. Perfect, right? Not quite. The house felt like it was missing *something* even if Ada didn't know what that *something* was.

"He was sleeping when I got home last night, and this morning he had to leave early to go back down to Jesse County for something at the distillery. He told me what for, but my brain couldn't hold on to it. I was too hungover. He woke me up to say he was leaving and left this on the nightstand with a note that said, *I think you'll like this, Caroline. Actually, I know you will.*"

"Romantic?" Ada asked carefully, not quite sure if Caro would agree.

"I mean, I guess," she said, as she finished putting out the cookies and stood back to admire them on the platter.

There was a knock at the door, then it opened. The alarm system chimed and Rosemarie's and Kasey's laughter lifted and fell, announcing their arrival.

———

"I know it makes you uncomfortable to be the center of attention, but I'm so glad to be looking at your face," Ada said to Kasey after they'd eaten. They were sunning by the pool now, drinking nonalcoholic fruity-spritzy concoctions Caro put together and called "spruitzers." Pineapples and cherries, ginger ale and peach syrup. It tasted like something Ada would've *loved* when she was a teenager, but she only sipped at it. She ate the sticky, slick cherry and put the glass down on the table.

"I'm so glad to be looking at *your* face right now and to be able to meet your boys in person. Ada, um, you have *four* boys," Kasey said, leaning forward.

"I know, right? Five, including Grayson! It's five against one in my house! Who let that happen?" Ada shook her head. It'd broken her heart that Kasey hadn't been in Goldie for the birth of any of her boys, never got to hold them when they were babies. Kasey had "met" the boys via texted photos and FaceTime, but seeing Kasey bend down yesterday to talk to them was so precious and surreal Ada had to blink fast to keep from crying.

"Kase, which one of these will look the best on me?" Caro asked, holding up three pinkish lip glosses she'd taken out of the LunaCrush gift boxes Kasey had brought for them.

"The brightest one. That's the one you have on now? Electric Raspberry?" Rosemarie went in her pocket for the same one and held it up, although she'd opted to put the pure red matte one on her own lips. Ada looked at the dip of Rosemarie's pretty Cupid's bow, watched it move.

"Agreed. I've got a couple more of those at the hotel. You can have them all. We'll change the name from Electric Raspberry to Caroppenheimer or Carofox if you want. It's lovely on you," Kasey said. "The *red* is made for you, Roses."

"It *is*. And nope. I'm Caroppenheimer forever, no matter what my married name is," Caro said.

"Love it. I love this light pink one too," Ada said, pointing at her own glossy mouth with both index fingers.

"I thought of you as soon as I saw it," Kasey said.

"Go ahead and name all the pinks *Ada Plum*!" Rosemarie said to Kasey before switching her attention to Ada. "And, girl, remember how you made us wear the same pink gloss on prom night because you said it was *good luck*?"

"Oh wow. You did!" Kasey said.

"I have no clue where I came up with that. Y'all know I just like it when we have the same thing. Plus, it matched my dress!"

"Well, it worked, because I did end up having a good night. We all did! I remember being worried we were all gonna start our periods that night like we did for junior prom. Of course my dress *had* to be white," Caroline said.

"Don't forget sophomore homecoming when none of us could go because we all had the same disgusting cough. I caught it from Leo and gave it to y'all. I'm still sorry for that. Forgive me," Rosemarie said.

"Forgiven," Kasey said.

"Senior prom night was a dream, though. Time stops at the Castelow lake house, doesn't it? Feels protected from the rest of the world," Caroline said, staring at the pool water—lucent and June blue.

"It really does. Grayson is there right now with the boys," Ada said.

"My mom was *so* paranoid I was going to get pregnant that night. I think she was worried about all of us," Kasey said.

"I remember her being like, *Y'all look way too good to let any of these Goldie boys talk to you, let alone touch you*," Rosemarie said, doing Angie's voice perfectly.

They laughed. Ada remembered Kasey's mom warmly. Her scratchy voice and white Keds. How she wore a bell on a twisted red-and-white cord around her neck every day during December. Ada would hear her jingle around the corner at the grocery store before she got eyes on her.

"Gah, she would've loved Devon, though. She loved Silas, but he's *Silas*, so that's a given," Kasey said.

"I do miss your mom so much, Kase. I miss seeing her around and how she'd say *Hey there, Rosiegirl* to me when I bumped into her at the store," Rosemarie said.

Ada was sure they were all sitting there feeling it, but Rosemarie was the first one to say so.

"Me too," Ada said.

"Me too," Caro whispered.

They were finally crying at the same time. It was a relief to let it out. Yesterday had been too busy and last night was too wild. In the quiet and sun of that backyard, they could let go.

"Well, since you brought Silas up, do inform us if the two of you are going to stay in touch when you go back to New York, since you're properly reconnected now," Caro said after a bit, smirking at Kasey. Rosemarie pointed at her in agreement and clicked her tongue.

"Yeah, I guess so? I wouldn't have blamed him if he never wanted to speak to me again, though. He doesn't owe me anything," Kasey said slowly. She pushed her sunglasses on top of her head and stretched out, crossed her ankles.

"Leo said Silas hopped on the drums for a gig he had the other night with my parents at Duke's. Is there anything Si doesn't do? He just stays out here in these streets doing *everything*? Like, does he sleep?" Rosemarie asked this so aggressively it made them laugh. She posed the question directly to Ada since Silas was her brother-in-law.

"He sleeps, yes. Sometimes on our couch, even though we have two guest bedrooms and he has his own place. He's just *Silas*," Ada said, shrugging. "He's forever trying to take the boys to do wild stuff, but I don't always let him. Uncle Silas can chill." Last time, it was extreme zip-lining in Tennessee, and while Ada (a bit reluctantly) didn't mind Grayson and Silas taking the twins and Gabriel, she'd said a hard no when it came to their youngest tagging along.

"He doesn't want to get married?" Kasey asked.

"To someone who *isn't* you? No, probably not" was Caroline's response.

"That's ridiculous! Trust me, Silas hasn't been holding his breath for *fifteen* years hoping I'd pop back up in Goldie one day."

Ada had already given Kasey the rundown of a few of Silas's girlfriends he'd had over the years as they happened. He was one of those guys who was *very* single when he wasn't dating someone, meaning he seemed content hanging out and not getting serious. All his real relationships seemed to take him by surprise.

"Right, but *first* love," Rosemarie said, like it was law.

"Mm-hmm. Like you and Leo?" Kasey said.

Rosemarie scrunched up her nose.

Ada shook her head at them and excused herself to go inside and use the bathroom.

*　　*　　*

She stopped at her bag first to check her messages and was texting Grayson some hearts when her mom called. Ada picked up.

"Do you know where your dad is?" her mom slurred.

Ada's stomach sank out of annoyance; she knew That Voice and she didn't have time for That Voice today.

"I thought Daddy was there at the house? That's where he told me he was going to be this morning," Ada said calmly. Through the tall glass door she watched her best friends sitting on the edge of the pool now, their bare feet flicking like fins.

"No. I've been looking for him and he's not here. I'm not crazy!" her mom said.

"Mama, I don't think you're crazy. I just thought Daddy was at the house." She went into the half bathroom in the hallway, pulled the pocket door closed. She balanced the phone between her ear and shoulder.

"No, you think I'm crazy."

"I don't think you're crazy."

An anticipated standoff. Ada let it linger while she used the bathroom. She was washing her hands when she heard her dad's deep voice through the speaker.

"Ada? I was out on the deck. Your mom must've thought I left. She shouldn't have bothered you."

"It's fine. Tell her it's fine," Ada said. "Tell her I'll call her later."

"All right," her dad said.

"Are you coming here soon?" her mom said.

"Maybe tonight, if I have time."

"Can you come now, so we can talk?"

"About what, Mama? I'm at Caro's right now. We're all here."

"I'm your mother and all I've asked is for you to stop by. Is that too much?"

"Mama, it's *not* too much—"

"In the next half hour would be good, okay?"

"Yeah. Okay. See you soon," Ada said, holding in her curses. She scowled in the mirror and turned off the light.

Ada told the girls she'd probably swing back by after going to her parents' to see what her mom wanted. The day was fairly lazy wedding event–wise, but there *was* some prep she needed to do for Taylor's second bridal shower tomorrow. Looking on the bright side, Ada could get that done at the house while her mom talked to her about whatever she wanted to talk to her about.

———

When Ada got to the house, she let herself in. Her dad was on the couch watching baseball.

"Hey, Daddy. Where is she?" Ada asked.

"Sleeping upstairs. Did you not hear your phone? I called you. Left you a message," her dad said. Ada sat next to him and put her bag on the floor.

"It's been, like, *ten* minutes, tops," she said, pulling out her phone to check the time, flicking away her dad's voicemail notification. "What did she want to talk to me about?"

"Probably something about Tay's shower—I don't know. This game is getting good. Want to watch it with me? There's a bunch of leftover food if you want too."

"I'm not hungry, Daddy."

Ada scanned the room. Most of the decorations from yesterday's bash were still up. She needed to refresh them a bit even though her parents had hired help to clean and set up again for tomorrow. Tomorrow morning she'd go to the restaurant to get the soft-bread finger sandwiches and salads, bottles of champagne for mimosas; Caro would bring the vanilla buttercream cupcakes.

She asked about her brothers, and her dad told her they were out on the water, fishing. She sat there next to him, watching the baseball game, feeling tissue-paper-thin.

"Daddy, what all is she taking? Her doctors shouldn't be writing those prescriptions anymore, should they? What's going on?" Ada asked.

"As far as I know, she needs them for her back, Ada. She says she's in pain all the time."

"Yeah, but there's physical therapy and she never does it; there are other things she can do. Seems like half the people in this town are addicted to pain pills and I..." Her voice got softer and softer until she stopped.

"Well, maybe she'll listen if you talk to her. She won't listen to me," her dad said.

Ada stood and went upstairs to her parents' bedroom.

Her mom was in a white ruffle sundress, softly snoring on top of the duvet. All three windows were open, breezing the dress fabric and curtains so prettily Ada stopped to watch.

Not even the rest of RACK knew what Ada's mom had been like lately. Grayson knew, but she'd been keeping some of it even from him. She hadn't told him about the time last month when she held her mother's hair back at eight in the morning because she'd taken pills without breakfast. She hadn't told him yet that she knew her parents didn't sleep in the same bed anymore. Ada didn't want to talk about how she resented how much her dad had checked out; her brothers had checked out too. Neither of them lived in Goldie anyway, and soon enough, Taylor—who had been so hyperfocused on her wedding for the past year she barely noticed *anything*—would be moving a couple hundred miles away too, leaving Ada alone with the burden of looking after her parents, on top of her own family, and the Plum empire.

Ada stared at the curtains and listened to the Goldie street sounds drift up—the church bells ringing, the crescendo of a motorcycle growl, a mockingbird cycling through its song. She planted herself on the corner of the bed and said, "Shit," under her breath.

2004

8

Ada had proposed they have a big dinner under a white tent in her backyard instead of going to one of the fake-fancy chain restaurants on prom night. The caterers were busy in the kitchen, and RACK was upstairs in Ada's capacious pink-and-white bathroom getting ready.

"Caro, Grayson *swears* Will knows what a corsage is. He asked him, like, five times and I told him to make sure it had some yellow in it to match your dress. Let's see if he can follow directions," Ada said. She leaned closer to the mirror with her mouth slightly open and put on her mascara. Caro was next to her, brushing powder across her face. The RACK mix CD they'd made together was on repeat in Ada's boom box on the floor—Usher, Mariah Carey, Tim McGraw, Christina Aguilera, and and and.

The girls were in their robes. Kasey had just shown up with her dress in her hand, backpack slung over her shoulder. Her stepdad must have been going through one of his more chill phases, because she hadn't been talking about him as much, and she'd been sleeping at home all week, not crashing with any of them. Never one for shyness, Kasey stripped completely naked, replacing her regular underwear with her special-for-prom matching underwear before putting on Ada's other robe, since she'd forgotten her own.

"I think Leo saw him picking it up from the florist, but Leo's such a hyper storyteller sometimes it's hard to get information in any sort of linear order. I'm pretty sure he mentioned seeing Will inside or outside of the florist doing...something," Rosemarie said. She was piling her hair on top of her head and then letting it fall, unable to commit.

"Half-up, half-down," Kasey said to her. Ada met Rosemarie's eyes in the mirror and nodded in agreement.

"I feel pathetic that you had to round up someone for me to go with. Why can't I have a normal prom experience like the rest of y'all?" Caro asked, snapping her compact closed.

"*They're* going with their boyfriends," Rosemarie said with a bobby pin between her teeth. She tilted her head toward Ada and Kasey. "My whole situation is weird. But! We're gonna have a good time anyway, damn it. You and I should've gone together, Caro. Screw it," she concluded. She rattled around in the box on the counter for another bobby pin.

"Yeah, screw it. That's totally what we should've done," Caroline said, making her eyes big. One of them was mascaraed and lined; the other wasn't.

"Ada, do my eyes," Kasey said, holding up a tube of liquid eyeliner and handing it to her. "Look, y'all, this is our last big thing together before graduation and before Rosemarie and I leave Goldie, and it's going to be awesome. Y'all look *beautiful*, and look at this." Kasey went to the open window and pulled back the curtain. The spring wind was light and warm; the sun was hanging out over the hills. Some of the caterers were lighting the hurricane lamp candles; others smoothed out the white tablecloths. The air twinkled. "*Best* night, bitches. Period," Kasey finished. Rosemarie and Caro said yes at the same time and jinx at the same time, which set them off laughing. Kasey moved to put her butt on the counter and Ada got in front of her.

"Close your eyes," Ada said.

———

Ada's mom had forgone the professional photographer after Ada assured her it wasn't necessary, and now she was in the front yard behind the camera, snapping plenty of pictures of the girls and their dates. Ada, in cotton-candy pink. Kasey, wrapped in blue. Rosemarie dripped in purple next to Caroline's canary yellow. Caroline's wrist was encircled by the white-and-yellow roses that Will had shown up with, and the girls were happy and smiling, standing in front of their dates in traditional, cheesy prom poses, then some individual pictures and silly shots. Rosemarie's and Kasey's moms stopped by to take some pics of their own, and so did Grandma Mimi.

By the time they were finished, Ada was so hungry she could've chewed off Grayson's gray-tuxedoed arm. He had it around her as they made their way to the backyard for dinner. Ada had invited six more friends and their dates so there'd be twenty people total.

"You are the prettiest little thing I ever did see," Grayson said in her ear as he pulled the chair out for her and kissed the top of her head.

"That's what I like to hear," Ada said to him.

Dinner was fried chicken and steak. Fries and asparagus. Biscuits and rolls. There was a "bar" with fruity virgin drinks and sugar cookies with *Class of '04* looped on the thick frosting. Holly Plum was aglow with her full house and her cold glass of moscato. She chatted with the other moms, while Mr. Plum was content standing back with his beer and buddies—as he did on all social occasions—watching his wife and daughters flitter and shine.

Taylor was only in middle school, but Ada hadn't wanted her to feel left out, so she said it'd be okay for her to dress up and invite some of her friends too. The little girls ate and giggled in their dresses at a smaller table next to the deck.

———

The prom theme was Cotton Candy Land, and Ada and her mom and the rest of the prom committee had spent weeks searching for the perfect pinks, lavenders, and blues for the decorations. Everyone who entered the Goldie Country Club had to walk through two huge arches wrapped in tulle to get to their table. Cellophane and twinkle lights were fashioned into fruity candy wrappers and strung on the walls. On the floor, big colored squares made everyone feel like pawns on a giant board game. Cardboard peppermints hung from the ceiling; over-sized lollipops were propped around the room. By the time the girls got there, a long line was already snaking around the cotton candy machine. The fog box smoked between two stacks of fat, oversized, sugared gumdrops; the room flashed with disco-ball light.

"Will is *truly* brainless, y'all. Damn. Ain't enough cute in the world to fix how dumb he is. Look at him," Rosemarie said later, after about an hour of dancing. She tilted her head toward him and made a grouchy face to prove how completely done she was with Caro's date. She mimed his erratic dance moves and said Caroline's name exactly how Will said it—all slow, like if he said it too fast, he'd get it wrong. Ada covered her mouth for a second so she wouldn't fall into a full open-mouth guffaw. Rosemarie laughed when she looked at her; they lost it together. They were by the punch bowl now, having decided to take a breather when the DJ put on back-to-back Justin Timberlake songs. Caroline and Kasey swished off to the bathroom, and their dates were scattered. Leo was talking to a friend of his from band class, and Silas and Grayson were out there on the dance floor, watching Will attempt to do the worm.

"He's just *so* weird, but he's nice! He's not a jerk, right? He told Caroline her dress was cool and that her hair looked fancy. It's really all we can ask for," Ada said. Rosemarie was still cackling.

"No, he's not a jerk, but bless his heart. That's where we'll leave it. Bless his heart," Rosemarie said as they watched Will lift himself from the floor only to hop down again with his legs positioned in some sort of half split. The Castelow brothers were doubled over in laughter, and when Caro and Kasey returned, they asked the girls what was so funny.

"Your future ex-boyfriend," Rosemarie said.

When Caro's eyes found him, Will was busy doing some twirls.

"He's said, like, *eight* words to me," Caroline said.

"Thank *God*," Kasey said. "You're blessed, girl. Don't jinx it!"

The Justin Timberlake faded into Norah Jones, and the fast, swooping lights changed from red to a slow, pale blue. Leo was the first to make his way to them, holding his hand out for Rosemarie. Next, the Castelow boys for Ada and Kasey. Will had disappeared.

"No way are we leaving you here by yourself," Ada said to Caro.

"Nope." Rosemarie shook her head. Kasey did the same in solidarity.

"Please don't be ridiculous. I'll scream so loud if y'all don't go out there. I'll be fine! He'll come back from...wherever he went. It's fine!" Caro said to them. She lifted a napkin from the table, started putting some pretzels on it.

Trey Foxberry, whom none of them ever talked to or even liked, appeared beside them in his tuxedo, craning his neck to see if the punch bowl was empty. Caro scooted over. The girls and their dates lingered awkwardly, not wanting to abandon their friend, no matter how much they loved the song. Ada pretended to brush something off Grayson's lapel, and he leaned down to kiss her.

"Are you not here with anybody?" Trey asked Caro. Ada's back was turned to them now, but she was using all her energy to hear every word.

"Oh...yeah, I am. Will Brody is my date. But, um, he's gone somewhere. I don't know where," Caro said.

"Do you want to dance to this song? You don't have to stand here alone waiting for him," Trey said. "I'll dance with you if you want."

"Okay," Caro said.

Ada turned to see Caroline smile at him, and they all walked to the dance floor together.

Trey was surprisingly fun and light on his feet, even taking the time to dip Caroline back like something out of a movie at the end of the song. When Destiny's Child came on, he stayed out there with them for that one and "Toxic" by Britney Spears too before disappearing.

By the time Silas and Ada were crowned the no-surprises-there prom king and queen, Will had returned from smoking pot with his burnout friends, but Caroline was ignoring him. Ada and Silas were on the stage while the principal finished his speech, and Ada could see her girls in the dark, doing their fanciest beauty pageant waves at her. Grayson won prom king last year with someone else, and now his little brother was winning it with *his* girlfriend. They'd been joking about it for the past week and now it was done. Mission accomplished! Ada and Silas slow danced together to Faith Hill while Grayson laughed and said, "Hey, watch your hands!" to his brother.

As much as she loved prom, Ada absolutely couldn't wait to get into the limo again. To get out of that dress and into something comfy at the lake house, so the real party could start.

The rustic Castelow lake house sat back from the water and far up enough so that if someone wanted to tuck right off the wraparound porch into the grass, they'd be rolling for a *while* before they got wet. Ada had spent so much time there for the past two years she and Grayson had been dating that it felt like home to her too. There was a fire pit, and white twinkle lights wrapped around the trunks of the two reaching walnut trees out front. The Castelows had old tobacco money and new money from construction, and Mrs. Castelow had decorated the house in her quirky country style. There was a red-and-black buffalo plaid welcome mat in front of the door and lanterns on the porch. And there was a black bear carved out of wood standing at the bottom of the porch steps, like at a lot of the lake houses, but the Castelows' was painted to look like it was wearing a baby-blue Marvin Gaye T-shirt and sported a pair of vintage '70s sunglasses.

Mr. and Mrs. Castelow were spending the night at their B and B, but Grayson told Ada that his dad said he'd be stopping by unannounced to make sure nothing got *too* out of hand. Grayson's buddies dropped off a few cases of cheap beer, and the boys sploshed them into the cooler.

Even before they'd gotten in the limos heading to prom, there'd been whispers of possible skinny-dipping. A group of guys Ada didn't know well were the first ones in, whooping and jumping off the dock, sending biggish splashes into the navy-blue darkness. The girls watched from the porch, all four of them in their tie-dyed senior hoodies and sweatpants, all four of them nursing cold, drippy cans of Goldie Light. Sparrow Kim walked out of the house, also in her senior sweatsuit. She scooched next to Rosemarie and took the can from her hand, drank some, and gave it back.

"Whose pale ass is that?" Rosemarie asked out toward the water.

"Are you serious? How could we possibly know which one you're talking about?" Kasey asked. "It's *only* pale asses as far as the eye can see besides Mateo and Cassius."

"True that," Rosemarie said, laughing. "You remember what Cassius's ass looks like, Ada?"

"We went on *one* date. One! *Freshman* year!" Ada said, swatting at her arm.

"So, you didn't see his ass? You're sticking to that story?" Kasey said.

"Don't act like I'm the only one who's kissed Cassius, because y'all know we *all* have. I won't allow this slander," Ada said, pointing at the rest of them.

"Again, I say true that," Rosemarie said.

"I don't regret it, to be quite honest," Kasey said.

"Me neither," Caro said.

"Nor I," said Ada. After the skating party freshman year, Cassius had asked Ada if he could kiss her and she said yes. It was the first time a boy put his tongue in her mouth, and she remembered the sound the rain made falling on the metal awning above them when he did it.

95

"Is Will even here? It's probably *his* ass," Caro said. She leaned back in the chair and tipped the rest of the beer into her mouth.

"He's here somewhere. He's *so* stoned. I saw him talking to the magnolia," Ada said.

"Who the hell is *Magnolia*?!" Kasey asked.

A sharp laugh shot out of Ada's mouth; she kicked the air.

"The *tree*. The magnolia tree! Yeah right, like there's some girl in the senior class named Magnolia and we hadn't heard of her until tonight!" Ada said.

"Oh wow, this conversation is wildly dumb," Kasey said.

"Magnolia's a really great name, but I have to agree," Caro said.

"Are you getting in?" Sparrow asked Rosemarie. Rosemarie shrugged and Ada wondered if she was loving this. If getting to skinny-dip with Sparrow like this was what she wanted. Ada had half expected Kasey to already be boning Silas in his bedroom, but so far Silas had shotgunned only one beer and was standing in the kitchen with Grayson eating pizza and being loud with their friends, listening to 50 Cent.

"Are y'all getting in?" Rosemarie asked everyone on the porch.

"Hey! How cold is it?" Caro hollered out, leaning over the porch railing. A loose knot of boys jumped and splashed, swam and bobbed, not too far out.

"That you, Red Delicious? You can get in here and warm me up!" one of them hollered back.

"How did he even hear you and how is that helpful?" Ada said.

"A horny boy can hear anything he wants," Kasey said.

"We doin' this?" Grayson asked through the screen door. He stepped out and took off his shirt.

"Aha, that's Leo's pale ass!" Rosemarie said, pointing.

"Took you this long to realize it? What a disgrace, Kingston. You're gonna hurt that poor boy's feelings," Grayson said.

"I'll try to keep better track of asses, Grayson," Rosemarie said.

"Thank you. Show some interest, y'know?" he said. He unbuttoned his jeans and leaned down to kiss Ada. "Come on, baby girl," he said to her. Ada stood and took off her hoodie.

Silas smacked the door open. "Why are you still dressed?" he asked Kasey with fake surprise.

"Because *you* are," she said.

"Not anymore," Silas said, taking his shirt and shorts off quickly.

The girls, including Sparrow, stripped down to their undies and left their clothes on the porch. The air was night-cool, the moon an almost-full pearl. The crickets were singing loudly. The light wandered across the black-as-nothing, splashing water. They took off slowly at first, then they were runningrunningrunning through the cool grass. As the wind whistled in Ada's ears, she knew she would always remember this, always remember *exactly* how she felt on prom night with everyone together with the perfect weather and the perfect sky, and she couldn't figure out exactly why those good, perfect things made her a little sad, but maybe it was because she knew that as soon as she'd realized how perfect the moment was, it was already ending. She promised herself she'd let the rest of the night stretch out like gum. Everyone would stay awake and watch the sun come up. Make the night last forever.

Grayson was next to her in his underwear, holding her hand. Caroline and Kasey were holding hands too. Silas was ahead of them and Ada laughed when he kicked his boxer shorts off before jumping into the lake.

When Ada was naked in the cool lake water, hugging Grayson around his neck, kissing him, she opened her eyes to look out into the yard and saw Rosemarie and Sparrow with their arms around each other, swaying to the music she couldn't hear. Awash in moonlight.

———

By 3 a.m., not only had Rosemarie and Sparrow kissed—for the first and second time, thanks to a lazy game of spin the bottle started by

Sparrow's date, Frankie, on the porch—but people who had only just dried off were running down the hill, splashing into the lake again.

"Don't drown!" Ada yelled through her cupped hands, feeling like it was good luck to say it.

Ada and Grayson snuck off to his bedroom to have sex and take a shower together. They'd been having sex-sex only since Christmas, but she and Grayson never had sex in her house. In Grayson's bed, in Grayson's bedroom, in the Castelow lake house, she could be the Ada who let him take off her panties in the dark. The Ada who let him touch and kiss her everywhere while she touched and kissed him everywhere before they stepped into the coolness of his bathroom and rained off each other's smells.

Mr. Castelow popped in once at the party to talk to his sons. Ada saw him as he was leaving, and he'd even been kind enough to sit and talk to a girl who was on the front steps crying. Ada heard it was about spin the bottle, but she couldn't put the pieces together and was too buzzed and sleepy to even try. When Mr. Castelow was gone, the girl came back inside with her friends and laid her cheek against the cool creek rock of the fireplace while one of her friends petted her hair. The big antlered head of the whitetail deer Mr. Castelow had put down years ago hung above them, its dark, glassy eyes staring out at nothing.

Now most of Ada's crew was in the living room, dancing, lying across the couches, drinking, and eating. More light beer and mini bottles of whiskey. Gummy bears and cold pizza. Spicy chips and chocolate cookies. "Hot in Herre" by Nelly was pouring from the speakers again. Sparrow and Frankie disappeared to one of the bedrooms, and Rosemarie was lying on Leo's chest on the couch. Ada couldn't *wait* until she could talk to Rosemarie alone about the Sparrow kiss. It was the first time Rosemarie had ever kissed a girl, and Sparrow wasn't just *a* girl to Rosemarie—she was *the* girl and Ada was happy for her friend. Kasey was across Silas's lap with her eyes closed, and Caroline was in the kitchen with some people, rooting around in the freezer for Popsicles.

"What was up with Trey Foxberry acting like a normal human tonight? Or at least for the fifteen minutes he was on the dance floor with us?" Ada asked the room.

"Who did he go to prom with?" a girl asked.

"I don't know," Silas said, shaking his head.

"Why don't we, like, *know* anything about him?" Kasey mumbled. Ada had thought she was sleeping, but Kasey sat up and leaned against the arm of the couch.

"I don't know," Silas repeated. "I've grown up with the kid my whole life, but we've never been friends. He's a dick."

"He *is* a fucking dick," Grayson chimed in, his voice deep and sleepy.

The Castelow boys got along with almost everyone, so the ease with which they fell into calling Trey Foxberry a dick was telling. No one in the room challenged them on it.

"I've never said one word to him, and we had three classes together last year," Kasey said.

"His dad's a dick too," Grayson said. He explained how Mr. Castelow didn't like Mr. Foxberry and how they'd played on the high school football team together.

"Caroppenheimer?" Rosemarie said loud enough so Caro would hear her from the kitchen.

"Yo," Caro said, swishing her red ponytail out and peeping around the corner.

"Come and tell us more about dancing with the devil," Rosemarie said. Ada was buzzed, not drunk, and so was Rosemarie. She could always tell from Rosemarie's voice first, how it crackled like a sparkler.

"Trey Foxberry," Kasey clarified.

"I knew who she meant," Caro said. She walked into the living room with her right hand spread wide, five raspberries stuck on the tips. She sat on the rug in front of them and ate the one off her thumb. "I don't know why he asked me to dance. Maybe it was a dare."

"Oh, please! Why are you doing that? No one has to be *dared* to dance with you! Quit it," Ada said.

"I'm sorry! I mean, I never talk to him. Right place, right time, I guess. Or wrong place, right time. Or right place, wrong time," Caroline said.

"Or *wrong* place, *wrong* time," Rosemarie and Ada said together.

They'd already talked about it as soon as they got to the lake house, but that was hours ago and now it was late enough to begin going over everything again in joyful, painstaking detail.

When they were finished, they came to the consensus that yes, absolutely, it was undeniable, and their years and years of research proved it—Trey Foxberry was indeed a colossal dick.

2019

9

KASEY

Kasey had spent the past few days having breakfast at Caroline's and lunch at Rosemarie's and dinner at either Ada's or Plum Eats. Caro always brought sweet treats to Rosemarie's, and Ada never showed up at Caro's place without something delicious.

Last night after stopping by Duke's house to visit and have cherry pie with him and his wife, Kasey caved and spent the night with Caro in the mansion because Trey was out of town and Caro begged her to. Even though her ridiculously overpriced hotel room was going to sit empty for a night, Kasey couldn't say no. Caro seemed like such a little girl in that moment, pleading in the same way she used to beg Grandma Mimi to ask Kasey's mom if Kasey could stay one more night when she'd already stayed two. Rosemarie had slept over at Caro's too, and Ada had hung around until she could barely keep awake.

Caro fell asleep first. Rosemarie and Kasey took the bottle of wine outside to continue their conversation, and Rosemarie told her how she peeked at Trey's texts on Caroline's phone. She talked about Caro mentioning that he could stay mad for days over the littlest thing. Kasey talked about how it bugged her that she didn't know more about Trey. The longest amount of time she'd spent with him was those fifteen minutes he was out on the dance floor with them at prom. She hadn't laid eyes on him since she'd been back in town.

Kasey had no place questioning Caroline's marriage or what Trey was like. Kasey had kept so much from everyone she had no choice but to believe that everyone had a right to their secrets. She hated when the girls got pushy with her, so she wasn't going to get pushy with Caro.

At least, not yet.

Rosemarie said she was only allowing herself to worry about Caro quietly for now, and Kasey said that was what she'd do too. They finished the rest of the wine by candlelight, sitting on the side of the pool with their feet glowing in the water.

It was the middle of Taylor's wedding week when Kasey finally worked up the nerve to go to the farmhouse. She hadn't been there since the night she graduated from high school, the night of the big party they threw in Ada's backyard. She called Devon from the car. She had the windows down and was wearing her dad's old, threadbare *Gremlins* T-shirt with her cutoffs. She'd been leaning into her Goldie wardrobe all week—humid, Southern summer and nostalgia.

"I hate thinking you're doing this alone. I know you're getting tired of hearing it from me. Am I getting on your nerves?" Devon asked with the same plunge of tenderness in his voice he always had when he was being patient with her. She pictured the face she knew he was making—his amber eyes, his rosy bottom lip in a straight line. He was by far the prettiest man she'd ever dated, somehow both pretty *and* handsome. Leonine. She'd been attracted to him immediately, leaving no wondering on that front. After discovering that he was intensely smart and kind too and that their personalities coalesced, staying together had been so easy. Staying together forever and dreaming of buying a brownstone in Brooklyn one day and having kids and making French toast on Saturday mornings in a Nancy Meyers–esque kitchen made the most sense.

"No, no," Kasey lied. "You're being very sweet and it's not like I *want* to do this alone, Dev. I *have* to do this alone." She let him know (again) that she could ask any one of her girlfriends to come with her and they'd do it in an instant.

"I miss you," he said.

"I miss you too." Her blood tingled cool when she made the last turn before the farmhouse driveway. She timed it so she would get there while the sun was up, get inside before it went down. She told Rosemarie, Ada, and Caro where she was going and left them chatting at the table at Plum Eats, where they'd eaten dinner together.

"I saw a Shih Tzu on my walk home this afternoon. Black and white. He was barking at the pigeons, but I could tell his heart wasn't in it," Devon said with his gentle *heh heh* of a laugh that Kasey loved so much.

"After I left Caro's this morning, I got to hang with Rosemarie's dog, Basie, at her place with my second cup of coffee."

"Kasey and Basie. Cute."

"I know, right? I'll send you a pic of her. She's so adorable it almost makes me want to get a puppy. *Almost*," Kasey said.

"Let's get a puppy the day we get back from our honeymoon. Seriously."

"Deal." The wedding was a year away; getting a dog then sounded lovely.

Kasey stopped the car at the end of the driveway. She didn't want to be on the phone when she drove the last quarter mile up to the house.

"I love you, Kase. FaceTime later and let me know how everything goes?" Devon said.

Yesterday morning they'd FaceTimed. She told him a lot of things, but nothing about Silas. Before she'd left the city, Devon had asked if there was an ex-boyfriend in Goldie he should be worried about. He'd said it tongue in cheek because Devon wasn't a jealous man. He was confident and coolheaded and he'd proven he could handle her and her emotions, even the sloppiest ones.

So why wasn't she telling him about Silas?

Was there anything to tell?

She could tell Devon she felt like she had the stomach flu when Silas said hey to her. That she felt like she had a high fever when he picked her up and hugged her. That the room tilted when they were at Duke's later that night and Silas handed her a fizzy Bellini because when they were in high school, she'd told him when she was grown-up, she wanted to be the kind of woman who drank Bellinis with her girlfriends and wore expensive heels and lived in New York. That her mouth dried out when he said goodbye to her at the end of the night. How he'd said, "I'll see you tomorrow, Fritz? Promise you won't disappear? I couldn't handle it. I thought I was going to die last time. I'm serious. I thought I'd legit die of a broken heart when you left. I thought I did something wrong or that I hurt you somehow, but I didn't know how. I couldn't eat for, like, a month." He was confessing because he was drunk at that point and so was she. He'd told her some of those things in a few emails they sent back and forth fifteen years ago after she left. He said some of it on the phone the handful of times they'd talked. But then Kasey stopped writing; Kasey stopped answering the phone. She forced herself to stop thinking about Goldie and him too.

They both moved on.

"Yes. I will. I love you too," she said to Devon, careful not to let her voice crack.

"Promise you'll let me know immediately if you need me? I'll hop on a plane so fast—"

"I promise, Devon. Thank you."

*   *   *

104

Kasey had been working with a Realtor friend of Holly Plum's for the past year to rent the farmhouse out from time to time. As her car's tires rolled over the gravel of the driveway, she imagined a family renting it in July—grilling hamburgers and corn, filling an inflatable pool with cool water for their kids. She pictured little ones catching lightning bugs in mason jars and their parents drinking sweet tea on the porch. Maybe they'd bring their boat or a pair of Jet Skis, or big black rubber tubes for floating away on lazy days.

Her daddy had been smart enough to set the house catty-corner on the land so it caught the best light, and if she squinted, she could see the Castelow lake house and acreage sprawling through the trees on the other side of the water. Her mom could've made good money if she'd sold the farmhouse, and she could've worked less, but she said she'd never sell it. The house meant so much to them because it felt like the thump of her daddy's heart was still knocking inside of it.

He'd made that house and he'd loved that house, so no, Kasey wasn't going to sell it now that it was hers. She didn't know what she was going to do with it. For as *adult* as she'd felt for practically her entire life, and for as long as she'd been living on her own and taking care of herself, being responsible for a whole-ass house felt a smidge too grown-up for her liking. She found herself more angry than sad as she pulled up and turned the car off, yanked the emergency brake.

Her mother's great-uncle didn't have any children of his own and left her mom that land when he died. Her family disapproved of her relationship with a black man, Kasey's daddy. Practically the whole family disowned her, so she moved two hundred miles away to Goldie, where her great-uncle was kind and welcoming and not a racist. He loved Angie a whole lot and left her forty thousand dollars too—all the money he had saved up—to help them get started on the farmhouse.

Angie's favorite rocking chair was sitting on the front porch right next to the door. Kasey didn't linger too long out there. It was time to get inside and get this over with. She hadn't put the farmhouse key on her key ring, because even that was too intimate, too much. She went in her pocket for the envelope it was in and pulled it out. When she turned the key in the hole, it made the same soft click she'd heard her whole life.

The threshold was a time machine—a portal to the fuzzy, haunted *beyond*.

In the corner of the living room: where Roy hollered at her for leaving her backpack on the couch.

In her old bedroom: where she slept with the TV on so she wouldn't have to hear her mom and Roy arguing. It was where she could have a semblance of peace, especially if she told Roy she was on her period and wanted to be left alone. It was even better when her cycle aligned with her mom's. Roy would leave the house entirely, sometimes for the whole week. Sometimes Kasey would lie, say she was bleeding when she wasn't, so they could get a break.

In her mom's old bedroom: where Kasey watched Roy put his hand around Angie's neck and where he broke their antique mirror. It'd been around since the Civil War but couldn't survive being in the same house with Roy.

In the bathroom: where Kasey would hide when things got too bad. The deep claw-foot tub she sank into when her mom and Roy were fighting. The place where she occasionally thought about slipping under and going to sleep forever.

In the bathroom, the window: she climbed out of it sometimes when it all got too much. Walked to Rosemarie's, Ada's, or Caro's and called her mom from their houses.

In the kitchen, the table: where Kasey and her mom had a lot of fun doing their weird taste tests. Daring each other to take one bite of Twinkie and one bite of pickle, to wash it all down with a big gulp of orange juice to see who'd be the first to chicken out.

Also in the kitchen, the sink: where Roy destroyed a lot of meals.

The garbage can next to the oven: where Roy destroyed a lot of meals too.

And on the kitchen floor.

Now on the kitchen floor was where Kasey finally lost it. She sat and let herself cry and cry and cry.

On the kitchen floor.

On the kitchen floor.

And on the kitchen floor.

On the kitchen floor.

No breath.

Kasey needed air. She stood and smacked the back door open, ran out into the yard and bent over, crying. She stood again, crying. There was the now overgrown patch of garden where the berries used to be. Another for the tomatoes. The sunflowers. The grassy shaded spot where she fenced in the rabbits they sometimes kept.

Behind the shed: where Roy shot her favorite dog because he said it was time, but it hadn't been time. Not yet. He didn't even let Kasey say goodbye.

After she cried it out, her stuffy head pulsed in the humidity. *Good Ol' Goldie. Looks like Stars Hollow but feels like Hell's Front Porch.* Even though it was hot, the fresh air was helping. Seeing the water was helping. Kasey walked toward it and sat, watching it move.

She didn't smoke but wanted a cigarette; it felt like a cigarette moment.

"Fritz?"

Kasey turned at the sound of Silas's voice. He was walking across the grass in a dark blue uniform.

"Uh . . . whoa . . . you're, um . . . a cop?" she said to him. Her cried-out eyes were hidden behind her sunglasses, but she was sure the tip of her nose was pink. Silas would know what was up, no question.

"Yeah. It's a brand-new gig. Only part-time. To help out my uncle, mostly. Do you remember him? My mom's brother, Mickey? He's chief now. I said yes as a joke, mostly, since I'm an outlaw at heart. That's what makes it ridiculous. I don't give a shit what other people do, honestly," Silas said. *Silas Hickory Castelow, the cop.*

He looked *real* good in that uniform, so she swapped it with an image of Devon in one of his suits instead—the slim gray one she loved, his brown double monk straps. Her mind was a mess. Her heart zapped back fifteen years.

Back in Goldie.

Still crying at the farmhouse.

Still thinking Silas Castelow is cute.

Still not knowing what to do about anything.

"This is all mine now," she said, holding up the key for him. She motioned to the house, the land, the water.

"Miss Nancy called. Said she didn't recognize the car, but she knew there weren't any renters right now. I figured it was you." Silas crouched next to Kasey and looked out at the lake.

"Right. Nosy Nancy. Well, it's good she hasn't stopped keeping an eye out. I do love that old broad."

"Remember how she didn't know it was us, so she called the cops that night we had the bonfire over there?" Silas pointed toward the Castelow lake house.

"When Grayson and Mateo were setting off bottle rockets at two in the morning? Yep. I remember," Kasey said.

Some quiet.

"You all right?" Silas asked.

"Will be."

"You're not selling this place, are you?"

"Never," Kasey said. "We're supposed to get our rafts out in the water sometime while I'm here." Silas knew that *we're* always referred to RACK.

"Glad to hear it. I'm sorry I interrupted. Are you okay alone? Did you want me to leave?" he asked.

"I'd like you to stay a little bit longer. If you can."

Silas jingled as he sat. He let his knees settle into the inside of his arms. He didn't ask Kasey any more questions. Instead, he told her stories she'd never heard. Stuff only Silas would know. Like how the woman who lived directly across the lake hit on his dad once when he'd gone to check on the construction team building her a new deck, and how the next time the woman called the B and B to book a room for her family, his mom had cussed her out. He told her about the kid who almost drowned in the lake two years ago because he and his buddies were having a contest to see who could hold their breath the longest.

"That was Jacob Stoeffer's kid. You remember Jake Stoeffer. Remember he stuck a fork in the wall socket freshman year? Real sparks and shit. Yeah, no surprise there—his kid's *also* an idiot," Silas said.

He kept telling her stories as the sun went down, streaking the deep-blue sky with outrageous shades of lavender and peach. Kasey felt small and insignificant under the glory of it, but she couldn't focus on that, because Silas was making her laugh so much she had to beg him to stop. She'd cycled through her entire range of emotions since she walked through that front door of the farmhouse.

"Si, I'm serious. *Please!*" She slapped his shoulder.

"No, now you missed a *lot*, Fritz, and it wouldn't be neighborly for me not to fill you in as best I can," he said.

Her eyes weren't hidden anymore now that she'd pushed her sunglasses on top of her head. She knew what was coming.

"Whew, I can't stand to see you cry," he said.

It was something he used to say to her when they were in high school. When he'd threaten to come to the farmhouse and beat Roy's ass himself if he had to. *Swear you'll tell me if he ever lays a hand on you,* Silas had said to her too often. By that time, Roy had stopped shoving Kasey around, but it made her feel guilty that her mom was taking the full brunt of his abuse.

Kasey remembered how Silas had asked her if Roy ever sexually assaulted her or tried to. She told him about the time junior year when

Roy was drunk and grabbed her ass in the kitchen. How she'd pulled the knife from the block and threatened him with it. Slept with it under her pillow for a week after. She never told her mom about that; she never told anyone about it at that point. Only Silas.

When she told him, Silas looked right into her eyes and said he wanted to kill Roy. She saw something in him that night she'd never seen before, and it didn't scare her one bit. She liked it. She *loved* it. Police uniform or not, Silas really was an outlaw. She felt it that night and had never forgotten.

"Don't tell me you're the cop who gets tenderhearted for every girl in Goldie as soon as they drop a few tears for you, Castelow. You're so soft," Kasey said.

"Nah, not *every* girl in Goldie," he said, shaking his head. "Oh. Wait! Did I tell you about Wallace Brody and how he got caught in what we'll call a *compromising situation* with Billy Boone's duck?"

Kasey's cackle shot out and bounced across the water.

———

The starry night of Taylor and Ben's wedding, Kasey and Caroline were alone at the reception in the Plums' backyard.

"Caro, I don't want you to get mad at me, but are you *sure* you're all right? I know Trey hasn't been around much and you get lonely in that big house by yourself. Does Mimi come stay sometimes? Is everything *really* okay? You seem a little...I don't know." Kasey could feel something wasn't right, and despite her best attempts to mind her business, she couldn't let this go. She'd thought she could worry about it quietly, but she couldn't. It was time to get loud. This wasn't leftover weirdness from her leaving Goldie; this was something else entirely. She knew her best friend, knew something was up.

Caro glanced down and smoothed her dress—Kasey noticed she was in long sleeves again, even in this heat. Her stomach twisted. Caro shook her head and looked at Kasey, quiet. Then her face changed completely and Kasey stood still, unsettled and waiting.

"There's Trey," Caroline said.

Caro waved at him as he walked toward them. She posted pictures of him on social media from time to time, but Kasey hadn't ever stood close to Trey on purpose. Also, Kasey hadn't seen him in person since high school, when she usually steered clear anyway. His hair was a slicked wheaty-gold color; his eyes were light blue and cool and Trey was long. Both his arms and legs seemed to be nearly double the length of most men's. He reminded her of a scarecrow that spent its evenings in the gym.

"Trey, it's finally time for you to remeet Kasey! Kasey, this is my Foxberry," Caro said. She kissed Trey and smiled up at him, moved her eyes to meet Kasey's. In Kasey's periphery, she could see Rosemarie and Leo on the stage inside the white tent. Kasey turned to watch Rosemarie adjust the microphone and sit on her stool; Leo was behind her with his guitar. Trey stuck out his hand and Kasey took it.

"You sat behind me in Spanish Two sophomore year because of our last names. That was a million years ago, wasn't it?" Trey said with a smile that Kasey could imagine being charming if she knew him, but there was a lightness in his voice that signaled to her that he thought what he was saying was more interesting than it actually was. Yep. She remembered clearly now. How confident he was in high school, how easily girls seemed to fawn all over him. It was still hard to believe Caro was one of those girls now. No matter how white his teeth were or how commanding his presence in a suit, how the hell did Caro end up married to *Trey*?

Kasey had a flash of fear and a quick flick that she was somehow living in a dream. A nightmare. Whose wedding was this? She hadn't come back to Goldie for Caro and Trey's wedding, so why was she here? There were pops of confetti, and Taylor and Ben walked out into the backyard with the warm evening wind in their hair, holding one hand, the others raised in triumph. Everyone looked over and clapped.

Kasey downed the rest of her champagne and set her glass on the table next to her. She clapped and clapped. Caro did her finger whistle. She was the only person Kasey knew who could do that; Mimi taught her how.

"It was a million years ago—you're right," Kasey said.

"You two chat! I'll be right back," Caro said, walking toward the caterers.

"One of the cupcakes is probably missing a sprinkle," Kasey said to Trey. She heard Silas's voice somewhere in the crowd behind her and felt better instantly. Felt guilty instantly too. She'd been thinking about him too much. She'd started pinching herself when she thought about how handsome he looked in his uniform. Started twisting her engagement ring when she thought about how long he stayed with her out at the farmhouse, making her laugh, making sure she was okay. How he hugged her in the driveway before they left. How they followed each other in their separate cars back into town. How she felt a sharp blip of sadness when he turned and disappeared as she drove straight on.

"She's always worrying about something. I tell her not to, but she's hardheaded," Trey said. Kasey hated that she'd made even a small, lighthearted joke about Caroline, giving Trey room to make it more aggressive. Kasey should've anticipated that; Trey *was* aggressive. His energy, his body. Leaching testosterone rolled off him like fog. "Your dad was black, right?" he asked.

"Uh...yeah? Yep, he was," Kasey said, knowing her loud face would betray her true emotions, but she didn't care. She heard Silas laugh at something. Grayson too. She looked up at the back deck to see Ada helping her mom inside. Maybe she drank too much already? There was a lot happening and Kasey was overstimulated. The one glass of champagne hadn't done much for her nerves. A caterer walked by with a tray and Kasey grabbed another and thanked her. When Kasey turned back to Trey, he had that dumb fucking look on his face she *definitely* remembered from high school. "You're not wrong.

My dad was black; my mom was white. I'm a biracial superhero," Kasey said.

"I remember your mom." Trey asked the caterer for a glass of water with extra ice.

"Angie," Kasey said, just to hear it. She thought of Mick Jagger's big, handsome mouth singing her mama's name.

"Holy shit, she was good-looking. You look *exactly* like her, except, you know, half-black," Trey said. Did he look at her ass when he said *half-black*? Maybe? Okay. Maybe not. Maybe she was overreacting. Maybe she'd only convinced herself she hated him. Maybe he was trying to be nice. Didn't she love Caroline too much not to at least *try* to be cordial to her husband? "Where's your man? You have one? I'm sure you do," he asked.

"I'm engaged to a man, yes. He's happily busy in New York City, waiting for me to come back home to him," she said, smiling.

"Good for him. I don't blame him one bit."

Okay, he *totally* looked at her ass that time.

Kasey let her face go plain, sipped her champagne. Whether other people thought Trey was charming or not didn't matter. No matter how hard she tried, she couldn't find anything *special* about him. He acted like a lot of guys she'd known and been bored by. She tried to imagine how Caroline could have become enraptured by him, as he took his water with extra ice from the caterer when she returned. He didn't thank her. Trey watched Kasey's face for a moment and then took his time surveying the people in the backyard. She made her move to walk away, but Caroline was coming toward them with an older woman.

"Kase, this is my amazing mother-in-law, Paula Foxberry. Paula, this is one of my best friends and sisters, Kasey Fritz," Caro said. Kasey said hi to Paula.

"Oh, of *course* I remember little Kasey Fritz from the grocery store. You and your poor mother," Paula said. "Bless her heart, but Caroline thinks I'm old and senile. Well, she *wishes*. I may not have been as young as *your* mother was when she had you, but I was young when I had my children too. I'm not dead yet," Paula said to Caro with enough nastiness on her tongue to let Kasey know that maybe everyone in the Foxberry family was trash.

"Well, Paula, Caro and I have been friends since we were babies. I love you, Caroppenheimer," Kasey said, taking her hand. "Foxberry," she said quickly, correcting herself. "*Caroline*," she added for good measure. Leo's guitar strums blinked the summer air as she and Caro hugged each other tight.

"Kasey Josephine Fritz, come here to me, right now," Mimi said when she appeared. Kasey's eyes filled with tears even though she'd seen Mimi earlier and more than once since she'd been back in Goldie. She and Caro had gone to the trailer park to drink sweet tea with her and sit out front and gossip. But hearing Grandma Mimi say her whole name like that? Kasey was overcome with nostalgia and emotion. She hugged her around her neck and stood back to hold her hands and admire her dress—coral vintage and beaded, like something right out of Old Hollywood. She wore a yellow rose pinned to it, the yellow matching the flowers on Caro's long sleeves.

Rosemarie's delicate voice met Leo's in harmony in the atmosphere, and it gave Kasey chills, the magic of it—the starry dome of night, the math of music.

"Look at you, so beautiful," Mimi said, kissing both of her cheeks.

"*You* are," Kasey said to her.

"Caro, come out here and dance with us. We're not going to waste one minute standing around tonight," Mimi said, reaching for Caroline's hand.

When they moved away from Trey and his mother, Mimi's lip rose in a curl.

"I know they're your family now, Ladybug, but they can be the *sourest* mess of people on God's green. All that money and no sweetness. Where is the sweetness, honey?" Mimi said to Caro.

"The sweetness is right here," Kasey said, pointing to Caro's heart.

Mimi's seventy-year-old self spun Caroline right around as Rosemarie stood on stage singing her heart out. When it was Caro's turn to spin Mimi, she added a slow, careful dip.

"I love both of you more than you'll ever know," Caro said.

"We're all a little *too* tender tonight," Kasey said, gently bumping hips with Mimi.

"Lotta love and feelings are in the air! Blame it on the wedding!" Mimi was snapping her fingers to the music.

Over her shoulder, Ada was on her tiptoes, talking in Grayson's ear. Silas was next to them; Kasey watched a woman slip her arm around his waist.

Kasey walked across the yard closer to the tent when the song ended; she clapped and whooped and Rosemarie found her in the crowd. Kasey blew her a kiss through the air. Pretty buzzed from the champagne, she walked up to the stage and told Rosemarie how lovely she sounded.

"You too, Leo Bell," Kasey said to him.

"Thank you, Miss Fritz," Leo said in the old-timey style that had always endeared him to Kasey. Leo Bell was a good one, through and through. There wasn't one thing she didn't like about him. His sisters opened Bell Books a few years ago and ran it together. Yesterday, Kasey stopped in to browse, and Leo lit up when he saw her face. This was who he was—a complete and total weirdo in the fact that he seemed like one of the last few decent men on earth.

Leo strummed his guitar again, playing the opening chords to "Cowboy Take Me Away" by The Chicks, and Kasey's heart beat faster. Her face got hot as a lot of couples who were sitting and eating and chatting stood to gather on the dance floor.

"Dance with me, Fritz? Please? Don't make me stand here by my lonesome," Silas's voice said from behind her. She was warmer than she wanted to be. She took Silas's hand and led him out of the tent so they could get some more air. She put her arms around his neck as they swayed in the cool grass.

"Look at us dancing to our song," she said. The first song they kissed to. The song that played again on prom night. The song that would forever remind Kasey of Silas and everything they were together. Devon was her fiancé and she adored him; Silas was the cowboy from her past, the cowboy she dreamt of taking her away, only he hadn't. He couldn't. Here they were now, *fifteen* years later, holding each other. The smoke of memory and their unfinished business so thick Kasey had to focus on her breathing so she wouldn't choke.

"Wasn't going to let the chance pass me by. Just don't tell your fiancé if he's the jealous type."

"He's not," Kasey said, thinking of Devon in New York, wondering what he was doing. "What about Miss Green Dress over there? Y'all were looking mighty cozy a few minutes ago." Kasey tilted her head toward where Ada and Grayson were standing. Miss Green Dress had a little girl on her hip now, and all four of Ada's boys were leading a short line of kids holding glow sticks and running quick through the tables until Grayson reminded them to slow it down.

Silas turned to look when he heard his brother's voice.

"That's my little girl she's holding," Silas said.

Kasey's stomach sank like a capsized boat. She opened her mouth to say something, anything.

"I'm messing with you, Fritz! Wow, you look mad. I made you mad. You don't like me teasing you too much, I remember," Silas said, smiling down at her.

"She's pretty. The little girl's pretty too," Kasey said after scrunching up her nose at him. Rosemarie's voice lifted and met the stars. Kasey looked up at them and felt so small again. Invisible. Thinking about her mom. *Are You There God? It's Me, Angie.* Thinking about her dad. *Are You There God? It's Me, Isaiah.*

Are You There God? It's Me, Kasey.

"I don't know her very well. She works at the courthouse," Silas said.

Kasey closed her eyes and put her head on his chest, only looking up at him again when the song was almost over.

"Thanks again for the other day at the farmhouse," she said.

"Stop thanking me for that. I've *missed* you," Silas said softly. "Devon's living the dream right now."

Kasey felt untethered hearing Devon's name come out of Silas's mouth for the first time, and her face was so close to his.

"I'm so sorry everything happened like it did back then. I didn't mean—" she said. Silas pulled her closer. "No, I'm serious. You would've never done that to me and I know that." Kasey shook her head. His hand stayed at the small of her back.

"Ah, I'm just glad to be here now."

She wanted to kiss him. She wanted to kiss him *really* bad. She wanted to stop time and return to those nights when it was just the two of them, away from the world. Those nights up late in his truck, those nights he'd sneak out and wait at the end of the driveway for her to climb out of her bathroom window. Those spring nights that stretched on forever and ever and ever until life ran through her like an EF5 tornado.

Kasey and Silas let their noses touch, and Silas moved his up and down, snuggling closer.

"Can we talk more now, though? I mean, when you go home, you won't disappear completely again? We can be friends?" Silas asked.

"Of course, Silas. We'll always be friends. You know I love you, right?"

"You know I love *you*."

When "Cowboy Take Me Away" ended, Rosemarie started singing "Strawberry Wine" by Deana Carter, and Kasey and Silas kept holding on. Kasey loved that song too much. They'd danced to it at prom, and it was one of RACK's permanent BFF songs. The lyrics were too much, the champagne was too much, everything was too much. Kasey couldn't help but cry. Silas held her tighter and asked if she was okay.

"Yeah, I am. Thank you," she said, the two of them tied together with a mile-long ribbon of words they wouldn't say.

When Rosemarie was finished singing, Silas put his hand on the back of Kasey's head and, softly in her ear, thanked her for the dance.

———

Before the sun came up the next day, Kasey called Devon and told him about Silas. Told him he was her first *everything important* and that being back in Goldie and seeing him was overwhelming, and not entirely in a bad way. In a way that left her feeling exhausted and confused, and she'd be even more confused if she weren't flying back tomorrow, but she was. Thank God she was.

Devon wasn't mad, but he kept asking Kasey why she hadn't told him about Silas earlier. What was the big secret? He had exes too. As a matter of fact, he saw his ex in the park recently and she was walking four dogs. Devon laughed because he thought she was allergic.

"I'm sorry I didn't tell you earlier, but I wanted to tell you now, while the feelings are fresh. I barely got any sleep last night," Kasey said.

"Look. Just come home. Goldie's got you in a fugue state, that's all," he said. "I love you." His voice was confident and relaxed. So *Devon*. She'd done the right thing by coming clean, and he reassured her of it.

Goldie's got me in a fugue state, she said to herself as she snatched open the hotel curtains. She closed her eyes and interrupted her bad memories of Goldie by instead remembering Silas's nose touching hers last night and Rosemarie singing those songs as the rest of the stars came out, slow, slow, and quick. When she opened her eyes again, she stared out at the dark hills without blinking until everything went blurry. She wanted coffee.

*   *   *

While she drank her dark roast, she scrolled through some work emails, not feeling the least bit guilty for ignoring them since she was on vacation. She wrote in the group chat she had with her girlfriends from the city, saying hi and that she was stoked to see them soon for drinks next week. She was interrupted by an incoming surprise text from Silas.

Your earring's in my pocket.

It's not even six yet. What are you doing up?

Early shift. Filling in for someone at the station. An outlaw never sleeps.

Why is my earring in your pocket?

Ada said she found it on the kitchen counter and I took it because I told her I'd see you before you left town. Was I right?

Were you?

I hope so, Fritz. I hope so.

Now why would I choose to hang out with an unrepentant thief?

Because ladies love cowboys and outlaws. Like Quick Draw McGraw. Do you need me to keep rhyming? Because I will.

Please don't! :P

Okay, but only for you. See you
soon?

Yes, please.

Kasey sat by the window and held her mug with both hands in the
dark, anxious for the first hint of morning light.

2004

10

Kasey and Angie were at the kitchen table with the last college loan application in front of them. Angie clicked her pen with one hand and dug into the cookie dough with the other.

"Mama, come *on*," Kasey said. She'd spent most of the afternoon tutoring and had been waiting all evening for her mom to get off work.

"I'm sorry! Okay. One last lick," Angie said, putting her finger in her mouth. She hopped up to get a dish towel so she could wipe her hand clean.

Roy hadn't been home for two days, so the farmhouse was like a whole new world. The music was on; the windows were open. The short kitchen curtains were blowing up and out, making the soft evening sunlight dance around the room. Yesterday, Kasey found out she'd gotten the market analyst research internship in New York City that she'd been stressing over for months. That, on top of getting into Greenlee—the Ivy League she wanted—had made both of Kasey's wildest college dreams come true already. The third step was making sure everylittlebit was covered financially, since her mom hadn't been able to save up much and Kasey was hoping to focus on school instead of having to worry about finding a job too.

The internship paid a little, not a lot, but being selected was priceless. She and her mom had gotten their favorite Thai takeout from the fancy place in Adora Springs and a dark green bottle of sparkling grape juice to celebrate. Angie brought home five different kinds of boxed cakes for them to decide on and three tubs of frosting to mix and match. Yellow cake with chocolate was usually their favorite, but last week when Roy was gone, they'd made a lemon-Sprite cake and slathered it with fluffs of vanilla cream. Angie nabbed the best cookie dough too, but so far, it hadn't made it into the oven. Kasey gave in and scooped some of it off the package with her finger, echoing her mom's *one last lick* after she ate it.

"Praise the Lord this is the last form we need to fill out. These things are hell," Angie said, clicking the pen again and beginning to write.

"At least we're on the good side of it."

"Yes we are, Kaseybaby, and I'm so proud of you I can't stand it. I could hardly sleep last night."

"I know. You were keeping me up with your wiggling and turning the light on!" Kasey said. They'd slept together in her mom's king-sized bed like they did so often when Roy was gone. Kasey didn't care where Roy had run off to and didn't ask.

"I'm sorry, but honestly, if *I* don't complain about your strawberry sleep toots, then *you* shouldn't complain about my wiggling or my sitting up and reading," her mom said.

"I wasn't the only one with strawberry sleep toots!" Kasey pointed at her.

"Then maybe next time we shouldn't eat a pint of strawberries before bed!"

"Okay, maybe not. That's reasonable," Kasey said, laughing. They'd never be able to stick to that, though, because strawberries were their favorite.

Her mom piled her dark-chocolate hair on top of her head, stuck it there with a pencil. Kasey and her mom had the same brown curls, the same brown eyes, the same gentle press in their chins. Angie liked to tell her that it meant they'd been touched by an angel before they were born.

"Hmm...what's your middle name again?" Angie asked, smirking and eyeing the form.

"Angelina," Kasey lied. Angelina was her mom's full name, but no one called her that. Her middle name was Josephine, like Kasey's.

"Josephine," her mom said slowly as she wrote it down. "When were you born? Ah, I remember and so does my vagina, since it's never been the same since, poor thing."

"Mama, can we leave your vagina out of this?"

"Hmm, we'll see. I haven't finished filling out the form yet. You basically have to sign over your life, so there could very well be a question about my vagina somewhere on here. Yours too, Miss Valedictorian."

"*Mama!*"

Kasey's phone rang next to her elbow.

"Speaking of your vagina, it's Silas Castelow calling right on time!" her mom said, sticking out her tongue.

"Gross! I'm calling Child Protective Services as soon as I'm off this phone," Kasey said, sticking her tongue out too. She stood up to go talk in her bedroom for a second.

"Gail's in town for the night and on her way here, so you and Silas can hang out guilt-free. Your poor mommy won't be so lonely!"

Gail was her mom's best friend, who lived down in Jacksonville. She was on her way through town to visit her parents like she did several times a year. When those days lined up with Roy's absences, Gail spent the night. When they didn't, Gail stayed at the Castelow B and B and met Angie for coffee and lunch at the grocery store. Kasey loved Gail, and Gail had been married to a kind man for years and years. Kasey wished her mom had met a kind man after her dad died. Even with the dark Roy-cloud lifted for the past few nights, Kasey could feel the impending menace of his return the same way animals could sense an earthquake days before it happened.

Roy had been behaving himself lately and ignoring Kasey for the most part. She'd been sleeping at home more. He hadn't been yelling at her mom as much. Kasey had learned not to be too optimistic about anything, but the news of the internship, which started at the beginning of July, was the flickering light she could see so clearly at the end of the this-part-of-her-life tunnel. It was almost June. Her mom kept telling her that she thought Roy would start acting a whole lot better once Kasey was gone, so not to worry about it. Her mom told Kasey that her and Roy's personalities never mixed and it wasn't either of their faults. She said Roy was a junkyard dog and Kasey was a kitten, and that was all there was to it. When Kasey had asked her mom what animal *she* was, Angie—without missing a beat—said she was a unicorn.

On the phone, Silas told Kasey his parents were gone for the night if she wanted to come over. She could even sleep there if she wanted.

"Will your mom let you? Ada's already here with Grayson and she said she invited Rosemarie and Leo. Caro's coming when she gets off work. Prom night part two?" he said. Prom night had been perfect; prom night part two sounded like a dream.

"She'll let me. Pick me up in twenty minutes? Come all the way up the driveway," Kasey said, pulling her backpack off the door handle.

"All right, *Dandelion*."

Kasey could tell how big he was grinning when he said it.

———

On prom night, Kasey and Silas had slept in bed together for the first time. Technically it was post-prom *morning*, since they'd stayed up so late and only gone to bed as the sun was coming up. They'd gotten kind of drunk on Goldie Light, skinny-dipped twice, listened to the same Nelly song one hundred times. She and Caro kissed twice during their game of spin the bottle, matching Rosemarie's kisses with Sparrow. Sparrow and Frankie disappeared after that, and Rosemarie snuck off downstairs with Leo. Ada and Grayson also disappeared to his bedroom. Caro camped on the couch with some of their other girlfriends but wound up sleeping with her head in Mateo's lap, which was mildly scandalous in a fun way, since they were exes. Caro also drunk-dialed Beau, leaving him an *I just called to say hi and that I like pie* voicemail at four in the morning.

Kasey had been about 90 percent sure she wanted to lose her virginity to Silas on prom night. Ada's virginity was lost over Christmas break to Grayson, and Rosemarie and Leo had totally done it for the first time—both of their first times—downstairs at the lake house on prom night. Caro lost hers to Mateo at the beginning of the year, so Kasey was the last holdout, but when she got in Silas's bed the morning after prom, she was drunker than she wanted to be. So was he. They were under his sheets, fumbling and sweating; she was naked and breathless underneath him.

"I'm leaving soon, and I promise we'll do this before I go...but not now. Not when we both smell like Goldie Light. God, I'd never forgive myself," Kasey said, shoving her head out of his covers.

"Okay," Silas said, breathing hard. "You're right. Are you okay? Am I being too—"

"No! I'm the one—"

"No! I'm happy. I'm so happy right now," he said, kissing her mouth, her ear, her neck. Kasey leaned over to retrieve her tank top and slip it back over her head. Silas was in his boxers. He was holding her face, and they laughed when they both got stuck in her shirt.

"Soon. I promise," she said, kissing him back.

"I don't want you to leave. I don't want you to leave Goldie," he said so earnestly Kasey thought she'd burst into tears.

"We'll be *us*, no matter where we go. I'll come back. A lot. You know I'm a mama's girl so I won't be able to stay gone too long without coming home anyway. It's the future and we have phones and email. Plus, I'll be here," she said, touching his bare chest. His heart.

"You'll be here," he said, putting his hand on hers.

"And here," she said, putting her hand between his legs.

He snatched her under the covers with him, tickled her until she begged for mercy.

2019

11

CAROLINE

Trey was in a mood at Taylor and Ben's wedding reception. After dancing to two more songs with her grandma, Caroline found him sitting with a few guys she barely knew at a table inside the tent.

"I saw you out there. Didn't want you to hurt yourself," Trey said to her when she sat next to him. She took his glass of icy water from him, sipped it. "Were you dancing with Nick too?"

Caroline tried to think of who her husband could be talking about. *Nick?* She didn't know a Nick.

"I was dancing with my grandma," she said, tucking her hair behind her ear. "Who's Nick?"

"Some guy who's friends with Ben. He worked at the distillery for a minute. Seems like your type. He's tall and his family has a lot of money," he said. "He'd definitely try to get under your dress if you weren't married to me."

Caro was glad he said it low enough so the other men at the table wouldn't hear him.

"I'm not letting *anyone* get under my dress," she said defiantly. She kept her eyes on Rosemarie, still on stage with Leo. Leo was whispering something into her ear and Rosemarie bent over laughing. She touched Leo's wrist. Roses and Leo were so gentle with each other, so kind. Trey had no idea that gentleness and kindness were Caro's type, *not* height and money. She put her chin in her hand and blinked back tears, touched the pearl necklace Trey had given her, rolled it between her fingers. What did it matter if he gave her something like that if he treated her like shit?

"Not even me?" Trey said softly, putting his hand on her knee.

"Not when you're being mean to me, no."

"Stop it. You're beautiful tonight. Don't look for a way to ruin it."

"*You're* the one, not me. Did you have a bad day or something?" she asked, looking at him again. She wiped her tear away. The guys who were sitting at the table with them got up and left the tent. Rosemarie started singing a Taylor Swift song, which Caro knew was going to make her cry even more. Every Taylor Swift song made her cry. Three years ago, RACK had gone to see her in concert up in New York. They'd screamed-sung the words and cried so much that night. They'd gone back to Kasey's place in Brooklyn and slept tangled together in Kasey's huge bed with little puffs of confetti still in their hair, the four of them spilling onto the floor next to the wide windows and gorgeous view of the blinking, colored lights of the city.

In the tent, Ada and Kasey hugged on the dance floor. Grayson and Silas were next to them, being goofy as always. Caro wanted to go over there with them, wanted to hug little Taylor again and swish around with her girlfriends, but she was stuck to that chair and she was tired. Last night she'd stayed up late putting the finishing touches on the wedding cake and cupcakes. She hadn't left the bakery until 2 a.m., and the girls had breakfast at Plum Eats before heading to the Plum house to get ready for everything. It'd been a really good day up until now.

That was how most of her days went. Things *could* be really good until Trey showed up.

They'd only been married for about six months. How in the hell was she supposed to do this for the rest of her life?

"Caro*line*," Trey said with the tone she was all too familiar with now. The tone she didn't hear until they returned from their honeymoon. It'd happened for the first time when she accidentally let the garbage leak out onto the kitchen floor. He yelled at her. "Caro*line*. Fuck! Why do you act so stupid? I don't have time to clean this up. Come here!" She felt like she had to pee; she thought she'd go on herself. She was so scared, her first reaction was to run. To leave that house forever, to go back to her grandma's trailer and hide.

She couldn't do that.

It was too late and she'd be too embarrassed and this was what she'd wanted. Right? Right. She had to stay. She had to. Maybe Trey didn't realize how he sounded or how scary he could be. He didn't understand what women needed. He didn't have a sister, and his mom had an iron heart.

He'd never known tenderness.

He'd never had it shown to him growing up.

How could a man learn to give away something he never had?

"I'm gonna go dance with Kase since she's leaving Monday," Caro said, standing.

"Okay. Then we'll head out," Trey said, leaning back and drinking his water. Trey was bone-dry tonight and Caro's legs got light and wobbly as she walked, thinking about what was surely going to happen again when they got home.

2004

12

Caroline and Beau were sitting outside the diner sharing a cigarette. She'd already told him about prom and what a dud Will Brody turned out to be.

"Something's wrong with that whole family, Muffin Mix. That boy ain't right. I thought you knew that! I thought maybe that was *why* you wanted to go with him!" Beau said.

"Beau, why in the *hell* would I want to go to prom with a boy who ain't right in the head? Why? Please tell me why!" Caro said, smacking his arm. "I hate you; I truly do." She laughed with him and took the cigarette back. She French inhaled flawlessly and he bragged about it, told her that he taught her everything she knew.

"Speaking of teaching, you're sure it's pastry school in Adora Springs for you? You're not tempted to run off and leave Goldie in the dust?" Beau asked.

"I don't know how I'll be able to afford it. My parents...well, you know they're no help. My grandma has some money, but it's not enough. And she's done too much for me anyway," Caroline said.

"What about a loan? I'm assuming pastry schools have financial aid and all that?"

"Yeah, I don't know. I keep playing wait and see, hoping I have a fairy godmother out there or someone who's gonna float down and tell me exactly what to do and how to do it," she said.

"If anyone was ever gonna have a fairy godmother, it'd be you. I'd bet on it." Beau's witchy hazel eyes sparkled in the sunset light. Caro pictured herself writing about his eyes in the margins of her baking journal. She was putting together a new recipe for Beau Bramford Pie. Something with supergooey dark chocolate and marshmallow cream. Cayenne pepper and chili flakes on top.

She was so hungry. For Beau, for dinner.

"I'm starving," she said, getting up.

"If you want me to make you a grilled cheese, just ask. Don't be all passive-aggressive about it."

"Beau, will you *pretty please* make me a grilled cheese?" She held up her hand to high-five him. He slapped it.

"Yes, ma'am."

——

That night, Kasey and her trying-not-to-cry face appeared at Caro's bedroom window. Caro slid the glass up.

"I can stay tonight?" Kasey asked.

"Of course, but girl, come around to the front door. You don't have to sneak," Caro said. She walked out of her bedroom, past her grandma on the couch knitting and watching the news with a pencil behind her ear. "Kasey's spending the night."

"All right, Ladybug," Mimi said. "Do y'all have homework or is that done now since school's almost over anyway?" she asked. RACK had a bad case of senioritis, but Caro had been studying for finals even when she half-assed it, and Kasey actually liked doing extra math homework, which never ceased to blow Caro's mind.

"A little studying. We'll do it—I promise. Right after I make this pie," Caro said.

Mimi nodded and took the cloth measuring tape from around her neck, held it against the yarn, counted her stitches.

"Hi, Miss Mimi," Kasey said when she walked in.

"Hi, Kasey Jo. That dumbass being a dumbass again?" Mimi asked.

"Yes, ma'am," Kasey said softly.

"Well, I love your mama and I wish she knew she deserves better. Remember I got that shotgun back there if you ever need to use it," Mimi said, looking at Kasey over her glasses.

"Yes, ma'am," Kasey said again.

The girls got to work in the kitchen. Caro pulled the pie crust she'd made earlier out of the freezer and told Kasey to get a knife so she could chop pecans.

"Do you ever think about how Roses and Ada have these, like, *perfect* lives and you and I—" Kasey stopped and shook her head like she was attempting to process the enormity of it. "I mean, *duh*—Grandma Mimi is obviously amazing, but—"

"Yeah, I think about it," Caro said. She thought about it a lot. She had no choice. An easy, unstoppable jealousy ran through her like a hot current when she saw Ada with her daddy. Mr. Plum was crazy about his kids, and not only was Rosemarie's dad so cool with Caro, but he was also cool with all of them. He never seemed to tire of them hanging at their house after school or eating everything they could find in the fridge, and although Ada's mom could be uptight, she was hella fun once she had her wine for the night. She let the girls get away with everything without a peep. And Angie. Kasey's mom, Angie, was, like, one of the nicest women Caro had ever met, so no, it didn't make a lick of sense that she'd tied herself to Roy, who was probably the meanest man on earth. Caro's parents didn't care about her, and she'd known that her whole life, but yes, she had her grandma, and Kasey didn't have much, but she had Angie.

An invisible thread that tied Caro and Kasey together a little bit tighter than it did with the others was that they knew exactly what pieces were missing in their life. Even so, they both tried their best to be grateful for what they had. To hold on to it, no matter what. They both knew how easy it could be to let that hope go and sink.

So they never let go.

"You know how much I'll miss this when I'm gone off to school, so let's agree to never talk about it, okay? You'll have to find a way to send a fresh, hot pie to me in New York, or I'll cry myself to sleep every night," Kasey said, chopping and carefully wiping away her tears.

"Okay, but I never want to talk about you leaving, so let me tell you about this pie instead. This is Beau Bramford Pie. Figured I'd call it that since I'm clearly in love with the damn boy." It was the first time Caro had said it aloud to Kasey (or anyone).

Kasey just smiled at her, and Caro loved that she didn't make a big deal about it. It was so obviously obvious it was ridiculous to point it out, and therefore, it required no response. Like Caro mentioning she had a human body or red hair. She moved to the stove and turned the burner down; the chocolate was melted and ready. The crusts already lined the pans. She was making two: one to keep and one to give Beau at work tomorrow. She'd lie and tell him she called it Almost Summer Pie, and he'd love it. She knew it.

"What would you put in a Silas Castelow Pie?"

"Apples. Cinnamon and apples. He's a simple man," Kasey said.

"Let's make one of those for him tonight too. Are you tired yet?" Caro said, going back for more pie crust. There were never fewer than four pie crusts waiting in the freezer.

"No. Let's stay up and bake. Then we can go drop it off on his porch like pie fairies."

"You know, despite everything we have to deal with, aren't we the best girls in the world?"

"Yes, we are. We're *the* best girls in the world."

2019

13

ROSEMARIE

When Rosemarie and Leo were finished singing at Taylor's reception, she checked her phone and saw three missed calls and voicemails from Esme. Esme thought she was mad at her, and Esme wouldn't take *I swear I'm not mad at you* for an answer, because she never did. Leo was at the table next to Rosemarie, leaning back with his tie undone talking to some guy she maybe half recognized but couldn't remember. Leo knew everyone; Leo talked to everyone. Leo Bell never met anyone he didn't find fascinating.

Rosemarie stepped left and scanned the scrum, finding her friends. Kasey and Silas were standing close to each other by the oak tree, their faces twinkled by the pink lights wrapped around the trunk. Silas was telling Kasey something funny enough to make Kasey touch his stomach and laugh. Silas was such an animated storyteller and so catholic in his interests he could've been talking about literally anything. Ada and Caro were obsessing over the cupcake display, which was decidedly not their job that night, but Rosemarie would never tell them that. They'd surely scratch and hiss if they couldn't fret about all things Plum Bakery together. Rosemarie stepped away to listen to Esme's voicemails.

Hey, Rosie. I hope tonight goes well! I'm so sorry I can't make it down yet. I love you, okay?

I'm assuming Leo is your date tonight. I'm excited to meet him soon. I'll be there soon.

I miss you. I've been so busy...you've been so busy...I'm not trying to blow up your phone...but I miss you. I want to know how you're feeling and that you're taking proper care of yourself. I know how important it is for us to be together right now...and I guess I just want to know that you realize that and miss me too.

Leo is my date, yes. And I am his.
Also, I am yours. And you are mine.
I am feeling okay and taking proper care of myself yes!
And of course I miss you (and realize the importance of spending time together). How in the world could I not miss my heart? Let's sleep and talk in the morning? x

Rosemarie knew Leo had been the one to ask the DJ to play "Purple Rain." It was no surprise when he found her outside of the tent and bowed to her, held out his hand. Over his shoulder, she saw Caro and Trey walking away. Trey had his palm pressed against her back. Rosemarie took Leo's hand but quickly let it go and stepped forward.

"Caro! Are you leaving?" Rosemarie said.

Caroline turned around and Rosemarie saw that she'd been crying. That asshole was *always* making her cry.

"Yeah. I'm tired. Call me tomorrow, though!" Caro said.

Rosemarie walked to her. Trey didn't look at Rosemarie. He was busy acknowledging someone behind him who'd said his name. She hugged Caro tight.

"You don't want to stay for the sparkler send-off? It's in, like, half an hour," Rosemarie said.

"I'm tired," Caro said again.

"Okay," Rosemarie said, wishing she could say something else. Wishing some Random Act of God would keep Caro from walking through the dark and getting in Trey's car.

"Love you, Roses," Caro said. "I'll see you tomorrow."

"Hey . . . you're okay?" Rosemarie asked.

Caroline looked at her and said yes.

"Love you too," Rosemarie said. Trey had turned around and was already walking away.

Rosemarie went to Leo and they danced to the rest of "Purple Rain," but it felt like there was a wet rope in her stomach that was only getting heavier. She had faith (didn't she?) that above their heads, the sky was still lousy with stars and that God was watching. Wasn't He?

14

Rosemarie and Sparrow were lying out on Rosemarie's trampoline because that was a thing they did now. Also a thing they did now, ever since the prom after-party: kiss. That was it. Just kiss. When no one else was around, they kissed, even though Sparrow made a point of telling Rosemarie that she wasn't a lesbian. The last time she said it, Rosemarie parroted her and said she wasn't one either, and she didn't even feel bad for the lie, because it wasn't a lie since she *was* technically a label-hating bisexual anyway.

That afternoon after school, they'd sun-kissed in the conversation pit, and they'd chocolate-kissed in the kitchen after they shared a pot brownie. Now they were on the trampoline, listening to Fleetwood Mac. Whenever Jerry Garcia brought the tennis ball back to her, Rosemarie would get it from his wet mouth, chuck it to the corner of the yard away from the greenhouse and chicken coop, and do the whole thing again.

"But, like, Leo is your boyfriend, right?" Sparrow asked.

"Not officially."

"Because Frankie is *kind of* my boyfriend, but, like, I don't tell him that we—" She moved her finger between her shoulder and Rosemarie's. "That you and I kiss," she ended.

"Right," Rosemarie said. She was hella stoned and the daylight swam around them in a blinding, yolky haze that made it hard for Rosemarie to focus on anything else. She could smell the sunshine— grapefruit and oranges.

"So please don't tell anyone that we kiss. Is that . . . okay?" Sparrow said.

Rosemarie *hadn't* told anyone besides the rest of RACK, but that didn't mean she liked it when Sparrow asked her not to. In fact, she hated it and it made her feel like shit because Rosemarie wasn't a liar. Being completely honest whenever possible was her thing, but she said okay anyway and was relieved when she heard her parents' car in the driveway and her big brother's voice around the corner saying her name.

She hopped down from the trampoline, bouncing Sparrow up in such a funny way it made them both laugh, and for a second, Rosemarie almost forgot Sparrow had just asked her not to tell anyone they kissed. Sparrow kept giggling and she was *so* cute. Jerry Garcia was at Rosemarie's bare feet barking like mad because she was holding the tennis ball but not throwing it. Rosemarie tossed the ball before jogging to the fence and saying her brother's name exactly like he'd said hers. She put her arms around his neck and hugged him.

"I'm stoned," she said to him.

"That you are," her brother, Rune, said as their parents carried cloth bags of groceries into the house. He said it again in a dumb voice; Rosemarie giggled. Sparrow turned the music up—Stevie Nicks and Lindsey Buckingham were rasping about how much they loved each other.

"I'm spending the night at Ada's," Rosemarie said.

"Are you eating dinner here?" he asked.

"Nope. At Myrtle's," Rosemarie said. She turned to holler, "Sparrow, are you ready to go? We should probably go." She'd walk Sparrow home, then meet the girls at the diner and eat while waiting for Caro to get off work.

"Okay!" Sparrow hollered.

Rosemarie's mom came out of the house, closing the screen door behind her.

"I never get to see you anymore. You'll be in Costa Rica soon, but you're like a ghost already," her mom said, taking Rosemarie's face in both hands. "You're blissed out and beautiful."

Rosemarie's summer would start with a mission trip with Goldie First Baptist Church and Leo and his family, since his dad was the pastor there. In the fall she'd head to Seattle to work with some of her parents' friends at a nonprofit hunger-relief organization, and travel the world with them until the following fall, when she'd start majoring in social work at University of Seattle.

"Our little ghost baby! Don't go! Don't goooo!" her dad said from the other side of the kitchen door.

"Y'all stay trippin'," Rune said. He put his hand on Rosemarie's head and messed up her hair. "See you later."

———

After packing her sleepover bag and kissing and hugging her family goodbye with fake dramatics, Rosemarie and Sparrow set off on foot through the neighborhood. When they were almost to Sparrow's place, she pulled Rosemarie between two houses, instructing her to stop behind the tall, fluffy bushes.

"Um, I love kissing you. It's fun and you're really good at it. Plus, your lips taste like peaches. Does Leo tell you that? I love peaches," Sparrow said.

"Sometimes," Rosemarie said, floating. Sparrow was holding her hand, tracing the lines on her palm with her index finger. Rosemarie tingled; she always tingled when Sparrow touched her. Sparrow put her hand behind Rosemarie's head and kissed her. Rosemarie let go, let herself *feel* how good it was to kiss a girl like this, to let herself be kissed by a girl like this. A girl as cool as Sparrow, a girl as pretty as Sparrow, a girl with a name like Sparrow.

Slowly, Sparrow put her hand between Rosemarie's legs, and Rosemarie let out a soft breath and put her hand between Sparrow's. Their backpacks sat in the grass at their feet. They kissed and kissed and touched like that until they both came, panting in the lush. On prom night when Rosemarie had sex with Leo, she imagined doing this with Sparrow but didn't feel bad, because she was thinking about Leo too.

"Promise never to tell?" Sparrow said, breathing hard in Rosemarie's ear.

Rosemarie's secret mouth said *promise*, but her secret heart was beating *no*.

RACK was up late at Ada's. Mrs. Plum had made Taylor leave the room and go to bed hours ago. Caro baked a blueberry pie she was proud of because it was the fourth one she'd made in a row that wasn't runny. She'd gone on and on about how potato starch worked better than cornstarch, and the girls were sitting in a circle on Ada's bedroom floor, eating her sugary success, sharing bites off two forks.

"So, Roy's still doing better?" Rosemarie asked Kasey.

"Barely," Kasey said.

"At least he has a job?" Caro chimed in.

"My dad said he saw him working on a car at the garage the other day," Ada said.

"I don't care anymore. I'm only here until July, then it's New York City, *baybee*," Kasey said.

"New York City?!" Rosemarie said in a fake cowboy voice. Kasey snorted.

"Caro and I will miss you both so much we'll die, but I am happy for y'all. I know you and Roses have to leave Goldie so you can take over the world," Ada said.

"Let's promise to always keep in touch, no matter where we are or what's going on in our lives. It might be hard sometimes, I know, but seriously, we *have* to promise," Caroline said.

Rosemarie's day had been full of promises. She thought of Sparrow and what they'd done. How good it'd felt. How huge that was for them. Finally!

Promising Sparrow she'd never tell anyone about it had been hard and stupid. Promising her girls she'd always keep in touch was an easy, best thing.

"Promise," the four of them said at the same time.

Quadruple jinx.

2019

15

ADA

Ada was upstairs, attempting to coax her mother out of the bathroom she'd locked herself in just ten minutes before Taylor and Ben's sparkler send-off.

"Mama, *please* unlock the door and get in bed. I'll tuck you in and it'll be nice and cozyyy," Ada said, trying to make it sound as appealing as possible. Her mother loved her bedroom and spent a fortune on the best sheets and downy bedding. She recently had a high-ticket Italian alabaster egg lamp shipped across the ocean for her nightstand.

Rosemarie had stopped in the hallway and asked if there was anything she could do, but Ada told her no and to go back and enjoy the rest of the reception. Rosemarie had left reluctantly, and now that Ada was on the other side of the door alone, she wished she'd asked her to stay. Grayson had taken the boys home already, put them to sleep. She needed to get her mom out of the bathroom and into bed so she could send her little sister off on her honeymoon with sparklers and go home.

"I'll...sleep in here," her mom slurred. Ada watched the light disappear underneath the rectangle slip of door.

"Mama, no. No. You'll be much comfier in bed. Please. Open the door for me and everything will be perfect. Don't you love it when everything is perfect? I do!" Ada said.

"Oh yes, I love it *wheneverthing* is...perfect," her mom said. The light flicked on again. The lock clicked. Her mom's eyes were closed and she was leaning against the wall.

"Why'd you drink so much when you knew you had to take your pills too?" Ada asked.

"I need them. I take them because I need them," her mom said with a thick tongue. Ada put Holly's limp arm around her neck and carefully guided her to the bedroom. Got her in bed, unzipped her dress, and shimmied it off, only then realizing she'd peed on herself.

Ada went to the bathroom and cleaned up the floor, got a soapy wet towel and wiped her mom's legs and in between them, positioned her on her side under the covers, naked from the waist down. She was snoring by the time Ada turned off the light. Her dad was out back with his friends; her brothers were out there drinking with theirs. Ada was upstairs alone, fixing everything. Again.

Outside, Ada grabbed a sparkler, found Rosemarie and Kasey, kissed her baby sister goodbye, and stood with everyone crying and waving as Taylor and Ben made their way down the sidewalk and got into the limousine. She told her daddy she'd put her mom to bed, then Ada drove herself home.

———

Everyone in her house was sleeping. She closed their bedroom door. Grayson was naked on his back under the covers. Ada woke him up by climbing on top of him and kissing him as she rocked her hips back and forth. Afterward, she cried. It happened sometimes.

"Are you okay?" Grayson asked.

"Yes. I'm just tired."

"Are you sure?"

"Yes. I'm sure."

2004

16

Holly Plum was the head of the PTA, so oftentimes, Ada would literally bump into her mom in the hallway at school. This time Ada was looking down at the stack of graduation flyers she'd copied in the office before first period.

"Oops! Hi, Mama," Ada said. Her mom's laugh was left over from another conversation that just ended.

"Hi, baby girl. I'm on my way out. Graduation committee meeting adjourned," her mom said, adjusting her designer bag on her shoulder. She'd gotten a new French manicure earlier in the week and her hands looked so pretty Ada had to tell her so. Her mom thanked her and they stepped aside so they wouldn't clog up hallway traffic.

"I need a white dress. Like, soon," Ada said. Next week was the senior trip, when they'd spend three days in Adora Springs and see the *Lion King* musical. Graduation was only two weeks away.

"We'll go to the mall after school," Holly said. A teacher and a counselor walking down the hall stopped to say hello to her and she beamed, touching Ada's shoulder.

"Okay. Thank you, love you, bye." Ada waved to her mom and headed to class. Grayson was closing his locker and she blew him a kiss through the air.

After finding a white dress in her size and going back home, Ada got picked up by Grayson and they went to the lake house, where they'd have two hours alone before his parents got there.

They had sex in his bed and when they were finished, he got up, put on his boxers, and went to the kitchen. He returned with two cold red pops and opened the window.

"When we get married, can I still have a pop after we bone?" Grayson asked, snapping the tab with a hiss.

"Ew, Grayson. Don't say *bone*." Ada put her pink bra and panties back on and sat up against his headboard.

"What am I supposed to say, *make love*?" He laughed.

"How about you shut up, you freaking dork?" Ada said, laughing too.

"No, but seriously," Grayson said, sitting on the edge of the bed. His shoulders, his arms, his bare chest: Grayson Castelow was exactly what she wanted her boyfriend to be. He was a dream. Her mom had told her once that Grayson was perfect, but Ada didn't need her mom to tell her. She knew it already and it didn't even matter if he was perfect to anybody else; he was perfect to her.

She watched him scratch at his earlobe, and even his earlobe was perfect. Life could maybe throw plenty of curveballs her way, but she knew she'd never forget how Grayson looked sitting on the edge of his bed with the warm spring wind blowing in. How dark his hair was, all of it—his head, his arms, between his legs. His blinking black lashes, the gentle scrape of his chin because he hadn't shaved. How his armpits smelled like trees; how their bodies carried the misty musk of both of them now.

"Seriously, *what*? Can you drink pops after we're married? What kind of question is this, Grayson?" Ada asked.

"Will you really marry me someday, though, when it's time?" Grayson asked, taking a sip.

They'd joked about it and her girlfriends teased her about it, but it wasn't like he'd asked her. It didn't matter yet. She was seventeen, not even out of high school! It wasn't like they were getting married next week or even next year, but it *did* feel like magic, Grayson sitting there in the golden light, being all serious about it.

"You know I will. Come here," she said, hooking her finger at him and kissing him once he was close enough.

"I love you, Ada Plum."

"I love you too, Grayson."

Unlike Kasey and Silas, who would be ripped apart in July, and unlike Rosemarie and Sparrow or Rosemarie and Leo, who weren't sure what they were to each other yet, and unlike Caro and Beau, who couldn't be what they wanted to be, Ada and Grayson had it easy—had it all planned out. They would get married and be as happy as her parents. They'd have babies. She and her mom would expand Plum Inc., and she and Caro would stay in Goldie and be best friends and small-town princesses, and Roses and Kase would come home a lot. They'd be friends and sisters forever, raise their kids together.

Why couldn't they have it all? Not everyone could, Ada knew that, but *some* people could! Somewhere, somehow, it had to be true. It was almost graduation, almost time for one chapter of her life to be over and for the next one to begin. She was ready.

She felt abuzz in Grayson's bedroom thinking about it. Thinking about everything. They kissed and kissed until their mouths were almost numb, and on the drive to her place, they rolled the windows down. Ada put her pink toenails up on the dash, and Grayson had his hand on her leg. The birds were singing, and she and Grayson were singing along with the radio too. Goldie was alive and shimmering— the air glowed yellow and orange against the fresh green like it always did in the springtime, like it always would.

Act II

There is nothing I would not do for those who are really my friends. I have no notion of loving people by halves, it is not my nature.

—Jane Austen

2019

17

KASEY

Kasey was leaving Goldie the next morning, so she headed to Caro's early to surprise her with strawberry muffins and coffee from Plum Bakery. It was the sort of thing Caroline would do for her, especially because Caro was a natural early bird and Kasey had to teach herself to be one. When they were in high school, Caro bribed Kasey with homemade doughnuts and treats and strong coffee with cinnamon and whipped cream to wake her up when she slept over in Caro's bed. And back then, when Kasey needed to talk about her shitty home life, Caro was all ears. Now, Kasey could sense that it was Caro who needed an ear bent for her. Maybe over coffee and muffins, she would tell Kasey the truth about her long-sleeved dresses, about her reluctance to tell any of them much more about Trey or what happened when they were alone together in that house.

Kasey parked by the double garage. One of Trey's trucks was in the driveway, but Kasey didn't know if that meant he was actually there. She got out of her car, stepped toward the door, and knew for *sure* Trey was inside because she heard him shouting. Caro's voice answered him, and she was shouting too. Kasey froze.

After a few seconds, she leaned over.

She could hear them well since the window was open a smidge, and if she stood to the side, she could see them because one of the curtains was twisted up.

Kasey saw Caroline walking away, saw Trey grab her arm and snatch her back.

"Trey, let me go! Let me go, Trey!" Caro said. She sounded so scared Kasey pulled out her phone. She could call Silas. He could help. She was looking down at it when she heard Caro scream. When Kasey peeked through the window again, Trey had Caroline pressed against the wall, holding her throat. He kissed her and asked her if she wanted him to say he was sorry. He kissed her harder and asked it again. Caro tried to wiggle away. "Please leave me alone!"

There were times when Roy was smacking her mama around and if Kasey interrupted, Roy got even madder and meaner. Kasey knew better than to knock on the door. It could make everything worse. Remaining calm—because she knew if she gave in to it, she'd have a full-blown, out-of-body flashback of growing up with Roy—Kasey knew what to do. She put her phone against her ear and called Caroline, who always kept her volume turned up.

Kasey heard the ring against her ear and inside the house at the same time.

"It might be the bakery. It's important, so let me go! Let me go right now, Trey!" Caro said.

Kasey watched Trey take Caroline's face with one hand and squeeze it.

"Stop fucking up!" he said to her before pushing her head back against the wall. The picture frame behind her smashed to the floor.

Caro disappeared down the hallway and answered Kasey's call.

"Hi, Kase," Caroline said, sounding so normal it made Kasey's heart ache. Her mind rushed to all the other times when Caro *sounded* normal too. Caroline had told Kasey to stop keeping secrets, but everything in the past six months had clearly been an act.

Kasey didn't have the time to sit with that sadness.

She stepped to her car and got inside. Started the engine, hoping and praying Trey wouldn't hear.

"Caro, I was gonna stop by with coffee and muffins this morning if that's okay? Or...we could meet up at the restaurant later for dinner? Ada said we should eat after the place closes a little early tonight so we can have it all to ourselves," Kasey said a bit breathlessly, trying her best to keep a lift in her voice even though it was shaking. Her hands were too.

"Thanks for the offer for this morning...but, um, yeah, let's do tonight. Dinner works best. I'll be there at nine. I can't believe you're leaving tomorrow. I miss you already."

"I miss you already too. Okay! Sounds good. How's your morning? How are you?" Kasey asked as she reached the end of Caro's driveway and backed into the street, drove away.

"I'm good. Going down to the bakery in a bit. Is it hot as hell out there already? Hmm, maybe I should swim first. Trey's leaving in just a minute," Caro said.

Kasey was scared to leave and scared to stay.

She took deep breaths. She glanced down at the two coffees in the cup holders, the muffins in the paper bag on the car floor. She thought of Caro alone in that house with that fucking monster. The same way her mom had been alone in the farmhouse with that other fucking monster.

"Enjoy your swim, Peach. I'll see you tonight. Can't wait," Kasey said.

"Can't wait!"

Kasey pulled far enough away from the house and off to the side of the road so she could watch Trey leave, and when he did, she followed behind him at a good distance until he turned and disappeared.

———

Kasey drove to the police station and asked for Silas. When he walked into the lobby, she handed him the coffee meant for Caro and held up the bag of muffins.

"Hi. I realized I don't know how you take your coffee or if you even *like* coffee now. It's been a long time. There are enough muffins in here for a few of y'all. I would've brought more but—"

"Thank you. I *love* coffee. This is amazing. My favorite kind of surprise," Silas said. Kasey remembered that he'd said the same thing to her that night he and Grayson came over to Ada's when they were in high school—that night they listened to The Chicks down by the lake and kissed for the first time. "And this is yours," he said, pulling her dangly pearl earring from his pocket and handing it to her. She took it and thanked him. Ordinarily she would have savored how he'd been walking around all morning with her earring in his uniform pocket, but she was still too shaken by what she'd witnessed.

"How *do* you take your coffee?" she asked him.

"How do you take yours?"

"With all the good stuff."

"I take mine black."

"Well, that has lots of sugar and cream in it."

"Delicious," he said, taking a careful sip. "Are you all right?"

"Sure. Yeah. Thank you. Um, Si, I feel like I'm waiting around for you to be mad at me, and I'm leaving tomorrow, so...can we go ahead and get it over with?" Kasey said, trying to focus. She couldn't tell him what she just saw at Caro's, because she had to tell Rosemarie and Ada first. She couldn't even sort out her feelings or the best thing to do about what she'd seen yet, and she knew it would haunt her. But yes, she could blurt out something else that was weighing on her.

So there she was, standing in front of Silas Castelow, wishing he'd fuss at her for running away. Wishing he'd tell her again how much she broke his heart. How he thought he'd literally die from it. Then, she could finally tell him she thought *she'd* literally die too.

But she hadn't died.

She was still here.

So now what?

"Yeah, um, step out here with me real quick?" Silas said, moving toward the door of the station and holding it open for her. She walked out and he followed her. She was clutching the bag of muffins with both hands like a little girl with her school lunch. A few cars whizzed by in the morning heat. One of them honked at Silas and the guy stuck his hand out of the window, waved. Silas waved back and then started talking. "Kasey, come on; we were kids. And you had to deal with entirely too much darkness growing up. Don't you think I know that? Don't you think I slowly realized all you weren't telling me? Yeah, it broke my heart when you left, because to me, we were golden. That's what made sense to me when we were in high school, but that was a long time ago—*fifteen* years. I don't blame you for leaving. I don't," Silas said, shaking his head.

"I should've kept talking to you. I shouldn't have shut you out. I shouldn't have shut the girls out so much. I didn't know what else to do except run away, but I didn't *mean* it! I didn't," Kasey said, clutching the muffin bag even tighter to keep her hands from shaking. Silas gently undid her fingers and took it from her. She let herself cry and it felt really good after the horror of what she'd seen at Caroline's.

"Look. I'm not saying you didn't break my heart. I think I've been clear about that, right?" Silas asked. "And I keep telling you I can't stand to see you cry, but apparently, you don't give a damn about that, do you?" He touched her shoulder.

Kasey shook her head.

"I don't want you to think I've been *mad* at you for fifteen years. How could I sustain that, Fritz? It's poison," Silas said.

"I don't know if I'll see you again before I leave."

"You've got plans with the girls tonight?"

Kasey nodded.

"Maybe I can swing by the hotel later? We can have a drink?"

Kasey nodded again. "The bar there is *too* nice. That place is ridiculous."

"*Very* ridiculous, so let's do it. I'll text you," he said. "Thank you for this and this." He held up his coffee and the bag. She got on her tiptoes to put her lips against his cheek. "Thanks for the extra sugar too," Silas said. He put his arms around her.

———

Kasey, Rosemarie, and Basie were in the sunny, soft conversation pit. Rosemarie had started crying when Kasey'd told her what she'd seen, which made Kasey start crying all over again too.

"I'll cut his dick off, and I swear to you I'm serious. Men ain't shit! I...I truly *hate* him," Rosemarie said.

"What should we do? What *can* we do?" Kasey said. She was petting Basie's head, rubbing behind her ears. Rosemarie pressed the heels of her hands to her eyes, and she seemed so tired. The week had wrung them all out. Every emotion was turned to high—fifteen years of feelings rushing through the Goldie streets like the dam had broken wide open.

"Convince her to leave him. She has to divorce him—she *has* to."

"Right, but that can turn into the worst time for a woman who's being abused. Trey will go ballistic if she tells him she wants out. He has to control her. If he feels like he's losing that control, he'll hurt her even worse," Kasey said. She paused. Everything she was saying was hitting too close. She saw her mom's face, fresh in her mind. Heard her mom's voice saying her name. Kasey took a shaky breath in.

"We'll...we'll hide her, then. Send her off somewhere until he calms down and finds someone else...but oh God, I don't want him to get with anyone else and do this to her either. I don't know. I don't know exactly what to do, but we *have* to do something," Rosemarie said. She stood and got Basie's leash off the hook by the door. "Let's take her for a walk. We need the swampy—I mean *fresh*—air. Come on, get up. Time for walk and talk."

Kasey stepped out of the conversation pit and slipped on her sandals.

———

Since Caro couldn't make it to the restaurant until nine, Kasey had told Ada that she and Rosemarie would be there at eight so they could discuss everything before Caro showed up. Ada had prepared a beautiful spread for them, but they only picked at it as Kasey and Rosemarie told her everything. Ada cried, distraught and blaming herself, claiming she should've noticed the signs. She and Caroline saw each other practically every day, and yet, Ada had so many other things on her mind.

Ada told them that her life hadn't been as perfect as it seemed lately, and she hated that people thought her life was so perfect anyway. Living up to that was impossible, and Ada had never asked for it. Her mom had chronic back pain, and after several surgeries stretched over the past fifteen years, recently, she'd been *really* struggling with needing more and more pain pills.

"Ada, stop. I'm so sorry to hear about your mom, and we'll do all we can to help you get through this, but what's happening with Caro isn't on you. This isn't *anyone's* fault but Trey's. He's an Earl, period. Like Dumbass and more than half the men in this town." Rosemarie said the last bit through gritted teeth.

"She's right, Ada," Kasey said.

The restaurant had been closed for thirty minutes, but it still smelled like good food, a packed house. Two small white candles flickered in glass on the table, and soft Sinatra floated from the speakers. Ada had made chicken piccata and lemon rice. There was an unopened bottle of chardonnay on the table; Rosemarie picked at the foil on the lip. Ada got up and walked away, returning with a wine key and four glasses.

———

Caroline showed up looking like she'd stepped out of a magazine— smiling in a light cowl-neck sweater, shorts, and a pair of espadrille wedges that wrapped around her ankles. "Why haven't y'all started eating? Were you waiting for me? Sorry I'm late," she said.

"You look good," Ada said. "I love your face."

"Aw, thank you," Caro said, letting her fingers brush her forehead. "So do y'all! Whew, it's a wonder I could pull myself together. It's been a *day*," she said, sitting and plucking an olive from the scalloped dish.

"Why? What happened?" Rosemarie asked so innocently that if the situation were different, Kasey would've wanted to laugh.

"Oh, just busy. Bakery stuff and I was at my grandma's helping her weed the gardens earlier and Trey—"

"Caroline, stop. Caro, I was there at the house this morning and heard Trey hollering at you. I saw him grab you and push you, and I don't want you denying it, because I *saw* it. I was standing at the door, and I could see through the window because the curtain was twisted up. You can't stay with him. You *have* to get out. Now!" Kasey said. She let the words fly without caring about what Caro would think.

It was scary how easily Caro could act like everything was fine. How long could she keep this up? It was by God's grace that Kasey had been there at that house at the wrong time.

"Caroline, I'm so sorry I didn't realize how bad it was," Ada said, putting her hand on hers.

"He's not gonna get away with this," Rosemarie said.

"I...I don't know what any of you are talking about," Caro said softly after looking at them in silence for too long. She took her hand from underneath Ada's with no expression on her face and calmly poured herself a glass of wine.

2004

18

Roy lost the garage gig and things got worse. Instead of hanging out at the bar and picking fights there, he took up permanent residence on the couch, and when he was awake—drunk or sober—he was starting fights with Kasey's mom when she was around or, when she wasn't, with Kasey. Ranting about how life dealt him a bad hand and being ornery just to be ornery because it was who he was, through and through. Even if she had a million years to think about it, Kasey wouldn't be able to find one solid, good thing about him.

She'd tried picturing him as a baby. He had a lot of family down in Florida, but Kasey had only met his mom twice—once at her mama and Roy's wedding and one other time years ago when she was traveling through town. She tried imagining that Roy's mother loved him, although her brain would lock on the impossibility of even that, since his mother named him Roymont Dupont, so clearly she *never* loved the boy.

When he wasn't hollering at home or telling her mom and Kasey how awful they were, he disappeared for entire days or for long stretches in the middle of the night. The week prior, Kasey had seen a gun in his top drawer when she'd gone in there to put away the laundry. Her mom hated guns; she told Kasey that her daddy did too. Roy kept a shotgun in the shed sometimes, but her mom wouldn't let him bring one in the house. And one time when Roy thought she wasn't looking, Kasey saw him stuff a box of plastic bags and three huge stacks of cash into his duffel bag before getting in her truck and driving away.

For most of the last two weeks of high school, Kasey stopped coming home completely. After returning from the senior trip to Adora Springs, she rotated nights between Ada's, Caro's, and Rosemarie's. One of those days, she went home for a change of clothes. Her mom was standing in the hallway.

"I . . . I didn't know you were here. I thought you were at work. Why aren't you at work?" Kasey asked.

Her mom pushed her hair from her face.

"I took a day off," she said, leaning against the doorframe.

"Is he here?" Kasey asked softly.

Angie shook her head no.

"Thank *God*," Kasey said. She walked past her mom into her bedroom and pulled her top drawer open. She turned when her mom came into the room, limping. "What did he do to you? Mama? What the hell did he do? Can you walk? Are you okay?" Kasey asked. The fear hung on her voice first, and when it reached the rest of her, she dropped her bag and helped her mom to the edge of the bed so she could sit.

Kasey knelt on the floor in front of her.

"Kick him out now. It's *our* farmhouse. It's *Daddy's* farmhouse! Roy has no right to it. Please, Mama. Please! I'm literally begging you to do this," Kasey said. And although she'd been trying to keep it to herself, Kasey told her mom how guilty she felt for not always being there to protect her, to help call Roy off, and finally confessed how conflicted she felt about leaving so soon for New York, about going away to college and abandoning her mom to suffer all alone if she wouldn't do anything about it.

"You don't have to do this because of what happened to Daddy! I know you're scared of Roy being gone for good one day, but you don't have to be. Roy leaving is the *best* thing that could happen to you! You're scared of being alone, I know, but you're not! But alone is better anyway, Mama. Aren't you so tired of this? He's never—"

"Kase, Roy isn't here, because he's at an AA meeting at the church right now. He apologized this morning. He promised he'd get sober and I believe him this time," Angie said.

"Mama, stop—"

"I believe him. We've been together for a long time. I don't want you to worry about me. He swore he'd never yell at you again or bother you at all. He'll change. He knows I mean it this time," Angie said with such serious, heartfelt emotion; if Kasey didn't know any better, she would've believed her.

———

RACK had a sleepover at Rosemarie's that night. They talked about how there wasn't much time left for sleepovers like this. Soon enough Rosemarie and Kasey would break away, and everything would be different. Earlier, Rosemarie's dad had gone to Adora Springs to pick up their favorite pizzas, then her parents went back to Adora Springs for a late gig and were spending the night. The girls had the house to themselves.

Kasey hated having to ruin their pizza-and-movie night with her troubles at home, but she couldn't hold it in. She finally told them everything—every horrible thing about Roy she'd been keeping inside, all she'd seen him do to her mom. All he'd done to her. *There's nothing good in him.* She cried telling them how scared she was to leave. How bad she felt for leaving.

She *had* to leave, didn't she? But what about her mom?

"Well, honestly, y'know...fuck it...maybe I have the answer. I was thinking about it and...I could 'Goodbye Earl' his ass," Kasey ended, half laughing. Everything sucked so much she couldn't help it. She reached to snatch a pepperoni off the pizza between them and ate it. Caro had made a dozen chocolate cupcakes, and she took them out of her bag, putting the box on the floor next to them.

"I can definitely whip up some rat-poison black-eyed peas for you," Ada said. She snickered and got a cupcake out, inspected it in the light. She asked Caro if she put red pepper in it, and when Caro confirmed, Ada gave the *okay* sign.

"Wrap him in a tarp...weigh it down and dump him in the lake?" Rosemarie said. "I'm in!" She leaned and turned on her CD player. "Goodbye Earl" started playing.

"I mean, I do *not* see another answer here," Kasey said quietly.

"Do you think your mom tells Duke about Roy?" Caro asked.

"I don't know. Sometimes when I see him at the grocery store, Duke asks me how Roy's been acting." Kasey paused. "Duke knows I hate him. He told me to stay away from Roy the best I could and if I ever needed anything, to let him know. He would help my mom out if she asked for it, but she won't! She acts like everything is fine, and if Duke ever tried to do anything to stop Roy, my mom would probably get pissed at Duke!" Kasey said. She told them about how Mrs. Castelow had also offered up the B and B to her mom if she ever needed to get away for a few days.

"I know Grandma Mimi and Myrtle have tried to get the police to arrest him for practically nothing, hoping it would help, but the police won't do anything," Caro added.

"I remember my dad telling me about seeing Roy's arms all scratched up at the garage and he'd hoped your mom had torn him up the last time they fought. He said he asked Roy why he didn't leave your mom if things were that bad, and Roy told him to mind his business," Ada said.

"My dad flat-out told him to his face he was a piece of shit last week," Rosemarie said. "He said he saw your mom crying on break at the store and asked if he could do anything. Your mom was telling him that she and Roy had gotten into a fight, but before she could finish, Roy showed up and interrupted them. Roy didn't do anything when my dad told him that either, because Roy doesn't fight men, only women. I'm sorry I didn't tell you before now, Kase, but I wanted you to get a break." Rosemarie slurped the rest of her pop through the straw and set her cup aside.

"It's fine. It doesn't matter. No one can do anything about it. I'm serious...the *only* thing that can fix this is if he dies. Like, the police can't do it, my mom won't do it, your parents and Grandma Mimi...Duke...it doesn't matter. He has to be dead! When he's dead, it'll be over," Kasey said.

"Know any hitmen?" Rosemarie asked.

Kasey shook her head.

"Don't people die by just, like...getting too drunk and puking in their sleep? Does he sleep on his back?" Caro asked.

Kasey shrugged.

"The world would be much, much better with a dead Roy than it is with an alive-and-well Roy," Rosemarie said, nodding and chewing.

"Sometimes I really do think *I* should do it," Kasey said.

"Kasey, stop!" Ada said, sitting up straight.

"What? It's not like it'd be the first time a daughter killed her abusive stepdad. This stuff really does happen all the time, and maybe someone would understand *why* I did it—"

"You wouldn't have to do it alone," Rosemarie said. Kasey locked eyes with her. The song ended and started again.

"You two! *Please*," Ada said.

"Ada, they're not being serious. Kasey, you're not being serious," Caro said. She looked back and forth between the girls and put her pizza down.

"What if she *is* being serious?" Rosemarie said for her.

"Then I'd say it's crazy...too crazy to talk about!" Caro said.

"Tell me where I'm wrong. Tell me where there's some happy-ending, silver-lining shit I'm glossing over, Caro," Kasey said.

Caroline watched Kasey's eyes.

"It's not worth risking your life and your *entire* future," Caro said. Kasey could practically see the scale in her mind, weighing everything.

"I don't have a future . . . not like this! Even when I come back home from school, Roy will be here . . . there's no end to this," Kasey said.

"I don't think it's too crazy to talk about," Rosemarie said. "Kasey, I promise we *can* fix this. We *will* fix this. I'm not saying I have a plan all laid out right now, but I'm just saying maybe it's not too crazy to talk about."

"Okay, so when the police come knocking at your door, Rosemarie Kingston, you'll be okay with getting carted off to jail or whatever for this?" Ada whispered.

"For one, that won't happen. For two . . . for *Kase*? For something I believe in as much as this? Yeah, Ada, I'll be okay with it."

"I'll be okay with it too, Ada," Caro whispered, suddenly serious. Kasey was surprised she'd gotten to their side so quickly, but she was grateful for it. Her heart kicked harder; her blood was radio static. Caro took another bite of her pizza and held it out for Rosemarie so she could nab a chunk of pineapple. "I know it's messed up to even be talking about this so seriously, but, like . . . it *is* the answer to Kasey's problems. Undeniably."

"It's not like I came up with this idea on the spot. I think about it sometimes. I've told Roses I've thought about it sometimes," Kasey said, motioning toward her.

"It's true," Rosemarie said.

"Well, you've never said that to me!" Ada said.

"Right. Because I didn't want to totally freak you out!" Kasey said.

"I'm not . . . *totally* freaked out . . . I just think you need to think about this from all angles—" Ada said.

"I have. Ada. I *have*," Kasey said.

"No, but, like . . . seriously, he needs to *actually* die," Rosemarie said. "Y'know . . . graduation night would be ideal, because everyone will be distracted and busy."

Kasey took her time making direct eye contact with her three best friends.

"Y'all . . . I swear I'm serious. I'll do it. It's the *only* way to make this go away. This would fix everything...like, *everything*," Kasey said. She was trying not to cry again.

A dead Roy—an end and a beginning.

"This would fix everything," Caroline echoed.

"Obviously, we'll do anything for each other. *Anything!* But this is like...this is like a *we can never go back again* thing," Ada said.

"I know that," Kasey said. "You don't have to be involved. Seriously, Ada, we need to stop talking about it in front of you so you can have plausible deniability or whatever."

"I didn't say I didn't want to be involved! I just said you...*we*...need to think about this from all angles," Ada said in another aggressive whisper. She glanced at the bedroom door and back at them. Rosemarie reminded her they were home alone.

"Chill out. And you're right. We really will do anything for each other," Rosemarie said. This time, the power of those words was like a smoky magic spell, filling the room with an intense, dark promise that encircled them. Something pliable. Eternal.

Kasey cried into her hands under the weight of it, and her sisters smooshed her up and hugged her so tight.

"We'll do it. Roy has to die," Kasey finally said softly, suffused with a new strength. Her heart was beating so fast she felt like she could hear it drumming behind the song on repeat. She searched her soul for every shadowed moment, every fear, every drop of hate she felt for Roy and stirred it up with the twisted light of love that poured between the cracks. The love she had for her mom and the dad she never got the chance to know. The love she had for her sisters, who would always have her back, no matter what. Kasey imagined Roy dead like she had so many times before, but this time...

This time it would be for real.

Goodbye Roy.

2019

19

CAROLINE

"Caro, we love you. Cut the bullshit. We *know* and we're not going to sit here and let this happen to you. You know we won't, so just stop it!" Rosemarie said. It was the harshest Rosemarie had ever spoken to her, but of course Rosemarie had gone right for the throat of it. Caro took a long drink of her cold white wine.

"You were *always* there for me when my mom was going through this with Dumbass," Kasey said. "*Earl*. We'll call him Earl. Caro, Trey's an *Earl* too. An Earl with more money than God, maybe, but an Earl all the same. Oh, honey—" Kasey stopped and gently touched Caro's sleeve. She sat unmoving as Kasey folded the cotton up to reveal a pastel splotch of purple wrapping Caro's forearm. Next, Kasey barely pulled down the neck of her sweater. Rosemarie shook her head and looked away. Kasey was quiet now, holding Caro's hand. Ada gasped and apologized profusely.

"Ada, stop. You didn't do anything," Caro said. Her voice sounded far away, like a whisper in a cave. She wasn't crying; she was stone. She was somewhere up by the ceiling fans of the restaurant, looking down on RACK. She didn't know how she got up there, but she wanted to stay.

"That's the point! I *should've* done something! I should've noticed the turtlenecks and your long sleeves and how unhappy you are when you're with him. I should've noticed that whenever he comes around, you're sad that you have to leave with him. My head's been all over the place with work and the kids and my mom—" Ada stopped.

"Why? Is she okay?" Caro asked, still somewhere up by the ceiling. She loved Holly Plum; Holly had her faults like anyone, but she'd been like a mom to Caroline while she was growing up and even now. She'd spent countless hours working in the bakery with Holly and had learned so much from her. Caro hated thinking of anything happening to her. That thought started to sink her back down to the table. She picked her wineglass up again and drank.

"She'll be . . . fine. I guess. She just needs to get some better doctors for her pain. It's a long story and I'll fill you in later. Right now, we have to remain focused on getting you out of this. First, you need to come stay with me," Ada said.

"Or me," Rosemarie offered.

"Or you can stay at the farmhouse. I don't know what I'm going to do with it. Maybe this is it. You can stay as long as you need to," Kasey said, rooting through her bag. She got out a key and put it on the table in front of Caroline.

"Whatever you want," Ada said.

"You're leaving in the morning. You don't have time to—" Caro said to Kasey.

"No. I'm not going anywhere until I know you're okay," Kasey said sternly.

"Girl, why are you acting like we aren't who we are? If that son of a bitch ever touches you again, my God!" Rosemarie said.

Why are you acting like we aren't who we are?

Why was Caroline acting like she wasn't who *she* was?

If she tried, she could remember who she used to be before Trey. She was a frail, shaking shadow of that woman now. How had that happened in six short months? Six short months that felt like six long decades of darkness.

Caro tried to put her wineglass on the table, but it slipped.

When it crashed to the floor, she lost it. She finally covered her face and cried, apologizing to Ada for breaking her beautiful glass. She apologized to Kasey for being snappy with her in the bathroom at the Plums'. She apologized to Rosemarie for acting like nothing was wrong. She was crying so much and so hard she got panicky, thinking she'd never stop. The back of her head hurt from where Trey had slammed it against the wall. He'd been so mad about the night before. How she hadn't been in the mood for sex after the wedding, but he hadn't taken no for an answer, and when she cried afterward, he told her she made him feel like a rapist and there were plenty of women in that town he could fuck who wouldn't cry afterward. He was constantly turning *easy* women down. They'd beg for it. They'd be grateful.

Her body ached. There were more bruises hidden under her clothes that the girls couldn't see and tender spots inside of her—painful, forever invisible.

Ada picked up the pitcher and poured a glass of ice water and lemons for Caroline. She took small sips and caught her breath, began telling them everything.

———

For years she'd dated mostly losers in town. Guys she knew she didn't love but who seemed good enough to pass the time with. Guys whose main personality traits were that they had a workout routine and always flipped a middle finger in the pictures they uploaded to social media. But Jay from the bakery wasn't a loser; he'd been nice and they stayed friends afterward. Caro had even made the cake for his wedding.

Leo's best friend, Samuel, had been kind too. He asked Caro if she wanted to come with him to Amsterdam when he left for a museum job over there. Caro went and stayed with him for a few weeks and came home brokenhearted after they'd talked about it, both of them realizing their relationship was ending. She'd been so sad and tenderhearted when Trey popped up in her life not long after that.

Maxwell Mason Foxberry III had come to her rescue. Caro had loved fairy tales her whole life, and finally she was getting her own. It *was* a fairy-tale dream that a man with so much money would want to heal her broken heart, sweep her off her feet, treat her with such care and attention.

Trey was kind and gentle with her in the beginning, both physically and emotionally. So generous too. He bought her a huge ruby ring and earrings to match. He gave her his credit card and told her to get whatever she wanted. They flew to California together, road-tripped back home. They went on a trip to Europe, and he proposed to her in the summer wind on their balcony in Paris, and after the wedding, they honeymooned in Aruba.

It was there that everything had changed.

Once Caroline was his wife, Trey became controlling. Hypercritical. Verbally abusive. The last night of their honeymoon, he'd grabbed her face and squeezed when she wasn't looking at him as he was talking. Caro's eyes filled with tears and fear flashed through her body like lightning, sparking every part. She was thousands of miles away from everyone she'd ever known, and no one had ever touched her like that. She'd never gotten one spanking growing up, not one smack. Mimi didn't take no mess, but she'd been as gentle as a butterfly with Caroline.

Caro was filled with so much shame she couldn't tell anyone what had happened. How could she? How could she tell anyone that on their honeymoon, when Trey wanted to have sex but she didn't—not after how he'd grabbed her—he had sex with her anyway, telling her over and over again that he was sorry it was happening like this but she was his wife now and that was what being a wife meant. He asked how she couldn't have known. He asked if she was stupid. He said that she hadn't gone to college, only pastry school, so maybe he should've known she wasn't the brightest light on the porch, but he figured someone would've told her what being a wife meant. What being married to a Foxberry meant. He said he knew she wasn't some precious virgin, so she shouldn't try to act like it. He knew she had sex with Jay and Samuel. Mateo in high school too. He was willing to forgive her for those. She grew up in a trailer and he was a Foxberry and now she was a Foxberry too. It was how she'd get fixed.

Caro felt the sludge of shame so thick in her blood she thought it'd stop her heart. She'd loved him and thought he loved her too. She had an over-the-top wedding and hadn't been shy about being proud of landing Goldie's biggest fish. Now she had him all to herself, this nightmare of a man. It had taken her so long to find someone, a relationship that stuck.

So, it was her duty to stay stuck to him.

She'd tried to focus on the positives of being married to a Foxberry. Trey's parents had bought them that big house, and she got to live in it with those new cars in the garage. She had a cleaning lady and a pool boy and a gardener now. And when Trey wasn't forcing her, she could remember the time and place when she wanted to be with him in bed. When she thought he was handsome and masculine and sexy. When she'd admired how much stronger he was than her, that he could hold both her wrists together with one of his hands, so tight she couldn't get free.

If they had kids—like she'd thought she wanted to, once upon a time—the Foxberry family could send them to the new private school on the other side of town and to college, too, without worries. The kinds of things Caro didn't even dare dream about when she was growing up.

She'd been witness to some goodness in Trey. Like how she told him how much she loved the line about Tom carrying Daisy down from the Punchbowl to keep her shoes dry in *The Great Gatsby*, so one time when they were at a fancy Foxberry party at one of their distilleries, he'd slipped Caro's heels off and carried her down from the punch bowl upstairs. Cradled her out to the car and placed her into the passenger seat. "I knew you'd like that," he said, all smug and sexy.

Caro wrapped up moments like that with bows of extra emotion and emphasis, and as time went by, she kept lying to herself, leaning into desperate math.

Only one month since they'd been married . . . only three months since they'd been married.

She made his favorite dinners, tried not to stay at the bakery too late unless it was absolutely necessary. She almost never turned him down for sex, never looked at other men, never interrupted him while he was speaking.

Not out of love, but for survival.

But no matter what she did, something would spark him. As the abuse continued, Caro got better at hiding it. Part of her felt like it was her fault for not figuring out his puzzle yet. Part of her held out hope that things would get better.

She was naturally optimistic and never realized how that could be a dark thing until Trey.

Only six months of marriage so far. That wasn't so long, right?

Perhaps if she kept loving him and tried again and again to understand what set him off, what displeased him, she could become the type of woman he wouldn't punish. She held on to any infinitesimal amount of sweetness he trickled out. Any day he didn't hurt her physically was a plus. Any day he didn't call her a bitch or tell her she was stupid was a good day.

She didn't love him anymore. How could she? He'd probably never *truly* loved her, not even before they were married.

Now that heart she'd once had for him was dust, blown away.

———

Ada asked Caroline more than once if it was okay, then called her lawyer and told her to put her in touch with the best divorce lawyer in Goldie. She knew the Foxberry family had a team of wolflike attorneys on retainer. Kasey called Silas and asked him to tell her exactly what Caro needed to do to get a restraining order against Trey. When she got the phone from Kasey and heard Silas's kind voice in her ear, Caro took a deep breath and asked if there was any way to keep it as quiet as possible; Silas said he'd do all he could to make that happen.

Making plans like this, Caro could see so clearly the dynamic of their sisterhood in action. Kasey, the brainiac, strategized. Ada, the businesswoman, executed and scheduled. Rosemarie, the heartbeat, steady and so honest and able to focus her emotions and search for solutions.

"Caro, Trey is a fucking rapist and an abuser. I can't fully explain how sorry I am that you've been living like this for six months. That's too long. No more. You're so good at looking out for us and taking care of us. Now it's time for us to take care of you," Rosemarie said to her, pushing her tears away.

"It's my last night at that god-awful boutique hotel. I'm supposed to meet Silas there for drinks after this but—" Kasey said.

"*Please* don't change your plans for me—I mean it. You two have so much to catch up on," Caroline said. Rosemarie and Ada echoed her until Kasey folded.

"Just hang out at Ada's or Rosemarie's and text Trey and say you're spending the night with us, since he thinks I'm leaving tomorrow. He won't know about the restraining order until the morning," Kasey said. Caroline said okay.

"Tomorrow we'll all go to the house with you to get your stuff. Or we could send Silas and Grayson. The whole police force," Ada said. "We'll do anything for you."

"No. No, I can do that myself; I can. Trey will be busy at the distillery. It'll be fine—trust me. He's barely home anymore, and I'll need the space and time alone to process everything," Caroline said softly. There were so many nights she slept in that big house alone, and when she told Trey she wanted to get a dog, he'd said no. When she asked why, he told her it was because there would be times she might pay more attention to the dog and not to him, and then he'd want to kill the dog. Her head was pulsing hot under the dim lights of the restaurant. The wine was helping. She took another drink and Rosemarie poured more into her glass, her own too.

"Fuck the Earls," Rosemarie said, lifting her wineglass in a toast. The girls lifted theirs and repeated it. They clinked.

Caroline felt her mouth lift into a small, surprise smile.

———

The next morning, after spending the night in Kasey's hotel room, Caro and Kasey met the other girls and Silas at the police station to file the restraining order. Now Caroline was upstairs alone in her bedroom in the big house, packing her sunflower suitcase. She would miss that house. It could've felt cold or too empty with only the two of them in it, but Caroline had warmed it up. She'd painted their bedroom walls the blue of the ocean and the kitchen a soft honey color that reminded her of pie crust. She'd baked so many pies in that amazing oven. That oven was as good as the ones they had at the bakery. She would probably miss the oven most of all.

When she heard a car in the driveway, at first she assumed it was the cleaning lady. Then Caro's blood cooled, remembering their security system. The way that Trey could connect it to his phone. The way he could be watching her pack her things right now if he wanted. Couldn't he, if he'd activated it? Maybe he put secret cameras in the bedroom. She scanned the corners, the top of the dresser, searching for anything that could be recording her. Caro crept out of the bedroom slowly and looked over the railing. She went down a few steps so she could peek through the window.

The door chimed.

Trey walked in and looked up at her.

"Where are you going, Caroline?" he said so calmly she knew he was going to kill her. This was it.

There was a T-shirt balled in the grip of her fist. What could she do with that? She stood frozen on the steps as he walked up them, and it was only when he got close to her that she thought to run up too.

When she ran, her toe clipped one of the steps and she fell.

As she was falling, Trey grabbed her. Not to catch her, but to hold her so he could push her properly.

Now his hand was on her face, punching and grabbing at her hair. She was hurt, but she fought him anyway. She remembered the self-defense Beau taught her in high school. How to get out of a pair of zip ties if she ever needed to. How she could use her body weight to break them apart over her knee. He taught her to roll if someone was ever sitting on her and wouldn't let her up. She thought about Beau and how he taught her those things because he said there were *a lot of crazy, evil assholes in the world.*

Caroline heard Beau's voice as that crazy, evil asshole she was married to put his hand around her throat. She tried to roll but she couldn't breathe and she was still falling. Trey kicked her and her body moved across the linoleum to the glass. Somehow, she got on her feet, but she couldn't see. Her body was cumbersome and numb. Glass broke and wrapped around her.

She felt the heat of the sun as she slammed back onto the driveway. Then.

Everything went gelid and black.

2004

20

Caroline couldn't believe how okay she was with the plan to kill Roy. She wasn't a violent person; she was painfully tenderhearted. Once, she found a dead butterfly in the gravel outside of their trailer and cried about it all day. She'd never been in a fight, never even come close. Grandma Mimi kept a shotgun in the corner of her bedroom, but Caro had never touched it and never wanted to. She hated guns and wasn't interested in any of the people who were obsessed with them either.

She kept telling herself that they were young, they couldn't get in too much trouble even if they got caught, but they *wouldn't* get caught, because they had it planned out. Everyone would think Roy died of a heart attack or something. Why would anyone suspect RACK? They were good girls, young lights in the community, top of their senior class. It would make no sense.

They'd talked over everything so much and for so long Caroline could see the plan played out in her mind, coming together the same way her best recipes did. Ada had made the rat-poison black-eyed peas with extra onions and jalapeños on top and given them to Kasey. Ada had swiped the poison from her dad's stuff in the garage because he had everything in there and wouldn't miss anything. They decided to use a *lot* of poison since Roy was a big guy and they certainly couldn't safely look up *exactly how much poison to kill a big man* on their computers at home or school. Kasey put the food in the fridge for later because Roy had a new job down at the Foxberry brewery across the lake and always came home for his break. Most of the time he'd want Kasey to get food ready for him with leftovers or make sandwiches out of whatever they had. Kasey's mom hated black-eyed peas, onions, and anything remotely spicy so much that Kasey was 100 percent confident Angie wouldn't touch any of it. They asked her a million times if she was sure, and Kasey never budged. She said they were her mom's three most hated foods, period. Angie would be at the ceremony later, even though Kasey knew she wouldn't see her, not until the party at the Plums'. Ada, Caro, and Kasey were going to get a ride with Rosemarie from the ceremony to the party, so they could be together and be in a car. So they could be alone. They'd go discover dead Roy together too.

Everything felt better when they were together.

———

Graduation went off without a hitch. The girls wowed at Kasey's ability to give her valedictorian speech so perfectly with everything weighing on her. They were all frazzled, anxious with nerves because of The Plan.

But.

Rosemarie's station wagon wouldn't start after the ceremony. She'd left the headlights on.

"Fuck!" Rosemarie said in the parking lot. "I'm so sorry. This is my fault! This is all my fault. Shit!" She smacked her hand on the steering wheel. Kasey was up there next to her; Ada and Caro were in the backseat. Ada was looking out of the window chewing on her thumb, and Caro had already popped the lukewarm bottle of cheap champagne that Ada's mom let them swipe and started drinking it. She handed it to Ada, who took a glug too.

"This is a sign. This is a *bad* sign," Ada said. Technically, Rosemarie giving them all a ride to Ada's wasn't an important part of the plan; it didn't matter how they got there. Roy would be dead whether or not they rode in Rosemarie's car. But it couldn't bode well for the rest of the night if the first thing they needed to get done had gone wrong.

"I said it's all my fault, Ada! I'm sorry!" Rosemarie said.

"Right. Okay. I'm sorry. I can call Grayson. He might still be here somewhere," Ada said.

"Nope. He and Silas are gone already. I saw them leave," Kasey said.

"We could get a ride with—" Caroline got out before hiccuping.

"No. I don't want to be around anyone else right now. Um...okay. Okay. Um...we'll just walk. Let's go," Kasey said confidently. She opened the door.

"Wait! Let us drink some more of this. It'll help. Do you want some?" Caro said, shoving the champagne bottle up to the front. Rosemarie took it, sipped. Kasey took a pull, handed it back to Caro. She'd shotgunned two Goldie Lights on an empty stomach with some guys from her anatomy class after the ceremony, which gave her more of a buzz than she expected. The champagne was already meeting the beer somewhere in the middle of her bloodstream, sparkling. She chugged and chugged, handing it to Ada one more time before finishing the rest. Rosemarie and Kasey were quiet up front.

"I'm so sorry, Kase," Rosemarie said softly after a moment.

"Don't be. We'll walk. It's okay. Roy might be dead already. It doesn't matter. Let's go," Kasey said.

They got out of Rosemarie's car in their white graduation dresses and started walking the two miles to Ada's place with the boys from their school honking at them and hollering, pulling over to offer them rides. There were cans tied to their bumpers, and the truck beds were filled with seniors in their graduation robes, seniors in their gold CLASS OF '04 T-shirts.

The sun was slowly slipping toward the hills, and wow, Caro was drunk. She motioned to the girls that she was going to duck into the alley by the diner to puke.

"Congratulations, Muffin Mix! What—" Beau stopped with a big black bag of trash in his hand.

Caro held her finger up to him. *Just a sec.* Her girlfriends were right behind her, glowing like angels. She got to the garbage can first and Kasey held her hair back.

"Yeah, she had beers…and champagne too. Bless her heart, she's a bit of a mess right now," Ada said.

"She'll be fine," Rosemarie said to Beau.

"Understood. Been there. You all right?" Beau said to Caro when she was upright again.

"Oh, Beau, you're so fucking *cute*," she said, wiping her mouth. She hadn't thought about the words; they fell out. When she hugged him, he dropped the trash.

"*You're* so fucking cute," he said with his arms around her. "I won't put my hands on you. They're dirty."

"I don't care! I'll be eighteen in July!" Caro said as she let him go, as if she'd invented birthdays.

"Whoa! Okay! Okay, Caro, let's go. We'll see you later, Beau! Bye!" Ada said, putting her arm around Caroline's shoulder and guiding her toward the street.

"All right, now," Beau said through his chuckle. "Congratulations! Y'all be careful."

"Bye, Beau," Caro said in a soft Minnie Mouse voice. She turned to wave as they stepped out of the alley, back into the light.

"Roy might be dead already. He's probably dead already."

Caro heard Kasey say it more to herself than any of them as Ada's big pink house came into view, sitting there like a parade float.

2019

21

ROSEMARIE

Rosemarie, Ada, and Kasey were standing right outside of the ICU when Mimi told them that not only was Caro still in a coma, but she was pregnant too.

Ada and Kasey gasped and anxiously asked questions; Rosemarie felt a stillness come over her. A few weeks ago, she and Caroline had taken Basie for a walk and talk by the lake. Caro mentioned thinking she was pregnant a couple months before, taking a test, and it being negative. Then she said she felt like it'd happen sometime soon, and she wasn't stressing about it. She told Rosemarie that Mimi let her know a long time ago that all the women in their family got red-hot cheeks to go with their red-hot hair in the first few weeks of their pregnancies. Rosemarie noticed Caroline's cheeks flaming like her hair for the past week, but Caro had been drinking a lot too, and it'd been so hot.

"Her cheeks. Her cheeks have been so red," Rosemarie said softly, shaking her head.

"I thought so too, but I wondered if it was the heat. I should've asked her. I should've said something. It's so early, but praise Jesus. Praise Jesus they're both alive in there," Mimi said, nodding. She took her glasses off, patted at her eyes with a tissue. Mimi filled Ada and Kasey in on the meaning of the red cheeks and they stood quiet afterward.

"I read his texts to her...they were so nasty. I should've—"

Mimi shook her head at Rosemarie. "No. Nobody to blame here but him," she said.

Ada texted Grayson the latest and sprang into housekeeping action.

"I know flowers aren't allowed in the ICU, but when they move her, I'll fill the room with sunflowers," Ada said. "We'll make sure they keep her curtains open, and she'll have a private room soon, right? We'll make sure she has a private room. Grayson and I don't mind paying for it, Miss Mimi." She took drink and food orders from everyone, and she and Kasey went down to the cafeteria for bottled water and tea, soup and crackers.

———

Rosemarie and Grandma Mimi sat in the waiting room holding hands. Rosemarie asked if Caroline's mom and dad would be coming up anytime soon. Caro had an icy relationship with both of them and so did Mimi, but did any of that matter anymore? Did any of that matter when Caro was in a coma? Rosemarie's spirit was filled with grief, and there was a righteous fire in her heart.

Mimi said she told Caroline's mother what happened and she was on her way down from Indiana and would be there later tonight. The last Mimi heard of him, Caroline's dad was in Mexico.

"Probably sitting half-drunk on tequila with a bag of coke in his pocket and his arm around some woman he just met. She's better off without him. We all are. Caroline accepts anything she *mistakes* for love from any man because her daddy's no good and she never got it from him," Mimi said. "He's no better than that Foxberry boy, he ain't. Her mama says she's been clean for a few months, but we'll see when she gets here. I don't trust her one bit," she said. "And any man who could do something like that..." Mimi began. "I've known a lot of women who tied themselves to bad men, and they never change. I've seen it too many times. My daddy was a bad man. Horrible drunk. And y'know, I must've asked Caroline a million times if that boy treated her right, if he was *good* to her, and she looked me right in the eyes and told me yes. Caroline's not a natural liar. She wasn't. Not until he made her into one."

Mimi dug through her straw purse and pulled out a pack of mint gum, offering a stick to Rosemarie, who took it. Both of Rosemarie's grandmothers had died when she was a teenager. Being around Miss Mimi was always comforting in the best way. She was funny and warm, and there wasn't a phony bone in her body. She called Rosemarie *Ro-Ro* when she was a little girl, and when she spent the night, Mimi would warm her apple juice in the microwave because she'd done it for her once and Rosemarie loved it. God had gifted Miss Mimi the ability to make people feel better simply with her presence, and Rosemarie felt it, holy and radiating in that hospital.

After Ada and Kasey came back and they'd eaten and drunk what they could, Kasey got a call from Silas, who was supposed to update them about Trey behind bars as soon as he knew what was up. Silas had been the one driving on that street in his patrol car, the one a neighbor flagged down because she thought she'd heard screams, the one to put Trey in handcuffs.

Kasey relayed the new info from Silas.

Trey was going to be kept in custody even though he claimed it was all an accident and that everyone knew how clumsy Caroline could be, especially if she'd been drinking. She'd fallen down the steps, and when Trey tried to catch and help her, she freaked out on him and panicked. Maybe she'd been sleepwalking? Either way, she pushed him off so hard she'd fallen against the window, breaking it. Her head, her eyes, the scratches, and bruises? Those were from the fall and the window glass. Trey was horrified anyone thought this was something he would do to his wife *on purpose*. Of course he loved his wife. This was all bullshit. Nonsense. He wanted out of there soon so he could get to the hospital to see Caroline. Silas told Kasey since the restraining order had been filed that morning, they could maybe find a reason to keep him locked up for a day or two, but probably not since Trey's lawyer was already down there raising hell. His parents too.

Of course Trey was going to be able to spin this. He was a Foxberry and they owned half the town. Their grandfather's name had recently been added to the new wing of the hospital they were sitting in.

The girls held hands and sank into a deep quiet when Mimi went back inside the room to sit with Caroline. Patients in the ICU could only have two visitors a day; any more would be too much overstimulation. Despite the fire burning and burning in Rosemarie's heart, Ada and Kasey told her they felt like she gave off the most natural, peaceful presence and should be the one to sit with Caroline right now.

When Mimi came out, Rosemarie went in.

———

"Caro, it's Roses," Rosemarie said, sitting in the chair next to her bed. She watched Caroline's chest move with her breath, and Rosemarie started crying all over again, this time out of gratitude. "I'm going to talk to you and Baby, okay? Your little Rosy Magnolia. Remember years ago when I told you I had a dream that you and I both had little girls we named Rosy Magnolia? And I heard Grateful Dead in my head, singing it like 'Sugar Magnolia'? Don't ask me how I know you're pregnant with a girl—I just do. Both my grandma Rose and my grandma Marie had The Gift about this, and I don't question it."

The machines next to Caroline did their work of hushing and

beeping, while the IV dripped. Rosemarie took a good look at what she could see of Caro's face. Her head was wrapped in gauze and her eyes were swollen, one of the lids tinted pale purple as if there were a lilac light behind it. A gnarly hot-pink scratch slanted across her top lip, and there were slices on her forearms and hands. Fingertip bruises on her neck. Her right arm and shoulder were wrapped up too. She looked like she'd been in an explosion, and when Rosemarie gave it more thought, she realized it was true—Caroline's emotional and physical world had blown up because of Trey, and he'd probably be out in the Goldie sunshine again soon like nothing had happened.

"In my dream, your Rosy Magnolia had hair as red as the strawberries on those teeny shorts you used to wear all the time when we were in high school, and she had big brown eyes like *my* Rosy Magnolia," Rosemarie said, wiping her nose. "You and I both know I'm not gonna have my Rosy Magnolia, Caro. I'm not able to...it won't happen, so yours is gonna have a double spirit for us, and I know she will. She lived through this, and you're gonna live through this too.

"I read Trey's texts last week...the ones he sent to you. I shouldn't have done it, or I should've done more about it. Or I should've asked you the right questions, and I'm so sorry I didn't do that," she said. "I'm gonna play a song for you and the baby now. *My* favorite. No worries, 'Ripple' is next." Rosemarie pulled out her phone.

She turned "Sugar Magnolia" on soft and low and set her phone in her lap. She closed her eyes and listened, kept them closed and breathed with Caroline. Prayed for Caroline. Felt the wildfires in her heart flicker and grow.

Rosemarie didn't know what time it was when the nurse came and woke her up, told her visiting hours were over. Caro was still breathing and sleeping as the sun went down.

———

Ada and Kasey had waited at the hospital. Mimi was going to sleep there overnight, and she let them know Caroline's mom said she'd be there sometime too.

Rosemarie, Ada, and Kasey went to Myrtle's Diner for coffee and to compose themselves the best they could. After they filled Myrtle in on the latest, she brought them coffee on the house and a plate of fries to share if they were hungry. They thanked her, and Myrtle said Caroline was a tough old bird and reassured them she'd be all right.

"I feel so *guilty* and I'm not making this about me, but I really should've been paying more attention—I know that," Ada said, unfolding the paper napkin and setting it in her lap.

"You have your own life, Ada. I know it used to feel like we were all the same person sometimes when we were kids, but we're not. This isn't anyone's fault but Trey's," Kasey said.

"Please don't say his name. Not anymore tonight," Rosemarie said, holding up her hand.

"You're right. I'm sorry. You're exactly right," Kasey said.

"When are you going back home?" Ada asked Kasey.

"I don't know. I canceled my flight without making a new one. Told Devon I'd let him know. I'm not leaving anytime soon. I'll be at the farmhouse. Free house, right? I'm the idiot who spent so much money crashing at the boutique hotel," Kasey said, picking up a fry and putting it down. She drank her coffee.

"Is Esme coming soon?" Ada asked Rosemarie, trying to keep track of everyone. Rosemarie knew that was another reason Ada felt so guilty about Caroline. Their entire lives, Ada had made it her mission to know where they were and what they were all up to.

"Yeah, but I don't know when. This film she's working on . . . constant reshoots or whatever. It's a mess, but it's okay. I kind of only want to be with y'all right now anyway. Well, and Leo. I'm supposed to record with him tonight, but there's too much on my mind. I'm supposed to be at his place right now," Rosemarie said.

"Go. Go to Leo's. Let's meet at the bakery in the morning, and we can take some goodies to the hospital for the nurses and everyone else. Caroline will probably wake up tomorrow, don't y'all think?" Ada asked, lighting up a bit since she was planning again. She ate one fry, then another.

"I think so," Kasey said, nodding. She was ripping the paper napkin in front of her to shreds, surely thinking about her stepdad, all the Earls in this world who weren't worth a shit.

"I'm praying for it. Hoping for it. I feel it," Rosemarie said, finishing her coffee and nodding too.

———

Caro's still in a coma. Going back
to the hospital in the morning. I
love you, Esme.

I love you too, Rosie. I'm so sorry
and I'll keep praying. I'll be down
soon.

Rosemarie didn't feel like singing, and she told Leo that first thing. Leo knew everything about what was going on, and he'd made tea and peanut butter cookies, but she didn't feel like drinking or eating anything. She forced herself to take small sips of water. She was so tired and her head hurt; she needed to sleep and sleep. She'd been avoiding the calls and voicemails from her doctor, and the day had been too much. She felt so fragile, like a feather could split her in two. They got on the couch with Basie snug next to them. Rosemarie lay in Leo's arms and he held her like that. She fell asleep quickly with her ear pressed to his chest, listening to his heartbeat thumping like a train over tracks.

2004

22

At the graduation party, Rosemarie found her daddy and told him that her car was in the school's parking lot with a dead battery. Sparrow had come up and hugged her before disappearing with Frankie, and Rosemarie hadn't sorted her feelings out about that yet. Those feelings were lighting up, humming through her like fireflies as she walked across the backyard toward Ada and Kasey. They'd put drunk Caroline upstairs in Ada's bed for a quick nap.

"I can't get in touch with my mom. She won't pick up," Kasey said. Her hands were shaking. "I...I don't know what to do, because she's supposed to be here. If she's not here—"

"She's supposed to be here," Rosemarie said. *Shit. Shit. Shit!*

"Right. But she's not," Kasey said. "She won't pick up."

Kasey may have been freaking out, but Rosemarie could tell from the look on Ada's face that Ada was in *supreme* panic mode.

"I keep telling Kase we need to go find her! I keep telling her maybe I didn't put enough onions and jalapeños on the black-eyed peas. I put a lot of hot sauce, but maybe she wouldn't know it's hot sauce. Maybe she'd think it was ketchup or something! Kasey, your mom *loves* ketchup. We have to go right now. Maybe she's—" Ada's eyes were watery. She was blinking too much and talking too fast and being too loud.

"Shh. *Shh*, seriously, stop," Rosemarie said, looking around to make sure no one was close enough to hear. She pulled them back a bit toward the garage. "Ada, she didn't eat the food." Rosemarie was 99 percent sure of herself. "Kasey, try calling again."

"Please call her again," Ada said.

"Ada, girl, you *have* to chill," Rosemarie said. She had to!

"Okay. Okay. I'm calling her again," Kasey said.

"She didn't eat it," Rosemarie repeated. She peeked around the corner and saw Grayson walking toward them. She nudged Ada, and Ada whipped her head around to look at him.

"Is she picking up?" Ada asked. "Fuck, Kase, does your mom sometimes not answer her phone? I knew this wouldn't work. This was so stupid! There's no way we could pull this off!"

"Sometimes she doesn't answer, Ada. Sometimes she's busy. She probably got stuck at the store . . . busy with . . . something . . . and look, Grayson will be over here in, like, three seconds, so shut up. Right now," Rosemarie said through gritted teeth.

"Kasey, is she picking up?" Ada asked.

"Mama?" Kasey said into the phone.

"Is it her?" Ada asked. "Kase, is it her?"

"Mama? Where are you?" Kasey asked into the phone. She turned to the girls with one hand on her heart. She gave them a thumbs-up.

"Oh, thank *God*. Tell her not to eat the *fucking* black-eyed peas!" Ada said with a strong snap of relief in her voice.

"What's up, y'all?" Grayson asked when he stepped to them.

"I'm dying of thirst. Come with me," Ada said, flipping the switch and beaming up at him. She linked her arm with his and pulled him away.

Rosemarie spotted Leo in the middle of a small crowd and returned the thumbs-up to Kasey before joining them. Leo was playing the sax solo from "Careless Whisper" for whatever reason. Where did he get a saxophone? Also, why? It was the only thing that had made Rosemarie laugh at the party, and she felt disconnected from reality when she did it, because they were just having a collective freak-out, and now she was laughing. Everything was so weird. There RACK was, deep into carrying out a legit *murder*, and Leo was as Leo as ever. So good at being funny, dancing, and playing the sax so effortlessly, the same way he played every instrument because God had apparently snatched talent from some other people and given it to him.

When it came to the legit *murder*, Rosemarie had made her peace with it. She was born and raised hating injustice. Her parents were black people from the Deep South, so obviously they had no real faith or trust in the justice system. So often women who had to deal with physical and emotional abuse in their own homes rarely ever told anyone, and when they did, no one did a damn thing about it! Roy needed to go. Period.

"My mom's fine and at the store doing inventory. She said it's her job now that she's assistant manager. I told her the food in the fridge at home was for Roy and Roy only. She said he probably has to go out of town or something. Maybe for the night. She apologized a lot and said she wants me to enjoy the party. Not to worry," Kasey said, stepping next to Rosemarie, still holding her phone by her face like she was frozen.

"So, what do we do?" Rosemarie said. She found Ada on the other side of the yard. Rosemarie tried to wave her over without making a big deal about it. Thankfully, Ada saw, said something to Grayson, and walked to them alone.

"Nothing. Forget it. Everything's...I don't even know where Roy is! The car not starting was the first thing to go wrong, and it set everything off crooked, and Caroline's drunk...and everything's ruined! Everything we were supposed to do, none of it is happening," Kasey said. "Rosemarie, it's not your fault—that's not what I mean."

"I know, Kase. I know," Rosemarie said, but she did love hearing it anyway.

"I'm so scared I can't even think straight. I've been smiling but I'm a mess, y'all. I don't think I can go through with this. Maybe we should do something else, but not this. I think I'm having a panic attack. Am I having a panic attack?" Ada said, breathing hard.

"Obviously yes. Just breathe slow. You're okay. Put your head down or something. Be cool, Plum," Rosemarie said. She put her hand on Ada's shoulder and pulled her close. Caroline's red hair swished their way.

"Slept some of it off! What's up? What phase are we in now? Operation what?" she asked, obviously half-drunk.

"Kase, tell us what we can do. We're not gonna let him get away with this. We—" Rosemarie said quietly as they tightened the circle. They were in the darkest part of the yard not lit by the lanterns or twinkle lights; everyone was drenched in the gray-dark now.

"My mom couldn't even make the time to come to my graduation party. She probably wasn't even at the ceremony. I've been planning this! For *her*! She can't even bother to show up," Kasey said. Her voice was wavy and angry; her hands were shaking again.

"Look, let's give it some time. Like, an hour. In an hour, we'll sneak out of here and go to the farmhouse to see what's up. It may be taken care of already. The original plan got twisted, yeah, but your mom's okay and—" Rosemarie stopped when she saw Silas walking up behind Kasey.

"Okay, yeah. I'm gonna get Silas to take me for a ride. Clear my head. I'll be back in an hour," Kasey said, after she turned and saw him. "Let's go. Let's get out of here."

"You all right?" Silas asked her.

"Yeah, I'm fine," Kasey said.

"Kase—" Ada said through the muffle of being smooshed against Rosemarie's shoulder.

"Like, seriously. *One* hour," Rosemarie said, holding up a finger.

Caro was in a daze, braiding her hair over her shoulder.

"I'm fine! Love y'all," Kasey said in a completely normal voice. She turned around and walked away.

23

ADA

Ada got up early and made breakfast for Grayson and the boys even though she hadn't slept enough. She and Kasey had stayed at the diner for an hour after Rosemarie left, and afterward, she followed Kasey in her rental car so she could drop it off in Adora Springs. Then she stopped at Plum Florals for fresh flowers and Plum Designs for a lamp and linens before taking Kasey to the farmhouse. She couldn't stand the thought of Kasey not having new, soft, cozy things for her first night sleeping in that house. Ada wanted to do all she could to fortify her best friend against that flood of awful memories.

In the morning, she had eggs, fruit, bacon, and biscuits on the table for her family although she ate none of it herself. She sat with them, drinking her coffee, watching the clock. In an hour, she'd meet Rosemarie and Kasey at the bakery, and they'd go back to the hospital together.

"You'll have to get some rest sometime. If you don't take a break, your body will do it for you," Grayson said to her across the kitchen table. Her husband looked good and bright-eyed, wearing a stylishly rumpled button-down shirt the color of a stormy sea with his shorts. He'd left the top two buttons undone; she loved when he did that.

When she'd told Grayson what Trey had done to Caroline, she had to beg him not to do anything stupid. "My God! I cannot *believe* she married that piece of shit!" Grayson said, as if their marriage just dawned on him. "I can't *believe* she's pregnant with that motherfucker's baby." He'd been so mad he left the house and took the twins out to his parents' to shoot cans.

"I know I have to rest, and I will. But not today," Ada said.

"Mama, are you sleepy?" her youngest, Pacey, asked. He rolled a blueberry up his chin, into his mouth.

"Mama's wide awake. Look at my eyes, buddy," Ada said, making her eyes as wide as she could and opening her mouth wide too. Pacey did the same thing and laughed.

"Daddy, I heard you snore last night, so you owe me five dollars," Gabriel said. He was six with the savviness of a sixty-year-old attorney.

"I *snorted*, like, once. Woke myself up. You'll have to record me in deep-sleep snoring like a big black bear to make those five dollars, kiddo. It ain't gonna happen, because I don't snore! I never place bets I know I won't win," Grayson said, tousling the little boy's hair.

"Is it almost time to go?" Noah asked.

"Can I wear my swim trunks?" Nash asked. He and the boys had already been in their pool once this morning, and now it was almost time for the twins to get to the music camp down by the lake that Rosemarie's parents were running with Leo and some teachers from the high schools.

"Is Auntie Caro still sleeping?" Pacey asked.

An elevator in Ada's stomach was going down down down.

"She'll wake up today. She'll be wide awake," Ada prayed aloud to him, making her eyes wide again. Pacey hooted like an owl.

She told Nash that wearing his swim trunks was fine. She told Noah they'd leave in ten minutes, but he needed to finish his breakfast first.

She told Gabriel to grab a crayon and sign his name on the card they'd made for Caroline. She told Grayson she'd drop the twins off at camp, but he needed to pick them up at three.

Ada felt guilty for being so absent—not only physically, but mentally too—this past week. She hoped that with the wedding being over and having sent Taylor and Ben off in style to honeymoon in Hawaii, she'd have more brain power for getting back to normal and dealing with her mom and work and *everything*. Now she was up from the table, putting breakfast plates in the sink, wondering if she should take flowers up to the hospital even if Caroline didn't get moved out of the ICU today. She could give them to the nurses. She should take some for the nurses anyway. That was what she'd do.

Caroline would wake up soon.

She would be out of the ICU soon.

Ada knew it and believed it. She had to.

She began doing the dishes. Moved a mug to the other side of the sink, tossed some forks in.

"Leave it. I'll take care of it. You go," Grayson said to her as she sprayed a splotch of jelly off a small plate. "Boys, go upstairs and get ready."

Ada thanked Grayson profusely for being amazing and kissed him. She told him she'd talk soon, keep him posted about everything.

———

Ada dropped the twins off with Mr. and Mrs. Kingston by the lake, then called her dad on her drive to the bakery. She told him it was time to think seriously about getting her mom into the rehab center in Adora Springs. Her dad did some hemming and hawing, but Ada raised her voice.

"Daddy! It's better to do this now before she gets worse. She drinks too much when she takes those pills. And what if she starts needing more? What if she gets desperate? She could take too many or get her hands on some bad stuff. All those overdoses...no telling what could happen. She could kill herself with them, and I already have my best friend in the hospital, I—"

"Ada, I'll talk to her. It's all I can do."

"That's a start. Do that. Please. I'll call back later," she said.

Her twin brothers had left Goldie the day after the wedding, returning to Boston and Chicago. She called them both at the same time and told them she needed them to talk to their parents and convince their mom to enter rehab. She told them about the four teenagers who overdosed in one weekend in Adora Springs and the other one who'd overdosed last week in Goldie. She considered the fact that maybe she was overreacting, but she was too tired to mince words anymore. Ada needed help. They needed to step it up.

"Don't leave me here to do it all by myself, y'all. Please," Ada said. Her voice was thin and shaky. She turned into the Plum Bakery parking lot and shut the engine off.

"Ada, I'll call him right now. I didn't know. How was I supposed to know how bad it'd gotten if you hadn't told me?" her brother Henry asked.

"Pay more attention, Hen," she said. "And thank you for calling him."

"Do you need me to come back down there? I'll get on a plane," Michael said. His husband was a pilot and they'd both spent the better part of their last ten years together on airplanes, so Ada knew he wasn't kidding.

"Maybe; I don't know. I just needed to call and yell at y'all because I know neither of you can stand it when I'm mad at you and I'm *so* mad at you right now! Taylor's not here and I'm doing this alone and I *need* you," Ada said.

Henry was more defensive than Michael, but he softened when he heard the hurt in Ada's voice. Michael said he'd work it out with their dad to make sure he was back in Goldie by the end of the week.

———

Rosemarie and Kasey were sitting at the bakery counter waiting for her. She waved at them as she walked to the back to grab two boxes of muffins and doughnuts she'd had set aside. Caroline should've been there in her apron, staring at a cake in the oven; Caroline should've been behind the counter greeting their regulars, like she always was, like she'd been doing ever since she graduated from pastry school.

Ada had been filled with rage about how Roy treated Kasey and her mom, but Ada was so young then, so unable to *truly* imagine what it was like to live with a man like that. Even seeing how different Caro's and Kasey's home lives were, Ada didn't fully realize how lucky she was growing up. She hadn't been raised in a *perfect* home, but she'd been raised in a *loving* home. Not one person in the Plum family had ever shied away from an argument or a confrontation, but they knew how to make up too. Even talking to her brothers quickly about how much she had on her plate helped settle her down. Now that she was a grown woman, she realized how heavy the weight would be if—like Angie or Caroline—she was scared to go home to Grayson at night. How much it would change who she was if he ever put his hands on her to hurt her.

When she motioned to Rosemarie and Kasey at the counter that she was ready to go, she thought about that panic attack she had the night of their graduation party. It was bad. Full-blown. She thought about that little girl crying in her white dress. How that little girl had turned into a grown-ass woman. She thanked God for refilling her with the power and strength she had now.

They walked down to Plum Florals to snatch up every sunflower they had, filling Ada's minivan with them and driving to the hospital.

———

Mimi had texted them on the way, letting them know Caro still hadn't woken up, but without wanting to say *too* much, the doctor felt like there was probably a good chance she would soon. Ada left one box of banana muffins and the flowers with the nursing staff. She imagined Caro seeing them and lighting up when she awakened, when they moved her to a regular room.

Ada and Kasey had talked it over, and Kasey was okay with Ada sitting with Caroline first, then Kasey would take the late shift. Caroline's mom called Mimi early that morning saying her car had broken down, but she was trying her best to make it. Mimi told them that was probably a lie and she wasn't even expecting her daughter to show up at all at this point.

While Mimi, Rosemarie, and Kasey went to the cafeteria for coffee, Ada walked into Caroline's room, getting eyes on her for the first time.

———

Ada was still crying in that beeping room when Caroline stirred a bit. She moved her fingers, then her feet. By the time she opened her eyes, Ada had already stood and called for the nurse.

Caro was talking through a groggy fog of tears, and Ada couldn't understand her. She asked her to take her time, say it again.

"Trey . . . he told me he'd kill me. He promised he'd kill me and find another wife who wasn't useless."

2004

24

Ada sat in the grass behind the garage, drinking a glass of water. She was holding it with both hands and Grayson was next to her, rubbing her back in big, soft circles.

"Feeling better? Seems like you're feeling better," he said.

"Mm-hmm." Ada let the sound come out of her mouth as she drank. She nodded for extra emphasis.

Yes, she was feeling better now that she knew Kasey's mom hadn't eaten the black-eyed peas and now that Kasey was gone and there could be a break from secret murder planning. She wanted Roy dead like the rest of them, but she also wanted to go to LA with Grayson. They were supposed to fly out to visit her cousins next month. She also wanted to talk to her mom some more about rebranding the Plum businesses in pale pink and a soft lime-green color that reminded her of the tropical beaches and salty air she wanted to experience with Grayson. All the beaches she wouldn't be able to go to if she got arrested for helping to murder a man.

Ada would turn eighteen at the end of July. What if they didn't get arrested until then? Would she be forced to wear orange? She hated orange. It would wash her out. She'd look ridiculous!

She hadn't told Grayson a thing about the plan, because they swore they wouldn't tell anyone. Besides, she didn't know if it was even happening anymore, so technically there was nothing to tell. So even when she was drinking the water in the grass and he was asking her what she was so upset about, she told him she didn't know, because she didn't!

She didn't know anything! Not really!

"Do you want to go upstairs and get in your bed? Try to sleep?" Grayson asked.

"There's probably a grass stain a mile wide on the back of this dress now," Ada said, since it was the first thing that popped into her head.

Someone turned the music up. Nelly. Apparently no one would ever tire of that song. Rosemarie had taken Caroline inside and put her to bed in Ada's room again. They were supposed to wait until Kasey got back from wherever she was. Then, Kasey would tell them what to do. They didn't want to take Ada's car to the farmhouse, since it was a hot-pink convertible that practically glowed in the dark; there wasn't another one like it in Goldie. They'd chosen to ride in Rosemarie's forest-green station wagon because it was so inconspicuous that even Rosemarie occasionally tried to stick her key into one that looked exactly like it.

The plan was to take Rosemarie's station wagon to the farmhouse, and Kasey would go peek inside to see if Roy was dead at the kitchen table, and if he was, Kasey was going to pretend to be surprised to find him like that. Kasey had said she was scared to do it alone, and she wanted RACK to stay together the whole time.

But now Kasey was gone.

"Did Silas take Kase home already?" Grayson asked, reading her mind.

"I don't think so. I think they went for a ride."

"Heh," Grayson said, chuckling. "Yeah, okay. A *ride*."

"Grayson Sycamore!" Ada said, putting the empty water glass between her knees.

"Do you think you can stand? Want me to carry you?" he asked. He was on his feet already, holding out his arms for her. Ada stood, leaving the glass in the grass. He scooped her up like she was already his bride and carried her through the dark toward the house.

"Ada, is Kasey here yet?" Rosemarie said when she saw them.

"No. She was supposed to be back in an hour," Ada said from Grayson's arms.

"Yeah, and it's been almost *two*." Rosemarie seemed super annoyed. She shook her head.

"Wait...it has? Uh...um...okay. Okay, you can put me down. Grayson, put me down, please," Ada said as calmly as she could. Once her bare feet were in the cool grass, she felt hot panic rising again.

2019

25

KASEY

On Wednesday after visiting Caroline again, Rosemarie, Ada, and Kasey went out to the hospital parking lot to talk in Ada's minivan.

"*You* heard her when she woke up yesterday, Ada. He beat her; he raped her. He said he'd kill her, and he will. He will *kill* her, and we will cry at the fucking funeral and act like we're so sorry it happened. We'll wish we could've done something about it, but we *can*! We *can* do something about it, and we *will* do something about it. Men kill women all the time, and no one does anything about it. Last month in New York, a woman was murdered on her way home from work, and the week after, some motherfucker killed his entire family before killing himself. His wife was pregnant. It happens all the time! We need to take care of this ourselves. We can kill an Earl and make the world a better place, period. That's what we're supposed to do. That's what—" Kasey stopped because she had to. She was hot, breathing hard. Ada had the engine on; the AC vents above her were blasting ice-cold air on Kasey in the backseat, but there wasn't enough AC in the world to cool her down.

She saw her mom's *before* face clearly in her mind. The *after* too.

Both visages so vivid Kasey's mouth crumpled. She sobbed and hid her face.

"Kasey," Ada cooed, putting her arms around her.

"Fritz, we love you so much, girl. Shit, I wish we could relax for, like, a minute and *be* together. Why do we have to be forever under the weight of...*everything?*" Rosemarie said. Kasey felt Rosemarie's arms around her too. Both Rosemarie and Ada had gotten into the backseat with her, and she laughed a little at the smooshiness of it.

Finally.

Finally, she confessed the heavy-hollow dark of what she'd avoided telling them for the past fifteen years.

2004

26

Kasey didn't know what time it was, and she didn't care. She was underneath Silas, kissing him like the world was ending. The frogs were singing so loud it felt like the sound would pull her and Silas under; the crickety heartbeat of the grass droned thick enough to spirit her away. They'd taken the flannel blanket out of his truck and laid it down on a patch of darkness far from potential prying eyes—a clandestine spot green-deep between the trees near the Castelow lake house that Silas knew well and had shown her that first night they kissed.

When she told him she was ready *forreal* this time, he wasn't slow about getting the condoms from the box in the glove compartment that she'd put in there a week ago, just in case.

She'd probably failed at planning a murder, but she succeeded in holding her breath so it wouldn't hurt so much when Silas moved inside of her at first. It got better very quickly. So good, in fact, that it didn't take long for Silas to finish, breathing hard in her ear. *Fuck, Kasey, I love you.* He pulled her on top of him and she moved her hips until it was her turn. *I love you.*

The heat was comforting, a Goldie constant in the spring and summer. Kasey would think of it often, no matter where she ended up in the world. It would feel good to know that no matter what, the Goldie wind would blow like honeyed breath. No matter what, the lake mist would always smell blue, and white clover would always play hide-and-seek in the green. Kasey lay in the afterglow on Silas's chest, wishing she could stay there forever. Her mind was whirring again. She considered a *Try to Kill Roy Part II* plan that she and the girls could throw together. Could they make it happen tomorrow? No. It would be bad luck to try the same thing twice.

But.

The food was still in the fridge and Roy could eat it at any time. Or maybe he was dead and her mom didn't want her to know yet. Maybe that was why she was being so weird. Maybe Kasey would look at her phone and see that her mom had texted *Roy is dead. Come home.* The darkness inside of her lit up thinking about it, listening to Silas's heartbeat as he played with her hair.

"I love you and I love this, and I know you're leaving soon, but I don't want to break up. Ever. Have I made that clear enough? Want to make sure there's no wondering on your part. You're stuck with me because I'm planning on loving you forever, without exception," Silas said against her ear.

Kasey locked the smell in her memory—eurythmic. A new sex-and-resin musk their bodies made together on that flannel under the trees. She moved her head to look at him. The moonlight rang slow through the leaves, giving him the dreamy look of being underwater.

"I don't want to break up either. Let's stay like this. I'm gonna love you forever too, so no takebacks. I promise. *You're* stuck with *me* now," she said, kissing him.

"I'll be miserable. I'll miss you so much. You promise you'll come home enough? I'll come up there too. We can make a schedule, and I know we won't *always* be able to stick to it, but people make stuff like this work all the time," Silas said.

He'd been accepted to Berry Bryn College an hour east in Berry County and would be living in a dorm, majoring in business. That hour got him one hour closer to where Kasey would be, and neither of them would let the other forget it.

"I'm not worried about us," Kasey said, kissing him. Kissing him and kissing him and sliding down.

She told the girls she'd be back at Ada's in an hour, but all Kasey cared about now was putting Silas Castelow in her mouth and spreading her legs and getting him inside of her again, thick and wet. Swallowed up and lost to forest-fecund lust, her body glory-blooming like a flower amidst those trunks and branches going up forever. It was slower this time, and she gave herself over to him completely. Let her thoughts empty out, refilling her brain with only the good, desperate sounds Silas was making in the dark and her own, rising to meet his.

After, they both fell into light, easy sleeps.

———

When they woke up, Kasey checked her phone, praying that her mom had left a message with some good news about something bad happening to Roy.

Five missed calls from her mom.

One voicemail.

Grayson had called Silas, and Silas was down by the water, folding the blanket and talking to his brother. Kasey was up by the truck now, trying to stop her finger from shaking so she could tap the voicemail button.

Kasey Jo ... it's your mama. I'm home now. I love you ... so much. Your daddy used to sing the chorus of "Moonshadow" by Cat Stevens to you when you were a baby. Remember I told you that? He'd press his nose against your little nose ... moonshadow ... it doesn't sound as good when I sing it. Remember how I used to try to sing it to you when you were little? Remember we'd sing it whenever we got MoonPies, and it made us happy and sad at the same time? I'm so glad you're getting away from here. Run, baby girl. You can do anything, be anything; you're going to do amazing things, and don't let anyone ever, ever make you feel any differently. You'll never be totally alone, because mamas should always look after their babies, even when they're gone. Your daddy loved you so much, and the way we love you is a special love that nothing and no one can ever take away—do you hear me, Moonshadow? I mean it. It's different than anything else in this whole wide world, and don't you ever forget it. I'm so sorry I—

The voicemail cut off. Her mom had been crying hard at the end. Kasey hollered Silas's name into the night.

———

She told him to stop before he turned up the driveway.

"You have to leave me here," she said, getting out of the truck.

"Hell no, Kasey! You're not going in there by yourself. Get back in."

Kasey lied and told him she needed to get right home because her mom was pissed, but she didn't tell him about *moonshadow*. That it was her and her mama's code word. They'd never had to use it in any real situation, and it started as a joke.

If I ever need you to help me get out of a conversation, I'll say, "Moonshadow."

Once, Kasey's mom picked her up from school in fifth grade, and some kids in class had been talking about zombies and how sometimes they take the form of people you know, and it'd scared Kasey so much that when she got to her mom's car, she told her mom to tell her something only *she* would know, something her zombie mom would never be able to figure out. Her mom said *Moonshadow* and smiled at her, easing her fears.

"Silas. I have to go in there by myself, but I swear I'll call you as soon as I can. It's just me and my mom. Roy's not here!" she said. Maybe. She didn't know where Roy was and she didn't care, unless Roy was dead. "I need to talk to my mom. She didn't show up tonight and I'm mad at her about it and she's pissed at me now and we'll probably have one of our fights like we always do...like sisters," Kasey said.

"Ah...I don't want you walking the rest of the way by yourself, though. Get back in. I'll drive you up," he said, leaning over and opening the door. Kasey slammed it closed.

"Silas! I love you. I'll call you soon—I mean it. *Very* soon! Please."
She started down the driveway toward the house.

Running.

Faster now.

"Kase! Kasey!"

She didn't turn around.

When she reached the house, Kasey ran past her daddy's truck, which was now wrecked. The front bumper was completely smashed, and the back wheel was sticking out in a way that a wheel shouldn't stick out.

It didn't matter.

She had to find her mom.

And she did.

Bloody on the kitchen floor with Roy standing over her. Her mom looked dead, but maybe she wasn't? She was pale and not moving. Maybe she was just unconscious? Kasey didn't even look for a gun or a knife in Roy's hand. She jumped on him and punched, clawed, bit, told him she was going to kill him. He growled it back to her. Told her he was going to kill her like he wanted to kill her mother. Like he wished he could kill all the whores on earth.

Where was her phone? She needed to call an ambulance. Not the police.

Her mom had told her never to call the police, because they weren't on a woman's side in cases like these. They'd find a way to blame her for everything. There wasn't even a woman on the force; it was all men.

Men could never understand. Men thought this was okay.

Fucking Earls.

Silas wasn't like that, though. No.

Maybe Silas was still at the end of the driveway?

Maybe Silas would hear her if she screamed?

She opened her mouth to let it out right as Roy knocked her off him and sent her flying. She felt the back of her head dent the wall, and she was falling asleep. She couldn't see, couldn't move.

Or maybe she was dying?

Maybe this was what it felt like. Maybe she'd meet her mama somewhere in the quiet, static dark. Somewhere in the moonshadow.

Kasey's body tingled and shook; the inside of her thighs warmed wet when her bladder let go. She tried to open her eyes, but they wouldn't work anymore. She heard Roy telling her not to tell anyone what happened. Didn't she? He said if she did, he'd kill her. Didn't he? She couldn't hear anything anymore. She fell inside of herself so deeply she kept right on going through the floor into cold layers of black nothing.

———

When she came to, Kasey saw her mom across the floor and Roy passed out next to an empty bottle of whiskey. She crawled to her mom and touched her arm. It was warm. Wasn't it? She checked for a pulse and found none. She checked again. And again. Kasey took her mama's head and held it to her chest, rocking back and forth as quietly as she could in silent agony for fear of waking Roy, who was only a few feet away from them. He could wake up at any moment, and when he did, he'd kill her too.

Or she could kill him.

If she could get up quietly enough and grab a knife. Be sure to stab him somewhere that would kill him immediately so she wouldn't only make him mad.

Run, baby girl.

Run, baby girl.

Kasey knew what she was feeling was total powerlessness—a potent, real fear. A fear more real than any other emotion she'd ever felt. A fear as real as a stopped heart. A fear as real as death. She kissed her mom's cooling forehead, sobbed with her hand covering her mouth to keep quiet. That real fear was what moved her body to get up and wash off, change clothes.

Run, baby girl.

Go to her bedroom for her backpack.

She filled it with what she could, including clothes, toiletries, and the six hundred dollars she'd saved from tutoring. She went to her mom's bedroom and took the money she knew she kept in a box of tampons at the top of the closet—five thousand dollars. She put the picture of her as a baby held between her parents and the picture of her daddy that she sometimes kept in the truck in her backpack. She checked the container of poisoned black-eyed peas in the fridge, and they hadn't been touched. She took it and her mom's cell phone from the table too.

One last look at her on the kitchen floor.

Roy made me an orphan. My mom is dead and I have no one. Alone. I'm all alone.

Never.

Run, baby girl.

She'd never come back to that farmhouse.

Never.

———

Kasey threw the black-eyed peas in the trash and walked the miles to Caroline's trailer in a daze. She tapped on Caro's bedroom window, hoping she was in there sleeping and hadn't stayed over at Ada's. Kasey probably didn't believe in God anymore after what she'd just seen on her kitchen floor, but there was a small godlike mercy when Caro opened the window.

"Kase. Oh no. What's wrong? Silas told us—" Caro said as Kasey climbed inside.

"My mom...I got in a big fight with my mom, but we made up.

It's fine now. I need to go to sleep," Kasey said. She hadn't seen herself, but her face must've been a hot, crying, snotty mess.

She crawled into bed with Caroline, thinking that she'd die because she probably had a concussion. She wasn't supposed to sleep, but she'd never been this tired in her life. She hoped it wouldn't scar sweet Caroline forever if she found her dead in the morning. She used up her last prayers praying for her mama and Caro as she sank into the black again.

———

When Angie didn't show up for work, Duke had been the one to tell Kasey that she needed to file a missing person report. She was too scared to tell anyone what she'd seen, what really happened; she was too scared of what Roy would do. He'd told her not to tell.

So she went along with it.

She didn't know what Roy had done with her mom's body. Duke had taken Kasey to the police station, and Mimi had been there with them too. After Kasey lied to Grandma Mimi and told her she'd fallen off a rope swing and hit her head and wanted to make sure she didn't have a concussion or anything, Mimi took her to the hospital so they could take a look. No concussion, but Kasey's heart rate was elevated, and her blood pressure was high. The doctor joked that she was too young to have high blood pressure and suggested she get some extra rest. As he said it, Kasey pictured her mom's lifeless body.

Eternal rest.

———

It was three days later when Angie was found downstream from the farmhouse. Her body was bloated and beaten up, as she likely went over a few falls and got snagged on the rocks. It was quickly ruled an accidental death. Roy told the police she'd taken the boat out alone after getting off work and never came back. He said he saw the boat floating out there, empty. He explained away his scratches and bruises by saying he'd gotten in a fight in a bar in Adora Springs.

—

After the funeral, when Kasey was leaving the bathroom alone, Roy came out of the hallway and pulled her inside the bathroom again, locked the door.

"Mama called me. She left me a voicemail. The police will know you're lying," she said. Her voice was barely there and shaking, but she didn't care. The fear of being locked in a bathroom with him was eclipsed by her hatred. She wanted him to kill her now; then at least he'd get arrested. He wouldn't be able to lie his way out of both murders.

"If you tell anyone about that voicemail or what you saw, not only will I kill you, but I'll kill your pretty friends out there too. I swear to God I will, and I know you believe me now," Roy said, like a scripted cartoon villain. Kasey felt as if she'd slipped into another dimension that night on the kitchen floor, and now she was stuck in this nightmare. "It's not just me you'll have to deal with. I know everybody in this town. Trust me—they've made sure this will not fall back on me. They owe me too much."

Kasey boldly walked around Roy without saying a word. She unlocked the bathroom door and stepped into the bright hallway.

She called the woman who ran the internship in New York and told her that her mom had died unexpectedly and she no longer had housing. She asked if there was any possible way for her to come up to the city early. She'd do anything—work anywhere, sleep on anyone's floor if she had to. The woman let her know there were some students who were in hard situations like hers and emergency dorms were available.

Kasey cried so hard thanking her that the woman told her to let her know as soon as she was safe in the city.

———

That night after taking a long walk around Goldie and having dinner and pie at Ada's, with Rosemarie and Caro too, Kasey asked Silas to take her for a ride. They drove out of town and back into it, talking about how things would be totally different now that her mom was dead, but Silas said she could stay at the Castelow lake house or their B and B anytime she came back home. Nothing felt real and Kasey was numb. Desperate to feel *something*, she asked him to take her to their spot and they touched in the dark again until they both felt good. Both of them crying at the shock of everything and hanging on to each other afterward.

She told Silas to drop her off at Caro's because she was sleeping there again. She kissed him and told him she loved him, that she'd love him forever. He returned her kisses and said the same.

Once he drove away, she walked past Caro's trailer down to the lake, threw her mom's phone in the water, and hers too. She walked to the bus station in her dad's *Gremlins* T-shirt and bought a ticket to New York. When she got on that bus, she put her iPod earbuds in and turned up "Wide Open Spaces."

She'd call Silas when she was safe in the city. She'd call Rosemarie and Ada and Caroline too. They'd be so mad at her, but she'd sneakily left them letters so they wouldn't think she was missing. She left Silas's next to the black wooden bear at the lake house. Rosemarie's, tied up with the lilac sundress she'd borrowed last month, and left on her doorstep. Ada's, underneath the windshield wiper of her pink car. Caro's, peeking out from underneath the trailer's ladybug rug.

Maybe if she and her mom had run away a long time ago, everything would be different, but it was too late. *Run, baby girl.* Kasey cried with her head against the warm bus window until Goldie and everything in it was gone gone gone gone gone gone gone gone gone gone gone gone gone gone gone gone gone gone gone gone gone gone gone gone gone gone gone gone gone gone gone gone gone gone gone gone gone gone gone gone gone gone gone gone gone gone gone gone gone gone.

2019

27

CAROLINE

In the hospital, Caroline dreamt she was married to Beau, not Trey. She and Beau had a baby, and Beau was holding the baby up in the air, swooping it back down. He put his arm around Caro and touched her cheek. He kissed her softly and called her *Muffin Mix*, and he held their baby's little foot in his big hand.

When she woke up in a regular room, her grandma was sitting in the chair right next to her bed, knitting and watching a cooking show. Mimi told her she'd said Beau's name more than once in her sleep.

"One time, it was so breathy I thought I'd teleported into my romance novel, Ladybug," Mimi said, motioning her head down at her lap, where a glossy paperback sat. Caro looked at it. The woman on the cover had red hair like hers, blowing in the wind. The man's face was hidden. He was kissing her neck. The woman was Caroline and the man turned into Trey. He put his arms around Caro's neck and started squeezing. Caroline sat up and gasped. She couldn't remember how long she'd been in a coma. Was it only one day? Someone told her that, but who? Those words, *in a coma*, on top of all the pain medicine running rivers through her blood and the strange, new surroundings of the hospital were creating a distress signal in her body.

Her grandma put her knitting down and reached out to touch her. "What do you need, honey? Some more water? I'll call the nurse," her grandma said, taking her hand.

"No...no. Sorry. I'm fine. I think I was half-asleep...still dreaming. I'm okay now," Caro said, taking a deep breath. She told herself she was okay now, safe. She had murky memories of being in the ICU. Of Rosemarie, Ada, and Kasey coming in and out. Of her grandma and possibly her mother too. She asked Mimi about that.

"Yes. She was here. She couldn't stay, but she was here. You talked to her. Does it feel like everything's okay with the baby? I love that baby so much. I've been talking to her while you've been sleeping, you know," Mimi said, winking at her.

"How do you know it'll be a girl?" Caro asked. She put her hand on her stomach. It seemed like magic how she could *feel* the flash of life inside of her now that she knew it was there. She had no clue she was pregnant until she woke up in the ICU. *Four weeks.*

She wasn't like her mother. Caro knew she'd be a *real* mom to her baby; she'd do anything to protect her baby.

Her baby.

The baby.

She didn't have time to talk to her grandma about the baby being a boy or a girl right now. First, she had to protect it from Trey. He'd kill it. He'd take it.

I have to protect the baby.

Grandma Mimi continued talking.

"Where's Trey?" Caro asked, interrupting her.

"I'm not sure, but you don't have to worry about him. He's not coming up here right now. Silas will let us know what's going on soon."

"Is he in jail?" Caro asked. Her bottom lip quivered quick. "Does he know about the baby?"

"No, and he's saying all this was an accident, honey. I don't want you making yourself upset over it, though. You're safe here. We don't have to worry about him right now. All we need to worry about is getting you better. And no, he doesn't know about the baby, and we'll keep it that way for as long as we can," Mimi said confidently.

Caro wanted to believe her, but Mimi didn't know what Trey was capable of. She hadn't seen the look in his eyes. Caro tried to reach her arm out to touch Mimi's face, but couldn't. She couldn't move like she wanted, and it hurt too much to think of trying again.

"Remember, day after tomorrow is the surgery on your shoulder," Mimi said, triggering Caro's memory. It was broken, her shoulder. They'd told her that yesterday. A fuzzy calendar flipped in her mind.

Yesterday was Tuesday. Today is Wednesday. It was Monday afternoon when I was at the house and Trey came home.

"I don't want him to know about the baby. He'll kill me if he gets the chance," Caro said. "*When* he gets the chance." The panic and the urge to cry had flown over. If Caro looked up, she could see it—a toy plane gliding through the blue and clouds of where the hospital ceiling should've been. It flew toward the door and slammed into it, crashed to the floor. A puff of black smoke sputtered from the back end and it disappeared.

She could also see Trey standing over her with both hands holding her hair, his fingernails pressing her skull, slamming her head into the concrete. Telling her he'd kill her because she was *so fucking stupid and hardheaded*, and he was *so fucking tired* of her.

"Not gonna happen, Ladybug. No way in hell, so stop that. All you need to think about is yourself and my precious great-grandbaby girl. I'm knitting this pink blanket for her," Mimi said.

There was a vase of sunflowers next to Caro's bed, another on the table underneath the TV. Another big one on the table outside the bathroom. A box of cupcakes from the bakery was on that table too. On top of her on the hospital bed, a soft, fluffy sunshine-yellow blanket. Ada Plum had worked her magic on the room.

Caro lifted her left arm—the one she could move freely—and touched her face.

"Careful, honey," her grandma said.

"Can I take this off and see it? Can I see my face?" Caro asked, gently touching the gauze. Her chin, her cheek, the spot underneath her eye that hurt so much. The urge to cry flew over again. The toy plane soared up and through the window next to them. The curtain blew in and out like the whole world was taking deep breaths. Caro looked at the sunset-sky. The horizon, an orange scratch. "Is this a bruise? A cut?" Caro pointed to her mouth and the skin underneath it that was unwrapped. Touched tenderly and winced.

"Both. He hurt you everywhere. He broke your bones. Tried his best to squeeze the life out of you, but he failed. Let's give your face a few more days to heal. No point in you looking at it right now and getting yourself worked up. We'll fix it, so give it time. Let's eat a cupcake. You know Ada has filled this place with flowers and treats. You should see the nurses' station. Well, you can't even *see* the nurses' station for all the sunflowers Ada hauled in here. The girls will be back in the morning. They've barely left your side. I had to *make* them go home and get some rest," Grandma Mimi said.

She pulled the cupcake box off the table and moved her chair closer to Caro's bed. Mimi poured some water from the pitcher into a cup and put a straw in it, held the straw to Caro's lips and she drank.

2004

28

The morning after Kasey left Goldie, Grandma Mimi handed Caroline a letter, telling her she'd found it under the ladybug rug.

Caroppenheimer,

I know how mad you'll be at me, but I also know that deep down (after you get over being mad!!) you'll understand. I don't want you to worry about me! I ditched my phone. I'll get a new one soon. When I'm settled, I will call you and check my email. I want to hear all your news! All your new pies and whether you ever work up the nerve to tell Beau how you feel about him! (You totally should, by the way! It's clear the boy is in love with you too, Caro!)

Tell Grandma Mimi thank you for everything. Please let her know I'm okay.

I love you, Caro. So much. I'm sorry we didn't get to do more together before I had to say goodbye.

RACK forever.
Kase

Caro was hanging at Rosemarie's until her diner shift. Ada had just taken a tray of fries out of the oven, and Rosemarie was digging into a small carton of chocolate ice cream with a big spoon. She let her dog lick some off her fingers.

"Roses, stop! Dogs can't have chocolate ice cream," Ada said to her.

"Oh, right," Rosemarie said, snatching her hand back and wiping the rest on her shorts. She breathed in and out—sad and dazed.

"Ada Plum, if you're eating frozen French fries, we're definitely in a *major* crisis. I mean, I'm a mess too, but we've *got* to hold it together," Caro said. Ada had her head in Rosemarie's fridge and didn't respond until she'd found the bottles of ketchup, mayo, and mustard.

"Kasey's gone and it calls for junk. Rosemarie, does your mom have Maldon salt? The big flakes? Where's the garlic powder? I can't find it," Ada said, putting the condiments on the middle of the kitchen table.

Rosemarie pointed to the cabinet that held the spices, told her everything was on the second shelf.

They watched Ada get the spices down and put the fries on a platter. She seasoned everything and put it on the table in front of them. Rosemarie scooped the ice cream and fed herself, then Caro. Ada made them plates and stole a spoonful of ice cream to dip one of her fries in.

"Like, what are we supposed to do now? Seriously. I don't know what to do," Ada said. She was eating and crying. Caro started eating and crying too. Rosemarie leaned down to pet her dog. Petting and crying.

"I wish we'd been able to kill that bastard. Maybe everything could've been different, and Angie wouldn't have gone out on the boat," Caro said.

"Do you *really* think that's how she died?" Rosemarie asked them. Caro didn't know what she thought.

"Everyone else might've lied about that, but Kasey? She wouldn't lie about it. Not to us," Ada said.

"Right, but it doesn't make sense. Where'd Roy go?" Rosemarie said.

Ada shrugged and got up to grab a box of tissues from the hall closet. She sat and snatched three out for them.

"He left right after the funeral. I don't know. He's into so much shady shit, but Kasey said he'll leave her alone now that her mom's gone. She said he probably has, like, a million women with terrible taste in men lined up to be his next old lady," Caroline said, wiping her eyes. "God, I'm so tired of crying."

"So, she told us all the same thing. That she'll call us soon, and she will. I have her dorm address and everything. She hasn't fallen off the face of the earth. She just needs some time, that's all," Rosemarie said.

"Right," Ada said.

"So why do we feel so awful?" Caro asked.

No one answered.

—

When Beau was going on break, he asked Caroline if she wanted to smoke with him, and she said yes.

"That Almost Summer Pie you made is my favorite, just so you know," he said, when he was finishing his cigarette. She was still smoking. She'd never smoked a cigarette outside of his presence, and she wondered if he knew that. If she should tell him. Shouldn't she tell him *something*?

"Kase and I call that one *Beau Bramford* Pie," she said. The air was heavy and humid, like they were inside a mason jar. A storm would be blowing over the hills soon, and Caro couldn't wait for the relief. It hadn't rained since Angie died, and Caro needed Goldie to be washed clean. She wondered if it was raining in New York where Kasey was. Caro worried about Kasey being lonely already and was sad for Silas being left behind. She wondered if he'd try to go find her or if he'd be too hurt.

"Wait. Do you *really* call it that?" Beau asked.

"We do. We were talking about you when I made it for the first time."

216

"Well, thank you. I've never had a pie named after me before."

"Aha, a first timer...so you're not a virgin anymore," she said. Hot damn, these things were pouring out of her mouth with the smoke.

"Look. You've done a good job of not getting me into trouble," he said, tugging at his earlobe. It was his tell when he was feeling shy. Caro had noticed it a long time ago—first when a customer would catch him at the counter and say something kind, then later when he and Caroline started smoking together on their breaks. She noticed Beau was looking at her in a different way now too. Like she was a woman. She wasn't in high school anymore. She was still seventeen, but she was *almost* eighteen and she wasn't a baby.

Mateo was the only boy she'd ever had sex with and that was only a couple times. What she wanted was to have sex with Beau. Didn't matter when. Now? On her eighteenth birthday? A year from now? Whatever! She'd been obsessed with the idea from the moment she laid eyes on him, and she thought about it every night when she was going to sleep. He was the kind of guy who made her feel *more* like a girl, and those were the kinds of guys she liked. She imagined the two of them having sex in his truck. Her, smacking her hand against the steamy glass like Kate Winslet did in *Titanic*. Could he guess what she was thinking about? Maybe if she blinked Morse code?

"Beau—" she said with a lot of breath, letting her eyelashes flutter.

"So, I have a surprise," he said at the same time. "Since Myrtle's in Alabama visiting her brother and can't be here to do it herself, she told me to give you something. Hang on." He got up and jogged inside the diner. Caro watched his cute little butt. The air smelled like rain.

When he came back, he put a brown envelope on the table between them.

"What is this?" Caro asked, touching it. She French inhaled again and put her cigarette out.

"You've gotta open it up to see. Don't make me do all the work. I'm the one who went in there and got it for you," he said.

Caro picked up the envelope and pulled out the slip of paper inside.

It was a check from Myrtle's Diner to her in the sum of thirty-five thousand dollars—the exact amount she needed for pastry school. She gasped and asked Beau what it was again.

"Someone who wants to stay a secret gave you the money. We were gonna give it to you as a graduation present the night of the ceremony, but I told Myrtle to wait a little bit after I saw you in the alley. Figured I'd let you sober up first. Then Kasey's mom and everything...it's been rough, I know...and I was gonna wait until later tonight when we were closing up, but I can tell you've been crying, and I know how much you miss your friend already, and I thought this would cheer you up, is all. You can go to pastry school in Adora Springs without worrying about the money, and you can focus on the next dessert you're gonna name after me," Beau said, smiling at her.

"Someone *gave* me this money? Just like that? Do you know who? Is it Louie and Pete? Please tell me who it is, Beau." Caro kept staring at the check and blinking to make sure she was reading it right. That she wasn't adding zeros that weren't there. That she wasn't hallucinating— it *really* was her first and last name on that line. Things had been so dark lately it felt crazy and stupid to let in all this light.

"Miss Myrtle's sworn to secrecy. You wanted a fairy godmother, girl. Now you got you one," he said.

"This can't be real," she said, shaking her head.

"Oh, it's real, Muffin Mix. We can run right down to the bank together and put it in your account if you want."

"Is that what I should do?" she asked. She'd never seen a check for this much money in her life. She should call her grandma and tell her before she did anything. She told Beau that.

"All right. Call Miss Mimi and then let's go prove that the check is for real American dollars," Beau said. "We'll take my truck so we don't get soaked." He glanced up as a fat raindrop smacked the table. Beau looked at it, then at her, still smiling with his whole face like *he* was the one whose dream was coming true.

2019

29

ROSEMARIE

Rosemarie had never 100 percent believed that Kasey's mom died in a boat accident, but Kasey's story hadn't budged over the last fifteen years, and none of the girls dared bring it up to her. So, when Kasey finally admitted that Roy had threatened to kill them if she ever told the truth, all the blurry puzzle pieces fell into place.

Kasey also told them Roy died almost exactly a year ago in Bluewood, a hundred miles away. Liver cancer. His mother found her online and contacted her, let Kasey know Roy left the farmhouse to her. His mother also told her that she had him buried in the small cemetery near the property where Angie was buried too, but Kasey had never been to either of their graves. Kasey knew Roy only left her the farmhouse as a fucked-up *thank-you* for never telling anyone the truth about what he'd done to her mom, and it was the *one* good and decent thing he'd done with his shitty life. It'd taken Taylor getting married for her to decide to come back and go step inside the house for the first time since that night her mom died.

They were still sitting in Ada's minivan outside of the hospital. Kasey apologized for keeping everything secret for so long, but Rosemarie stopped her.

"You did what you had to do, Kasey. That was too much put on you. You're an amazing, strong woman, and I will pinch you hard if you say sorry one more time," Rosemarie said, pretending to squeeze Kasey's arm.

"*You're* an amazing, strong woman, and so are you, Ada. I *literally* can't imagine my life without y'all in it. You're my family, and I don't have another one. Even when we're apart, y'all stay right here," Kasey said, touching her heart.

"Oh, I love you so much," Ada said, taking Kasey's face in her hands and kissing her mouth. "Kase, we all thought part of the reason why you left was because you were mad at us for not killing Roy that night. For not making it happen."

"No! Why in the world would I be *mad* at you for something like that? We were teenagers! *Teenage* girls planning a murder!" Kasey said.

"Well, now let's be *grown-ass* women planning a murder," Rosemarie said.

"Wait. Seriously? Last time—" Ada started.

"Last time we didn't know what we were doing, and *this* time we will," Rosemarie said.

"And *this* time we would definitely all be tried as adults, and my boys would have to come visit me in prison," Ada said.

"That's not going to happen. We're all too pretty to go to prison, so that alone...and also, we won't get caught. *Also*, your family is superrich, and superrich people rarely have to go to prison. It's the reason Trey will never pay for this unless we make sure he does," Rosemarie said.

Kasey's phone lit up.

"Si's going to call me soon, but right now he says they had to let Trey go. The judge denied the restraining order because Trey said she was lying about everything. He says she's mentally ill and needs help," Kasey said after reading the text.

"Okay, good. This is good," Rosemarie said.

"Wait. Explain what's good about this!" Ada asked. She twisted her face up in confusion.

"Because we can't kill the son of a bitch if he's in jail or at the police station, can we? We need him out and now he's out. The Foxberry lawyers worked their trash magic, and now we'll work ours," Rosemarie said.

No more wasting time wondering if this was what they should do.

No more wasting time waiting around to see what would happen next.

Trey needed to die.

"Tomorrow. That's when it needs to happen. Seriously, Caro may lose the baby if she's overwhelmed with stress, thinking Trey's coming up here to kill her. He can come visit her if he wants. He's a free man right now," Kasey said.

"That's probably what he'll do, but that's perfect too. Mimi will be here all day tomorrow, and we'll ask her to let us know when Trey comes. When he does, Kasey, you'll bump into him and invite him to dinner at the farmhouse tomorrow night so you can talk to him. Let him know this was a big misunderstanding and now that you're back in Goldie, you want to get to know him better," Rosemarie said. "Ada, what's he order when he comes into the restaurant?"

"Usually pasta. Last time he got my mushroom lasagna. He loved it so much he ordered an extra to take home," Ada said.

"My dad still grows psychedelic mushrooms, so we'll make it with those. Spike his Foxberry Bourbon with LSD I'll get from my dad too. Let's make sure he's *really* tripping. Which pie is his favorite? It's pretty poetic if we make him a poison pie too for what he did to our pie queen," Rosemarie said.

"Pecan," Ada said.

"Would he taste mushrooms in it?" Kasey asked.

"Not if I use enough sugar, right?" Ada said.

"Use a *lot* of sugar," Rosemarie said.

"He won't taste the LSD?" Ada asked.

"No," Rosemarie said. "And all these questions...does that mean you're not against this idea?" Ada had freaked out so much last time that if she didn't want to help, Rosemarie wasn't going to try to force her. Although it would be easier with her on board, Rosemarie and Kasey could do this alone if they had to.

"I'm not against the idea! Obviously I think he's a total piece of shit who deserves this. Not only for what he *could* do to her in the future, but for what he's already done! It's just...it's just that everything went completely sideways last time, and I want to make sure—"

"That's not going to happen again," Rosemarie said, interrupting her.

"Okay, so what—we're gonna wrap him up in a tarp and dump him in the lake?" Ada asked. "We've gotta have more than one country song to talk us through this."

"Actually, there are a *ton* of outlaw country songs about killing people, so we're plenty covered," Rosemarie said.

"Trey doesn't know how to swim," Kasey said. "What if he 'drowns'?" Kasey made a show of her finger quotes around the word *drowns*.

"They'll still check his blood for alcohol or drugs. They'll be able to tell by looking at his lungs or whatever. I may not be a master murderer but I do watch a lot of *Dateline*, y'all," Ada said. "Can't we plant some of the LSD in his car or something to lock that down?"

Rosemarie got chills and looked at her, impressed. "How much *Dateline* do you watch?"

"A *lot*," Ada said.

"Damn, girl. That's brilliant. I'll do that," Kasey said.

"I'll get it all from my dad and he won't blink. And don't tell any men about this right now. Even your handsome Castelow boys. Not yet. We'll figure out the rest later. I don't care how it happens...at all. He's gotta go," Rosemarie said, shaking her head. Her phone vibrated with another call from her doctor and she shut it off. She was so tired. None of these things would matter when Trey was dead. Everything would be better. Caroline would be free and they'd figure their way out of it. "There's probably no end to the people who want Trey Foxberry dead, to be honest. They'll have no shortage of suspects. Tomorrow morning we'll meet at the farmhouse and start cooking," she said.

Kasey's phone rang and she silenced it.

"Who's that?" Ada asked.

"Devon. I'll tell him everything later. I mean, about my mom," Kasey said. "I love him. So much. But there's no room in my head for him right now. Not until after tomorrow."

"Are we sure we have to do this so soon?" Ada asked.

"Ada, we don't have time to lose, and I wouldn't blame you if you didn't want to be a part of this. You have so much more at stake. Do *not* do this if you don't want to," Rosemarie said. "I'm serious."

"She's right. Please don't," Kasey said.

"Well..." Ada said, looking out the window. She closed her eyes.

"Well, what?" Rosemarie asked after giving her some time.

"Well, if I don't do it, who's gonna make the lasagna? And Caroline certainly can't do it, so who's gonna make the pie?" Ada said, rolling her eyes as if she were giving them the easiest answers to the dumbest questions ever asked.

Rosemarie and Ada stopped to pick up Basie at Rosemarie's parents' place, then Ada dropped them both off at Leo's. He'd made a big pot of chicken noodle soup and biscuits too. Rosemarie's appetite had been funky and sometimes nonexistent, but that didn't stop Leo from trying.

"How are you real?" she asked him, sitting at the kitchen table.

"I like taking care of you. You know that," he said. He took his glasses off and rubbed his eyes, put them back on. Basie pawed at him, and he gave her some sweet talk and love.

"You also know I can take care of myself, but gimme that," Rosemarie said, reaching for a biscuit and putting an unholy amount of butter on it.

"You're welcome."

"Thank you, Leopold," Rosemarie said with a full mouth. Maybe she could live on Leo's biscuits and not have to worry about her appetite anymore.

"So that's it? Trey walks away like none of this happened?" Leo asked.

"Y'know what? Here lately, whenever I think of Trey, I think of Odetta singing 'God's Gonna Cut You Down.' God's gonna cut Trey Foxberry down—trust me. It's what happens in this world eventually, even when it takes too long." She drank some water, ate some more biscuit. She also swallowed all she couldn't tell Leo yet, even though she wanted to.

"*I* want to kill him. So, I can't imagine how someone feels who, you know, actually kills people or has ever been in a fight or isn't, like, a peaceful, bookish musician," Leo said. The hair on Rosemarie's arms stood up when he said the word *kill*.

"You wouldn't last a minute in prison," she said, petting her arm without being too weird about it, and eating more. It was the best food she'd ever tasted.

"Watch it. You're dangerously close to hurting my feelings."

"Come here." Rosemarie motioned to him, and he leaned into her. She rubbed her nose against his and kissed him.

———

Later, after they smoked a bowl and sang and recorded two songs, they went to Leo's bedroom and moved together, slick and breathless in the dark. She lay on his chest afterward with Basie at her feet and listened to his heartbeat. It was the only way she could fall asleep lately. It was where she felt the safest.

Trey would die, but he wasn't special. Everyone died.

Rosemarie would die too—possibly soon.

Being in Leo's arms was where she felt good, even when she knew she didn't have much time left.

Even when she knew her body was soaking up her cancer like a sponge now that it'd returned. Only Esme, Esme's oncologist brother, and Leo were aware.

It was three years ago when she was first diagnosed, got the double mastectomy and reconstruction surgery. It was three years ago when Ada, Caro, and Kasey had come out to Seattle to be with her. Leo had been there too, barely missing meeting Esme for the first time because she was off doing reshoots in Vancouver.

It wasn't long after that when Esme was in Portland and Leo had come to Seattle again, fresh from divorcing Annie. Back then, Leo got in bed with Rosemarie and pulled her on him just like this, holding her, protecting her from the rest of the world. Making her feel better. Leo had taken time off from touring and made his way back to Goldie because Rosemarie had returned to die. And no matter when or where they were, like always, Leo's music and keen light never failed to keep the darkest dark away.

2004

30

Roses,

I know you'll find me first. It's who you are and I love who you are. I fully expect the first email in my inbox to be from you and you won't let me down. You and I are going to be on opposite sides of the world for a bit, and then, opposite sides of the country. I miss you already. I miss the sunny patches of your magical house and feeding treats to Jerry Garcia while we lounge on your trampoline in our bathing suits and sunglasses, drinking clinky lemonade like Hollywood starlets.

Please write me and tell me EVERYTHING about EVERYWHERE you're going in the world and EVERYTHING you're feeling. And! Let me know what Sparrow says after you tell her how you feel because I know you're going to do that before you leave, because I know you. I'm sorry I had to leave like this and I love you madly.

RACK forever.
Kase

To: KaseyJosephineFritz@gmail.com
From: RosemarieCloverKingston@gmail.com
Subject: Yep

226

Kase,

Yep. I came right back inside after I got your letter and sat at my computer to email you. I'm pissed you're gone, but I understand. I wish I wasn't so mature!!! God has cursed me with this advanced brain and heart!!! And since I'm so ahead of Ada and Caro when it comes to emotional intelligence, the price I pay is totally getting why you can't be in Goldie right now. Of course you can't. I won't even pretend to imagine what you're going through and all I care about is that you're safe and doing EXACTLY what you need to do.

I'm praying that your heart (spirit! mind!) gets everything it needs in your grief, Kase. I am grieving with you across the miles, holding your hand.

I will most definitely write you from the other side of the world/ country. Please write me back sometime. The sooner the better. I won't tell you what Sparrow says unless you write me back. How's that for incentive? (I haven't told her yet, but I will!!!)

Love you so so so much.

RACK forever,

Roses

——

Rosemarie and Sparrow were making out in the conversation pit, and when they took a breather, Rosemarie went to the kitchen to get two peaches and handed one to Sparrow.

"I'm going to miss you a lot when we leave Goldie," Rosemarie said to her. Sparrow had gotten an athletic scholarship to a big university three hours away.

"When do y'all leave for the mission trip?" Sparrow asked, taking a bite of the fruit and wiping her mouth. The sun was lighting up her eyes—flickers of green jasper.

"Two weeks."

"I'm going to miss you a lot too, nerd," Sparrow said and kissed her. "See? Now my lips taste like peaches too."

"I love you. Do you know that? Like, I love you the way people who are dating love each other. I love you the way you *may* love Frankie—I don't know. Do you love Frankie?" Rosemarie said.

It felt like a wild cricket was hopping around in her stomach when she said this, but she said it anyway. She was proud of herself for it. The windows were open and she was starting to sweat. She was thirsty. So thirsty. She bit her peach again for the juice.

"I know you love me," Sparrow said.

"Good."

"I love kissing you and hanging out with you. Like, so much. Have you told anybody about this?" Sparrow asked, pointing down as if the couch were their secret.

Rosemarie shook her head and looked at Sparrow's pointing finger, trying not to cry.

"I'm going to miss you *so* much," Sparrow said, stepping out of the conversation pit. She went to look at one of the picture frames hanging by the bookshelf and turned to ask Rosemarie where she and her family were in that one.

"California," Rosemarie said.

———

Later, after going to the gas station for a cherry slushie and stopping by Myrtle's with Ada to visit Caro on her break, Rosemarie went to Leo's to swim. She was wearing a teeny lavender bikini underneath her clothes, and Leo gave her a bright wolf whistle when he saw it. He took his shirt off and dove into the water like an arrow, barely making a splash.

"I'll be reporting you to the police for harassment, just so you know," Rosemarie said when he came up for air. The water was tinted orange in the sunset light. She dove in after him.

"Forgive me, Kingston. You do look amazing, though. Congrats on that," Leo said, shoving off with his feet and floating on his back. Rosemarie loved seeing his no-glasses face. It was like seeing him naked, which she also loved. She'd seen Sparrow half-naked, but never all at once.

She didn't want to think about Sparrow, so she thought about Leo instead.

"Leopold, am I your girlfriend?" Rosemarie asked. She backstroked to where he was and floated.

"Hmm. I don't think so."

"You don't *think* so?"

Leo flipped and swam to the edge of the pool. Rosemarie watched his back muscles; she loved how his long body moved. He climbed out and sat dripping, kicked his feet.

"You're in love with Sparrow, Ro. I mean, obviously I know that."

Soon, Rosemarie and Leo were going to be spending every waking moment together for the entire summer before he went to school in Boston. They rarely argued, and even when they did, it was usually something small that could blow away like a bubble. Rosemarie didn't want to get in any sort of minor disagreement with Leo right now or ever. Her relationship with Leo was so pure, precious, and easy it had to work smoothly or her whole life would be thrown out of orbit. Kasey was gone now; Kasey's mom was gone forever. Life could rumble off the tracks at any minute, so yes, everything with Leo *had* to remain smooth. Rosemarie depended on him too much.

He was squinting in the sun, avoiding her eyes.

"It's...obvious that I love *you* too, Leo," Rosemarie said gently.

"Right." He nodded, refusing to look at her. "Just don't let her mistreat you or, like, break your heart or whatever."

"I won't." She thought of how hot she felt confessing her feelings to Sparrow earlier in the afternoon compared to the coolness coming off her in the water now. She wanted to remember everything, even the things that hurt, so she could tell Kasey all of it like she promised. "What about Claire?" Rosemarie asked him. Claire was a girl from church whom Leo used to date, and Rosemarie didn't realize she was jealous of Claire until Leo told her Claire wasn't going on the mission trip and Rosemarie's body flooded with relief.

It was selfish to want Leo all to herself this summer, but so what? He wanted her all to himself too. It was how their relationship worked even if it didn't make sense to anyone else. It didn't have to.

"You *love* Claire," Rosemarie forced herself to say, scared of what Leo's response would be. She flipped and went underwater, swam across the pool and back again. She popped up and sat next to Leo, nudging him playfully with her shoulder.

"I only love Claire a little. I love you a lot," he said finally.

"I love you a lot, too," Rosemarie said to him, touching his wet face.

———

Rosemarie was already in her pajamas when there was a knock at the door, and it was Sparrow. Rosemarie asked her if she wanted to go outside and talk on the trampoline, and Sparrow said yeah, sure.

"What's up?" Rosemarie asked once they were out there lying down. The sky was full of stars. She couldn't stop looking up at them; Sparrow was looking up at them too.

"I was thinking maybe this should be it for us. Like, whatever this weird thing is we've been doing, I think I'm done with it. When you go to Costa Rica and when I go away to school, maybe we should leave it here in Goldie and not talk about it anymore again, like ever. Because I'm not gay, Rosemarie; I'm not. Like, I had sex with Frankie *today*. I have sex with Frankie, like, every day." Sparrow said the last part softly, and when Rosemarie looked at her, by the light of the kitchen-window glow, she saw a tear smooth down into Sparrow's ear.

"Okay," Rosemarie said. She said it again. It was all she could say. She didn't want to ask anything and she didn't want to hear any more either. After a couple minutes of quiet, Sparrow got up. The fence lock opened and closed.

—

Rosemarie cried in her bedroom with the light off, but it wasn't all because of Sparrow. It was because of Kasey and Kasey's mom and high school ending, and her aunt too. Her mom had told her earlier that her aunt's cancer was back, and she imagined her aunt dying and Rosemarie wanted everyone to stop fucking dying.

She cried because she knew she was hurting Leo and she didn't want to hurt Leo. She got her phone off the nightstand and called him. She didn't try to hide that she was crying when she told him she was sorry.

"For what, Ro? Did you think we were in a fight earlier? I didn't. It felt like we were just talking," Leo's sleepy voice said. There was a blankety muffle on his end of the line.

Rosemarie told him about her aunt and she told him about Sparrow too. When she was finished, she heard a bit of rustling and then quiet guitar strums. Leo was playing "Pink Moon" for her. She cried some more because it was so soft and pretty and she loved that song so much and it was Just So Leo for him to play it for her in the dark when she'd called him crying about the weight of being human.

"Do you want to stay on the phone together until we fall asleep? Let's stay on the phone together until we fall asleep," Rosemarie heard him say when she was nearly knee-deep in a dream.

2019

31

ADA

Thursday morning, Ada called Grandma Mimi first thing and asked her to please text or call them when Trey was up at the hospital. Mimi promised she'd do it.

Rosemarie brought the mushrooms in a little cloth bag. They were on the counter next to the sink alongside wedges of Gruyère and Parmesan cheese, a bag of mozzarella and fresh herbs. A cold bottle of white wine and a box of noodles. Butter, olive oil, a lemon, eight cloves of garlic. Laced or not, Ada wasn't skimping on taste.

"*Psilocybe ovoideocystidiata*," Rosemarie said, pointing. "This is our answer. These mixed with the LSD bourbon will make him so out of it that it'll be easy to convince him to go down by the water and get him in. The drugs will have him thinking he can swim."

"Explain this to me like I barely got a C in biology, because I barely got a C in biology," Ada said.

"They're psychedelic magic mushrooms. Eating them won't be what kills him; they'll make him high on shrooms. Like being stoned on weed, except more intense and totally different, and the odds of them turning up in an autopsy report or anything is pretty low. They're *magic*," Rosemarie said. She explained that cooking the mushrooms made them less potent, so they'd be sure to use a *lot*. "And *lysergic acid diethylamide*: LSD. For our Foxberry Bourbon–Tripping Balls Cocktail." Rosemarie held up a small glass vial of clear liquid. "Kase, you'll have a knife on you in case he tries to fight back?" she asked.

"Right. I'll flirt with him, though. I'm going to do and say everything he wants," Kasey said confidently.

"So, I'll put some in there and sprinkle some on top too. I'll use all of them with some extra sauce," Ada said about the mushrooms. "Extra sugar in the pie, just in case." She'd get the lasagna in the oven and start on the pie filling. This plan wasn't like the old plan. This was going to work. It had to work. Every time anxiety crept in, Ada visualized squashing it with a pink four-inch heel that said *this has to work* on it in a fancy script.

"I know it may be wild, but I don't have any weirdness about doing this whatsoever, do y'all? People get sick and die all the time; actual good people are *murdered* all the time. Trey doesn't get to live when other people have to die. He tried his best to *kill* Caroline and he said he'd do it. I don't have any weirdness about doing this at all," Rosemarie repeated, shaking her head. "I thought about it a lot last night. I barely slept."

"I didn't sleep a lot either," Ada said. Grayson, like most men, could sleep through anything. She didn't have to worry about disturbing him as she sat up for hours the night before with the lamp on, mindlessly scrolling through her phone. He'd only mumbled nonsense and rolled over when she got up and cleaned the coffeepot at 3 a.m., just for something to do.

"Me neither," Kasey said. "And I don't have any weirdness about it, no. We don't have a choice anymore—we don't. *Fuck* him."

"We can't wait around for something to happen," Ada said. "*Fuck* him. This will work. It will. It'll be fine." Ada had weighed everything, holding on to the belief that Rosemarie was right. The Plum family had money and good lawyers, and no one would suspect her. She was a mother, a major figure in the community. Her reputation spoke for itself. Her privilege was a shield. *This has to work.*

"*Fuck* him," Rosemarie said. "Except, no, Kasey, don't *actually* have sex with him or anything. That's crossing a line. He's disgusting. If it comes down to that, walk away. There *are* things you can't come back from, you know."

"Please don't make me puke while I'm cooking," Ada said, getting an onion from the fridge.

"That's probably the *only* thing I wouldn't do for Caro," Kasey said.

How could their mood be so light? How could they be cracking jokes and having such a good time when they were planning what they were planning? If they shouldn't do this, Ada would feel something, wouldn't she? Wouldn't she feel bad? Wouldn't she have a panic attack like she did the night Angie was killed?

She knew the Bible said, "Vengeance is mine; I will repay, saith the Lord," but she also knew that it said humans should love mercy, and killing Trey was showing Caro the mercy she needed. She knew God would forgive them for what they were about to do. His forgiveness was the only forgiveness that mattered. This was what had to be done, and doing it would right at least one thing in this crooked-ass world.

They got to work in the kitchen, and when both the pie and the lasagna were cooling under the window, Mimi texted:

> I told Trey he shouldn't be allowed anywhere near Caroline, but the police said there was nothing I could do since the judge denied the restraining order.
>   Trey said he had a right to see his wife.

He said his lawyers would get
involved if we didn't let him.
He's on his way up here now.

The girls left to go meet him.

———

The girls were all genuinely surprised when they spotted Beau(!) Bramford(!) walking across the hospital parking lot. Beau Bramford, whom none of them had laid eyes on in years. Kasey said hi and hugged him before stepping away to go upstairs to catch Trey. Ada wanted to distract Beau. *Had* to distract Beau.

"Wow, Beau! It's so good to see you back in Goldie! You're here to visit Caro? She's doing better now," Ada said, hugging him. Kasey turned around and Ada waved at her to let her know it was okay. Rosemarie stepped forward to hug Beau too.

"Okay, good. Yeah, my aunt told me Caro was in the hospital, and I've been meaning to get back anyway," Beau said. He had an unlit cigarette behind his ear. His hair was a little longer now and barely graying at the temples; his beard had some gray in it too, but not a lot. He had a pair of Wayfarers pushed on top of his head, and Ada thought of that pic of Devon that Kasey had on her phone. Devon had called twice while they were making the lasagna, and Ada had watched Kasey ignore it both times, but she texted him, promising to call soon.

"She'll be *beyond* stoked to see you, Beau," Rosemarie said.

"Honestly? One reason I came to Goldie is because I wanna kill that dude. I got a gun in the truck," Beau said. His voice was soft, but his energy was loud. "I'm serious." His aggressive little nod shook his sunglasses.

"Your aunt told you—" Rosemarie started.

"She said Trey's saying Caroline fell, but no one believes that, do they?" Beau said.

"He's up there. Trey's up there right now," Ada said.

"He's *here*? They didn't keep him locked up?" Beau asked. His voice got louder. He moved toward the hospital, but Ada reached for his arm and gently pulled him to her.

"Hey, Beau, come here. Come sit in my van. Let's talk. Plus, it's fixin' to rain. Come on," Ada said, looking up at the sky. Somewhere between the farmhouse and the hospital, the clouds had taken on an ominous dark gray hue; the air was warm as breath.

The three of them got in and Ada turned on the AC. She looked in the rearview, wanting to catch Kasey or Trey whenever one of them walked out.

"Married anybody in a Vegas drive-thru lately?" Rosemarie asked him, checking out the bare ring finger on his left hand.

"Nah. Actually, my ex has a kid with some guy in Colorado now," he said.

"Oh wow. Is that weird? I'm sorry," Ada said.

"Don't be. It's not weird. Good for her. Everybody ain't meant to be together forever and that's okay," Beau said, like some kind of country sage. He had a soothing presence; Ada had always thought that. His voice was deep and calming; he didn't waste words or energy. It was part of the reason Ada felt compelled to get him into her van when he started talking about killing Trey, because she'd never felt that hyped-up zappiness coming off him.

"True that," Rosemarie said. "I like you, Beau."

"I like you too. I'm glad I saw y'all," Beau said and paused. "Caroline *is* doing a lot better already, right?" His voice hitched and for a split second, it looked like he might cry. He blinked quickly.

"Yes. And you'll have to get in line if you want to kill Trey, because basically anyone who's not a Foxberry or in the Foxberry pocket wants that boy dead," Rosemarie said.

Ada wished she could tell Beau outright that they were taking care of it. Beau would be a good person to have in their inner circle. She also wished she could tell him that Caroline was pregnant—but sharing any of that right now would be really dumb, so Ada just smiled at him.

"Y'all trying to keep me in this minivan so I won't go up there and kill him?" Beau asked, smiling back.

"Basically. Not to protect him, to protect *you*. Although I'm sure the boys at the penitentiary wouldn't mind if you got twenty to life if it meant they got to eat your grilled cheese every day. Seriously! You made the cheese goo out perfectly, not too much and not too little. Still to this day the best grilled cheese I've ever had," Rosemarie said. Beau laughed and leaned back. He was the *anti*-Trey, all sweetness and heart. Ada might not have known him super well, but she knew that.

Beau was telling them about life in Nevada and showing them some pictures of the Toiyabe Range on his phone when Ada saw Trey in the rearview mirror. He was walking toward their side of the parking lot, and Ada kept watching him, her heart like a hammer. It was raining now.

"So, like, do you go to Vegas a lot or is that not your style? I've only been once," Rosemarie was saying when Ada gently nudged her arm. Rosemarie looked at her, then turned to see Trey. When they turned, Beau turned, and before the girls could say anything, he was out.

Rosemarie and Ada hopped out too. Beau already had Trey pressed against his truck. Beau's forearm was at Trey's throat and Trey was frozen for a second, then he shoved him off.

"Who the fu—" Trey said. "You're . . . you're the guy who used to work at the diner? Why are you here? What the hell is your problem?"

A small group of Castelow Construction guys were walking past, and once they realized what was happening, they stopped. Ada recognized two of them.

"Everything all right?" one of the guys asked.

Ada shrugged, and they came over.

"How'd you like it if I tried to kill *you*, you piece of shit?" Beau said to Trey. "Beating a woman like that—"

"How'd you like to get arrested for assault?" Trey asked him. One of the construction guys got in between the two men and wrapped his arms around Beau, moving him back. It started raining harder, and Kasey came out of the hospital, right into the chaos.

"I'll see you around, Foxberry," Beau said to him as Trey got in his truck.

"Beau, you all right?" Kasey asked him.

"I'm all right. I'm good. I'm gonna go up there. I'll see y'all soon," Beau said to them. Ada didn't know where or when they'd see Beau again, but she believed him and she liked that he said it. He jogged away from them and ducked inside the hospital.

The construction boys were gone now and so was Trey. Once all three girls were in the minivan together, Kasey told them Caro said Trey barely touched her arm when he was in her room and she freaked out and scratched him. Kasey saw those fresh scratches on Trey when she was talking to him in the hallway. He stayed out there while Kasey listened to Caro talk about how she was worried he'd try to use those scratches against her and claim that *she* tried to attack him. Kasey attempted to calm Caro down, telling her it'd all be okay. There was heat pouring off Kasey, and Ada turned the AC up.

Kasey told them the plan had changed. Tonight was tornado weather, so they'd move it to tomorrow. It'd been all over the news on the TVs inside, and as soon as she mentioned tonight for dinner, the weatherman talked about how bad it was going to be, so she asked Trey if Friday would work better. He said yes.

"I hate to change plans, but I also don't want to deal with wrestling with a tornado *and* Trey Foxberry at the same time. Plus, it'd look weird if I insisted it had to be tonight. Flexibility is key here," Kasey said, tucking her rain-wet hair behind her ears. "But I don't want to wait around to see what tricks he has up his sleeve either."

Kasey was right. If they waited ... if Trey got another chance ...

The wind was picking up; Ada craned her neck to get a good look at the sky.

"We're not spooked by changing the plan, are we? Because I'm not," Rosemarie said. "This isn't like last time."

"No, it's not. Plus, Caro's got her surgery tomorrow. She'll be out of it for most of the day. That's even better. The less she knows, the better," Kasey said.

"Was he weird about it?" Ada asked Kasey.

Kasey shook her head. "He asked if I was flirting with him," she said.

"Are you *fu*— Are you kidding me?" Ada asked, whipping around to look at her.

"Nope. He said it real quiet so no one else could hear him. I told him no, I just wanted to hear his side of the story—that was all. Give him a chance, since I don't know him or anything. Also, wasn't that a shame we never got to know each other in high school?" Kasey said, making her voice different and batting her eyelashes.

"Excellent. When it stops raining so hard, Rosemarie and I will go in there and see Caro. I bet she was so scared when Trey was here," Ada said.

"Yeah, but I told her Beau was with y'all and that helped. And Mimi never left her side," Kasey said.

"I'm so glad Beau came. He said he wants to kill Trey," Rosemarie told Kasey.

"No shit. Did you tell him to wait his turn?" Kasey asked.

"Actually, yep. We did," Ada said as the windy rain slid across the minivan like a curtain snatched back.

2004

32

Ada,

I'm sorry I didn't tell you I was leaving, but I will email you properly soon. And call! We'll see each other soon, somewhere. You're such a city girl I'm sure you can already hear NYC calling your name. Ada, you're the Princess of Goldie and that's one thing I'll love about Goldie forever. Goldie is good as long as you're in it. Although I do hate to leave like this, I know you and me will be fine. I hate that I couldn't tell you beforehand, because I know how much you love a damn schedule!!

Please tell your mom and dad thank you so much for everything. For feeding me and for letting me practically live at your house sometimes. Please tell Taylor I love her too. Tell Grayson I love him too, but wink when you say it, because that's what I'd do. He's my buddy and the two of you are going to make the prettiest babies someday, I know it.

About Silas . . . I've written him a long letter. He'll probably hate me forever, but I'll love him forever anyway. You can tell him I said that. I also told him that in the letter. I will email him or call him when I can. I promise.

Talk soon.
I love you so much.
RACK forever.
Kase

———

With Kasey gone, Ada spent a lot of time talking Silas down. The morning after he'd found Kasey's letter by the bear outside the lake house, he stopped by Ada's and asked if she knew exactly where Kasey was going, and Ada told him that she only had the address for the building her dorm would be in when school started. He said he was going to drive to NYC and go to the dorm, try to find her. Ada explained to him that Kasey wouldn't be there yet, because the internship was somewhere else. Ada figured she'd worked out something until it started. Kasey was smart and resourceful by nature and made even more so by how she had to learn to survive under such awful circumstances growing up. Ada had been surprised Kasey left Goldie without saying goodbye, but also, Ada hadn't been surprised at all that Kasey left Goldie without saying goodbye.

"I don't understand why she broke up with me. Why couldn't she tell me she was leaving?" Silas said, sitting on Ada's front porch. It was only the second time she'd seen him cry. The first was at Kasey's mom's funeral.

"Y'all will talk soon, Si. She meant it when she said she'll love you forever—trust me. Kase doesn't say stuff like that about everybody. They have to earn it," Ada said.

———

Once July rolled around, Silas started hanging out again with a girl named Lane he half dated before Kasey, and one night at the lake house when Mr. and Mrs. Castelow were out of town, Silas got the drunkest Ada had ever seen him and he called Lane *Kasey* more than once. She got so furious at him she slapped his face and left the party early. Ada and Grayson put him to bed, and he kept asking them to find Lane and tell her he was sorry. He said Kasey had run off with his virginity and his heart, and he felt like he was stuck in a *bad fucking rom-com*.

He hung out with Ada and Grayson a lot after that, and they didn't mind. Silas also picked up extra work with his dad, building decks and fences in both Goldie and Adora Springs, and Ada even gave him some work to do at the bakery sometimes, having him help her take inventory and entertain the kids when she and her mom had birthday cake tastings for persnickety parents.

———

With Rosemarie gone on the mission trip to Costa Rica, it was just the AC of RACK left in Goldie, which brought Ada and Caro closer than ever. Ada fussed at both Caroline and Taylor easily when they were in the kitchen with her while she was trying to finish dinner. Taylor's new collie puppy was circling Ada's feet, jumping up at her apron strings.

"Y'all! There are too many people and dogs in here. Caro, I'll keep an eye on your cake; step out for one second, please! Taylor, take the puppy outside and go invite one of your friends over because I made way too much potato salad again," Ada said, shooing them out. Taylor scooped the puppy up and ran to their daddy, asking him to go pick up her friend.

Caro sat outside of the kitchen.

"Good. Stay right there." Ada held her hand up at her. "You're too tall to be in here right now." She went into the fridge for the romaine lettuce and tomatoes. She'd already grilled the chicken, and next, she'd slice it for the salad.

"I still can't *believe* somebody gave me all that money for school. Myrtle won't tell me who it is, and Beau swears he doesn't know, but I can't tell if he's just a good liar," Caro said.

"I'm so excited for you, no matter who it is," Ada said, going in the knife drawer.

"So, should I remind Beau that I turn eighteen next week?" Caro asked.

Ada started chopping but stopped to check Caro's coconut cake in the oven. "Looks almost ready. And yes. Get a T-shirt that says OF LEGAL AGE right across your boobs in big red letters with an arrow pointing up at your face and another arrow pointing down at your itsy-bitsy, Caroline," Ada said. "I'm serious. Well, half-serious. Let's throw a party at the lake house and invite him, and I'll order a big *one* balloon and a big *eight* balloon, and we'll tie them to the posts out front. He won't miss that. He probably has his own countdown going."

"He does *not*," Caro said, shaking her head.

"Do you want me to throw you this party or not? You'd said something about having a small one, but let's have a huge one. Everything's been so sad lately. Let's make it happy," Ada said.

"Okay," Caro said.

"Okay!" Ada said. "Now get your bony ass in here and pull the cake out of the oven, please."

Ada was extra excited about the party since that meant she could plan two birthday parties back-to-back. First Caro's, then hers. Anything to take her mind off Kasey and Kasey's mom and her own mom was a win.

The week before, Holly Plum had drunk one and a half bottles of red and tripped over the puppy and fallen down their front steps, throwing her back out so bad she needed surgery. She'd been laid up, high on pain pills, and although they had a nurse and a maid and plenty of help if they wanted, Ada and her dad had been doing everything the maid didn't do. So, Ada had been either going to the restaurant to get meals or making them all herself in their kitchen.

She heard Grayson and Silas walk up the deck steps, meaning that soon there would be more tall people filling the room. She chopped faster.

33

KASEY

As predicted, on Thursday night there was a small tornado in Adora Springs that uprooted some old trees and tore part of the roof off a high school. On Friday morning, Kasey was out by the lake behind the farmhouse—mostly for the fresh air and distraction—moving some smaller branches away from the big ones that had fallen during the storms. The water would rise soon. She envisioned herself a few hours into the future, down there with Trey, luring him closer and closer until he was wet and wetter, going under. She wondered if she'd have to hold his head, if he'd make a lot of noise. If Nosy Nancy would be able to hear him yell. She remembered all the times Roy yelled. All the times her mom screamed. No one seemed to care.

Her mom had told her that after he finished building it, her dad said the farmhouse felt like the only farmhouse in the world. That was what her daddy meant it to be, and there *was* something hidden and untouchable about it.

That was the attitude Kasey had to keep if she was going to do this right.

"This is the only farmhouse in the world," she said aloud to no one.

She heard Silas say, "Hey, Fritz," and turned to see him walking

244

across the grass. She was relieved he wasn't in his uniform for reasons directly related to murder and prison.

"Hey, Castelow," she said. He got next to her and pulled a big broken branch out of the tree, down to the grass. She thanked him.

"I'll finish doing this. I can bring the truck back later today and take care of it for you."

"Not today, no. Don't worry about it. Later this weekend, maybe?" she said, not wanting to be too weird about it, but she definitely couldn't have Silas popping up tonight.

"All right. Sounds good," Silas said. "Do you know when you're going back to New York? You're hanging around until Caro's out of the hospital?"

"Yeah, I don't know. I have a *ton* of vacation days saved up, and I can work from home a lot and make my own hours anyway," she said. She'd had a conference call with a few of her coworkers that morning, and she was grateful everyone was so understanding about everything. She'd told them a little about the farmhouse, a little about Caroline. One coworker went above and beyond and even ordered flowers from Plum Florals and had them delivered to Caro's hospital room.

"Your man's not stressing yet?" Silas asked.

"My *man*," Kasey said with a snicker. She thought of Trey calling Devon her *man* when he'd asked about him at the wedding reception. When Trey said it, it was annoying. When Silas said it, it was cute. She'd taken her engagement ring off. When she looked down at her bare finger, Silas did too. "He's fine. He's very patient and busy. He has plenty of things to do with his brain."

"Right. Well, I heard Beau tried to beat Trey's ass in the hospital parking lot yesterday. Were you there for that?" Silas asked.

"Yep. I wish he had."

"Grayson wants to kill Trey too. I mean, he wants to *forreal* kill him. I had to stop him from coming into the police station the other night when Trey was there."

"Okay, so, I guess y'all need a sign-up sheet for people who want to kill Trey Foxberry, and go ahead and put everybody but his mama on that list," Kasey said, with ice water in her veins. She wondered what time it was. Trey wasn't coming over until nine, because he had to go to the distillery in Jesse County.

Maybe he'd die in a car wreck on his way. Her daddy died in a car wreck; the drunk driver died too. If her daddy could die in a car wreck, so could Trey.

"This cop buddy of mine wants to kill him too. He and another guy are taking shifts at the hospital, watching and making sure Trey doesn't try anything with Caro. Although, he'd have to get past Mimi first, I know," Silas said, letting out a short, breathy laugh.

She loved when he laughed like that after making a dumb joke. She remembered it from high school, and she remembered it from the other night when he came by the hotel, the night before Trey put Caro in the hospital. They'd had two beers and shared a small plate of devils on horseback in the bar downstairs—all swank with bare, hanging lightbulbs. They played two rounds of pool and listened to Neil Young and Aaliyah. P!nk and Gorillaz. James Brown and Kings of Leon and the Notorious B.I.G. and Kenny Chesney. Kasey's mind was full of worry about Caro, and Silas knew that. He distracted her by telling her more funny stories about the Goldie stuff she missed over the past fifteen years.

What *really* happened to Katie Brunswick's houseboat last summer and how the insurance company didn't believe the lie. How Stanley Morrison saved a man's life in Myrtle's Diner when he choked on a meatball. Why the mayor ordered the fountain in the town square to remain empty for the second half of 2012. Silas had done The Smile and his breathy laugh then too. He'd smelled so good— woodsmoke and apples—like he always did. Once, when she was bending over to aim at the corner pocket, he walked behind her, and someone accidentally bumped him. *My bad, Castelow*, the guy said. *No worries* was Silas's reply. Kasey felt the warmth of the front of Silas's thigh on the back of hers and he said, *Sorry, Kase,* touching her shoulder. She denied herself the pleasure of pushing her body against him. To tell him she remembered. She remembered everything.

The sexual tension had been stupidly, syrupy thick, and she was grateful they were so far away from her hotel room. What would've happened if they were closer to it? She was grateful that Caroline would be spending the night with her. What would've happened if she weren't? Would Silas try to kiss her? Would she let him? She'd had plenty of surprise dreams about him over the years. Dreams where they'd only kiss or only have sex or only talk all night. Dreams that left her frustrated and sometimes touching herself awake in the morning. That hungry high school energy they'd had for each other sizzled on the back burner of her heart as she watched Silas leave the hotel. She'd gone upstairs to her room alone, and while she waited for Ada to drop off Caroline, Kasey had called Devon to let him know how much she loved him. Told him about the dalmatian puppy she had seen in front of the firehouse.

She'd finally called Devon back earlier this morning too because his nonstop texts were driving her crazy. She told him she needed two more weeks and she'd return to NYC. It seemed like a decent amount of time to give herself. If she needed more, she'd figure it out then. She didn't have a reference point for how she'd feel after murdering a man, even if he deserved it.

Kasey pressed her lips together so she wouldn't say the word *murder* aloud. She watched Silas's arms as he pulled some more branches down; his sun-kissed biceps were annoyingly attractive against the salty white of his shirt. She could watch him do that all day, but she forced herself to look away.

"Caro's shoulder surgery is this afternoon. I'm gonna pop in to see her. I made lemonade. Want some?" Kasey asked. Wanting him to say no. Wanting him to say yes.

"No, but thank you. Grayson and I are taking the boys go-carting in Adora Springs, so I gotta get going. I was just thinking about ya and wanted to say hey because I can, since you're still here and everything," he said, smiling at her.

"Hey," she said, smiling back.

"Hey," he said. "Talk at me later?"

They were hugging now. She nodded against him.

———

Trey had been a fortress when Kasey first approached him about coming to the farmhouse for dinner. They'd stood outside of Caro's hospital room and he'd leaned against the wall with his hands in his pockets.

"I know none of Caroline's friends are interested in getting to know me. Especially now that you all believe anything she says about me," he said, not breaking eye contact with Kasey. She got chills looking back at him. How he could stand there and lie like that without blinking. How he was so calm. How he didn't seem desperate in his attempt to convince people he'd never hurt Caro. He simply *expected* everyone to believe him.

"Trey, I haven't been back to Goldie in fifteen years. I haven't had a chance to get to know you! You don't know me either! So let's fix that. I know you love to eat," Kasey said, quickly poking at his stomach.

He smiled a little then, softening. That was when he asked her if she was flirting with him.

"No, and don't you *dare*," she said, widening her smile even more and swatting at his unscratched arm. "I'm serious. There has to be a way we can fix this."

Let's fix this, Kasey thought, picturing Caro's swollen face. *Let's fix this*, she thought, picturing her mom's headstone, the one she hadn't seen yet.

Yes, let's fix this, Trey.

The mushroom lasagna was hot hot hot. Kasey left it in the oven to reheat for too long. She opened the kitchen window and set the dish on the counter.

She put on the red sundress she'd thrown in her suitcase but hadn't worn yet. It was a smidge too short, which meant it was perfect for convincing Trey she'd slipped it on especially for him.

Now Trey was standing in the doorway wearing a Foxberry Distillery T-shirt. Kasey would never forget that shirt—the tomato red of it, screaming hot summers. She'd never forget how that red was the same red as her dress and the same color of the fresh scratches on his arm. Their Caroline, fighting, even still. Even with one arm out of order, even from her hospital bed. Never giving up.

Trey was wearing a ballcap too, but he took it off and put it in his back pocket when he stepped through the door. Kasey wondered if his mom or grandma taught him that. If someone had told him it was rude to walk into somebody's house with a ballcap on. If they did, why didn't they tell him it was rude and wrong to fucking rape and beat your wife too while they were at it?

"Caroline's surgery went well. I'm guessing Mimi told you?" he said, not moving from where he was.

"Yeah, I went to see her earlier. I'm glad it went so well."

The way he said *Caroline* made Kasey's skin crawl. He said it like he didn't like her name. She wondered if he always said it like that, but she couldn't even remember it coming out of his mouth before.

The lasagna was still too hot. Kasey was going to have to keep him talking for a bit longer. She'd sprinkled some mushrooms on top and put extra sauce over them like Ada suggested. She hadn't bothered reheating the pie; it was on the counter next to her. She'd also put together a salad for herself. The lasagna made the whole house smell delicious; she fanned the platter with the cookie sheet, hoping it would help cool it down.

"I'm sorry she got hurt so bad. She reminds me of a clumsy kitten sometimes. Or a colt, learning how to walk," Trey said.

"Tell me exactly what happened, please...if you can," Kasey said. "Here. Have a glass of bourbon. I'll have one too. We need bourbon for this." She poured some Foxberry Bourbon from the laced bottle into one short glass for him and explained that she was drinking the cheaper kind so he could have the good stuff as she opened a new bottle for herself. She motioned for him to sit across from her at the kitchen table.

Kasey sipped at her bourbon while Trey told her the same load of bullshit he'd told everyone down at the police station.

He drank. Kasey drank too.

"But Caroline said you did it. Why would Caroline say *you* did this?" Kasey asked.

"Honestly? I think she *thinks* I did it because she's mad at me all the time for being a man, because her daddy ain't worth two dead flies. She hates men. She expects me to be an asshole every second of every day, and I'm not beyond criticism by any means, but neither is she. Nobody is," Trey said, knocking back the rest of the bourbon. Kasey did hers too, matching his pace.

Trey kept talking. This was all Caroline's fault, but he felt sorry for her. He was only trying to help, but she made things harder for herself. He said it was probably because her parents didn't want her and she only had Mimi in the past. Now she was a Foxberry, so he didn't know what the problem was. Kasey listened patiently, fighting the urge to claw his eyes out.

"Thanks for telling me your side, Trey. It's hard on all of us. I mean, you know how close we are," Kasey said, getting up to grab the laced bourbon bottle. She asked if he wanted some more, and when he said yes, she poured it in his glass.

Kasey had lit candles, and two were flickering on the table in front of them, others on the kitchen counter. She dimmed the overhead light and only had the lamps on in the living room. She wanted Trey to feel relaxed; she wanted the mood to be romantic enough to fool him. He didn't need to know she'd puked twenty minutes earlier thinking about him coming over and what she was going to do.

"Yeah, I know. She loves y'all a whole lot," Trey said.

"Well, she's forever our sweet Caroline."

"Sweet Caroline," Trey repeated with a chuckle. "That's her, all right. Ha!"

Kasey pictured Trey as a little boy, wondering if he'd *ever* been sweet. Caro said he had. She'd mentioned a handful of times when he said nice things or did nice things, and Kasey squinted her brain to try and see those things the same way she tried with Roy. Tried to *force* herself to see him as a person worth loving, as a person who could love.

"Sweet Kasey," Trey said, leaning over to put his hand on her bare leg.

She let him.

She sat still.

"You're truly beautiful, Kasey. Lord have mercy, that dress. That dress is a problem, you know that? I mean, I know how much you love Caroline and I love her too. You and I weren't friends in high school or anything, but I remember thinking Silas was *the man* for bagging you. Honestly. But I mean, you're way hotter now."

"Oh...well...thank you, Trey," she said, looking down at her legs.

"You're welcome."

"You hungry?" she asked, licking her bottom lip and biting it slowly. She stared into his blue eyes. She hoped Caroline's baby had her warm eyes and not Trey's cold ones. Kasey made sure her face wasn't as loud as her thoughts. She softened it some more.

"I am," he said.

"For what?"

"For whatever you want me to eat."

They both let the tension thicken.

When she stood and turned, she heard Trey get up too. He put his arm around her waist.

She let him.

Maybe there was some other way to do this. Maybe they could... maybe she could—

He grabbed her ass, squeezing gently. Both different and the same way Roy had done it the time she pulled a knife on him. Everylivingthing inside of Kasey flashed to that moment. How scared she was. How alone she was. How she'd wanted to die. How she prayed for God to kill her so she wouldn't have to live one more second like that. She wished she'd never been born. She wished she'd been in the car with her daddy when he died so she could've died too. How she went to her room and put that knife under her pillow and cried so hard she made herself sick.

She gasped and snatched Trey's wrist away.

"Ah. Let's eat first, right? Then dessert," she said to him. She felt like a different person putting that voice on and that was good. She imagined herself as a smoldering actress, playing a part. It wasn't her voice; it was the actress's voice. Frangible, feigned. The voice that was going to get her through this.

"All right," Trey said, smirking at her and leaning against the counter.

She got her salad and put his lasagna on a plate, telling him she wasn't that hungry yet since she'd done all the cooking.

———

It was after Trey had drunk the rest of his bourbon and eaten one big slab of lasagna, half of another, and a huge piece of pecan pie that he'd gotten up and tried to sit on Kasey's lap. She had dark ripples of worry earlier, thinking that they hadn't put enough LSD in the bourbon or that they'd cooked the mushrooms too much, but Trey was giggling and completely spaced out now. Everything had worked properly.

"Trey, you're a big boy. You need to sit in your own chair," Kasey said, making herself giggle back at him.

"You're so fucking good-looking, though. It's been a *hell* of a few days. My wife is good-looking too, but she's in the hospital," he said.

She saw Caro's disfigured face in her mind. Heard the doctor saying the words *almost fractured an orbital bone.* Pictured the surgeon putting a metal plate in Caro's shoulder. Saw the deep cuts on her arms, the dark bruises, the violet swell of her eye.

No. Kasey couldn't let fear in. Her focus had to be revenge and revenge only.

"Right. She's in the hospital," she said, pushing him gently, fighting the urge to stab him to death at the table. "Hang tight, I'm going to the bathroom." Kasey got up. Trey was back in his chair now, completely zoned out to everything but the rest of his lasagna.

Behind the bathroom door, she texted Rosemarie and Ada in their group chat.

Go look at the moon.

It was the code for the girls to meet her outside in ten minutes. They knew to leave their phones at home so no one could place them at the farmhouse. Now it was time to get Trey near the water.

He was at the kitchen counter, sloshing more laced bourbon into his glass.

"It's been a *long* time since I drank this much. I'm drunk off my ass. Sorry about that. Want some?" he said, slurring. He shoved the glass at her but she said no thank you. "This farmhouse is *amaaazing.* Your dad built this? Sorry, your *black* dad built this?" Trey said.

"Yep. My black daddy built this house, Trey, and you're right. It *is* amazing. Come here and I'll show you something," she said to him, taking his hand and leading him out the back door. She pointed at the roof and told him about the rain barrels her dad had painted, but none of it registered one bit to Trey, because he was tripping balls on another planet. He was putting his hands all over her and Kasey let him, not worried he'd feel the knife.

Wouldn't matter if he did.

Wouldn't be much longer now.

"Whoops. Stars are spinning and I'm seeing all kinds of weird... like...glowing turtles. Did you see a glowing turtle up there? I think I need to sit," he said, pointing at the roof, then down at the ground.

"Let's do that, cowboy," she said, pulling his arm toward the far end of the property where the water licked at the rocks. "Let's go out on the dock and do it. It's prettier."

They walked up the steps and down to the edge. She sat first and tugged on his jeans so he'd sit too. Then, she climbed on top of him, laid him back and leaned down. He closed his eyes and kissed her.

She let him.

Wouldn't be much longer now.

"Do you feel good?" she asked.

"Yeah," he said softly.

"Do you want to come with me no matter where I go?"

"Hell yeah, Kasey. Kasey Fritz. Your name feels so good to say. My mouth. Feels good in my mouth, Frasey Kritz."

"So, let's pretend to go to sleep so we can catch those turtles, okay? Let's go swim with the turtles. It's turtles all the way down. Will you come with me?" she said into his ear as a soft, weird snore escaped his mouth. He moved his head with his eyes half-closed and mumbled something about not being able to swim. "I know. That's okay. I'll go tell those turtles we're on the way. They'll take good care of us." After waiting until it seemed like he was asleep, she stood and walked toward the farmhouse, *pssting* for Rosemarie and Ada.

They stepped into the moonlight.

"He's completely out of it, so we need to get him in the water now," she whispered to them.

"God, he's huge, though," Ada said.

"We don't have to put him in far. It's deep," Rosemarie said.

"I'll jump in with him. Come on," Kasey said.

When they got to Trey he was kind of awake again and the expression on his face had changed into a smug half smile. He was moving his head back and forth on the wood like it felt good to do it.

Kasey remembered the ballcap in his back pocket and pulled it out.

"Trey," Rosemarie whispered, "we're your sirens, here to sing you a song about how you can't get away with raping and beating women. Those women will make sure you can never do those things again." She got close and, after taking the ballcap from Kasey, tucked it onto his head. Trey mumbled something but he was deep in the depths of bourbon LSD magic mushroom land.

They pulled and pushed him so he was sitting up. He slumped again and his ballcap fell off. Kasey turned and watched it floating there in the dark water, then it was gone.

"Okay, help me—" Kasey said to the girls, but she stopped when Trey sat up again and grabbed her leg.

"Don't!" Ada said.

"Trey, *relax*. Let's swim," Kasey said to him. He got on his feet and put his arm around her.

"Sit down, Trey," Rosemarie said coolly.

He turned to look at her. He didn't ask what she was doing there. He didn't react at all; he just obeyed.

"Sometimes the sirens get bossy," Kasey said, relieved he'd let her go. She motioned to Rosemarie and Ada to stay back, and she sat next to him.

He looked right through her before he grabbed her hair and yanked. Kasey suppressed the scream.

It was happening again. Everything was going wrong. He'd kill her. He didn't even know what he was doing and he was too strong. He pulled her hair again and held her arms.

The knife.

If he let go even for a split second, she could get the knife out of her pocket.

But he didn't let go.

He wouldn't.

She felt the girls move toward them. Trey shook Kasey so hard she bit her tongue, and he was mumbling something she couldn't make out. She said his name with blood in her mouth and prepared herself to fall in the water.

She thought of ways to keep from drowning during a struggle, of ways to fight him off. She thought of her mom's last moments. They were like this too, hopeless and scorching in the red-hot anger of a violent man.

She'd scream.

She had to! Someone could come and help them. Kasey opened her mouth to do it and turned her head. Suddenly, Trey let her go and Kasey moved behind him.

She watched Rosemarie put her foot on the small of Trey's back and Ada lift a big rock with both hands. Ada brought the rock down on his head like an egg cracking on the rim of a bowl.

That quick, Trey fell forward and the lake swallowed him up with a gushy gulp.

"Ada!" Rosemarie said.

"Shit, Ada!" Kasey said.

"Kase, are you okay?" Rosemarie and Ada asked her at the same time.

"I'm fine. I'm fine," she said, wiping blood from her mouth.

"I'm sorry...I was scared he'd grab you again...that he'd hurt you...I wanted to make sure...to make *sure*...he'd be dead," Ada said too loudly, wiping her hands on her jeans. She had wild eyes and Rosemarie went and hugged her, pulled her head close, and shushed her so she wouldn't make any more noise.

Kasey threw the knife in the grass and jumped in after him. Rosemarie and Ada jumped in too, but he was gone already and so was the rock. Trey had slipped under the black to the sound of

Cat Stevens singing *moonshadow* as she thought of Roy throwing her mama's precious body in that lake like a bag of trash.

What he'd wronged—*moonshadow*—they'd made right.

If there were an atomic flashlight in her heart beaming the dark, it wouldn't find a drop of remorse for helping Trey get to where she knew he was going. They knew the world would be better without Trey Foxberry, and now the world was better! Simple as that.

Maybe no one would ever find him. Maybe it wouldn't matter that Ada didn't stick to the plan. It was done.

~~Wouldn't be much longer now.~~

It was finished.

"Where's the knife? I had the knife in my pocket and I threw it out here and *fuck* if it fell in the water—" Kasey said quietly when she was out of the lake, but her head was roaring.

"What knife?" Rosemarie asked.

"Rosemarie, the *knife*! The folding knife you made sure I remembered to have on me! I can't see. I can't find it," Kasey said, scanning the ground beneath her. She told them she'd put the knife in her pocket, didn't she? Of course she did. And she threw it before she jumped in, didn't she? Of course she did. She remembered. She squatted and felt for it.

"Right, right. I can't believe I forgot about that. I'm sorry. There's kind of a *lot* going on! Um, I'm sure it's down here," Rosemarie said, squatting too. Feeling.

"Where'd you get the folding knife?" Ada asked.

"Ada, does that really matter right now?!" Rosemarie said.

"It's been in the kitchen drawer my whole life. I put it in my pocket and I need to find it," Kasey said.

"Okay. Well, we can't use a light," Ada said, squatting with them, patting the grass.

"Kasey, how big is it?" Rosemarie asked.

"It's . . . the size of a folding knife, Rosemarie, I don't know! Not too big, not too little. *Knife*-sized," Kasey said. They were all trying to keep their voices as low as possible, all trying to steady the shaking sounds that came out when they opened their mouths.

The three of them moved slowly, feeling around in the grass and rocks for how long? A minute? Two? Once, Ada and Kasey accidentally touched fingers in the dark and Ada almost screamed, but Rosemarie put her wet, muddy hand over her mouth and stopped her.

When Kasey felt the cold plastic and metal, she gripped it as hard as she could and snatched it up, pulling some weeds along with it.

"Found it! I have it," Kasey said, clutching it like a crucifix, swallowing blood.

Before going inside to clean up, the girls stood wet and shaking, holding hands. Kasey's dress dripped and stuck to her like a petal. The water near the farmhouse was rougher since it was closer to the falls, the rocks. It was why they'd wanted to put Trey in there as opposed to anywhere else.

The moonlight cut the lake like a deck of cards, and they watched it chop and run.

Trey's car door was unlocked, and quickly, quietly—after she was in a new, dry change of clothes—Kasey put the smiley-face LSD stickers Rosemarie gave her in the glove compartment, careful to wipe her fingerprints away. They put what was left of the lasagna and pie down the garbage disposal bit by bit and shared two bottles of wine afterward, crying. High on their dark and temporary mania, going over the lies they needed to tell again, talking about what'd happened like they'd done it years and years ago. Like it was already a Goldie legend.

"I can't believe we actually did it," Ada said, wrapped in a blanket, dazed and drunk on the couch.

"I can," Rosemarie said. She let herself fall across Kasey's lap and closed her eyes.

"I can too," Kasey said, so wired she thought she'd never be able to sleep again. So tired she could barely stay awake.

Trey returned to her immediately in a dream, the first part of the night replaying on a loop, but this time Trey wouldn't die, no matter what they did. Once, he turned into Roy. That was when Kasey woke up crying, with her heart pounding so hard she could feel it in her teeth. She stayed awake in the dark until the first hint of light.

As the sun rose, Kasey stood at the window drinking her coffee carefully because her tongue was still sore from biting it so hard. How long would she be haunted by that first taste of blood and the slash of moonlight on his face? She stared toward the dock—her heartbeat galloping a wordless prayer—keeping watch while Rosemarie and Ada slept. Making sure Trey hadn't risen from the water, bedraggled and zombied.

2004

34

From: KaseyJosephineFritz@gmail.com
To: SilasCastelow@gmail.com
Subject: [no subject]

I wanted to email you again and say I'm sorry. We've been over it, I know! But I wanted to say it again. I'll call your phone soon so you can have my new cell number. I'll understand if you don't answer or call me back.

I love you.

From: SilasCastelow@gmail.com
To: KaseyJosephineFritz@gmail.com
Subject: Re: [no subject]

I heard "Running" by No Doubt in my truck this morning and you love that song so much it felt like you were right there in my passenger seat. This time I was paying so much attention to what she was singing, I had to pull over.

Kase, I would've run with you. You didn't have to do this alone.

Of course I will answer when you call. I love you too.

GOODBYE EARL

From: KaseyJosephineFritz@gmail.com
To: RosemarieCloverKingston@gmail.com,
AdaPinkPlum@gmail.com, CarolineCaroppenheimer@gmail.com
Subject: Kase and the City

Hi y'all. I've attached a few pics for you.

#1 is of my dorm room. It's tiny, but cozy. My roommate's name is Betty. She's from Rhode Island and she's fluent in Japanese. She's also quiet, which is like The Dream. I think we're officially friends now, which is pretty great.

#2 is a selfie of me in Central Park. It's hella hot here but not Goldie-hot so I can walk around during the day and not want to straight-up pass out.

#3 is a selfie in front of Magnolia Bakery to prove I'm not scared of the subways anymore! I get lost sometimes but it's okay! Takes me about twenty minutes to take the train from the financial district to the bakery. Their cupcakes are the closest I can get to Plum Bakery's or yours, Caro! Whenever y'all get up here, we'll go and (probably?) won't get lost. (Although I make no promises!)

Now, it's your turn. Send me pics, please! I promise to write back even if it takes me forever.

Sometimes the grief is waiting for me when I wake up in the morning. Sometimes it's unrelenting in the middle of the night. Sometimes it's not until the afternoons that I sink in it.

I know it's taken me too long to write back this time and I'm sorry.

I don't want to talk about how much I miss y'all because it makes me too sad.

I love you and RACK FOREVER. RF!

Xo

Kase

PS: PLEASE tell me everything about both of your birthday parties,

Ada and Caro!! Rosemarie please send me pictures of the flowers in Costa Rica!

From: RosemarieCloverKingston@gmail.com
To: AdaPinkPlum@gmail.com, CarolineCaroppenheimer@gmail.com, KaseyJosephineFritz@gmail.com
Subject: Re: Kase and the City

Hello lovelies!

It's the "sweet spot" of the rainy season down here so everything is green, green, green but we get some dry days too. Kase, I'm attaching pics of lushy green and flowers for you and a pic of me and Leo from last week when we went to Monteverde. Cloud forest!

Honestly, I guess I'll go ahead and marry that boy someday because besides y'all, he's the only person on earth I can spend this much non-stop time with. He's sleeping on the floor next to me right now. Laid down in a patch of sun and fell asleep with his glasses on, like a cat (who wears glasses)!!

I've gotta hop off because we're organizing a taco dinner for the church tonight...providing free childcare too. So I'm in charge of like, twenty (!) five-year-olds. Pray for me, y'all!

And yes, Ada and Caro, happy happy birthdays one week apart if we don't talk before then! TELL ME EVERYTHING. CARO TELL ME IF BEAU KISSES YOU AT EXACTLY MIDNIGHT WHEN YOU TURN EIGH-TEEN AND ADA TELL ME HOW PERFECT (AND PINK) YOUR PARTY IS BECAUSE I KNOW IT WILL BE!

Kasey, more pics to prove you're not scared of subways please! Love y'all so so so much miss you so so so much!! More soon!

RF.
Xoxo
Roses

———

Every night before bed, Kasey would think, *If we'd killed Roy first, he couldn't have killed my mom; if we'd killed Roy first, he couldn't have killed my mom; if we'd killed Roy first, he couldn't have killed my mom; if we'd killed Roy first, he couldn't have killed my mom.* So, she swore to herself if she were ever in a position like that again, she'd *do* something about it, instead of waiting. The waiting had killed her mom.

Now she had no mom, no dad, no family at all.

Sometimes she talked to her mom's best friend, Gail, but most importantly, she had her sisters.

We'll do anything for each other.

Even when she was too tired in the evening to respond to their emails and even when she was so tired and sad that she ignored their calls. Even when it was weeks or months.

Even then.

She'd always have her sisters.

2019

35

CAROLINE

"Caro, Trey's dead," Kasey said softly.

Caroline's eyes were closed and although her bloodstream fizzed with pain medicine, her shoulder throbbed somewhere deep inside, somewhere she didn't even know she could hurt.

"He's dead. We did it. You're free," Kasey said.

Caroline opened her eyes to see a blurry Rosemarie sitting on her bed. Blurry Kasey was in the chair next to her, and blurry Ada was standing on the other side, holding a blurry batch of sunflowers. She remembered her grandma telling her she was going to have breakfast with Myrtle and that her girlfriends were here right before she fell asleep again. It must not have been long ago. She'd seen a glimpse of her face in the mirror, and when she cried, her grandma shushed her and said it always looks worse before it gets better. Caro knew it was morning and that it was Saturday. Yesterday was surgery day.

And Trey was dead.

Trey is dead.

Trey was dead?

"What?" Caro asked them.

"Trey's dead," Rosemarie said, holding her hand.

"Soon, people will start looking for him, saying he's missing, but he's not. He's dead," Ada said.

"Wh— What? What happened?"

"*Goodbye Earl*," Kasey whispered.

Trey's dead. Goodbye Earl. Trey's dead.

Trey's Earl. Goodbye Trey. Earl's dead. Trey's dead.

The sentences rearranged themselves repeatedly in Caro's mind. Each letter was a block, stacking; the words smashed together and broke apart.

Trey's dead. Goodbye Earl. Trey's dead.

When it sank in as much as it could, Caro gasped.

"Y'all...y'all will have to go to prison and you did this for me and I won't be able to live knowing that. I won't. Me and the baby will die too," Caroline said, sobbing.

"Caroline, we won't! You won't! Stop. Listen. It'll look like an accident. That piece of shit killed my mom and made it look like an accident and we're righting the world with this one," Kasey said. She was crying too.

"*What?* Roy really did kill...your mom? But you said—" Caro said.

Kasey filled her in as quickly as she could.

"Obviously, we weren't going to let anything like that happen again. Ever," Rosemarie said when Kasey was finished.

"For right now, the less you know, the better. Whenever they come around asking questions, tell them the truth. That Trey came up here to see you and that's the last time you saw him. Tell them again how he said he'd kill you. He never knew about the baby, right?" Ada said in between nervous glances at the door.

Caroline shook her head even though it ached. She'd been so scared a nurse would come in and blurt it out when Trey was there to visit her, but it hadn't happened. She cried in relief when he was gone. *We'll get you back home and get you the help you need*, he'd said, and she said, *No, Trey, you're the one who needs help.* He was quiet, touched her arm. That was when she scratched him. He told Mimi she was acting out of

265

her mind again and it was probably the medicine. Or maybe she was having a total mental breakdown. He said he'd ask for a psychological evaluation. Grandma Mimi couldn't stop him from coming up there, but she told him to leave because Caroline needed to get her rest.

"So, the Foxberrys will never know the baby is Trey's. Beau's here. Say it's Beau's. You aren't obligated to have anything to do with that family ever again," Rosemarie said.

"Say it's Beau's baby?" Caroline coughed out. Her mouth was dry. Rosemarie poured her a cup of water and held the straw to her lips; Caroline drank and thanked her.

"Say it's Beau's baby," Kasey repeated. "Tell Beau to go along with it. He'll do it. He'll do anything for you."

"That baby will look just like *you*, so it won't matter anyway. You know she's gonna have your hair, Caro," Rosemarie said. "Her name's gonna be Rosy Magnolia, so you know she's gonna be a Reds."

"Her name is Rosy Magnolia?" Ada cooed.

"Rosy Magnolia. Oh God, I love it," Kasey said.

"Rosy Magnolia," Caroline said with her hand on her stomach.

"She'll be here when the early spring magnolias bloom again," Rosemarie said, putting her hand on Caroline's.

"Did he hurt you?" Caroline asked Kasey. They didn't have to tell her that Kasey had been the one to get close to Trey. The one to do what needed to be done. Caroline knew it'd been her. The thought of what Trey could've or might've done to Kasey sent ice-cold needles down her back. Her arms, her legs.

"No," Kasey said, shaking her head. "I promise."

"How did you—" Caro stopped when Rosemarie looked at her.

"We can't tell you now. Not until we get past this part. We're almost past this part," Rosemarie said.

"Are you hungry? These are vanilla orange cream. They're not as good as yours, but I tried," Ada said, reaching for a cupcake to hand to her.

———

Beau came to visit Caroline right as Mimi and Myrtle were walking out. She'd gotten a little sleep after Rosemarie, Ada, and Kasey left, and she thought maybe she'd want to get some more until she saw Beau standing there holding a big bouquet of daisies wrapped in Plum Florals paper.

He asked her if Trey had been there again and Caroline told him no. She told him what Mimi told her, that there was a cop in the parking lot keeping an eye out for him.

Trey's dead, Trey's dead, Trey's dead, Trey's dead, Trey's dead.

After they chatted a bit and watched the TV together, Caroline turned it off.

Trey's dead, Trey's dead, Trey's dead, Trey's dead, Trey's dead.

Kasey's words were on a loop in Caro's head, and there was a heavy weight inside of her—a hot, glowing orb of worry and anxiety she couldn't sort out, because she didn't know anything. Grandma Mimi and Myrtle hadn't mentioned Trey being missing, and the girls had told her no one else knew about their plan. But everyone *always* found out about *everything* in Goldie, didn't they? When would *she* find out what happened to Trey?

Her shoulder throbbed; the tender space under her swollen eye did too. *My whole body is an exposed heart, painfully beating.* The word *beating* sent her right back to those steps. Right back to Trey's face pressed against hers, his gritting teeth and the hate in his eyes although she'd done nothing to deserve it except exist.

She kept waiting to feel sad when she heard *Trey's dead, Trey's dead, Trey's dead, Trey's dead, Trey's dead* spinning in her mind, but she didn't. She felt a lot of things, but none of them were sad.

Many times—only after their big fights, when she felt the most like a small, caged animal—she'd imagined Trey dying in a horrible freak accident at the distillery so she could have a new beginning. She'd imagined someone killing him in a road-rage incident or him getting hit by a truck as he crossed the street.

Trey dying only meant she was free. It didn't mean anything else to her. He'd stopped being a person she could muster up compassion for. It was either him or her. He tried to kill her. He said it with his own mouth; he couldn't gaslight her out of knowing that. He couldn't do anything anymore, because he was dead, and most importantly, he couldn't hurt the baby.

One day she'd tell the baby the truth—she would. She'd have to.

Right now, she needed Beau to do something for her. Something that made her feel crazy for asking, but the pain medicine helped get her there. She closed her eyes and pictured her and Beau sitting outside somewhere by the water. Instead of beeping machines, there were birds. Instead of that hospital bed, grass. Instead of the white ceiling, nothing but blue sky and fluffy clouds. She'd make a Beau Bramford Pie for him and he'd make his grilled cheese, and nothing else in the world would matter.

"Beau, can I ask you a wild favor? Before I even say what it is, I want you to know that I *know* it's crazy. Everything is crazy right now. When Kasey told me you were out in the parking lot the other day, the floor opened beneath me. I...I couldn't believe you'd come all the way to Goldie just to see me. I still can't believe I'm looking at you. It's—" She stopped, trying not to cry. She was so tired of crying.

"Hey. I'll do anything for you, Muffin Mix. You know that. You've always known that," Beau said.

"I'm pregnant. And because of that and everything...could you...if it comes up, act like...this baby is yours? It's part of my plan to get away from Trey. You don't have to do anything. I'm gonna say it and I would just need you...to go along with it," Caro said, watching his eyes.

"Done," Beau said plainly. "It'd be my pleasure."

"Well, only if—"

"Done," Beau said again.

"Her name is Rosy Magnolia," Caro heard herself say. She was so sleepy, and her body felt like it was soaring cloud-high.

"That's a real good name and I know you'll be an amazing mama to her."

Caroline reached for his hand and Beau took hers, squeezed it.

"Thank you, Beau. I'm going to take a nap now," she said.

"Good. I'll be sitting right here when you wake up," he said.

———

Caroline didn't know how long she'd been sleeping when Trey's mother, Paula, showed up at the hospital. Caro had woken up before and Beau left, saying he'd see her again later. Somewhere after lunch, she must've fallen asleep again.

She was scared to be alone with Paula, but she was alone with Paula now and her face was twisted into a snarl. Her eyes were red and wet.

"Nobody's seen hide nor hair of Trey since last night, Caro*line*," she growled. She said her name the same way Trey said her name, and Caroline's heart was kicking so hard she figured a nurse would be in soon to check on her.

"What? What do you mean?"

"You heard me. I filed a missing person report. He'd never skip town without telling me where he was going. What did he say when he was up here? What did you say to him?" Paula asked. She was pacing in front of the hospital bed, twisting a tissue in her hands.

"He told me he wanted to get me the help I needed, and I told him I didn't need help. I told him *he* needed help," Caroline said defiantly.

"Why'd you tell him that? He's probably upset about it. That's a terrible thing to say to somebody," Paula said, stopping to stare at her.

"Because he tried to *kill* me, Paula."

"He didn't." Paula shook her head angrily. "*You* did this to yourself! If you—" Paula stopped. "Oh God, if—"

"He goes to Jesse County all the time—"

"He's not there. We already checked."

"Well, he hasn't been up here today. I haven't seen him. He hasn't called either."

Paula wiped her nose, threw the tissue in the garbage can.

"We'll find him. When we do, I'll let you know," she said, regaining her composure.

"Okay," Caroline said as Paula moved to leave the room.

Trey's dead, Trey's dead, Trey's dead, Trey's dead, Trey's dead.

"Trey's dead," Caroline said softly to herself as Paula walked out, and the darkest part of her hoped that she'd hear her.

2004

36

Ada had done the Castelow lake house up so pretty for Caro's birthday it brought tears to her eyes. Ever since graduation, everything had been making Caroline cry. Anytime she thought about Kasey in New York, anytime she thought about Kasey's mom being gone, she had to focus on swallowing the lump in her throat. She stood out front looking at the porch wrapped in twinkle lights and the big *one* and *eight* balloons tied to the railings.

"We're doing a sparkler countdown at midnight," Ada said proudly. Caroline would officially turn eighteen in a few hours.

"We are *not*," Caroline said.

"Oh yes we are! And this green looks so amazing with your red hair. I knew it," Ada said about the sundress she'd given Caroline that morning. Caro agreed and thanked her again. Ada touched the strap of it and swatted Caro's butt. Caroline smacked hers back before Ada went up the steps.

"Happy almost birthday, Caro!" Grayson said to her, following Ada. Silas wasn't far behind. He hugged Caro and said the same thing.

"Thank you, Grayson. Thank you, Si. Have you—"

"Nope. Not talking about that tonight. Birthday stuff only," Silas said. They'd spoken about Kasey only a little bit, Caroline being very careful bringing her up to him, knowing how brokenhearted he was.

Caroline pretended to zip her lips.

Mateo walked up the driveway hollering her name. He handed her a six-pack of Goldie Light and wrapped her in a bear hug, planting kisses on both cheeks. He was tipsy already. Their relationship had been fun and playful, and neither of them was crushed when it ended. The bonus was that they could still be friends. Caro wiggled and giggled in his arms.

Ada ordered a ton of red-velvet cupcakes from the bakery; Caroline was peeling the paper off her first one on the front porch in the sunset light. When Beau came around the corner in a white pocket T-shirt and jeans, every cell in her body warmed and purred.

"The almost birthday girl," he said. He was holding a big bouquet of daisies and a small box. He walked up on the porch and put them both on the table. "You look really pretty."

"Thank you, Beau," she said, hugging him tight. "Want a bite?" she asked when she pulled away, offering him the cupcake. He took a small bite and sat. She sat next to him. "Thank you for coming and for these too." She motioned toward her presents.

"Open it," he said.

She opened the box to find a paperweight—a glass ball with a yellow flower in it; it was cool and heavy in her hand.

"Wow. It's beautiful. Thank you, Beau," she said, hugging it to her chest.

"I saw it in the antique shop and it reminded me of you."

"That's a high compliment. I love it."

"Good. That's how I meant it."

"Do you want a beer?"

"Yeah."

"Come on," she said, taking his hand.

———

From: CarolineCaroppenheimer@gmail.com
To: RosemarieCloverKingston@gmail.com, AdaPinkPlum@gmail.com,

GOODBYE EARL

KaseyJosephineFritz@gmail.com
Subject: Sparkler Kisses

Okay y'all, so Ada's already heard this story a hundred times so Ada IGNORE THIS IF YOU WANT!!!

But yes.

Yes. YES! Beau DID kiss me a little after midnight on my birthday like it was FREAKING NEW YEAR'S EVE and y'all it was the BEST KISS OF MY LIFE. Ada made everything so perfect and we really did do sparkler countdown with everyone and then like, twenty minutes later Beau and I went to sit on the dock and share a cigarette. Beau lit two sparklers for us and when the sparklers went out and we were done with the cigarette, I told him to kiss me. I literally said it! I said KISS ME BEAU and he did !!!!!

It was SO romantic. I keep thinking about it. He's an amazing kisser and if I hadn't been sitting, I would've fallen over. We laid down and kissed and kissed and kissed for SO LONG...I don't even know how long. Just kissing. That's all we did and it was the best night of my life!! We fell asleep out there and didn't wake up until almost sunrise.

I don't know what we are. I don't know what's gonna happen, but since it was one of the best nights of my life y'all are gonna have to get used to me talking about it A LOT!!

CAN YOU BELIEVE IT.

I'm attaching a pic of me in the sundress Ada got me for my birthday which from here on out will be called the SPARKLER KISS DRESS. And another one that I took of me and Beau sitting by the water.

Rosemarie, your mom dropped off your gift for me and thank you so much! It's such a beautiful cookbook and I can't wait to make everything in it.

Kasey, I got the ribbons and the apron you sent me too! Thank you!

I LOVE Y'ALL TALK SOON RACK FOREVER.
Caro

———

Three days after Caroline's birthday, when she got to work, Beau was sitting out back of the diner with a sad look on his face. When she asked him what was up, he told her he was moving to Carson City, Nevada, in two days to go help his dad take care of his grandmother.

"Fucking *sucks* because I was looking forward to a lot of stuff," he said, smoking.

"Yeah, I was too," she said, without knowing how it came out of her mouth when all she wanted to do was scream and cuss and cry.

For two days they took kiss breaks in his truck, and he promised he'd write and be back in Goldie sometimes, told her that he was crazy about her.

"I mean it, Muffin Mix. I'll talk soon," he said, kissing her goodbye for the last time.

2019

37

ROSEMARIE

Well, shit. They hadn't planned on Trey's body resurfacing so quickly. They'd killed him on Friday—making it Good—and there he was on Sunday, like Jesus.

Except Trey was, like, the literal opposite of Jesus.

Kasey told the police that Trey had come to the farmhouse on Friday night. That he'd been upset about Caroline being in the hospital and wanted to talk. She told them he was a little drunk when he showed up and he kept drinking. That he admitted what he'd done to Caroline and he was torn up about it. Kasey told them he was distressed and out of it, wandering the property, wondering aloud if the Foxberrys should purchase it and use it as a small distillery since it was right next to the water. He was being so weird it scared Kasey, so she went inside and locked the door.

That was the last she saw of him.

She figured he didn't want to drive since he was so drunk and he'd wandered off somewhere. That he'd come back for the car later, but he never did. On Saturday, when Caro let them know Trey's mom had opened a missing person report, Kasey called the police station to report Trey's car being there. By Sunday, the cops had towed it away.

"Trey's mom asked me if I was a lesbian. She asked if Caroline was my *girlfriend*, or if she ever had been," Kasey said. She was sitting on the counter in the farmhouse kitchen, eating cherries out of a green glass bowl.

Rosemarie was sitting at the table, nursing a glass of ice water. She'd had no appetite for the past few days, and sometimes even forcing herself to drink water was a hassle, even when she was thirsty. Esme's brother Ambrose, her oncologist, texted earlier that morning, asking if she'd adjusted to the new meds he'd called in for her, but she hadn't even gone to pick them up yet and she wasn't going to. They made her puke and she was tired of puking. She was tired of chemo cocktails. She was a hippie about that stuff and always had been. She'd tried it when she was first diagnosed in 2016 and they made her feel *awful*, but at least they worked.

They couldn't work the same way now because her cancer was back, everywhere, and it'd kill her if she wasn't killed by some Random Act of God first. Her cancer wasn't a Random Act of God; it was the same cancer that killed her aunt. Once she'd stopped thinking of it as simply "cancer" and instead as "*her* cancer," she realized that she finally accepted it for what it was.

This cancer was *hers* and the double mastectomy didn't fix it and no medicine would fix it either. *Her* cancer was *her* death and all she had to do now was wait for it. In the meantime, she'd try to love the people she loved as much as she could love them. Protect them. Try to make the world the best she could. So no, she didn't think twice about killing Trey Foxberry, because that was an Act of Love. They made Caroline's world better by doing it. Esme's brother could call in whatever prescription he wanted; it wouldn't matter. Rosemarie had returned to Goldie to hang with her parents and her sisters, to sing with Leo, to die in the sunshine.

When it was time, she'd tell her parents. She'd tell her sisters too.

But it wasn't time. Not yet.

"Was she serious?" Ada asked, chewing on her thumb. It was what she did when she was nervous, and although she'd handled everything way better than Rosemarie had ever imagined she would, she was easily the most anxious of the three of them since she had the most to lose if they got caught. Kasey was born scrappy and Rosemarie was obviously hyperaware of her numbered days, but Ada had Grayson and those four boys and Plum Everything to think about.

All three of them lost it in their own way after killing Trey. Ada got drunk fast and cried a lot; Kasey had nightmares and woke up early. Rosemarie had been the most stoic, only fully breaking down in the shower, but even then, more out of relief than fear. Most of the fear had burned out of her now. If Caroline was okay, if Rosemarie knew God would forgive her for everything, *Whom (or what) shall I fear?* she thought.

"Oh, she was definitely serious. She said I was probably in love with Caro and that we were *weirdly* close when we were in high school. She said that about all four of us, actually," Kasey said. "Then she said I probably held a grudge against Trey for taking *my woman* away when he married Caroline. She said maybe that was why I didn't come to Goldie for the wedding."

"Are you serious?!" Ada asked.

"Ada! Girl! She's *obviously* serious!" Rosemarie snapped. So far, they'd done a good job of not snapping at each other under the stress and they rarely argued, but Ada's anxiety was spilling out and Rosemarie was tired of having to clean it up. The room spun a little and she picked up her water glass again and drank.

"I'm sorry. Right," Ada said, nodding. "Sorry."

"She said stuff about how, yeah, I grew up in this town, but I've been gone so long, and she threw some wild, out-of-pocket stuff in there about how my mom worked at the grocery store on Sunday mornings and never took me to church and that everyone knows my mom never went to church anymore after my daddy died anyway," Kasey said. She was eating while she talked and not showing any real emotion. Rosemarie knew it was what she had to do to get through it. She'd seen Kasey pull this move a million times. She could push through until things were taken care of. It was how she dealt with Roy growing up and Rosemarie could see how effective and economical that attitude would be working in New York finance too. Kasey could do it without seeming cold and Rosemarie loved that about her. It was truly *inspiring*.

"Like the Foxberrys are an ideal Christian family? Oh, please! No one in that family is a Christian," Ada said.

"At this point y'all are right outside the police station?" Rosemarie asked.

"Yep," Kasey continued. "She said Caro wouldn't get one penny of Trey's money and they'd decided that a long time ago. She called Caro 'gold-digging trash looking for a payday' and said that was the only reason she married Trey anyway," Kasey ended.

"Are you s—" Ada stopped herself.

"That *bitch*," Rosemarie said softly.

"What did you say? What did you do? The whole time you were just standing there listening to her say all this? How?" Ada asked. She stepped over to the cherry bowl and got one out, started chewing on that instead of her thumb.

"Because I was exhausted from the cop's questions, and the less said, the better. I don't give a shit what she thinks about me. She can look as hard as she wants for someone to blame this on, but she knows in her heart that Trey did this to himself by being who he was. Exactly who she raised him to be," Kasey said.

"Go back to her saying you're a lesbian right quick, because honestly, I'm jealous she didn't mention me. How am I the only one sitting here with an *actual* girlfriend, but no one accused *me* of being a lesbian? Please make it make sense," Rosemarie said. She finished her water and got up slowly.

"Are you okay? You look a little tired, Roses, and I know that's not a thing we're supposed to say to people, but—" Ada said.

"I'm fine. I just haven't eaten anything decent," Rosemarie said, digging in the cherry bowl for a couple. She could probably do some fruit. She steadied herself against the counter and ate one.

"When was your last scan? I'm sorry I can't remember. I write them down when you tell me, though. In my calendar at home," Ada said, touching Rosemarie's shoulder.

"Around Christmas. Ada, I'm fine, but thank you. I just need food," Rosemarie said.

"Welp, so yeah. There you have it. Trey's mom for sure thinks Caro and I are secret lovers. Sorry you missed out, Roses. Feel free to join us, though. Lesbian throuple. Or a rectouple, if you want in, Ada. *RACK*touple," Kasey said.

"You're not freaking out about the police questioning you?" Ada asked. "I'm freaking out." She looked at the clock on the oven. She was due at the police station in twenty minutes, and later, Rosemarie would go. No one was forcing them to go in, but Mrs. Foxberry had told the cops to ask them some questions and they were going willingly. All they would tell them was that Caroline had been keeping the abuse a secret and they knew Trey was an asshole—that was it. How could they possibly know anything else?

"Not really," Kasey said. "It'll look like he fell and hit his head and drowned. We didn't try anything too fancy and that's good. Accidents happen. Life's a bitch."

"That's New York City talking," Rosemarie said. She reached for another cherry.

"I couldn't have dealt with it if we'd done some *gruesome* thing. If we'd, like, chopped him up or something. It was downright peaceful until he pulled my hair and . . . the rock. He saw glowing turtles, then thought he was going to get laid by his wife's best friend. We showed him mercy. I know! I *know* I may have to deal with the trauma of all this some more later down the road. But I've dealt with worse. I mean, no, I don't want to spend the rest of my life in prison, but y'all, my mom died right there and I saw her. I held her body as it cooled and her murderer got away with it. I couldn't let that happen again. No fucking way. I'm different now," Kasey said, pointing to the spot on the kitchen floor. Rosemarie and Ada turned to look at it. Kasey ate the last cherry. She hopped down off the counter and put the bowl in the sink.

"So the cops already talked to Caroline and they'll hear from all of us too. Do you know who else they're talking to?" Ada asked.

"If Trey's mom has it her way, everyone in Goldie," Kasey said.

"Good. The more people talk, the more crooked leads they'll have, honestly," Rosemarie said. "And what about Devon? Where's your engagement ring? What's happening?" she asked Kasey.

"I took it off to do some yard work on Friday and didn't want it on for...everything. It's safe! On the dresser!" Kasey said, pointing down the hallway.

"And what about Devon?" Ada asked her again.

"I *love* Devon and I *miss* Devon and Devon is driving me *crazy*, but I can *handle* Devon," Kasey said.

They stood in a circle, held hands, and prayed. Ada left for the station. When she was gone, Rosemarie and Kasey put on the *American Beauty* album and sat on the back porch sharing half a joint that Rosemarie had gotten from her dad.

———

Roses, I'm flying to Goldie on
Friday morning.

You mean to Adora Springs.
Goldie doesn't have an airport,
Esme. :P

Yes. To Adora Springs.

Okay! Ilu. Call me later?

I will. Love you too.

Silas was standing outside of the police station.

"Hey. So, I have a feeling none of this is going according to protocol. A private citizen can *suggest* that we come up here and give statements, although it has nothing to do with us? Is this a murder investigation or what? Who said *anyone* killed him?" Rosemarie asked him quietly after they hugged.

"It's a death investigation right now. They're doing the autopsy soon, but besides that, I don't know what's going on. When I do, I'll tell you. You know I will. How's Caro doing today?"

"Grandma Mimi says she's fine and should be out within the week. I'm going to see her after this," Rosemarie said, motioning her head toward the building.

"Good," Silas said. "A friend of the Foxberrys said they heard Beau Bramford ask Trey, 'How'd you like it if I tried to kill *you*, you piece of shit?' in the hospital parking lot last week, so Beau's in there right now, talking."

"Really?" Rosemarie's mostly empty stomach dropped. She might puke. She should stop by the bathroom first, just in case. Beau would be fine, she knew it, but a *lot* was happening all at once. *Whoa.* She hadn't gotten properly stoned at the farmhouse, but the edges of the world still curved and fuzzed a little—a good thing.

Silas nodded. "What's up, Bell?" he said over Rosemarie's shoulder, and she turned to see Leo standing behind her.

"What are you doing here?" she asked him.

"I was going to sit and read until you were done. Moral support," he said, holding up a James Baldwin paperback. She'd called him on her way and let him know what she was doing, but she hadn't asked him to come along.

"Good man," Silas said, shaking Leo's hand. "Want some coffee? Bottle of water?" he asked him.

"Coffee, yeah. I'll take it. Thank you," Leo said, sitting on the bench in front of the police station. Silas went inside and Rosemarie sat next to Leo. He put his arm around her and she stayed there until it was time to go in.

2006

38

In Seattle, no women asked Rosemarie to keep their kissing a secret. No women in London asked her that either. Or Paris, for that matter. It was studying abroad in Paris where she met Mélanie and kissed Mélanie and let her tongue taste every part of Mélanie in Mélanie's art studio. It was where Mélanie would go down on her for twenty minutes at a time while Rosemarie closed her eyes to writhe in ecstasy, then opened them in a shock of pleasure to gasp up at the skylight. Blue sky or gray clouds. Moonlight and raining stars. It didn't matter, because time froze in Mélanie's art studio.

Mélanie was the sister of Rosemarie's brother's friend, and Rosemarie met her one night at a party her brother's friend threw. Rosemarie loved that she and Rune were in Paris at the same time, especially since it'd been sort of an accident. He'd gotten a semipermanent DJ gig, and she was there for two months in the spring, studying art history.

Leo was in music school in Boston, and she had plans to visit him on her way home when she left Paris. He'd been dating a cellist from Wisconsin for the past few months—a girl called Annie with dark bangs that got caught in her eyelashes. Rosemarie studied every picture she'd found of her online. Rosemarie lied and said yes when he asked if she wanted to meet Annie when she was in town, but Leo knew that, so he laughed when she said it and she laughed too.

Rosemarie could completely let go in Mélanie's world because it

283

didn't feel like a betrayal to Leo. Nothing sapphic felt like a betrayal to Leo and never would. *Bifurcation.* Paris, like Seattle, was decidedly not Goldie. Rosemarie could comfortably be exactly who she was, all the time. She and Mélanie walked hand in hand up and down the streets of Paris and along the Seine, sat outside cafés feeding each other strawberries and Chantilly cream.

From: RosemarieCloverKingston@gmail.com
To: AdaPinkPlum@gmail.com, CarolineCaroppenheimer@gmail.com,
KaseyJosephineFritz@gmail.com
Subject: Salut!

Okay, I'm sending a pic of Mélanie FINALLY but she prefers to be behind the lens. She's aggressively sexy and smells like vetiver and violets most of the time. Sometimes, smoke and rain. I don't know how she's real. I took this pic right outside the café we go to most often. (I've also learned to love extra-frothy cappuccinos.)

Caro, how's it feel to be almost done with pastry school??? Do tell!! And Jay! I hope everything is good there with that cutie.

Ada, you're taking a color class right now? Mélanie's been teaching me about different kinds of paint. Gouache vs. tempera, etc. Don't tell my mom that because she's tried to teach me about paint my whole life, but I wouldn't listen.

Kasey, I know you're busy and I know you're not emailing us back right now even though it's been TOO LONG, but I'll never take you off here because I know you're there I KNOW YOU'RE READING THIS. We love you so much. Hope you're having so much fun when you're not working or studying and I hope you are so excited about life that you're never sleeping in never-sleep NYC.

TALK SOON RACK FOREVER.

Roses

The breakup with Mélanie was torturous and Rosemarie sank into it, letting herself really *feel* it. Even though it was only two months, it was the longest time she'd been in an open, real relationship with a woman, and weirdly, Rosemarie wanted to remember even the bad parts, as a guide for something she knew would happen again. She found a hope in that—that she'd get to do it again. Rosemarie was returning to the United States and Mélanie was going to Vienna to live with her sister, and they said they'd call and write. Lied and said they'd meet up again one day when they could.

Rosemarie missed Mélanie the whole flight to the United States and missed her more when she was at Leo's door in Boston, meeting his girlfriend for the first time. They hung out as a trio for a day, and Rosemarie was glad to get Leo all to herself for two days too. She was surprised how hard it was not to think about him having sex with Annie and Annie's rosin fingers scratching down his back. Her curves like the cello she played, her hands in his hair.

Or how hard it was not to be able to kiss him.

But they rubbed noses and shared beers on rooftops, looking out over the city. One night, she told him about Mélanie and Leo said he was sorry but he also said "good for you" and they sang together up there under the stars. Just the two of them.

"KASEY FRITZ, IT'S ROSES! I LOVE YOU AND I FOUND YOU!"

When Kasey poked her head out of her dorm window, her smile was so big Rosemarie couldn't wait for her to get down there so she could hug her. The next morning Ada and Caro were in New York too, and

285

the first thing they did was take the subway to Magnolia Bakery, only getting lost once. Then RACK spent the day wandering the city in the spring air and spent the night holding hands and singing at the Chicks concert at Madison Square Garden, together again for the first time since Kasey left Goldie.

2019

39

ADA

Ada told the cop she didn't know anything about how Trey had ended up in the water, but she did tell him Caro had bruises on her arms and neck the night before she was admitted to the hospital and how she'd been wearing long sleeves more lately in this heat. Ada told him how upset Caroline would be after one of their rows and that whenever Trey came around, her mood would change. How she'd shrink herself. Ada mentioned that Trey hated Caro working at the bakery and wanted her to stay home all day so he could control her.

The cop was a friend of her dad's, and Ada had made his son's Spider-Man birthday cake last month. He was gentle in his questioning, although Ada's tears were real. She was tired and stressed and only a few days out from her first murder, so she allowed herself to feel paper thin without struggling against it too much, assuming it was an important part of the trauma-healing process. Or at least, it sounded like something one of those mental health influencers would post in a colorful square of text on Instagram.

After hugging Silas and telling him she'd talk to him later, she saw

Leo Bell sitting on the bench outside of the police station reading. She sat next to him.

"Hey. Are you here to talk to the police too?" Ada asked.

"Nah, just waiting for Ro. I think my mom is coming by later, though. She said she had something to say about the Foxberrys and Trey, specifically, but she didn't want to say it in front of me because she'd have to use bad words," Leo said, raising his eyebrow.

"Okay, she cracks me up. Does she know you're *thirty-three* years old?" Ada said.

"Guess not."

"Wow. I've never heard your mom cuss. I can't even picture it. Seems like the world would split in two or lightning would strike the church or something. I've never heard your mom say an unkind word about *anyone*. This is beyond intense," Ada said.

Her blood tingled. Something was happening and she could feel it the same way she could feel the sweat behind her ears sitting out in the Goldie afternoon sun. Her anxiety had certainly quelled a little upon hearing Leo's mom was coming down unprompted to let the police know that when Trey Foxberry died, maybe it wasn't the Good Lord who had called him home. Maybe it was the devil himself.

"Tell Roses to call me later?" Ada said to him, standing.

"Absolutely. Also remind your husband that anytime he wants a disc golf rematch, he knows where to find me," Leo said.

"Absolutely."

———

Ada was walking into the hospital as Beau was walking out. They stepped aside to talk.

"How's our girl?" Ada asked.

"She's good."

"And your baby?"

"She's good too," he said, tugging at his earlobe and chuckling a bit.

"I'm so relieved for Caro. That she doesn't have to worry about Trey. I mean, it's *truly* for the best."

"Yeah. I'm not wasting any grief on that man, and I hope she doesn't waste too much either. When I look at her face and think about him doing that...I wish he'd come back to life so I could be the one to kill him this time. *If* somebody killed him," Beau said.

"Well, I hope you didn't tell the cops that," Ada said, swatting his arm.

"No. Not yet, at least. They've got me on a list because of what happened out here the other day," Beau said, motioning to the spot in the parking lot where he'd confronted Trey. That day seemed like a lifetime away to Ada now; Trey was alive then and now Trey was dead. "Do y'all think I killed him?" Beau asked her.

"No." Ada shook her head. "Absolutely not."

"I swear I didn't."

"Trust me—I believe you, Beau," Ada said, thinking of a day in the future when she could have a good laugh about him saying that.

"My aunt Lucinda's the coroner now, so she'll be doing the autopsy," he said.

"How did I forget Lucinda's your aunt? *She's* the one who called and told you about what Trey did to Caro."

Something was *definitely* happening. Ada's toes buzzed.

"Oh yeah. She loves her some Caroline. She used to get on me real bad saying I should've moved back to Goldie and married her, and well, yeah, I probably should've if she would've had me," Beau said.

"Don't you dare say *if* she would've had you! You and I both know how easy that would've been, Beau Bramford. How long are you staying in town?" she asked.

"I don't know. Long as I need to. I'd hate to run off like a deadbeat dad or something. Gotta stay. I'll be around," Beau said.

"Good," Ada said, hugging him.

———

After getting all four boys to sleep, Ada fell on their bed and let out her breath.

"Ugh. I don't want to stress you out any more than I know you already are, but yeah...I've gotta tell you something," Grayson said, sitting next to her.

"Go right on ahead," Ada said. No use fighting it. Everything was happening at once, and this was how it was going to be for who knew how long. Her anxiety was a washing machine inside of her stomach, swishing and shaking—a violent maelstrom attempting to suck up all the good and calm. She had to fight it off. *Had* to. She closed her eyes and, as much as she could, tried to focus on how comfortable that bed was. So big, so soft. It made her feel like a little bunny tucked into a giant nest. A little sleepy bunny in a peaceful forest, surrounded by fluff.

"It's the Foxberrys funneling the drugs into Goldie. Through the distillery. Some of it goes all the way back to Kasey's stepdad, Roy, growing weed for them. That's why their lawyers protected Roy from ever being charged for Angie's murder. The Foxberrys knew he did it, but they covered it up. It used to be mostly weed, but now it's opioids. The Foxberrys are probably the ones selling the same pills that killed those kids that one weekend in Adora Springs. No telling what they put in there," Grayson said. Ada opened her eyes and watched him rub his forehead.

Ada tried to be that little bunny as she let it sink in.

But that little bunny was getting stomped by the fucking Foxberrys. She knew every last one of them was complicit. In covering up Angie's murder, in pumping drugs into Goldie and Adora Springs and killing those kids. Now she was paranoid her mom would get mixed up with it too. What if? Ada didn't know anything about how that stuff worked! But what if the pharmacy was closed one night and her mom got desperate? What then?

And Trey! He'd tortured Caroline. Ada was so glad *she'd* been the one to bring the rock down on his head. For everything! For every woman on earth who'd had to put up with a no-good man!

Thank God her husband was a good one.

Ada sat up.

"Grayson, it was us. It was me and Roses and Kase. We did it. We killed Trey."

2006

40

Caro had moved from Myrtle's Diner to Plum Bakery halfway through pastry school. The original plan was that when Ada graduated with her degree in interior design, she and Caro would start planning for Oh Plum. But when Ada asked her if she'd be okay with taking the reins to Plum Bakery herself so Ada could focus on Plum Designs and Plum Florals, Caro's face had turned red and her bottom lip quivered like a Disney princess.

Ada told her that this didn't mean they couldn't have their dream together one day; it just meant she had something else she needed to do first. Caro didn't say anything, just left, even though Ada begged her to stay and talk about it some more.

From: AdaPinkPlum@gmail.com
To: RosemarieCloverKingston@gmail.com,
CarolineCaroppenheimer@gmail.com, KaseyJosephineFritz@gmail.com
Subject: [no subject]

Hey.

I'm gonna come right out and tell y'all that Caro isn't speaking to me at the moment and hasn't been for the past two weeks because for now (and only for now!) Oh Plum is a bust. It's a long story and I'll spare you in this email. I've included you here, Caro, because I want to tell all three of you this at the same time.

I had an abortion last week.

Honestly, I never thought of keeping it and I didn't tell y'all before because I didn't need advice. Grayson is the only person who knows. We went to Adora Springs for it on Monday and I stayed in his room at the lake house with the "stomach flu" for three days.

We want to have babies someday! A whole bunch of them.

For now, I really-really want to stick to the plan and I've made my peace with God about it. Grayson has too.

We're okay.

I wanted to tell y'all, although y'all have to swear not to make a big deal about it right now because I won't be able to handle it. So, tell me your stuff instead please! I mean it. Don't dwell on this. Tell me something else that's going on.

I love you and miss you all so much and Caro, I especially miss you because you're so close, but still so far away. I'm sorry! I'm so sorry! Please, let's talk?

RACK FOREVER. And ever.

Ada

From: RosemarieCloverKingston@gmail.com
To: AdaPinkPlum@gmail.com, CarolineCaroppenheimer@gmail.com,
KaseyJosephineFritz@gmail.com
Subject: Re: [no subject]

Ada,

I love you so much. I'm here and here anytime if you want to talk about this more. Understood if you don't. (But seriously call me call me call me soon.)

Okay . . . if you want a distraction, we can talk about how Leo casually mentioned that he and Annie were talking about getting engaged after they finish school which is equal parts way too much planning ahead and way too fast in my opinion even though it's not fast at all?? Yeah . . . I have a LOT of feelings about that. Some of which I can attempt (???) to distill. Do I want him to be my boyfriend or my best friend forever, why have I never known this? Am I jealous of Annie? YES. Will I always be? I DON'T KNOW!

Also, I can't stand the fact that you and Caro aren't speaking so FIX THAT IMMEDIATELY OR I'M FLYING HOME IN THE MORNING. I could probably talk Kasey into THAT. Or call me on three-way so I can talk you through this? Please! (Remember we used to switch off and do that in middle school whenever we had fights? Whenever two of us are fighting, we have to figure it out together! Nothing's changed!)

RF.

Roses

From: KaseyJosephineFritz@gmail.com

To: RosemarieCloverKingston@gmail.com, AdaPinkPlum@gmail.com, CarolineCaroppenheimer@gmail.com

Subject: Re: [no subject]

Ada, I love you too. I believe in you and trust you to do exactly what you need to do. You've made like, the most consistent, best decisions of anyone I've ever known. And same re: being here if you want to talk about it.

Or! For *my* distraction, I can tell you about the terrible date I went on last night and how he ignored me for the second half of it because his friend showed up and they zoned out playing *Call of Duty*. He forgot I was there!!! I give up.

Roses, you and Leo are obsessed with each other and always will be. It's a lot for anyone to handle so yeah!! Buckle up, Annie!!

Also, MAKE UP YOU TWO. I cannot come back to Goldie right now or anytime soon to fix this. I NEED MORE TIME.

I LOVE YOU. RACK FOREVER.

Kase

GOODBYE EARL

From: CarolineCaroppenheimer@gmail.com
To: RosemarieCloverKingston@gmail.com, AdaPinkPlum@gmail.com,
KaseyJosephineFritz@gmail.com
Subject: Re: [no subject]

Ada, OH MY GOD. Well now I'm only mad that you didn't tell me this so I could cook and bake for you while you were at the lake house. What in the world did you eat? I love you so much and we'll talk about everything in like a minute, because I'm coming straight to your house after I stop at the bakery for a pie.

TALK ABOUT EVERYTHING ELSE SO SOON, GIRLS. Rosemarie, your Leo...and Kasey, your bad dates!! Ahh!!

LOVE AND RACK FOREVER.

Caro

Act III

But if the while I think on thee, dear friend, all losses are restored and sorrows end.

—William Shakespeare

2019

41

CRESSIDA BELL

Officer Duncan: Mrs. Bell, why have you decided to come down to
the station today?

Cressida Bell: Because I know y'all are trying to figure out what
happened to that Foxberry boy. My son, Leo, was in the same
graduating class. Is this a murder investigation?

OD: It's simply a death investigation at this time.

CB: Okay, well I was curious because *if* it becomes a murder investigation, I think it's best that y'all know Trey Foxberry could be a
horrible person who said *horrible* things. I'm praying for his mother,
I really am, but that boy had the devil in him when he wanted to.

OD: Could you elaborate for me?

CB: Once, when he was in high school, he and some of his friends
were walking past when I was locking up the church for the
night. Trey asked me if...

OD: Asked you if...

CB: He asked if me and my husband...ever had sex in the church.
There's a couch in the lobby outside the sanctuary...and he
asked if we'd ever...done it...there. But that's not exactly what
he said.

299

OD: What did he say, exactly?

CB: He said… "Do you and Reverend Bell… *f-u-c-k* on the couch after service?"

OD: Well, that's an awful, inappropriate thing for someone to say to you, Mrs. Bell, I agree.

CB: Let me tell you the *worst* part.

OD: Go ahead.

CB: His daddy heard him and didn't say a word! I looked up and saw him. He didn't correct the boys at all. He was sitting in his truck, watching it happen. I couldn't believe it. That family gets away with *everything* big and small, and maybe if it was someone else, you could chalk it up to him being young and stupid, because Officer Duncan, I raised a teenage boy, so trust me—I know what they can be like. But Trey Foxberry has never been held accountable for anything in his life and neither has his daddy. Same probably goes for his grandfather too, if you ask around enough. I wish my mama was still on this earth to tell me some stories because she lived in Goldie her whole life and she used to go to school with Trey's granddaddy. So, can you take my statement and keep it in a file somewhere in case anything comes up? Again, I'm sorry he's dead. I don't wish that on a mother, ever. I have the Holy Spirit and the Holy Spirit won't allow me in good conscience to wish that on anyone. But *if* somebody did hurt Trey Foxberry, maybe it was because no one had ever told him no, not once in his life. He thought he could do and say anything. And what he did to his poor wife—

OD: What he *allegedly* did.

CB: What he *allegedly* did to his poor wife. Either way, Reverend Bell wouldn't feel comfortable doing the funeral if the Foxberrys asked, although I doubt they would. And I heard Mr. Foxberry was raised Episcopalian, not Baptist. I figured they wouldn't have a big funeral anyway, maybe just a little memorial service later...after this is settled. I won't take up any more of your time, but all I'm saying is that God has His own way of making things right, even if we don't like how He does it.

———

NAOMI BROOKS

Officer Duncan: Naomi, why have you decided to come down to the station today?

Naomi Brooks: Because I heard people were giving statements about Trey Foxberry. Is this a murder investigation?

OD: No, it's not. It's simply a death investigation at this point.

NB: Oh. So, can I tell you what he did to me when we were in college since he's dead now? I never pressed charges back then because he said he'd ruin my life if I did. His mom and dad told me that too. Can you believe that? I was only nineteen and here were these...*parents*...these *adults*...with a *lot* of money telling me they'd take joy in ruining my life if I lied about their son, but I wouldn't have had to lie. I would have been telling the truth. They gave me fifty thousand dollars to keep quiet, and I'm not really allowed to talk about that to anyone, but I can tell y'all, can't I? You won't tell?

OD: Correct. We won't disclose that information to anyone.

NB: I was at a frat party with my friends and I know...I know how generic it is to start this story off at a frat party...but that's where we were, and Trey was a big shot in the frat—I mean, of course he was. So, that night, I drank too much and my friend Sparrow was in town, and she took me upstairs to lie down and I fell asleep. When I woke up, Trey was on the bed with me and he was putting his hand up my skirt. I screamed because he scared me and...I'd never talked to him or anything...I went to South Goldie and he went to Goldie . . . I saw him around, but I didn't know him. None of that has anything to do with what he did, but do you know what I mean?

OD: I understand, yes.

NB: So, when I screamed, he asked why I screamed . . . he asked what was wrong with me. He said he saw how I was looking at him downstairs, but I wasn't looking at him in any way downstairs when I saw him . . . I was only looking around because it was so packed. Then, he told me he loved how short my skirt was . . . but it wasn't that short and that's not the point.

OD: It's definitely not the point. He had no right to touch you without your consent.

NB: I pushed him off, but not before he kissed me and . . . *touched* me . . . he sexually assaulted me, and later when he was gone, Sparrow came back and she was drunk too, and I told her what happened, but I made her swear not to tell. I didn't tell anyone else, but the next day, Trey found me and said he barely remembered what happened since he was pretty drunk, but I was a slut and that's what he'd tell everyone. The day after that I saw his mom at the grocery store and she basically said the same thing to me. A week later, his dad came to my dorm and asked me to sign a form and said he'd get me fifty thousand dollars, so I did it because my parents barely had money to afford the *books* I needed, let alone the classes. I lied to my parents and told them I got a scholarship. I never told anyone but Sparrow until this morning when I told my parents and my great-aunt Myrtle.

OD: I'm sorry this happened to you. Please tell Miss Myrtle and your parents hello for me.

NB: Thank you, Officer Duncan. I will.

SPARROW KIM

Officer Duncan: Hey, Sparrow. I talked to your dad yesterday at the restaurant, by the way. Had to shake his hand. He made me the best spicy kimchi tofu stew I've ever had in my life. I had a dream about it last night—I'm serious.

Sparrow Kim: Ha! I'll tell him you said that. He'll love it.

OD: What brings you down to the station?

SK: Oh, I thought everyone who knew Trey Foxberry was supposed to come down and talk about him because someone killed him?

OD: We haven't determined the manner of death or if a crime has even been committed.

SK: Well, specifically, I told my friend Naomi I'd come here and corroborate her story. She didn't ask me to, but I wanted to.

OD: Okay. Go ahead.

SK: When we were in college, Trey sexually assaulted her, and I saw him as he was coming out of the bedroom. I was with Naomi right afterward...she was a wreck and kept blaming herself, and I told her to stop. I told her it wasn't her fault. How could it be her fault? She was *sleeping*. And y'know, it's not like Trey was one hundred percent terrible one hundred percent of the time...that wouldn't be realistic, right? He was charming enough sometimes—that's how he worked. Like, in elementary school, he helped me get gum out of my hair one time. Also, early senior year of high school, I went on one date with him, but when I said no to another one because I thought we'd be better off as friends, he called me a lesbian in front of everyone. His wife, Caroline...she's best friends with Rosemarie Kingston, who used to be...well, she used to be one of my best friends in high school...but I screwed that up. I owe her an apology, actually...but yeah, from what I know of Caroline, she's a sweet person and I keep thinking about what everyone's saying he did to her. A *lot* of people would've wanted to kill Trey for doing that to Caroline. I mean, *if* someone killed him.

OD: Thanks for coming in, Sparrow.

SK: Of course. You can put this in some sort of file somewhere? I know there's nothing to be done now about what Trey did to Naomi back then, but...it's still important for women to tell the truth, even if it's late.

OD: I agree with you.

42

KASEY

On Monday night, Silas showed up at the farmhouse unannounced, and Kasey zapped with wild panic that maybe he was there to arrest her.

No. He was the same Silas she'd known back then. Right? But what if—

No.

He'd traded the cop car for his black truck and gotten a haircut. He'd swapped his uniform for a T-shirt and dark jeans, a pair of all-white slip-on sneakers. Tonight? He was *annoyingly* handsome. Why these irrational, conflicting feelings? Why tonight? Her heart had been jumping rope lately anyway, from the murder and the new Trey nightmares, but now it was going double-speed double Dutch for too many different reasons.

Her hands were shaking when she let Silas in, but she tried to act as normal as possible. He didn't *seem* any different. Everything about him was still familiar. He still smelled the same and had the same scampish look in his eyes.

"I'm assuming you know all about how the Foxberrys knew Roy was responsible for your mom's death and helped cover that up?" he asked after they exchanged *hey*s.

"Yeah, I know. Is that why you're here?" Kasey was about to ask him if he wanted to sit down, but he kept talking.

"Grayson said some guys from construction have been bringing it up again lately and apparently they've all known for years, but there was nothing they could do about it. The Foxberrys had the police force in their pocket back then."

"Yes. I just got off the phone with Ada," she said. Ada had FaceTimed her, and she ignored a phone call from Devon to keep talking to her. Ada also let her know that she told Grayson what happened to Trey and he was obviously sworn to secrecy, but maybe he told Silas anyway? Didn't they tell each other things?

"Okay. I figured as much," he said. "I...I am *so* sorry."

"Sorry we skipped the whole part where I tell you the truth about how my mom died, because I should be the one who's sorry," Kasey said. Couldn't she just tell him *everything* and be done with it? "Do you want a beer?" She walked into the kitchen and he followed her.

"Something stronger?"

"Even better."

Kasey had hated buying that bottle of Foxberry Bourbon last week, and she'd poured the rest of it out after Trey was in the water, ripped off the label, and recycled the glass. There was a non-Foxberry bottle of Tennessee whiskey in the cabinet and she got it down, held it up for Silas.

"Yes, thank you, and you don't have to apologize for anything. It was a long time ago," he said.

"I feel like we've been saying that to each other a lot lately, haven't we? Everything was a long time ago. But if it was *such* a long time ago and we should be over it, why the hell aren't we?" she asked.

Kasey steadied her hands as she poured two short glasses of whiskey and tried to calm herself as they clinked.

This is Silas. Silas is one of us. Always has been, always will be.

They went into the living room and sat on opposite ends of the couch. She put her back against the side and stretched her legs out toward him. When she looked down at her fingers, Silas did too.

"Where's that big ol' rock that's usually blinding me, Fritz?" Silas asked and drank.

"On my bedroom dresser. Or *the* bedroom dresser. Feels weird to say *my* about anything in this house yet, although it is...mine," Kasey said. The last time she'd lived there was *a long time ago*.

Everything was a long time ago and everything is right now.

"Why aren't you wearing it?"

"I took it off to move those branches and I decided to keep it off because I've been doing other stuff around here." Kasey looked at him as she drank. *I took it off so I wouldn't lose it while we were killing Trey.* Could Silas read her mind? His eyes crinkled in the corners now; she loved those new crinkles. He also had a new, small scar on his right forearm that hadn't been there fifteen years ago. She wondered what differences he'd noticed about her.

She'd filled out a little, but she liked it. When she was a teenager, she didn't love being so skinny, *too* skinny. She'd secretly wanted a body more like Ada's because she looked more like a woman and less like a little girl. Kasey had a baby face, but her body finally gave her the breasts she'd wanted when she was in college. The first time he'd seen her completely naked, Devon had told her that he wished he were a better artist so he could draw her properly because she had the most beautiful body he'd ever seen. She laughed and told him it was a brilliant line, but she'd already slept with him so he didn't have to try to get her in bed anymore. He told her he was serious, and got out a pencil and a pad of paper and sketched her by the lamplight. She still had the drawing pinned on the wall above her bed.

She missed Devon. During their last quick call, he'd pressed her some more about when she was coming home to New York, and she'd been as gentle as possible with him, understanding his anxiety. She imagined another timeline where they were sitting in shorts in the sunshine at a Vampire Weekend concert with their friends, sharing a tall boy. She put herself in his Brooklyn apartment in the dark, thought about how his place was her second home. Her bamboo toothbrush in the cup next to his, as well as her tube of LunaCrush salt toothpaste he hated so much it made her laugh. How much she loved how he sat in a chair, resting his hand on his thigh. His *thighs*. She thought of his sister, Honora, her colleague who'd also become one of her close friends and who had texted Kasey yesterday saying hey and asking what was up. Kasey had written her back quickly saying things were okay and she would talk more soon. She sent her a picture of the lake with heart emojis, successfully compartmentalizing the fact that Trey died in that dark water.

When Kasey was on the phone with Devon, he told her about a Boston terrier puppy he'd seen on his run and that he tried to take a pic of it, but it was blurry. He sent her the blurry pic anyway, the pup a black-and-white smudge in the corner. It'd broken her heart, that smudge, because Devon was trying *so* hard. He was doing the right things. He knew how much she loved dogs even though she didn't have one. He knew how scarred she'd been when Roy had killed her dog when she was a kid. Talking about the dogs they saw was a fun thing they'd always done together, and Devon was still doing it even though she'd been avoiding him, because he was Devon and her pain didn't scare him and neither did the walls she put up.

Kasey was thinking about all this as Silas watched her eyes and barely smiled. He threw back the rest of his whiskey.

Slowly, the smile disappeared. Maybe this was it.

"Kase, the Foxberrys are gonna keep pushing. They probably would be doing it anyway, but Trey's car being in your driveway and his body found downstream from here...they're not gonna let up. If there's something you need to tell me, I need you to go ahead and do that so I can help you out best I can. I'll do that—you know I will. I'll do anything you need me to do, but you have to be straight with me," he said.

"The night Roy killed my mom, I tried to scream for you. Just in case you hadn't driven away yet. Just in case you could've heard me," Kasey said, pointing over Silas's shoulder. He turned around to look at the wall. "I *felt* you out there. Did you stay?"

"I sat at the end of the driveway for thirty minutes, and when you didn't come back out, I left. I didn't hear you," Silas said softly.

"I tried to scream but couldn't, because when Roy slammed me into the wall, I was out cold, and when I woke up, he was passed out. I wished he was dead, but he wasn't. My mom was."

"Kasey—"

"Thank you for staying out there, for waiting for me. I don't know how long I was out...time meant nothing anymore. I grabbed some of my stuff and left for Caro's." She finished her whiskey and wiped her eyes.

It was painfully unfair that the first night she and Silas were together like that was also the same night her mom died. She wondered if he was thinking about that too. They were so quiet she heard the train whistle. Most of the time it was too faint to hear from the living room.

"There were some different footprints on the side of the house and by the dock, meaning there might've been *three* people out there with Trey, walking around the backyard. Could've been from another night if you had the girls over but I saw the prints and I didn't say a word about it to anyone else at the station just in case, and I won't. I even made a mess of it so no one else would notice. Kasey, I put...I put a bag of confiscated pills I stole from the evidence room in his car, just in case I needed to...protect you, so you need to tell me *exactly* what happened so I can help you," Silas said gently.

One big *ha* came out of Kasey's mouth. Silas Castelow had planted *extra* drugs in Trey's car. Ridiculous! She'd been so stupid to panic. Of course Silas was who he was. She *knew* him. Now everything was happening exactly as it should. She laughed some more. She couldn't help it.

"What's...what's funny?" he asked, tilting his head.

"I . . . it's just . . . wow . . . thank you, Silas. For thinking of me. But—"

"But what?"

"You don't have to—" Kasey said.

"I think I do."

"Did you see some smiley-face stickers in Trey's glove compartment?"

"Yeah, why? What—"

"Did you put them in a little bag and seal it? Take them down to the station?"

Kasey watched her words register on his face. He shook his head no. "I guess that's because at that point I wasn't thinking about him. I was thinking about *you*," he said.

"Y'know, when you pulled up . . . for a second I thought maybe you were here to arrest me."

"Do you *really* think I'd do that?" he asked. He put his hand on his thigh and rubbed.

"Well, people change. Don't they?"

"Nah. Not all that much. I haven't. Have you?"

"I don't know. Have I? Is this conversation going anywhere?" she asked.

"I think it *can*, Kase."

"How else are you going to help me?"

"By making sure they don't look harder at this farmhouse. By making sure anytime anyone brings you up as having anything to do with this, I divert their attention. By making sure the women coming forward to tell their stories are heard. By making sure my uncle, the police chief, knows that this was an accident and will stay an accident forever."

"If I'd killed Roy, he wouldn't have been able to kill my mom."

"You were a kid. That wasn't on you."

"I was scared to let you come in here with me that night. Scared of what could've happened to you, scared of—"

"Hey . . . I understand. I understand why you did what you did. Everyone does."

"I left her dead on the floor and I lied about what happened to her," she said.

"She wouldn't have wanted you to do anything different, Kase. You know you did the right thing."

"I'll never forgive myself for it."

"You *have* to," Silas said, reaching for her.

"Well, I can't."

"Come here." He leaned forward. "You *have* to," he said again.

Kasey, crying, crawled closer to him, and he pulled her the rest of the way into his lap. She was *so* tired of keeping secrets.

———

"I've only trusted a handful of men my entire life and you're one of them," she said when she was finished telling him everything. "I should've told you how I saw Trey acting when I went to Caroline's that morning. Maybe you could've—"

"What he did is not your fault," Silas said.

It was too much, they were too close, she was running on too little sleep.

The kissing wasn't an accident.

The lean-in started at Taylor's wedding, dancing to "Cowboy Take Me Away" and "Strawberry Wine," and ended with Silas's whiskey-tongue in her mouth on the couch. They tussled tenderly, kissed some more. Now he was on top of her, with his arm around her waist. His hands moved to her face. In her hair, behind her head. His mouth was on her neck, his breath hot. She opened her legs so he could sink and settle there. Her body was a question in lightning and his was attempting to answer in thunder. She could feel him. She remembered.

Cowboy, take me away.

No, don't.

"Shit. Shit! Si, you have to go. Like, now," Kasey said, pushing him.

"I have to go?"

311

"Yes! You have to go. Right now!"

"I have to, um...*physically* get off this couch and leave the farmhouse?"

Kasey nodded aggressively and stood.

How long had they been kissing? What happened now?

Silas sat up and put his head in his hands. He stood too.

"Um, all right. I'm obeying your orders and leaving the farmhouse. Right now. Can you please call or text me later? We're nowhere near finished—"

"Yes. I will call or text you later. Go! Rightfuckingnow. I mean it," Kasey said. She pointed and he moved toward the door. She was right behind him. "Wait...you're not going to say anything to anyone about any of this, right? Not what I told you, not the kissing—nothing. Silas, please don't."

"Are you serious? Hell, Kase—"

"Just say you won't, then leave."

"You know I won't. Why do you keep—"

"Okay. Thank you. Bye."

She opened the door and Silas let her push him onto the porch. He turned and put both hands on the doorframe.

"Remember how I used to call you Dandelion? Kase, I love you. I'm in love with you. Look, if you decide not to put that ring back on, that's something you should know," he said. In a small, almost imperceptible movement, he leaned in. She noticed. She noticed everything about him. She'd never be able to forget any of this.

"Silas, go! Of course I remember that! Now, leave before we mess everything up."

She needed to talk to Devon; she loved Devon. She needed to put her engagement ring on and call him. *I love Devon.* Yes, she'd love Silas forever, but Devon was her fiancé and she loved him. She loved him!

Kasey put her hand on Silas's chest and gently pushed.

"All right. I'm leaving. I love you and I'm leaving," he said.

Kasey watched him drive away and closed the door. She put her back against the wood and touched her cheek, feeling like she was in a movie. She went to the bedroom and slipped her engagement ring on. She poured herself another glass of whiskey and called Devon, but he didn't answer. She tried again. And again. She *had* to talk to him. Her body ached with the overwhelming need of it.

When Silas knocked on the door, she snatched it open, ready to yell at him.

But it wasn't Silas.

It was Devon.

There was a little white hatchback in her driveway. Would the porch crack and swallow her up? Had she summoned him with wishes? Devon and his soft eyes, looking tired and handsome, shaking his head at her?

"Kasey, you *gotta* tell me what the hell is going on," he said. He took her face in his hands and kissed her with apocalyptic ardor. Like she was the last woman left on earth. Like he'd been shipwrecked for weeks and there she was, shining on the shore.

2016

43

After being set up on a blind date by his sister, Kasey and Devon hit it off quickly. He was droll and kind, charming in a seemingly effortless way. Kasey liked a lot of small things about him immediately. Like how he said her name and the way he held his fork. He had an easy presence about him, the same way Silas did. Kasey tried to imagine a woman breaking up with Devon and not looking at him on a regular basis like this anymore, deciding she was done with how good he looked in that suit and how pretty his hair was or how much emotion he could convey with his wide eyes. Kasey tried to imagine it but couldn't. She found him quite lovely.

Once she mentioned she was from a small, Southern town, he asked her a lot of cute questions about Goldie. Whether everyone knew everyone (seemed like it, yes) and whether they had festivals all the time (yes) and if she liked living there (sometimes). He was from Long Island and hadn't spent much time in the South, but he told her that he always romanticized it and said he considered *her* romantic by default since she was from a town called Goldie because of how the sun lit it up.

Kasey loved how he shared things about himself but didn't hog the conversation like some of the other men she'd dated. She told him that he was *really* good at this. *This* being a first date, *this* being drinks, *this* being a man in this world who was obviously handsome and successful and smart but who also didn't seem to think the sun rose and set on his watch either.

"Honestly? This is by far the best first date I've ever been on," Devon had said as they were leaving the bar.

"Honestly? Same," Kasey said.

They kissed on her stoop at the end of the night. Kasey had been wanting to do it since the moment his sister showed her the picture. His mouth was dark beer and peppermint. It was two in the morning, and she was exhausted but all lit up with excitement for this newness, and Devon's shirt smelled so good—like some sort of ridiculously expensive cologne, but only faintly, as if he'd simply walked past someone who whispered the name of it. She was debating between saying goodbye and inviting him inside when her phone vibrated. Kasey checked it immediately since it was so late.

It was Rosemarie.

Are you awake?? Can you call me
ASAP? Please?

Yes. Just a sec.

"I'm sorry. It's my best friend and I need to call her right now. You can, um...you know what? Just come up," Kasey said, motioning for Devon to follow her. She was a smidge drunk and trusted that he wouldn't murder her, confident that Honora certainly wouldn't have set her up with her brother if he were a murderer. Right? Right.

Once they were inside her apartment, Kasey put Devon on the couch with a glass of water and the remote in case he wanted to watch something. Quickly, she showed him how to turn it on and flip through. He was easygoing and content, leaving his shoes by the door and settling in, making himself at home. She excused herself to the bedroom and called Rosemarie.

"Hey—"

"Kase, I have breast cancer. It's treatable but I have to get surgery and chemo and I know I'm telling you at two in the morning. I'm sorry...I didn't forget about the fact that you're three hours ahead of me, but I wanted you to know. I'm weirdly okay right now...although I know I won't always be. Esme's brother is my oncologist and she's with me. My parents are on the way here," Rosemarie said.

The room spun; Kasey had to sit to stop it.

"Roses, I'm coming too," she said as soon as she could string the words together through the thick cloud in her head.

"Okay," Rosemarie said.

After she got more details and told her how much she loved her, Kasey went to the couch and blurted everything out to Devon, who leaned forward and got such a sad look on his face Kasey started crying and couldn't stop. He opened his arms and she curled into his lap. He held her there, listening and telling her everything was going to be all right. Kasey was a wreck, but she forced herself to think of things that were fixed and true. She had to.

Rosemarie will be okay. We can get through this. We'll do anything for each other. We can get through this. We can get through anything.

We can get through anything.

She cried herself to sleep on Devon's shoulder, and when she woke up in the morning, he was still asleep in his suit underneath her. He hadn't budged.

2019

44

JOANNA CASTELOW

Officer Neil: Mrs. Castelow, what was it you wanted to discuss?

Joanna Castelow: Just doing my part when it comes to the Trey Foxberry murder investigation if it helps.

ON: It's a *death* investigation.

JC: Right. *Death* investigation. My sons told me Trey couldn't swim, which I always thought was the oddest thing since they live so close to the lake. I mean, not *on* the lake like we do, but I don't think I know *anyone* in this town who can't swim. Makes no sense.

ON: Someone said he liked being on the water, like fishing and boats, but never cared for being in it. He might've had a cousin who drowned when he was a kid? I don't know. Everyone reacts differently to those sorts of things.

JC: Well, I guess that makes sense in a strange way, doesn't it? Figures. He was a strange man.

ON: How do you mean?

JC: He had no choice since he got it from his mama and daddy, I guess. My husband and I grew up with his daddy, Max. His mama grew up in Adora Springs. Max threatened to kill the girl he dated before he met Paula. Did you know that? That was in high school, but I'll never forget it.

ON: No, ma'am, I didn't know that, but you know that doesn't pertain at all to this investigation.

JC: Right. Of course not, but this is really close to my heart because Caroline is one of my daughter-in-law Ada's *dearest* friends. Those two have been inseparable since they were babies—all four of them have been. Rosemarie, Ada, Caroline, and Kasey. Kasey's poor mother...everyone says that Roy Dupont killed Angie, but Roy never spent one day in prison, because the Foxberrys made it all go away. Well, I guess you know all this, don't you?

ON: I can't speak to any of that, Mrs. Castelow.

JC: Of course you can't. Well, I saw Caroline and Trey arguing once right outside the B and B not too long ago. She was crying. I was at the window watching. I thought about it as soon as I heard what he'd done to her.

ON: What do you mean?

JC: How he beat her up and pushed her through a window.

ON: *Allegedly.*

JC: Uh-huh. My brother is the chief of police, so trust me, I get it. I know the language and I said what I said. Maxwell Foxberry *allegedly* threatens to kill a woman forever ago and no one does anything about it since it was just an allegation, right? Like how Roy *allegedly* killed Angie Fritz and was never even investigated for it? So, it's all this *allegedly* that's mucking up the truth. Men keep getting away with it. So, whether Trey drowned on his own or whether someone wanted him dead, the Foxberrys have pissed off a lot of people in this town and I wouldn't mind seeing them run out of it, to be quite honest. Does this help? Can you put this down somewhere for someone to read later? I'm not even scared for you to put my name on it. I'm not scared of the Foxberrys. Never have been. Never will be.

ON: I've got it down, Mrs. Castelow. Thank you.

———

CLAIRE MILLER

Officer Neil: Hi, Claire. What brings you down today?

Claire Miller: I want to talk about Trey Foxberry and...

ON: And?

CM: This is hard for me.

ON: Take your time.

CM: I feel terrible. It's terrible, what I did...I don't know if I can...

ON: There are usually bottles of water in here, but we've been busy today. Let me go get some more. Would you like one?

CM: Yes, please.

ON: There you go. When you're ready, continue.

CM: Thank you. I...I dated Trey for a little bit when we were in high school. I was in love with Leo Bell, but he and Rosemarie Kingston are...well, no one could ever get between them. It's like this *supernatural* thing they have together that used to *torture* me when I was a teenager, but you force yourself to get over those things to survive. So yeah, Trey and I dated and broke up. Got back together and broke up. Sometimes when we were both home from college, we'd hook up. I liked him a lot, and he did have a way of making me feel like I was the only girl in the world sometimes...but he could be really jealous. He'd lose his mind if I talked to certain guys. Like Leo, for example, since he knew how much I liked him. Once, when Leo's band was in town, I went to see them at the amphitheater, and after the show, I gave Leo a hug, and later, Trey grabbed my face and smacked me for it. I smacked him right back too.

ON: Good for you.

CM: I was stupid enough to keep going back to him. Most of the time he kept me a secret, but I didn't care, because I was kind of seeing someone else. I'm not proud of any of it, but it's what happened. With Trey and me it was mostly sexual, because that's all we did toward the end. Some of it was while he was married to Caroline, and when I got pregnant, he said if I didn't get an abortion, he'd tell everyone at the church about us and share private photographs of me. I've worked there for so long...I couldn't bear the thought of letting the Bells or my family down like that, so I did it...I got the abortion. That was three months ago. I stopped sleeping with him after that, and I felt awful every time I saw Caroline at the bakery, because she is such a sweet person and she deserved so much more than him. Or what I was doing to her. I'm guessing he probably got meaner after I stopped seeing him—I don't know. Maybe he was upset because I ended it. It was hard to know what he was thinking most of the time. But I believe it if Caroline says he's the one who beat her up, because he did have such an awful temper. Maybe he got tired of being that way and maybe he jumped into the lake to end it.

ON: Is that really what you think happened?

CM: Yes. It is. I don't think someone should have to get in trouble for killing him if he did it to himself.

ON: That makes sense.

CM: I'm sad. I'm sad it ended this way.

ON: I understand, Claire. Thanks for letting us know.

LEILANI KINGSTON

Officer Neil: Mrs. Kingston, you're here to give a statement on Trey Foxberry?

Leilani Kingston: I am.

ON: I know your daughter, Rosemarie, and Caroline are very close.

LK: Like sisters, right.

ON: What is it you want to talk about?

LK: Trey's father threatened my husband's life years ago over selling weed in Goldie. Not a big deal and the cops always looked the other way for the most part, since they were buying it sometimes too. I mean, of course, it's been legalized and everything now, but before all that, my husband used to grow small amounts to sell. All organic, mostly to the hippies here who didn't grow their own and to cancer patients, the *occasional* college kid if they looked over twenty-one. Maxwell Foxberry didn't want my husband selling weed here, since he wanted to be the only source, and he told my husband that. It was around the same time he got Roy Dupont involved in running stuff back and forth from here to Adora Springs and Jesse County, all over these hills. Roy would do anything. The man had no morals. Did you know him?

ON: No, ma'am, I didn't.

LK: You're lucky. Anyway, my husband didn't stop, just went more underground, made a few deals with some big dispensaries. I thought maybe Maxwell had moved on, but one night he came to our house, and thankfully Rosemarie wasn't there, but he told my husband if he didn't stop selling weed in Goldie, he knew some guys that would make sure he couldn't do it anymore.

ON: Y'all took that to mean he was threatening your husband's life?

LK: Right. Then the next week when I ran into Maxwell on my walk, he said that maybe he and I could work out a deal.

ON: What did he mean by that?

LK: Maybe he meant sex? Maybe he meant ... I don't know. I ignored him, but at that point I think Max saw that weed wasn't making enough money anyway, because everyone wanted pills. None of this will leave this room, right?

ON: Everything you and I are discussing will remain confidential.

LK: Thank you. The Foxberrys operate differently and everyone in

Goldie knows it. It's not just Goldie, though; it's all these little
towns. If someone killed Trey Foxberry, it could've been anyone.
Do y'all think someone killed him or that it was an accident?

ON: Right now it's a death investigation.

LK: Well, nothing would surprise me. I'm not one to willingly come
down to the police station and tell anyone my business, but we
love Caroline like she's our own. There have been other . . . things
that have happened in this town . . . things I wish God had
reached down and stopped. Like what happened to my friend
Angie Fritz. I miss her. So much. She didn't deserve that and
neither did Caroline. I wouldn't be surprised if God Himself
came down this time around and snatched Trey away to make
sure he couldn't touch Caroline again. I bet, as long-suffering as
the Bible tells us He is . . . that even God can only take so much.

45

CAROLINE

Caroline was released from the hospital on the Fourth of July. Grandma Mimi took her to the trailer and had a big pot of Caro's favorite home-made vegetable soup on the stove and a berry flag pie cooling on the counter. Caroline's shoulder was secure in a sling, but her eye was still swollen enough that looking through it made her feel dizzy, and the dizziness gave her a headache. Had it really been not even two weeks ago that Trey had done all this? *You're the one who needs help* were the last words she ever said to him, and she hated herself for not saying more. For not telling him that no one had ever crushed her like he had and she'd make sure no one ever could again. When she checked her heart for grief, she didn't find any for Trey or even for what they once had, because those fleeting moments felt foolish and one-sided now after all he'd done.

What she found was grief for the woman she was before she married him. The woman she was in that trailer with her grandma and the woman she was when she was with her sisters. She wanted to make sure her sisters never had to suffer for protecting her. It'd be too much to bear.

She'd gotten into the habit of putting her hand on her stomach to protect the baby, even though she knew it was safe and snug. Trey could never hurt either of them again. The urge to cry about it was overshadowed by the flood of joy she got thinking about how quick and easy Beau had agreed to pretend to be the father. That filled her aching bones with light.

Kasey had invited her to come stay at the farmhouse, and Ada told her she was welcome to stay with her if she didn't mind the boys tearing through the house or the noise that came with it. Rosemarie also offered up her parents' place, which had always been a spot of comfort for Caroline with its rainbow colors and clucking chickens. But it felt so natural and normal to be back in Grandma Mimi's trailer, even though Caro had been living in that big house for the past six months or so—a big house she'd never set foot in again. She was glad it was tucked away on a side street she didn't ever have to drive down if she didn't want to. The house was never hers to begin with; her name wasn't on anything. It all belonged to the Foxberrys. Caroline didn't have a house, but she'd get one. She'd get a little house and raise her baby in it. A little house on the water, nowhere near where they found Trey.

Caroline kept telling Paula that she didn't know what happened to Trey, but Paula was having none of it. She'd been in a rage after they found Trey's body, and made such a scene at the hospital that an officer had to tell her to calm down or he'd have to ask her to leave. He apologized when he said it, but hospital security was involved at that point, and Caro's doctor had told Paula the stress would be too much for her; Caro prayed she wouldn't put it together that she was pregnant yet. She was so grateful when Paula left. But before she walked out the door, Paula told Caroline that she had warned Trey he shouldn't marry her, because she came from nobody, and that if anyone had harmed her son, she'd find out. Caro felt nothing. She was floating, and the painkillers either emptied her out completely or turned up her emotions as high as they'd go. She was up by the ceiling while Paula went on and on about how worthless she was, and Caro's feelings circled the drain and disappeared.

324

*   *   *

The feelings were back now, and she felt a lot of them about being on the couch in Grandma Mimi's trailer again. She felt a lot more *complicated* feelings when Beau stopped by later to see how she was doing.

"I'm not gonna stay too long; just wanted to drop by. I'm glad you're home," Beau said, standing by the door. The trailer park was filled with firework smoke already, and Caro could smell it slipping inside. The word *home* smoked through the air too and wrapped itself around her. She was tired and thirsty, and this was home. She was tired and thirsty, and Trey was dead.

"Come in here and sit down, Beau Bramford," Mimi said, waving him all the way in. A small, rowdy group of laughing children and a yellow mutt tore through the gravel behind him. Caro watched them disappear.

"Yes, ma'am," he said, obeying. "I was thinking about you the other day when they had that tornado in Adora Springs. You always run right out of here when the weather's that bad?" he asked Mimi.

"I do. I usually go to Myrtle's when they start talking about tornadoes, but the other night I was still up at the hospital with Ladybug," Mimi said.

"Good. I don't want to have to worry about you," Beau said.

"No, don't you worry a *bit* about me," she said back to him, slapping his shoulder.

"Thank you for coming to see me," Caroline said.

"How are you feeling? Better?" Beau asked as Mimi handed him a piece of pie with a big scoop of whipped cream on top. He thanked her and she motioned for him to go have a seat next to Caroline. Mimi sat at the table in the kitchen and took the pencil from behind her ear, scribbled on her pattern. Her grandma had been listening to a new romance audiobook in the hospital when Caro was trying to get some sleep. Mimi turned it on now and put her earbuds in, started knitting.

"Is it good?" Caro asked him after he'd taken a bite of pie.

"Of course it is," he said with his mouth full. He put some on a fork and offered it to Caroline, held his hand under her chin to catch the crumbs. He made a joke about her eating for two, and it was awkward and tender and funny, like so many of their encounters had been the past week. When she was in high school working at the diner, their relationship had been oiled-up and easy. She never had to think about it. Now he was divorced and she was a pregnant widow and her grandma was surely listening to everything they said.

"Beau, when I asked you to say the baby's yours, I wasn't meaning you had to stay around or anything...I just meant if anyone asks. That's the story I'm gonna tell because it's the best thing for me and the baby right now. I need to get a lot of distance from Trey's family, and this is the best way," Caroline said. Her head was gauzy and the pain medicine made her tongue thick. She'd spent a lot of energy focusing on speaking clearly when she told him all that, and now she wanted to sleep for a week.

"I understood you and I plan on staying around for a little longer if that's okay."

"That's okay," Caroline said, putting her head on his shoulder. She couldn't keep her eyes open. The sun was out but it was raining now too, soft patters against the window, and Beau's shoulder was warm, and the berries—the whole trailer smelled like berries.

———

The next morning, Kasey stopped by bright and early, and because Caroline had known Kasey her whole life, she quickly recognized Kasey's *something awful has happened* face. Although Caro was sitting on the couch, she touched the side of it to steady herself in case she fell.

The girls must've gotten caught somehow, and Kasey was there to tell her about it.

She wouldn't let them take the blame alone. She could lie and say she asked them to do it. This was partly her fault. At least her grandma was young; she could help raise the baby while Caro was in prison. And Beau. Beau said he wasn't leaving. Beau would help. The pain in her shoulder sharpened, and although she could tell her eye was healing, the room was a little dim when she looked out of it.

Grandma Mimi was knitting another piece of the pastel layette for the baby, watching the television. She offered Kasey the pancakes she'd just made and some coffee.

"No, ma'am. Thank you," Kasey said. Her voice was weird, but Mimi wouldn't notice. Only Caroline. And although Caro assumed Mimi would figure out what happened to Trey soon enough or maybe already knew, Caro hadn't said anything about it to her grandmother yet.

"Let's go to the bedroom," Caroline said, getting up.

Not much had changed about Caroline's bedroom since she moved out. She felt a little behind and immature, living back and forth with her grandma up until she married Trey in her thirties. She and Jay shared an apartment off the town square for about a year, and before she went to Amsterdam with Samuel, they lived together in his house on the other side of the lake.

But it seemed like no matter what happened, she ended up back in her bedroom in that trailer. The same bedroom with the window Kasey would climb through when she didn't want to stay at home. The same bedroom where Caroline would flip through magazines and cut out pictures and come up with pie recipes for all the people in them based on their looks. The same bedroom where she and the rest of RACK would stay up all night making lists of the boys they liked and looking at stuff on Caro's computer and listening to the same songs on repeat.

Caro was awash with the sticky nostalgia of their high school memories—both good and bad—as she sat on the bed and steeled herself for what Kasey was about to tell her. Those memories could keep her going. She needed to picture them one more time so she could store them away and go back to them later. She looked around the room, trying to hold on to every last bit. Caro could feel her life about to change, and her life had already changed so much since Trey put her in the hospital she wasn't quite sure how much more she could take. How many life-changing moments could a woman have before she was altered completely? Could she get far enough away from who she was that she couldn't even feel who she *used* to be again, no matter how hard she tried?

"Caro, Rosemarie's cancer is back and this time... it's not going away," Kasey said as she sat on the bed. "I didn't want to have to tell you. I wanted you and the baby to rest and you have enough on your mind—"

"What... what do you mean it's not going away?" The fogginess was almost unbearable. Nothing was making sense and her head was hurting again. Her shoulder was hurting. Her entire body. The air was painful. *Everything.*

Someone outside was setting off fireworks a day late; a loud boom spilled across the sky followed by a shimmery hiss.

"It's metastatic. Spreading all over her body now. There are some treatments that can help, but—" Kasey said.

"But what? What? She'll die anyway?" Caro asked, trying to make sense out of something that would never make sense. Imagining a world without Rosemarie was impossible, so Caroline shut the door on it immediately and stared straight ahead.

"She's in the hospital right now for exhaustion and dehydration, basically. No one knew about it besides Leo and Esme and Esme's brother, but only because he's her doctor. I'd have to assume that her mom must've known *something* was up, but... I don't know. She looked a little skinny to me, but she's always been a little skinny and she didn't *seem* sick. Did she seem sick to you?" Kasey asked, shaking her head to answer her own question.

Caro shook her head too and asked if she could go to the hospital and see her.

"Of course. We can go right now. Everyone's up there," Kasey said.

"How did you get here?"

"Silas dropped me off."

"I thought you were here to tell me the cops know about Trey," Caro said.

"It's actually a murder investigation now."

"What?" Caro's blood went thick and cold. "What? Why?"

"The Foxberrys were able to get an independent autopsy. I don't know how they did it so fast, but...that person said Trey's skull was cracked by something deliberately."

"What are we going to do?"

"I don't know...we'll figure it out. Beau's aunt is doing an autopsy too. She's on our side. Try not to worry. Okay? *Try*."

"On the way to the hospital, tell me exactly what y'all did to him. Promise?" Caro said, standing next to Kasey outside of Grandma Mimi's car. Shaking, she handed Kasey the keys to it.

"Okay. Promise."

2016

46

Beau had shown up back in Goldie. A sweet surprise. He'd come to visit his family after his divorce and stopped in the bakery to say hey, then hung around until they closed. Afterward, he and Caro ended up at Duke's. Half of the night was a blur, but Caro remembered dancing to the Spice Girls and Beau had his arms around her, and she was scared she'd melt right through the floor. She wanted him to kiss her so bad, so she told him she needed to get some air.

They stepped outside and she told Beau that Samuel was her boyfriend, but he was out of town and she *wished* she could kiss him. She wished she could be with Beau, but he ran off and got married and now he was back and the timing was wrong. Again. The timing was always wrong for them.

"Yeah, but maybe it won't always be," Beau said, after listening to her holler at him for a while. She was drunk and he told her that, which made her laugh.

"I loved you *so* much when we worked at the diner together," she said to him.

"I loved you too, Muffin Mix," he said.

They went back inside Duke's and danced together some more even though Caro thought she'd burst into flames. Like she'd split in two for wanting him so much and for loving Samuel, even when he wasn't there. Beau had taken her to Samuel's house and gotten her inside. He put her to bed and left a glass of water on the nightstand.

"Maybe it won't always be," he said softly when he thought she was sleeping.

Oh Plum wasn't happening, Beau wasn't happening, but the bakery was "basically" hers, and Samuel was great.

Every time Caroline thought about how boring and bad things were, she found herself thinking, *Yeah, but maybe it won't always be.*

To: BeauBramford@gmail.com
From: CarolineCaroppenheimer@gmail.com
Subject: Friends

Beau, I forgot to say something when you were in town so I want to say it now. No matter what... I want us to be friends. I love being your friend. You're one of my favorite people in the world. So there... I told you. Next time you're in town, I promise not to drink so much and by "so much" I mean not at all because I'm well on my way to realizing that I can't hold my alcohol. Such a lightweight! You told me that when I was in high school and okay whatever, you're right! :P

I hope Nevada is good to you.

Everybody/everything should be good to you. Always.

Love,

Muffin Mix

To: CarolineCaroppenheimer@gmail.com
From: BeauBramford@gmail.com
Subject: Re: Friends

Muffin Mix,

Anytime, anywhere you are, no matter what, you just say the word and I'm there. I mean it.

If that ol' boy Samuel (or any boy) don't treat you right even for one second, you'll let me know? Promise?

Damn straight we'll be friends. Forever.

Love,

BB

To: BeauBramford@gmail.com

From: CarolineCaroppenheimer@gmail.com

Subject: Re: Friends

PROMISE! Xoxo

2019

47

CHERRY NICHOLS

Officer Stewart: Miss Cherry, you're down here to talk about Trey
    Foxberry?

Cherry Nichols: Yes. How did you know that?

OS: Because everyone's coming down here to talk about Trey
    Foxberry.

CN: They are?

OS: Yes, ma'am.

CN: Well, I figured *some* people were talking about him, but I didn't
    know *all* those women out there—

OS: I can only assume.

CN: Every last one of them?

OS: Just about.

CN: Does it even matter if we tell you this stuff, though? I mean,
    if someone killed him and there's a trial, this isn't the kind
    of thing they could even use in a trial, right? You know I
    was raised in the funeral home business, so I don't know a
    lick about the legal stuff, although you'd be surprised how
    hand in hand our businesses do go along sometimes...well

333

you wouldn't be *surprised*, I guess. You see a little bit of everything every day, don't you, Wyatt? I mean, *Officer* Stewart?

OS: You can call me Wyatt.

CN: Okay, let's do that.

OS: What did you want to say about Trey Foxberry, Miss Cherry?

CN: There's always been a lot of gossip about how Roy Dupont killed Angie Fritz fifteen years ago, and you know Duke and Angie used to work at the grocery store together before he opened up the bar. Here lately, people are saying the Foxberrys knew all about what Roy did to Angie and helped him get away with it, and that crushed my soul because I loved Angie so much. She was a special friend to Duke and me. Kasey was left alone—that little girl disappeared and only popped up again a couple weeks ago. It was so nice to see her. She came over for cherry pie. I would've brought you some pie, Wyatt, but we've been so busy at the funeral home the past week. Robert Birdwell fell off that horse and I know you heard Elliott Maplethorpe finally died. He was one hundred and eleven, and did you know last week he told me he was starting to get his feelings hurt since he felt like God must not want him in heaven? It made me laugh out loud. He was such a kind old man. Oh and! That poor young girl who overdosed in that god-awful boutique hotel...she was from Adora Springs, but her family wanted us to handle the arrangements. See, I heard the Foxberrys have something to do with those opioids running through Goldie now, and it was probably some of those opioids that killed that poor young girl. Anyway, Trey Foxberry used to knock the headstones over in the cemetery on a regular basis when he was a kid, and I know kids do dumb things, but he was the only one of those boys who didn't apologize to my family for it. His parents never punished him for anything. They let him run amok, and that's what made him grow up to be a man who thought he could get away with anything. So, *if* somebody killed him for what he did to Caroline, it wouldn't surprise me. Or maybe he started taking those opioids too and fell into the water. Like I said, I know you might not be able to use this, but I figured I'd tell it anyway.

OS: Thanks for coming down, Cherry.

CN: I'll be back tomorrow to bring y'all some pie.

———

HOLLY PLUM

Officer Stewart: Hi, Mrs. Plum. You—

Holly Plum: Want to talk about the Foxberrys? Yes. How are you, Wyatt? How's your grandmother? I saw your parents at the farmers market and I meant to ask about her then. She's still causing a ruckus down in the Keys?

OS: She is. She's happy down there. Like a fancy lizard soaking up the sun.

HP: That's the dream. That's what I need to do. Someday soon, right? I don't have all that much to say about Trey Foxberry, and I certainly don't have anything nice to say. I dated his dad when we were in high school. Caroline is like a daughter to me and has been her whole life. She and Ada and Rosemarie and Kasey . . . I helped raise them all. Barely a day went by without having those girls in my house when they were growing up. Caro's mama didn't raise that girl and Mimi did an amazing job with her. I understand why Caro thought marrying Trey could give her the life she'd always dreamed of, and well . . . have you seen her? Have you seen what Trey did to her face?

OS: *Allegedly* did—

335

HP: Cut the bullshit, Wyatt. You and I both know he did it. Tell me. Have you seen her face?

OS: I have.

HP: Do you think a man who does something like that deserves to stay alive?

OS: I don't know how to answer that—

HP: Lemme just say this. Angie Fritz was my friend and I loved her. I came down here right after her body was found and told the police they needed to look closer at Roy Dupont and ask him some more questions. I wasn't the only one who did that, but no one would listen. No one would listen because the Foxberrys—that family...that family is the kind of family that wants to look good on the outside...one of those families that pretends to be one thing, but the inside is rotten. Now, I'll be honest with you and say that my husband's family obviously had to exploit good, hardworking people to get all the money they were able to pass down to him. Slaves... tobacco farming...coal mining...the Plum family was into a little bit of everything. Railroads too. Same stuff the Foxberrys did, but the Plum family has never run drugs and that's what the Foxberrys do. Why didn't anyone do anything about Roy killing Angie? Why can't anyone in this town do anything about the Foxberrys? And I know it's too late to fix what happened to my friend, but maybe if y'all let this whole Trey thing go away, the Foxberrys will move their shit out of this town and leave for good. Don't you think that'd be the best thing?

OS: It's a murder investigation now, so we're obligated to investigate it, Mrs. Plum.

HP: Sure, but if someone killed him...no telling who it was. All those drugs and all that money? Sometimes those kinds of things never get solved, because no one wants to say anything about them. Look, all I'm saying is that Trey Foxberry did a terrible, awful thing when he beat Caroline to a pulp, and that was the cherry on top of what he's done in this town... what his family has done all through these hills. I wouldn't sleep with his daddy in high school, and do you know he told everybody I did anyway? My husband knows all about it and that was a long time ago, but that's who Max Foxberry is and that's how he raised his son to be. I know some people may think I'm no better, because I do love my wine and I'm not perfect. I can see how somebody could get addicted to those pills they sell, because it starts with pain. Opioids are prescribed for pain. If you've been in enough pain in either your body or your soul, you'll do anything to stop it. *Anything.*

———

DAHLIA AND VERITY BELL

Officer Stewart: Both of y'all want to come in here together?

Dahlia Bell: Is that okay?

OS: Sure.

Verity Bell: We want to tell a story about Trey Foxberry, and we were both there when it happened.

OS: Is this something recent that pertains to the murder investigation?

VB: Was he *murdered*?

OS: We believe so.

DB: Oh okay. Well, no. This happened when I was seven and Verity was nine.

OS: And how old are you now?

VB: Twenty-eight.

DB: Twenty-six.

OS: All right... um, sure. Go ahead and tell me what happened.

DB: Trey Foxberry was the first boy who ever said something nasty to me. I ran out of the front door chasing Verity around back so we could go swimming, and Trey was walking past with his friends. We were in our bathing suits, and he told us to pull them down and show him—

VB: He used *filthy* words. Do we have to say them? I refuse to say them.

OS: You don't have to say them if you don't want to. I think I get your point.

DB: One starts with a *c*.

VB: Dahlia! Don't!

DB: I'm not. I only said one letter!

OS: That's plenty. That's all right.

DB: Trey was fourteen. I remember because our brother, Leo, was fourteen too. Well, you know that. You're friends with Leo, right?

OS: Absolutely. I'm glad he's back in town for a while.

VB: Me too. We put him to work at the bookshop, but he's easily distracted. He'll see someone he knows walking past and *poof*— he's gone! He's always been like that. He's like a bunny or something.

OS: I'll remember to call him that the next time I see him.

DB: He'll know you've been talking to us, then. Call him Bunny Bell! That's what we do.

OS: Leo Bunny Bell.

DB: Yep.

VB: I know it doesn't matter if Trey said something nasty to us when he was a teenager, but if it helps Caroline for us to come and tell you things like this, to prove he without a doubt could be the kind of person who could do awful things...who could put her in the hospital...

DB: I mean, no matter how he died...it seems like God would only let him act like that for so long...

OS: Yeah, your mom said sort of the same thing when she came down, and she wasn't the only one.

VB: I mean, if I had to choose between Trey or Caroline being alive...all I'm saying is that I'm *super* glad Caroline is alive.

DB: Right? I'm so glad she's alive.

OS: I can't argue with either of you there.

48

ROSEMARIE

Esme was shaking her head, on the phone with her brother in Rosemarie's hospital room.

"Rosie, he says the pharmacy claims you never picked up the prescriptions? Here, you talk to him," Esme said.

There was a small gap between Esme's front teeth, and Rosemarie had remarked on it within five minutes of meeting her for the first time; she loved that little gap. She'd missed that little gap. She'd missed her face, the pale coral blush of her cheeks. Esme was wearing a loose-collar T-shirt the same color of her blushes. Rosemarie had missed her stylish black glasses and the thin slip of prematurely gray-white hair she kept tucked behind her left ear. And she missed how she smelled—like some sort of biblical fruit and musk Rosemarie could never place, and Esme couldn't tell whether it was her shampoo or her soap or a mix of both, so the smell was a mystery. A chemical reaction that only happened when they both met Esme's soft, tawny skin.

"Hello, Dr. Eden, how are you this afternoon? Your sister got here five minutes ago and she's already ordering me around. Can you please inform her I'm busy dying?" Rosemarie said, looking at Esme the whole time she was talking. Esme took the hand that wasn't holding the phone.

"Rosemarie, the medicine can make you feel better. It *will* make you feel better, but you have to take it," Esme's brother, Ambrose, said gently.

"You know I know that, right? I also know you're just doing your job," Rosemarie said to him.

"And I love you," he said.

"I love you too, Ambrose. You're an excellent doctor. Thank you for calling in my medicine and for taking the time out of your busy day to talk to me on the phone because your sister refuses to let me die in peace," Rosemarie said.

"I don't like your jokes," Esme said.

"I know you don't, and I like that you don't like them. It's how we work," Rosemarie said.

"Please go pick up the pills, and let everyone take care of you while you're in the hospital. Let me know if they need anything else. Your doctor out there is the best. Are you comfortable right now?" Ambrose asked with extra tenderness.

"I am. I am happy to be looking into your sister's big brown eyes, and the curtains are open. The room is filled with sunlight. My friends left to let me get some sleep when Esme showed up, and I'm going to take a nap on her. I love sleeping on people," Rosemarie said.

"Good. Sleep on her a lot, okay?" Ambrose said.

"Talk soon," Rosemarie said, handing the phone back to Esme.

When Esme was off the phone with her brother, she got into the bed carefully with Rosemarie, and Rosemarie put her ear on her chest, listening to her heartbeat. Esme put her hand on Rosemarie's head.

"I *finally* get to meet Leo today?"

"Yes. He'll be back up here soon. He slept in that chair all night," Rosemarie said, moving her head a little.

"How are you feeling right at this moment?"

"Like I'm dying," Rosemarie said. She'd been inching that way for a while, but the stress of the past week or so had definitely fast-forwarded her pain and feelings. She accepted the fact that cancer would kill her as soon as Ambrose said the word *metastatic* right after Christmas. She responded, *Happy New Year*, and sat there looking at him across the desk. Esme was next to her, holding her hand. Rosemarie told Esme she'd never speak to her again if she pressed Pause to come to Goldie with her and not finish her film. She'd worked so hard, and Rosemarie was more than well taken care of when she was near her parents and Leo, with the added bonus of being back in town with Ada and Caroline, and now even Kasey too. She never had to worry about a thing with her real and chosen family so close, besides dying of the cancer that stalked the women in her family.

Rosemarie couldn't say *exactly* what dying felt like for her, but it didn't feel the way she'd thought it'd feel. Her bones ached and sometimes she couldn't eat for days. She was overly thirsty, and occasionally her heart would flutter like a small bird taking flight. She'd slowly become more photosensitive than she'd ever been in her life, so much so that sometimes she had to wear sunglasses inside, but she loved the sun anyway and refused to give it up. The hospital room was a tad too bright, but Rosemarie relished the discomfort. She was cold sometimes, even in the hell-hot Goldie summer, but she'd taught herself to be thankful for that, because soon she wouldn't be there to feel it.

Soon her soul would escape her human body like smoke.

This whole *slowly dying* thing was more useful than she'd thought it'd be. The bare fact of it had eclipsed the fear that at any second, the cops could show up and handcuff her skinny wrists to the hospital bed for killing Trey, now that they'd opened a murder investigation.

How could that scare her?

The only thing that scared her was the people she loved not knowing how much she loved them.

The only thing that would've scared her would have been not being brave enough to do what they had to do to protect Caroline.

Rosemarie woke up and squinted as the sunset poured into the room like water. So close to full gloaming. Rosemarie loved the gloaming. Leo and Esme were talking softly to each other in the chairs next to her. When she'd met and fallen in love with Esme three years ago, she imagined that it'd be a long time until she wanted Esme and Leo to meet. Like always, Rosemarie wanted Leo all to herself—which, admittedly, got a bit thorny when he was married to Annie for six years—and she liked having Esme all to herself too. She liked the two of them living in separate worlds, and although she never intentionally or actively tried to keep them from meeting, she didn't mind that, serendipitously, it hadn't happened before this.

Now, Leo and Esme were chatting like old friends, and they'd been doing it for how long? They both looked at her, loving her. She could feel the love in that hospital room. It spilled across the floor like the gloaming, splashed up on the walls and ceiling. She could sense that Ada, Caro, and Kasey had recently been in the room too or were somewhere near. Her terminal cancer diagnosis kicked in some extra Spidey-Senses for recognizing good things, and when she'd mentioned it to Ambrose once, he couldn't give her any scientific reasoning to prove she was *wrong*.

"The rest of RACK was here, but they didn't want to disturb you, so they went down to the cafeteria. Your parents are right outside. Rune left to go to the Burrito Barn. My sisters brought books, if you want books," Leo said, holding up two matte paperbacks Rosemarie had seen in the bookshop window the last time she walked past. "And Esme...well, I'm in love with Esme and I told her that already, so don't worry—it's not weird," he said.

"I already love you too," Esme said, holding her hand out at Leo. He took it, kissed it.

"This is a wish I didn't even know I had until it came true," Rosemarie said softly. Although it was almost too painful to bear, she imagined Esme and Leo left in this world without her but connected forever *through* her. She was crying now. She'd cried a lot when her mom had insisted on bringing her to the hospital too, because Rosemarie's headache was so bad, because her mouth was so dry, and because Rosemarie finally told her mom what her mom suspected all along.

Esme and Leo moved to sit on opposite sides of the hospital bed with her and held her hands.

"How do you feel? What do you need?" Esme asked, crying too. She flicked her dark hair out of her face.

"I feel like I want to go home," Rosemarie said.

"Tomorrow. Tomorrow we'll take you home," Leo said.

The door opened and the rest of RACK came in, her parents too. Rune was behind them with his sunglasses on top of his head and a bag of food.

"Are there too many people in this room?" her mom asked.

Rosemarie shook her head and held her aching arms out wide enough for all of them.

———

When Rosemarie was released and her parents took her home, Esme and Leo were there too. When she returned to Leo's, Esme came with them. Kasey wanted Rosemarie at the farmhouse, and that was the plan for next week. Once she could muster up the energy, she and Leo sang together in his kitchen, and she finally told Esme about the album they'd been recording. The cover songs and the three songs they'd written together.

Rosemarie took some of the pills Ambrose had called in for her but refused to follow the label directions. She took the pills with wine instead of water and made a mental note to take them every other day instead of once a day. It was enough to get Esme off her back. Esme was a control freak about her dying, and Leo was much more laid-back about it because he knew there was no point in arguing with her; he knew her better, full stop, since they'd had more time together.

She wished she and Esme could have more time together.

She wished she and Leo could have more time together too.

She wanted more time with Ada. And Caroline. And Kasey.

She'd had a peace about killing Trey ever since they decided to do it, and even now with the investigation still open, Rosemarie found that her brain couldn't hold on to worrying about it, like the floors of her mind had been slicked with grease. She wouldn't be alive long enough to face any real consequences, and she'd do all she could to make sure the other girls would be okay. She prayed continuously that things would right themselves properly and for it all to be over soon so Caro and her baby could be free from it. So Ada and Kasey could relax.

Rosemarie wanted more time with her parents. And Rune.

Everyone she'd ever known and loved.

She'd been so nervous about Leo and Esme meeting because she didn't want Esme to be jealous of Leo and she didn't want Leo to be intimidated by Esme, but now that she'd seen them together, she wanted them to stay connected, even after she was gone. Be friends forever. She wanted them to text each other at Christmas and on their birthdays or randomly when something reminded them of the other, or of her.

It was one way she'd stay alive.

———

Leo and Esme sat on the floor and Rosemarie lay on the couch with Basie the night they listened to their album for the first time together in its entirety. They shared a bottle of wine and passed around the organic weed her dad grew in the greenhouse in their backyard, which was something that Ambrose had actually said she should do—and *that*, she agreed with. They got stoned and talked and cried, and instead of feeling like everything was ending, there were cracks in the black when Rosemarie felt brand-new. Like she'd just been born. A second wind for a shortened life.

On that afternoon Leo sat outside of the police station reading and waiting for her, she'd told him the truth about what they did to Trey. Leo listened patiently, not nearly as freaked out as he could've been, telling her that he understood why they did it and promising he'd never say a word. He told her that his ex-wife, Annie, was engaged and pregnant and he had conflicting feelings about it. She mentioned that his confession was nothing compared to murder, and they laughed. They laughed about these huge, dark things that were stored up in their hearts because it was what they did. It was who they were.

She also told Leo that, heaven forbid, if the Foxberrys wanted to come after the girls once Rosemarie was gone...if things got really bad and it looked like the girls could get in trouble, that it'd be okay for him to tell the police Rosemarie killed Trey on her own. A crime of passion—she drugged him and hit him with a rock for what he did to Caroline. It was her alone. Leave the girls out of it. Leo said it wouldn't come to that, and Rosemarie didn't think it would. Ada, Caroline, and Kasey would be so mad at her for it and probably wouldn't let Leo do it anyway, but she still made him promise. With pinkies and everything—no takebacks.

When Leo asked her again what she wanted to name the album, she said *Roses in Space* because that was where she felt like she was, listening to it in Leo's living room. Later, she and Leo and Esme crawled into Leo's big bed together with Rosemarie in the middle and Basie at their feet, sleeping with the surround-sound crickets singing loud. Strong and steady as their three human heartbeats for now, before they were two.

2017

49

From: RosemarieCloverKingston@gmail.com

To: AdaPlumCastelow@gmail.com, CarolineCaroppenheimer@gmail.com, KaseyJosephineFritz@gmail.com

Subject: Over Noodles

Hello you beauties!

So y'all already know Esme and I met at the dog park right after I adopted Willie to give him a little love in the last year or so of his life. I couldn't imagine a break from traveling and feeding people for the non-profit and being in Seattle for more than a year without the comfort of a dog. Even when I was in Costa Rica after high school, Leopold and I found a puppy and fed and loved it while we were there. And in Paris, Mélanie and I "adopted" a long-haired chihuahua we brought in from the rain sometimes and fed it French dog treats made of honey and coconuts.

The first time I ever saw Esme cry was when Willie died.

After the cancer and everything, I told Esme that Leo used to be my boyfriend and that we were friends now, but I didn't tell her that when I went to visit Leo in Boston later that year after he divorced Annie that we had sex. A lot of sex. I didn't tell her that I hadn't been able to be around Leo (outside of his marriage to Annie) without having sex with him.

Y'all...I know he may not look like it because he's always like, holding an instrument or talking on and on about something he's read, but Leo is VERY good at like...giving himself over completely to my pleasure. He always has been! Reconnecting with him after Annie felt a lot like I was reclaiming him and his body. Like, sure it was Annie's cock for a minute, but like, now it's mine again and I've only had one before...but I love it. I love Leo's. So, yeah.

Last night we went out for noodles and I DID finally tell Esme I was *aggressively bisexual*, but basically only when it came to Leo. I told her *everything* about us and him and that we'd always be more than friends and how it was weird fate that they didn't meet when Leo was in town when I was first diagnosed. I would've been honest with her about this way sooner and I wanted to, but I didn't want to hurt her feelings! I made it worse by not telling her. That's on me.

Point is, she cried again the same way she cried when Willie died. Esme's not a casual crier. I think we'll be fine? I'll never choose between them? Esme's never been with a man, never been interested. She doesn't care about them and I love that about her. I clearly don't care about any men (romantically) but Leo. I've never (really) bothered trying.

I love Esme so much and want to be with her forever. I love Leo so much and we'll be what we are to each other forever too.

I'm attaching a pic of Esme in her black overalls because she's so beautiful in her black overalls. Her hair is longer now and I bought her those earrings when we went to Portland for the weekend last month. And! She finally got the green light for her new film !!!

I LOVE YOU AND NOW I'VE TOLD YOU MY LATEST STORY SO TELL ME YOURS.

Also, my last scan was clear! I guess I could've started the email with that, right? Ada, don't be mad at me! :P

RACK FOREVER.

Roses

GOODBYE EARL

From: CarolineCaroppenheimer@gmail.com
To: RosemarieCloverKingston@gmail.com, AdaPlumCastelow@gmail.com, KaseyJosephineFritz@gmail.com
Subject: Re: Over Noodles

Oh Roses, YAY A CLEAR SCAN!!!

Esme looks so pretty in this picture!

I'm glad you told her your Leo feelings. I also remember you reenacting the first time you saw Leo completely naked when we were in high school. THE GASP!!

I know you know Leo's back in Goldie for the week! After the show in Nashville yesterday, he crashed at our place for the night and he got up and made pancakes for Samuel and me this morning. He talks about you all the time. He played part of a song he said y'all have been working on long-distance together for like, five years. I loved it. I want to hear the rest!

Samuel is considering the job in Amsterdam and I told him he should take it. I don't want him staying in Goldie for me. I love him and we'll see... but I don't know. I'll talk more about it when I know what to say.

One more thing: guess who came into the bakery the other day and PLEASE don't kill me but he looked (a little?) cute and I hated myself for thinking it.

Do you know who I'm gonna say?

Shit. Y'all are never gonna let me live this down but...

Trey.

Trey Foxberry.

I'm signing off right now so I don't embarrass myself anymore.

RACK FOREVER.

Caroppenheimer

2019

50

MYRTLE CHILDRESS

Officer Castelow: Hi there, Miss Myrtle, how are you?

Myrtle Childress: Hi, Silas. I'm better now that Caro is back home, but poor Rosemarie...well, of course you know...

OC: Yeah...everyone's surrounding Rosemarie with a lot of love, and she's easy to love anyway. Seems like everyone in Goldie believes in miracles, don't we? We'll never stop believing in miracles. And Caro...well, I'm glad she's back home too.

MC: Caro's the reason I came down here to agree with what everyone else said on the record.

OC: All right...understood.

MC: Y'know, I always hoped Beau would move back to Goldie one day and sweep her off her feet and marry her. Remember how they were at the diner together? I knew then they were a perfect match, and now Beau's back in town...so maybe when she's healed up, something'll happen.

OC: It's really nice for him to come back to Goldie for her.

MC: Isn't it? Did you have some of the pie I brought? It's peach. I left it in the break room for y'all.

OC: I smelled it in there, but I haven't had a piece yet. Thank you, Miss Myrtle.

———

MIRIAM "MIMI" HARPER

Officer Castelow: Hi, Miss Mimi. Myrtle left not five minutes ago. Did you see her?

Miriam Harper: Oh yes, she's waiting out there for me right now. She brought a peach pie and I brought apple for you. I know you like apple.

OC: I do love apple pie, Miss Mimi. Thank you.

MH: I know this is a murder investigation now, but that's nonsense. Y'all don't really think somebody killed Trey, do y'all, Silas?

OC: Miss Mimi, I—

MH: Trey died because God don't like ugly. Nobody *killed* him.

OC: That just might be true.

MH: Everything Caro said about what Trey Foxberry did to her is true too. I grew up with a daddy like Trey. Did you know that?

OC: No, ma'am.

MH: One night my mama poured a pot of boiling water on him. Can you understand why a woman would snap and do something like that?

OC: I sure can.

MH: Right. Because she came down here to this police station when Trey's great-uncle was chief, and she told him everything my daddy was doing to us, terrorizing us in our own home, and do you know what Trey's great-uncle did?

OC: No, ma'am.

MH: Trey's great-uncle went right over to the mill where my

daddy was working, and he told my daddy exactly what my mama had told him, and my daddy went home and beat my mama up so bad she lost the baby she was pregnant with. My little brother. That's why I'm an only child, Silas... because the police didn't help us. The men on the police force knew exactly what was happening, but they didn't do a thing about it, and I protected Caroline from all that. She doesn't know that happened. Maybe I should've told her. Maybe it would've helped her out. I wanted to trust her when she told me Trey was a good man. I wanted to trust that there was something underneath that I couldn't see...I wanted to believe her so bad I guess I fooled myself. But Lord have mercy, I wish somebody would've killed my daddy instead of my mama having to try to do it on her own. She wasn't the same after all that. My daddy obviously wasn't either. He never put his hands on her or me again. He drank himself to death the year before she died, and he never told nobody what my mama did to him. He lied and said he'd had an accident himself because he knew he deserved it for everything he'd done.

OC: This is all so terrible, Miss Mimi. I'm sorry.

MH: Maybe in his heart, Trey *wanted* to die for what he'd done.

OC: Maybe you're right.

MH: We all tried to help Angie and Kasey back then too, but...we couldn't.

OC: That's a shame, I know.

MH: Just make sure you also put down there that Rosemarie, Ada, and Kasey were at my place for a long time.

OC: Mm-hmm. When was that?

MH: Whatever night Trey went missing.

OC: Oh, okay. They were?

MH: Of course they were, Silas. I wouldn't say it if it wasn't true, would I?

—

NANCY SIMMONS

Officer Castelow: Hi, Miss Nancy.

Nancy Simmons: Hi, Silas. Don't forget I remember when you were in diapers...I even changed a few of them when I'd stop at the B and B to drop off lavender from my garden when you were little and your mama and I would get to talking.

OC: Ha! I do love your stories, Miss Nancy. Thank you for sharing them with me. You know just about everything that happens in this town, don't you?

NS: Sure do.

OC: You said you had something important to tell us about the night Trey went missing?

NS: *Very* important. This is a murder investigation now, is that right?

OC: Yes, ma'am.

NS: Okay then. Since you like my stories so much, I got another one for you. I saw Trey Foxberry skulking around behind the Fritz farmhouse that night. No one came to ask me about it, which I thought was odd since obviously I know everyone in this town calls me *Nosy* Nancy, and I'm okay with that because I don't mind keeping an eye on Goldie. You know it was my great-grandfather who was so nosy he found out that those caves in Adora Springs made the water taste so good? But we got good water too, don't we? I know everyone loves Adora Springs because they got that big shopping center and they're talking about building the baseball stadium there, but that's what makes Goldie the magic that it is...it's smaller and off the beaten path and unexpected. Those are the best things in life sometimes...the good, unexpected ones. That's Goldie, one hundred percent.

OC: I agree with you on that. Did you want to tell me more about what you saw Trey Foxberry doing on... what night was it, Miss Nancy?

NS: Friday night. The day after the tornado in Adora Springs. I remember it because I'd stepped out front to see if that big tree in our yard still had that long branch hanging down like it was fixin' to fall off, and I hollered for Donnie to come look at it too. He asked about you, by the way, since he hadn't seen you in what—a week? Y'all never go too long without bumping into each other. He said to tell you hi.

OC: Tell him I said hi back. We've been friends for a long time.

NS: You sure have... since y'all were both toddling around. That's how I remember how old you are, Silas, because you were born the same year as my grandson—1986. Although his birthday is right there at the end; he barely made it in time. Anyway, Friday night I saw Trey's car in the driveway, but I didn't see him until it was dark... he's tall and long and I recognized him by how he was walking. I remember when Trey was born too, same year as y'all. He was a pretty little baby, but he never acted right. Anyway, I'd know him anywhere, even in the dark. He was out back of the house wandering around, but I never saw Kasey or anybody else out there in case y'all were thinking she had something to do with this; she definitely didn't. Kasey Fritz was raised in that hell of a household with that man Roy, and I used to see him acting a fool over there. I called the police several times, but Angie would never press charges; she just sent them away. I talked to her about it time and time again, begged her to let somebody help her, but she seemed determined to love that man no matter what. And Kasey's not violent. I would see Roy snatch her in the backyard, and that little girl didn't even fight back. I wish she would've! I called Child Protective Services once, but I hung up because I didn't want Angie to get in any trouble for what Roy did. It made me feel better that I saw Kasey sneaking out of that house so much. I knew she had safe spaces to get to. She went to the Plums' or the Kingstons', or Mimi kept an eye on her. I know you know I have my sons and grandsons, but I had a granddaughter die a day after she was born that same year in 1986. My other son's child. The one who lives way up in Ann Arbor. Anyway, I always kept an eye on Kasey and thought about my granddaughter... how she'd be that same age too.

OC: I'm sorry to hear that. I didn't know about your granddaughter.

NS: Thank you, Silas. I just wanted y'all to know I saw Trey walk up to the edge of the dock with my own eyes. I got my binoculars out because I wondered what the devil he was doing out there. Donnie got me a new pair of those binoculars that make it so I can see in the dark... everything glows green. I looked right through that green and saw Trey fall in the water. I figured he'd find a way to get himself out, but I guess he didn't. I didn't know he couldn't swim. I would've got down here earlier to tell y'all what I saw, but I was under the weather. I was in bed and didn't know Trey was missing, then I was gonna call, but I didn't even have a voice. Laryngitis. Happens every time I get sick. And when I did call... did you know they told me there was a waiting list to sit down with somebody? I can't sit too long because of my hip. I have to lie down. I can stand, but I figured only the Lord knew how long I'd have to stand down here. My hip's aching right now sitting here with you like this, but it's worth it. Anyway, I figured since it was a death investigation maybe it didn't matter what I saw... but when I heard it was a *murder* investigation, I said, *Nancy Frances Simmons, you better get your butt down there, aching hip or waiting list or not, before somebody gets in trouble who shouldn't.* Back when it happened, I tried coming down here and telling someone that although I had no proof... I was pretty sure Roy Dupont had killed Angie Fritz, but they wouldn't let me see anyone. Can you believe that? What a racket. I would've been down here earlier this time, but I thought everybody else had handled it. I thought it was over like it should be. I want to make sure the right thing happens this time. No one did this. It was an accident. I know it because I saw it with my own eyes. Do you understand?

OC: I understand.

NS: And I'd say it's a damn shame Trey never learned to swim, but I heard what he did to Caroline, and I don't think it's a shame he's dead. He just . . . walked too close to the edge and . . . *fell* in . . . that's all.

OC: Something in your eye, Miss Nancy?

NS: Oh, nothing. Looks like I'm winking at you but it's just my allergies, ain't it? Or at least I hope so. Hope I'm not getting sick again.

OC: All right. Thank you for coming down to tell us this, Miss Nancy. I probably shouldn't say this to you, but I agree that Trey probably fell in the water on his own.

NS: Well, and you know Kasey and the girls much better than I do, so you know they're telling the truth about everything too. Speaking of . . . I saw you at the farmhouse late the other night, and right after you left, a little white hatchback pulled up that I'd never seen before. You and Kasey used to be so cute together in high school. I remember y'all holding hands walking down the sidewalk with ice creams from the Dairy Dee like something out of a movie.

OC: Kasey's a real sweet person, and I'm glad to have her back here in Goldie.

NS: She still engaged? I saw that big ol' rock on her finger. Was that her fiancé driving that hatchback?

OC: Yes, she's engaged, Miss Nancy, and I'm not sure if that was him or not.

NS: Well, they're not married *yet*, so don't you let the chance pass you by if you get bit by the love bug again. Seems like the two of you were meant to be together, with her and Ada being so close and Ada being married to Grayson. It'd be peachy if you and Kasey were together too. It'd make a lot of sense, wouldn't it?

OC: Well, I don't have anything much to add to that.

NS: The look on your face, Silas Castelow! The look on your face says it all.

OC: Does it now?

NS: Sure does. And my story should put an end to all this, shouldn't it?

OC: Good chance it might. Thank you for coming down, Miss Nancy.

———

OFFICER CASTELOW'S ADDITIONAL NOTES

I've fully disclosed the fact that Ms. Kasey Fritz and I were once sweethearts fifteen years ago when we were in high school, but we haven't been in any sort of considerable contact since then. On the Monday evening following Trey Foxberry's disappearance, I revisited the Fritz farmhouse where his vehicle was found and saw no further evidence or reason to explore that led any further. Nothing on the scene pointed toward foul play, and Ms. Fritz has been cooperative. After several more interviews today, I've been made aware of additional evidence that points to Mr. Foxberry's death being an accident. Nancy Simmons claims to have been an eyewitness and is willing to come back in for another interview.

After hearing her story, as well as finding the drugs in Trey Foxberry's vehicle, it is my belief that Mr. Foxberry's death was an accident, not a murder, and no further investigations need to be made.

51

ADA

The rest of RACK visited Rosemarie at Leo's on Sunday morning. It was their personal church. Ada had scooped up Caro and Kasey and they'd stopped by the bakery on the way, although they knew Rosemarie wasn't up for sweets or anything heavy. She'd also gone by the restaurant for a cup of chicken noodle soup in case Rosemarie wanted the broth. She grabbed turkey sandwiches and Waldorf salads, strawberries and cheese, in case anyone wanted more. She went inside the grocery store for ginger ale and apple juice, too. The last stop before Leo's was Plum Florals to get Rosemarie some pink and white roses. Making sure everyone was fed and comforted and surrounded by beautiful things had never made a situation worse.

Rosemarie looked really good considering what they all knew, and she felt okay enough to sing with Leo a song they'd been working on in secret. A song about a small town in the sun and a group of girlfriends who would love one another forever. Rosemarie could barely get through it because it made her cry, but Ada heard every word loud and clear. They were all crying by the end. Esme sat on the floor in front of Rosemarie, with her hand on her bare foot, and Leo kept his wet eyes on Rosemarie as he sang.

Not wanting to stay too long and tire out Rosemarie, the rest of the girls left after picking at their lunches, and Ada dropped Caro off at Grandma Mimi's first.

"Everything is too much," Ada said in a thin voice. Her minivan was parked right outside of the trailer; Mimi's wind chimes brightened the air. Silas had told them that Mimi had given them an alibi just in case and that Nosy Nancy came forward to say she'd seen Trey fall into the water. The investigation *felt* close to being closed, but they still had to hear official word. Ada couldn't worry about the investigation and Rosemarie at the same time, so she shifted it all to Rosemarie. Once she did that, she realized she preferred worrying about going to prison over worrying about Rosemarie dying. Ada's sleep schedule was nonexistent, and she couldn't focus on anything. Grayson had been doing most of the work taking care of the boys, but she was trying her best. She was trying and trying and trying.

"She could live *five* more years...she could," Kasey said, nodding.

"Fuck that. That's not enough," Caroline said.

"Of course! Of course I know it's not enough, Caro, but it's better than thinking she'll die tomorrow!" Kasey snapped.

"So then let's not talk about her dying at all!" Caro snapped back. "I don't want to."

"Okay. I don't want to either," Kasey said. A dark, soft energy coursed through the car.

"I'm...I'm so scared y'all are gonna get in trouble for what you did for me; I can't even process anything right now. It's too much. I'm gonna lose this baby—I know it. It's bad enough I was drinking when I was pregnant, but I didn't know. I didn't..." Caro said, crying again.

"Of course you didn't. Stop that. This baby's gonna be just fine. You're *not* gonna lose this baby," Ada said, touching Caro's hand. "And you know about all the women who are going down to the police station in your defense, and Trey's not even here to be on trial. They can't help themselves. Kasey, tell her what Silas told you." Caro's chin was trembling as she looked out the window.

"It's true, Caro. Leo's sisters, Rosemarie's mom, Nosy Nancy...all of them. Everyone wants to make sure the police know Trey's not the victim here. We had to do what we had to do, yes, but that's only because women know that men always get away with this shit, and we're tired of it," Kasey said.

"You know good and damn well Nosy Nancy saw us do it," Ada said. Nancy made it her life's work to know everything about everybody in Goldie. Ada pictured her with those military-grade night-vision goggles, watching it all go down. All those women waiting in line to defend them gave her so much hope she could feel it steadying her, soothing her heart, even when it was racing.

Kasey nodded. "She's on our side, Caro. *All* the women in town are."

"Did y'all ask them to go down there and do that?" Caro asked with tears in her eyes. "I mean, Grandma Mimi and Myrtle...they all knew what happened to Trey...I didn't even have to tell them. I started to and Mimi stopped me. But what about everybody else? Did y'all say anything to them?"

Ada shook her head. "Girl, we didn't have to."

———

Kasey was talking to Ada about Devon on the drive to the farmhouse. How he was feeling now that she'd sent him away and he was back in New York.

"He's a little...confused, but he's not *mad*," Kasey said.

"Well, he's not *mad*, because you didn't tell him about the kissing," Ada said, driving down the road that led to the long farmhouse driveway. On the left—the Coxes' white picket fence and horses. On the right—rows and rows of knee-high-by-the-Fourth-of-July corn on the Markel farm. The greens and golds of summer in Goldie were as dependable as the heat. Ada turned up the AC. The stress, the past two weeks, everything was overloading the heating and cooling system in Ada's body too and surely sending her into an early menopause.

"Ada...I'm aware."

"I'm a big fan of the kissing, by the way. I'm just sorry that it's going to be a mess when you do eventually talk to Devon about it. There's enough going on without you having to do all that too. I get why you're putting it off!"

"Wait. Did Silas say anything to you about the kissing? Do you think he said something to Grayson?"

"No, and he won't. He's probably in a daze right now, thinking he dreamt it."

"He is *not*! Why do y'all act like I'm the only girl in the world when it comes to him?"

"Because you kind of *are*," Ada said, taking the turn up the driveway. She thought of the dark night they killed Trey and the police investigation and Rosemarie's cancer ticking her life away and taking time from them. She shoved those thoughts aside again. She'd much rather talk about Silas and Kasey kissing, so she leaned into that. "Why do you think he hasn't gotten married and hasn't kept a girl-friend for more than, like, a year?"

"Silas hasn't *not* gotten married because he's waiting to marry me! He hasn't! That's ridiculous!"

"No, what I mean is that he obviously measures his feelings for other women by his feelings for you, and when they don't match up, he doesn't stay interested for long. Miss Myrtle's been trying to marry him off to every woman who comes into the diner for years! Whenever a single woman stays at the B and B and starts chatting her up, Mrs. Castelow always throws in that she has a single son who's handsome and kind and good at, like, everything," Ada said.

"You'll like Devon too. He's also handsome and kind and good at, like, everything."

"Maybe, Kase, but I haven't met him yet, because you keep him from us."

"I do not *keep* him from you!"

"Kasey, you do! He was here in Goldie for, like, *two* days and you hid him!"

"I didn't *hide* him. You said yourself that there's enough going on here right now. How am I supposed to explain it all to him? I can't! I finally told him about Roy and what he did, and I told him I need more time with everything," Kasey said.

"Silas knows Devon was here. He figured it out."

"Figured it out how?"

"Well, Miss Nancy saw Silas over here and then she saw a mystery car come after Silas left. She told him that."

"Did Silas say anything else about it?"

"Not really."

"Not *really* or not at all?" Kasey asked.

"Do you *want* him to feel a certain way about it, Kase?"

"No! He can feel however he feels. I didn't know Devon was coming here! I didn't plan that."

"Why does it feel like we're fighting? I don't want to fight. I don't have the energy to fight," Ada said, stopping the van by the house. She was exhausted—the sort of exhausted that felt permanent.

"We're not fighting. We're hungry. Just come inside and eat," Kasey said.

Ada grabbed the bag of leftover food from the backseat. She'd left some at Leo's and given some to Caro, but there was still plenty for her and Kasey to right their attitudes.

———

Later, Grayson and Silas showed up with Beau, and the men got the fire going in the pit outside. Beau had been hanging out with Caro and Mimi, and he'd left after Caro had fallen asleep. On the walk to his mom's house, he'd bumped into Silas leaving the police station for the day. Ada and Grayson's boys were spending the night with

Grayson's parents; they'd FaceTimed Ada and Grayson at bedtime, and Ada kissed the screen saying goodbye. Life had felt so tenuous lately, and she was anxious to hug her sons again in the morning, glad they were happy and safe at their grandparents' watching superhero movies and staying up too late eating junk; it was exactly what they should be doing on a summer night. Ada had been an absolute mess about everything that was happening, but her children would never know that, because like most mothers, she'd learned to compartmentalize her feelings and wants into one small section of herself and leave the rest open for being Mama and Mama only.

When Beau was in the bathroom and the rest of them were sitting around the fire, Ada said quietly, "And we're sure Caro will be okay with us telling Beau?"

"She'll be okay with it," Kasey said.

"I think so too," Ada said.

"Maybe Caro already told him?" Grayson said, crossing his legs at the knee. Ada loved it when he crossed his legs like that. Once, she'd seen a picture of his great-grandfather sitting in a chair with his legs crossed, and she thought of his great-grandfather a lot when Grayson did it too. How relentless and strong the Castelow DNA was, how it'd completely taken over her DNA and created four little Castelow clones in their children. She pictured her dark-haired boys as grown men with their long legs crossed. She often thought about the men they'd grow up to be. Her first thought after she brought the rock down on Trey's head was that she didn't want to be taken away from Grayson and the boys. Not ever.

This has to work.

"I don't know, but he's basically in this with us already, so it's a bit late to act like he isn't," Kasey said. She took a drink from her bottle of beer.

"Y'all know I can't work at the station anymore, right? I mean, obviously I'm quitting soon," Silas said. He was drinking whiskey; he was exhausted. Ada knew the look on her brother-in-law's face, even in the firelight. "I'm in it with y'all too, and I've been listening to these women telling their stories all week."

"Well, don't quit right now. Wait a little bit or it'll look bad," Ada said.

"All the women coming in...that'll make a difference, right? Especially Nosy Nancy's story? They don't have a case, do they?" Kasey asked him.

"If the women want to keep talking, we'll let them talk. It certainly doesn't hurt that Nancy says she watched it happen. The rest depends on what the coroner comes back with," Silas said.

"We didn't ask those women to step up; they did that on their own," Kasey added.

"I know y'all didn't," Silas said. "You didn't ask our mom to go down to the police station either, but she did what needed to be done anyway."

Ada had been praying that his answer about the Foxberrys having a case would be an easy *no*, but she also thought about her mother-in-law, Joanna, and how she'd never backed down from a fight in her life. Grayson told her that Joanna had sat in front of her brother's desk with that chief of police nameplate on it and had once again given him the entire rundown of everything the Foxberrys had ever done wrong, going back at least fifty years.

Ada thought about Beau's aunt doing the autopsy—prayed that what she came back with held more water than the other autopsy report. For anything the Foxberry family tried to throw at them, there was a woman on their side who could throw just as much or more back.

"The Goldie coroner's not going to find anything that'll get y'all in trouble." Beau's voice in the dark startled them all. He was standing next to them now. "My aunt Lucinda already told me she was going to make sure it was airtight for now and later if anybody comes sniffing around. I told Caro that tonight, but I don't know if she heard me...maybe she was already sleeping. But really, don't worry about our coroner one bit. My aunt was married to an abusive asshole once too."

"Caro told you—" Ada said.

"I know enough," Beau said. He sat in the chair next to Ada and she offered him a beer. He took it and drank. "I was *real* close to telling that cop to his face that I'd wanted to kill Trey myself. Honestly? I just wish y'all had told me about it in advance so I could've helped."

"That's the same thing I said to Ada. I don't even want to think about what could've gone wrong...what he could've done to them if it'd gone sideways," Grayson said, rubbing his face. Ada knew that move and heard the change in his voice. Grayson wasn't scared of a lot of things, but he'd do anything to protect her and the boys. Ada had seen that *what-if* fear in his eyes when she had told him what they'd done. It was the only thing he'd been angry about, really—that Trey could've killed her or Rosemarie or Kasey. That he wouldn't have been there to stop it.

"So don't. We don't have to think about it," Ada said, putting her hand on her husband's knee. Hoping the words *we don't have to think about it* would help put an end to her own intrusive thoughts.

"Damn. Y'all love people the way people are supposed to," Beau said. "That's how you're supposed to love your friends, your family. Anything less and what's the point?"

"You can't tell anyone any of this," Ada said to him.

"I'm an outlaw, Ada; don't worry about me," Beau said, smiling at her. "I ain't saying shit."

"I'm an outlaw undercover for about another month," Silas said, causing Beau to let out an easy laugh. The boys shook hands. Beau asked Silas if he'd ever put anyone in handcuffs besides Trey, and Silas said no, but he *was* tempted the one time he saw Lawrence Acklin going a smidge too fast on his horse.

"There wasn't another choice here," Grayson said after some quiet, touching Ada's knee for reassurance, just in case she needed it, and she did. She was so grateful for their telepathy; she put her hand on his.

"Y'all, I can't even picture being in New York right now," Kasey said. "Like, being out here...Goldie on a summer night...I feel like a completely different person. I don't know which part feels more like the dream, though. Here or the city. Just listen to that," she said, tilting her head. They sat there with the sound of the water, the low hum of the night, all of it churning around them the same way it had when they were growing up. The same way it would when they were gone.

"I like you," Silas said, putting his arm around her.

"I like you too," Kasey said, leaning in.

"Will you tell your auntie that we'll owe her forever?" Ada asked Beau. "I want this all to be fucking *over.*"

"I'm betting it will all be over soon. This is for y'all and this is for Caro, but also, this is bigger than all that. It's bigger than everything, honestly," Beau said.

2018

52

From: AdaPlumCastelow@gmail.com

To: RosemarieCloverKingston@gmail.com,

CarolineCaroppenheimer@gmail.com, KaseyJosephineFritz@gmail.com

Subject: Hey Ladies

I'm bummed we can't all find a time to meet up anytime soon. I know everyone is busy, though! And Kase, Caro told us you're not able to come back to Goldie for the wedding this Christmas and I know how much I hated not having you here when Grayson and I got married. It's hard without you here! I don't want to make you feel bad about it, but you know it's not the same without you, and we all want to meet Devon too. Maybe next year when Taylor and Ben get married? I'm genuinely keeping my fingers crossed for that, although I know it's a long shot. I know there are things here you'd rather forget . . .

I miss RACK. I barely get to take a breath with work and the boys. Earlier today I was thinking of those days between junior and senior year when we'd launch our rafts off the Castelow lake house dock and float all day. Remember that?

Let's promise we'll do that again. One day.

I love you so much.

RF.

Ada

From: RosemarieCloverKingston@gmail.com

To: AdaPlumCastelow@gmail.com,

CarolineCaroppenheimer@gmail.com,

KaseyJosephineFritz@gmail.com

Subject: Re: Hey Ladies

I wish we could get together soon too! I haven't even seen much of Esme lately, she's working so much on film stuff.

Leo was in town last week. He was playing a string of shows on the coast.

I'll deffo be at the wedding, Caro! I cannot BELIEVE you're marrying Trey Foxberry!!!? Maybe now we'll learn the secrets about why we've never known anything about him. And MAKE SURE he knows that if he ever hurts you, we'll kill him! ☺

Of course I remember Raft Summer, Ada!

Also, I promise.

LOVE AND RF.

Roses

From: CarolineCaroppenheimer@gmail.com

To: RosemarieCloverKingston@gmail.com,

AdaPlumCastelow@gmail.com, KaseyJosephineFritz@gmail.com

Subject: Re: Hey Ladies

RAFT SUMMER!!! *squeal* I promise too. Let's do Raft Summer ASAP!! Kasey, it's mandatory, so no excuses.

And yeah...becoming Mrs. Trey Foxberry...I didn't see that on my Bingo card either, but here we go.

Kasey, my heart is broken you can't be here, but I understand. Or I'm trying my best to understand!! I'll miss you so much.

LOVE AND RACK FOREVER.

Caro

From: KaseyJosephineFritz@gmail.com
To: RosemarieCloverKingston@gmail.com,
AdaPlumCastelow@gmail.com, CarolineCaroppenheimer@gmail.com
Subject: Re: Hey Ladies

I'm sorry I can't be there but! Just picture it's Raft Summer again and we're not busy anymore and nothing bad ever happened in Goldie. It's only us and the lake. The Chicks and Popsicles. Caro's chocolate chip cookies and Ada's strawberry lemonade. "Crazy in Love" by Beyoncé + that day Caro's bikini strap broke and she had to run up to the lake house to fix it! Me and Rosemarie mega-stoned on her dad's weed, pretending like we were Ariel from *Little Mermaid*...that same night the boys were lighting off fireworks and Mateo kept playing the *one* Coldplay song he knows over and over again on Leo's guitar. Also, Ada, you made the BEST tacos that night. I'll remember those tacos forever.

We can make it all happen in 2019! Let's plan for 2019, somewhere! I promise.

I love y'all so much.

RACK FOREVER.

X

Kase

53

LUCINDA BRAMFORD: CORONER (ADDITIONAL NOTES)

Although the final autopsy report will not be available for six to eight weeks, my preliminary findings (which conflict with the Foxberrys' independent findings) are that Mr. Maxwell Mason Foxberry III died as a result of drowning.

He appears to have suffered no real harm to his body before his death. The scratching and bruising as well as the damage to his skull appear to have occurred postmortem when his body went over the falls and (presumably) hit the rocks.

Lysergic acid diethylamide (LSD) as well as traces of Psilocybe ovoideocystidiata were found in his system according to the hair test results. Traces of opioids were also found.

The stomach contained mushroom lasagna, pecan pie, a hamburger, and fries.

In summation, it is of my opinion that Mr. Maxwell Mason Foxberry III drowned because he was so inebriated he fell into Lake Goldie. (Corroborated by the Nancy Simmons eyewitness account/interpretation of blood alcohol report to follow.)

FINAL NOTES ON THE MAXWELL MASON FOXBERRY III INVESTIGATION, FROM THE DESK OF CHIEF MICKEY JOHNS

Closed. After reviewing the autopsy findings and blood alcohol report, I find no further need for investigation. It was an accident, not a murder. Unfortunately, Mr. Foxberry never learned to swim. (His death will also be listed as misadventure, since perhaps there's a chance he was so inebriated he forgot that fact and jumped in anyway.)

54

KASEY

"Caro's husband *died*? What happened?" Devon asked over the phone.

"He drowned. It's a long story...well, no, it isn't. He drowned. That's it," Kasey said. She was standing outside the farmhouse, looking at the water.

He drowned. That's it.

"Kase, everything sounds crazy right now and being there with you for a couple days didn't make me feel any better about it. I have no clue what's going on and you won't tell me," Devon said. His voice was sharp and dark, a tone she'd only heard a few times in their relationship. She understood how he was feeling, and if she could stop it, she would, but she couldn't.

"I don't know what to say, Dev," she said.

"Are you having second thoughts about us? Is that what this is about?"

"Devon—"

"Tell me how I'm supposed to feel, then."

"I can't tell you how to feel!"

"I feel...well, I feel terrible, Kasey. I love you and you ran away from me."

"I did not run away from you and I love you too! You know how much I love you!"

"Do I?"

"Yes! You do!"

"Enough to marry me?"

"Yes!" Kasey said. Yes. She loved Devon enough to marry him. That was the plan.

———

Devon had shown up on the farmhouse porch and they'd talked and kissed and had sex in Kasey's old bedroom. After she told Devon the full, truthful history of the house and why it was so hard for her to come back, he chilled out. After she talked some more about what had happened to Caro and told him that she and Rosemarie and Ada were trying to help her get out of her marriage, he chilled out even more. But when she couldn't tell him *exactly* when she'd be coming back to New York, he got upset and confused, and nothing she said could make him feel better.

Kasey explained to him that her friends were really busy, and Caro was still in the hospital and everything was weird. She and Devon had gone for one walk through the town square, and Kasey showed him the diner and Plum everything and Goldie High and her other high school haunts. She distracted him when he got too close to the copies of the *Goldie Gazette* in the newspaper box so he wouldn't see Trey's face splashed on the front page. She didn't want Devon asking questions; she didn't want to talk to him about it yet. Instead, they went to the dog park and peeked at the puppies. They got japchae and triangle kimbap from Korean Gold and ate on the back porch of the farmhouse, looking out at the water. Having Devon in Goldie was jarring, but no more jarring than killing your best friend's husband or finding out that your other best friend was dying of cancer.

And fast-forwarded: definitely not more jarring than the Goldie police deciding that the coroner's report was complete, the murder investigation was closed, and no crime had been committed. Trey Foxberry had drowned, plain and simple, and RACK had been so overjoyed about it they were speechless. They'd gathered at Leo's and sat in silence, holding hands while Leo softly played George Harrison on the guitar and Esme made holy basil tea in the kitchen.

Before Kasey knew that relief, she and Devon had talked and eaten and reconnected in that bed in her old bedroom a lot. It'd only been a couple of weeks, but she missed his kisses and tried her best not to think about the Silas kisses on the couch. She missed sex with Devon and eating with Devon and laughing with Devon, but she also asked Devon to please go back to New York so she could figure Goldie out on her own, and he agreed to that.

"I'm going to my mom's grave today. I've never been," Kasey said to Devon on the phone after they'd talked some more.

"Will you call me later?"

"I will. I promise," she said.

———

Kasey went to Roy's grave first. It wasn't right next to her mom's, but it was too close and she hated that, but also, *anywhere* on the planet would've been too close.

Kasey hated spit—even the word *saliva* grossed her out—but she spit on Roy's grave because she'd been wanting to do it since she was in high school, and it was one thing she could do now as an adult that she couldn't make happen when she was a kid.

Her mom was closer to her dad's grave, where she belonged. She walked over to her dad's and sat there for a bit, looking at his name. *Isaiah William Fritz.* She got up and sat in front of her mom's headstone and cried. Grandma Mimi and Duke had helped her pick out the headstone, and Duke had paid for it, promising Kasey he would take care of everything. When she'd gone to Duke and Cherry's for pie, Duke had let her know he kept an eye on Angie's grave and made sure it always looked as pretty as possible.

And it *did* look pretty.

The grass was cut short, but there were some pokes of violets and clovers and a tight bunch of wildflowers growing up behind it. When Kasey got up the courage, she touched the ANGELINA JOSEPHINE FRITZ carved into the stone. She was wearing a crescent moon necklace she'd brought with her to town but hadn't put on until that morning. She pulled another like it out of her bag and draped it over the headstone. She got a jingle bell necklace out of her bag too and put it there with the enamel snack food pins she'd ordered. She lined them up in a neat row on top of the stone—a tiny MoonPie and a tiny Twinkie. A little pickle and a translucent glass strawberry that caught the sunlight. She kissed the headstone and told her mama she loved her. She left flowers in the grass—red roses for Rosemarie, pink ones for Ada, sunflowers for Caroline, white peonies for herself.

She went back to her dad's grave and left him the third moon necklace she'd brought with her, kissed his headstone too. Kasey wasn't a cemetery person and neither was her mom when she was alive, but being there brought Kasey an unexpected peace in the middle of the raging storm of emotions inside of her.

Moonshadow.

Kasey imagined both of her parents looking down on her, knowing what she'd done for Caroline, knowing what she wished she could've done for her mom, and she didn't feel condemned. She sat there for a long time, waiting for it, but it never came.

———

On the way home from the cemetery, she called Devon and told him about the moon necklaces and attempted to soothe him as much as she could, promising she'd talk again soon. When she spotted Paula

Foxberry on her phone in front of the courthouse, Kasey walked right up to her.

"I know what you did. I know what your family did for Roy Dupont...I know *everything*. Everyone knows now. Everyone knows what kind of family y'all are and what kind of son you raised, and there's nothing we can do about any of that now, but I know. We *all* know," Kasey said to her. The peace of the cemetery was running warm and smooth through her veins. It made her voice lower than she thought it'd be, and it was steady, not shaking a bit.

"I have not one clue what you're talking about, Kasey Fritz, and I'm a grieving mother. How dare you—"

"I know all about *grief*, Paula. You're not special."

"Trey would've never gone to that farmhouse unless you lured him there. Don't you think I know that?"

"I have not one clue what you're talking about, Paula Foxberry," Kasey said, turning.

Her body attempted to process the encounter as she walked. Her hands were trembling now and her blood got cold, but the Goldie afternoon sun warmed her up again as she headed toward Rosemarie's.

55

CAROLINE

Beau was giving Caro a ride to Rosemarie's house. He was driving his uncle's old truck, and he apologized for the bumpiness.

"You sure you're all right?" Beau asked, putting his hand on Caro's thigh for a split second. She wanted him to keep it there for longer. She wanted to ride around in trucks with Beau Bramford for the rest of her life with his hand on her thigh, and she was so elated from the investigation into Trey's death being closed that for a fleeting moment, she'd forgotten Rosemarie's cancer was back.

The sun had pleasantly warmed up the inside of the truck and the windows were down. The wind blowing through Caro's hair made her feel like a teenager again, going for rides in Ada's pink convertible or Rosemarie's old station wagon or Kasey's truck. She tucked her hair behind her ear and touched her stomach, thinking about the baby, wishing it were really Beau's so they didn't have to pretend.

She was more than all right. Her face hurt and her shoulder hurt and the pills made her dizzy. Her vision was still a little blurry, but even in the half dark, part of her spirit was light and lifted, and she hadn't felt that way in a long time. Even if it would only last for a few seconds, she let herself feel it glow.

"I'm all right, Beau," she said. "And I can't thank you enough for everything you've done for me. Y'know, I never imagined my fairy godmother would look like a guy from Goldie, but I'm okay with it. I'm totally okay with my fairy godmother being *so fucking cute.*"

Beau was drinking water and he almost spit it out. They were close to Rosemarie's, but he pulled over on a side road and turned the truck off.

"When'd you know?" he asked, scratching his head.

"Myrtle told me not long after you left for Carson City, but she made me promise not to tell. I can't even imagine what happens to a person if they break a promise to Miss Myrtle Childress. An angel probably gets kicked out of heaven or something. I asked her yesterday if it was okay for me to finally say something to you, and she was really excited when she told me yes. She was always expecting you to come back on a white horse like some country song and whisk me off somewhere...but then, I mean, you got married and had your own life...and I had mine. But Beau, that was *so* much money you gave me and it made my life so much easier. And this...what you're doing for me now. I owe you—" Caro said with her hand on her stomach.

"I'd do anything for you, Caroline. That's been clear. You don't owe me anything. I got some money when my grandpa died and I didn't need it. *You* did," he said.

Caro quickly looked around for a Foxberry, and when she didn't see one, she kissed Beau for the first time in fifteen years, and it felt like everyone else in Goldie had been raptured up. His hands were in her hair and he was careful not to touch her shoulder and he was telling her how much he cared about her and she was saying it too. She imagined being with Beau for the first time. How she'd want to wait until after the baby was born. She wanted that one day. She wanted everything good with Beau so much she thought she'd never stop crying thinking about it.

56

ROSEMARIE

Rosemarie was in her black one-piece bathing suit when everyone got to her parents' place. She was standing in the living room next to the conversation pit while Basie barked up at her for the treat she was holding. She handed it over and rubbed behind her ears.

"Well, now that I think about it, this is completely backward. If we're gonna do surprise Raft Summer, we should've met at the Castelow lake house. Forgive me. Cancer makes my brain soupy," Rosemarie said.

She'd gotten in a habit of letting cancer take the blame for everything. There was *literally* nothing in her life she couldn't blame on it. Feeling tired? Blame the cancer. Emotional? Cancer's fault. Couldn't remember what she'd gone into the kitchen for? Damn cancer.

It was cancer that had her forgiving and hugging Sparrow Kim the day before when Sparrow had stopped by the house and apologized for breaking her heart in high school. It was cancer that had Rosemarie and Sparrow laughing and crying about their tangled teenage lives and how quickly it'd all gone by.

Fuck you, cancer.

"Do you feel like getting on the water? Is that..." Ada directed the

380

last part at Esme, who was in her bathing suit too and a pair of cutoffs. She looked over her aviator sunglasses at Rosemarie, then at Ada.

"I talk to my brother about Rosemarie every day, and every day he tells me whatever she wants to do is perfectly fine. I'm convinced she's put a spell on him," Esme said, shaking her head.

"She puts a spell on everyone," Leo said, stepping closer to them. He was wearing his swim trunks and a Bell Books T-shirt.

"All right. You make the rules," Kasey said to Rosemarie.

"I'm glad you're all here anyway, so I can feed you," Leilani Kingston said, waving them into the kitchen, where she had a whole spread set out on the table. Thinly sliced meats and vegetables for sandwich fillings. Whole-wheat bread. Pickles and lettuce and tomatoes from their backyard garden. A wide array of condiments—the hippie stuff Rosemarie's mom loved, like liquid aminos, SunButter, and cheese made from cashews. "Special brownies if anyone wants some," she said, pointing to the fudge in the purple glass.

"Thank you, Mama," Rosemarie said, immediately grabbing a piece of one and putting it in her mouth.

"We'll eat and meet up at the lake house. Caro, come home with me; I have a bathing suit for you," Ada said. Most of Caro's stuff remained in that big house she shared with Trey. It was easy to see that for Ada, focusing on fixing a small problem like that made her feel so much better about the world.

Yes, Rosemarie was dying, but even in that dark, there was light and stubborn hope in their group. No one was going to be carted off to prison for Trey's death, and Caroline's face was glowing.

"I'm going to say something...blame it on the cancer," Rosemarie said when she was finished chewing. Esme put her arm around her waist and kissed her cheek. Rosemarie looked at her dad in the doorway. Her brother, drinking water by the sink. The room could explode with love at any minute; the house was swollen with it. Rosemarie couldn't conceive of better circumstances for what she was dealing with. Even under the hovering doom, she felt blessed in God's warmth. "When I knew that this was it for me...that my cancer would kill me, I made myself one promise. To love the people I love as much as I can, no matter how much it scared me, no matter how much it would hurt, knowing what I knew. And I love you...I love *all* of you with every part of me. In a way that changes us...that changes who we are for the better every single day," Rosemarie said, putting her hand on her heart. The heart that one day, possibly soon, would stop beating. All their hearts would stop beating eventually, and Rosemarie prayed to see every single one of them again on the other side.

"I love you," she said to Esme, and Esme said it back.

"I love you," she said to Leo, and Leo said it back.

To her mom and dad. Her brother. Ada, Caro, Kasey. They all said it back.

Rosemarie was tired and wanted to be in the sun. "We promised we'd do Raft Summer, so let's do Raft Summer. We don't break our promises," she said.

57

ADA

"The lake is lazy today," Ada said from her raft with her fingertips in the cool water. It was something Grayson said on days when the water didn't move as much. They were all in their rafts in front of the Castelow lake house.

Ada let herself think about Trey for a split second before she closed her eyes and made him go away. She wasn't worried about him anymore. She wasn't worried about her mom anymore either. Holly Plum had made a promise and she'd kept it when she checked herself into rehab in Adora Springs. Ada and Taylor and their brothers already had plans to go visit her together next week, after she had some time to get settled.

Rosemarie was dying and there was nothing Ada could do about it, but no one knew when. As much as an unscheduled life terrified Ada, knowing that today didn't *have* to be the day propelled enough hope for tomorrow.

She looked at Rosemarie, remembering their Raft Summer back in high school. How blissed-out they were, knowing they'd be friends forever, no matter what.

"We were right," Ada said loud enough for everyone to hear.

"About what?" Caro and Kasey asked at the same time.

"About everything," Rosemarie chimed in, just knowing.

EPILOGUE

KASEY

Devon took the breakup really hard, but not any harder than Kasey, although she'd known it was coming. He returned to Goldie and she gave the engagement ring back to him. When he left, she cried herself to sleep for a week straight. Ada brought food and flowers like it was a funeral, but Kasey couldn't eat. She visited Rosemarie and Caro but didn't stay too long.

Silas came by the farmhouse and helped her fix the gutters and the post that needed to be replaced on the back porch, but they didn't kiss, no matter how much she wanted to. He let her know he was waiting patiently, like he always had been. She wanted to honor what she'd broken with Devon and needed more time.

Maybe Devon was The One.

Maybe in a bit, she would realize it and he'd take her back. Maybe.

———

Once she decided to make her new life in Goldie for good—and after she'd gone to New York to put everything in order for the move—she kissed Silas on the porch for a long time right next to the sign she'd made that said RACKRose Farm on it.

"RACK for Rosemarie *and* Baby Rosy, Ada, Caro, and Kasey," she said to him.

She could still work for LunaCrush from Goldie and she'd do that. Caro and her growing belly were going to live with Kasey in the farmhouse, and Beau was back in Nevada for now, finishing out his work contract. He and Caro talked a lot and there was a bright, heavy hope there. They'd discuss that hope when they both had some more time to breathe about it. He would return to Goldie when the baby came, when Caro was planning to start up the pie-delivery business she'd been talking about. Ada had also connected Caro with a publisher who wanted her to begin working on a cookbook as soon as possible. Kasey would help too. Happy work for everyone, little calm eyes in hurricanes of sadness.

Kasey was determined to rewrite the story of that land and that house her daddy built. Maybe she and Caroline would get their happily ever afters someday with the men they chose, but even if they didn't, they had each other. Baby Rosy would grow up with more than one mom watching out for her, just like they all had.

Kasey had spent so much time awash with regret and couldn't touch the bottom, but now she was finally ready to forgive herself for running away and choosing survival, for not doing enough to save her mama all those years ago.

When Kasey was a little girl, whenever she got down or frustrated about something, her mom would tell her, *Take a break; don't let it break you.* She started thinking of her leaving Goldie after high school as a break so it wouldn't break her. And Caroline's broken shoulder had healed and was like new again.

There were so many hearts and spirits and bones breaking and healing at the same time, every day.

Rosemarie was sicker now, and she'd asked Kasey if she would take care of Basie. Kasey loved that dog to bits; Basie followed her everywhere and had plenty of room to run and roam on the farm. Grandma Mimi knit Basie a patchwork blanket for her dog bed, and she knit Rosemarie a bigger one to match. Sometimes when Rosemarie felt like it and it was warm enough, she sat in Angie's chair on the porch with the blanket over her lap. Rosemarie had also told Caro that she wanted her to have all the money she'd saved up, and once again, Caro was overwhelmed by how much and how well they loved one another, the lengths they'd go.

We'll do anything for each other.

Trey's parents sold their houses and moved to Adora Springs, and although it wasn't far enough, the distance made it easier for Caro to dream and breathe.

They all knew Rosemarie would be gone once the early spring magnolias bloomed again, and they leaned into loving her as much as they could. Life had proven that RACK was forever, and death would prove it too.

Not only was RACK forever, but it was protected from the rest of the world, the same way RACKRose Farm was protected from the rest of the world—right there on the edge where Kasey's daddy had put it. Like the women it was named for and all the women of Goldie who'd stepped up to protect them—the women who knew the truth, the women they would owe and thank with smiles and winks all over Goldie as long as they lived, the women they'd swap stories about with Nosy Nancy when she visited once a week with tea and cookies—that farmhouse and that land were staunch and steeled against anything life had waiting for them.

Even the ethereal, incongruous stretch of an *impossible* goodbye.

ACKNOWLEDGMENTS

As always, thank you so much to my literary agent, Kerry D'Agostino, for everything, everything! To my editor, Elizabeth Kulhanek, thank you so much for everything, everything! And thank you so much, Alli Dyer! All of you! LAKE FOREVER!

Huge thanks to Andy Dodds for everylittlebit.

Huge thanks to Theresa DeLucci for everylittlebit.

Huge thanks to the art department and everyone at Grand Central Publishing.

Huge thanks to Tareth Mitch and Kristin Nappier.

Special thanks to everyone at Temple Hill Entertainment.

Special thanks to everyone at Curtis Brown, Ltd.

Special thanks to Simon Lipskar and Writers House.

Special thanks to nostalgic country songs and Rissi Palmer and Brittney Spencer and Mickey Guyton (&c) and "Back Down South" by Kings of Leon and Kentucky sunsets and Ghibli clouds and iced yuzu tea with keto honey in a strawberry glass and crispy quinoa peanut butter cups and K-dramas and webtoons.

Wow, lots of big love and !!! and gratitude to The Chicks for making my girlfriends and me smile and laugh and cry with your beauty and music!

ACKNOWLEDGMENTS

Thank you, dear reader. Thank you, Sarah "Muffin Mix" Mimnaugh.

A very sweet important thank you to Kim Namjoon, Kim Seokjin, Min Yoongi, Jung Hoseok, Park Jimin, Kim Taehyung, and Jeon Jungkook for your music and hearts and inspiration and love. And a very sweet important thank you to Lim Jaebeom, Mark Tuan, Jackson Wang, Park Jinyoung, Choi Youngjae, Kunpimook Bhuwakul, and Kim Yugyeom too.

As always, thank you so much to my family for your love and support. I love you so much!

And finally, Loran, I couldn't do any of this without you and I often say you love me like Jesus does and it's still true! Thank you for taking care of the house while I lock myself away to write books. Thank you for sandwiches and tea and dinners and and and. Thank you for kitchen kisses and and and. I love you forever. I'm yours. And to R & A, I love you madly and forever. Thank you, thank you. xo

ABOUT THE AUTHOR

Leesa Cross-Smith is a homemaker and the author of *Every Kiss a War*, *Whiskey & Ribbons*, *So We Can Glow*, *This Close to Okay*, and *Half-Blown Rose*. She lives in Kentucky with her husband and their two teenagers. Find more at LeesaCrossSmith.com.

Facebook: LCrossSmith
Twitter: @LeesaCrossSmith
Instagram: @LeesaCrossSmith